Of Closures and New Beginnings

SANIYA is an established writer of short fiction, fiction and non-fiction in Marathi and the recipient of several awards for her novels and collections of short fiction, including the Maharashtra State award for literature. Her writing reflects her concerns and preoccupation with issues dealing with human relationships, and the predicament of the modern urban Indian woman coming to terms with her surroundings and reconciling her upbringing with her environment. Her work includes the novels *Avkash* (2010) and *Sthalantar* (2014), and the short story collections *Omiyage* (2004) and *Pratiti* (2012).

KEERTI RAMACHANDRA is an experienced and accomplished editor and translator. She has taught English at various levels, worked as an editor with Katha, Indialog, and as a freelance editor for various publishing houses including Harper Collins, Penguin, and Sahitya Akademi. She has translated several short stories from Kannada, Hindi, and Marathi, for *Katha Prize Stories*, various journals, magazines and anthologies, and a Marathi novel by Vishwas Patil, *A Dirge for the Damned* (2014).

MAYA PANDIT is a poet, translator, teacher developer and an activist who has been involved with the women's movement in India and alternative theatre movement in Maharashtra for the last three decades. An accomplished translator, she works with Marathi and English and has translated several plays, autobiographies and fictional narratives across the two languages. She has published research papers in feminist and Dalit studies, translation studies and English language training (ELT). She is a professor at the English and Foreign Languages University, Hyderabad.

Of Closures and New Beginnings

SANIYA

Translated from the original Marathi by
KEERTI RAMACHANDRA

Orient BlackSwan

OF CLOSURES AND NEW BEGINNINGS

ORIENT BLACKSWAN PRIVATE LIMITED

Registered Office
3-6-752 Himayatnagar, Hyderabad 500 029, Telangana, India
e-mail: centraloffice@orientblackswan.com

Other Offices
Bengaluru, Bhopal, Chennai, Guwahati,
Hyderabad, Jaipur, Kolkata, Lucknow, Mumbai,
New Delhi, Noida, Patna, Visakhapatnam

First published by Orient Blackswan Private Limited 2019

ISBN 978-93-5287-791-1

Typeset in
Book Antiqua 10.5/12.6
by Le Studio Graphique, Gurgaon 122 001

030273

Printed in India at
Akash Press, Delhi

Published by
Orient Blackswan Private Limited
3-6-752, Himayatnagar, Hyderabad 500 029, Telangana, India
e-mail: info@orientblackswan.com

Contents

Acknowledgements

Nothing is ever the result of a single individual's effort—there are always so many active participants and silent supporters in the completion of a project. In this case, too, there were many, and I would like to thank them all:

Saniya, who not only let me translate her stories but held my hand throughout the process;

Dr Maya Pandit, for agreeing readily to write the introduction;

Vidya Rao, for approving the manuscript and accepting it for publication;

Noella James and the editorial team, for using the most fine-toothed comb on the text;

Not to forget all those at Orient BlackSwan who will make the book available and visible;

The support of my friends who have faith in me as a translator (you know who you are!) and who encourage me to venture into doing more translations...

To all of you, a heartfelt Thank you.

Saniya: An Introduction

Maya Pandit

Saniya is a well-known literary figure in Maharashtra whose short stories have changed the map of gendered imagination and expression in contemporary Marathi literature. She has not only contributed significantly to the tradition of women's writing, but also changed the contours of fiction writing itself in Marathi. Her three novellas, eleven short story collections and two collections of prose writing have left an indelible stamp on the Marathi literary world.

Saniya's journey as a writer began with the publication of a short story, 'The Lost Path' ('Harawleli Paulwat', *Shree*, 1968). Most of her stories have been published by popular magazines, because of which Saniya has been a major influence in shaping the literary tastes of the Marathi middle-class readership.

Since Saniya's short stories spring from the Maharashtrian woman's social, psychological, aesthetic and cultural-political experiences in the post-Independence period, it might be helpful to look at the factors that went into redefining the role of women of that time. The discourse of modernity had initiated the process of recasting women into different moulds as complements to the new man. Women, who had so far been illiterate and unknown to the outside world, had to be educated. They were expected to be understanding companions to their husbands, and yet be docile subjects to the power of patriarchy and empire.

The climate after the two World Wars compelled women to come out of their homes and take up employment in factories, offices and other public spaces. Gradually, the joint family gave way to the nuclear family, and the struggle for survival in the new urban ethos completely changed women's public and private life. And yet the injustice and oppression on ideological and practical levels of existence continued, shattering their dreams and aspirations. Despite their education and work outside their homes, women were expected to be good housewives and create good homes to bring up good citizens to strengthen the new nation, rather than be equal partners in the process of nation-building. As a result, a feeling of isolation, marginalisation and alienation crept in.

During this time the reform movement in Maharashtra, with thinkers like Mahatma Phule, Gopal Ganesh Agarkar, Pandita Ramabai, Maharshi Karve, and many other pioneers of women's emancipation, had introduced women to the idea of resistance. They learnt to aspire for individual freedom and equal rights. The discontent and frustration that they felt led to many struggles, spilling over onto the streets, which challenged the entrenched oppressive patriarchal attitudes and strategies in social, economic, political and cultural fields. The women's movements also questioned patriarchal controls over women's sexuality and the institutional mechanisms that society had put in place to control it.

Maharashtra has always had a strong oral tradition of creative articulations by women saint poets. Writers like Kashibai Kanitkar, Pandita Ramabai, Tarabai Shinde, Laxmibai Tilak, Geeta Sane, Vibhawari Shirurkar represented a tradition of resistance to the dominant ways of thinking about women in society. Their literature was their attempt to subvert the stereotypes popularised through the hegemonic Marathi literary tradition by writers such as V. S. Khandekar, N. S. Phadke, Gangadhar Gadgil and P. B. Bhave among others. The women writers found a platform to air their concerns in the numerous women's magazines like *Stree, Stree Muktichi Lalkari, Stree Uwach* and *Milun Saryajani*.

Reared on cultures of subversion in the past and the contemporary women's movement against inequality and exclusion from citizenship, women writers in the seventies looked at developments in the outer and inner spheres of culture around them differently than their male counterparts.

Their writing represented gestures of defiance in terms of themes, characters, problems and resolutions. Writers who articulated this new subversive idiom include Vijaya Rajadhyaksha, Kamal Desai, Shanta Nisal, Gauri Deshpande, Ambika Sarkar, Priya Tendulkar, to name a few.

Saniya belongs to this social and literary ethos. Her stories articulate middle-class and upper-caste women's personal experiences within the institution of family and home. They demolish stereotypes of doting mothers, good submissive housewives, bad dominating ones, and prim single women. Her protagonists are mature, educated, independent, and sometimes also self-willed. Her narratives focus on the internal world of women, their emotional ties, their loves and frustrations, and their relationships with the men and women both within and outside the family. Through their stories Saniya explores the myriad conflicts in a woman's everyday life and traces her journey towards a world of choice, liberty, agency and individualism. On the way, one sees a breakdown of the family as an institution that defines women's lives.

The five stories and one novella included in this collection are fairly representative of Saniya's preoccupations.

The first story, 'A Matter of Choice' ('Apaple Prashna') deals with a complete role reversal between men and women. The protagonist, Vaijayanti, is a widow who chooses to live by herself, is reserved, and not fond of children, debunking the romanticism around motherhood. Vaijayanti guards her independence, her job and her privacy, and will not allow anyone to invade that space or take advantage of her just because there is no man in her life. However, this changes when Makarand, an old friend, turns up at her house one night with a sick child. He has no qualms about playing on her sympathy and basic kindness to make himself at home in her house. In the end, he offers to live in as a caretaker-cum-'wife' in return for a roof over his head. Saniya thus presents an alternative ideal of a 'family' in which two people can live together, working, eating and sleeping in the same space without love—physical or mental—coming into it, suggesting a radical re-interpretation of man-woman relationships as well as the traditional notion of 'family'.

The second story 'Bequest' ('Varsa') brings out the limitations of middle-class norms and values, their hypocritical stance, and the predicaments of educated and 'cultured' human beings desirous of joining politics. This seems to be the weakest link in this chain of stories as neither friendships nor family relationships, nor the nature of politics and its demands in the real sense of the term seem to have been fully explored in the story.

The protagonist of 'Bhumika' ('Bhumika'), Vasu finds herself expected to fit the role of a stepmother to her friend Shrirang's unexpectedly orphaned child. Neither Shrirang nor his mother, or for that matter Vasu's mother, understand why she is totally against the idea. Her successful career, her independence, her choice to remain single become irrelevant in their scheme of things, illustrating how women are often taken for granted by family members, and even by educated male friends and colleagues.

'The Love Gene' ('Premache Januk') is as much about the father-wife-daughter relationship as it is a portrayal of a typical man fitting a traditionally accepted role in the family. When young and ambitious, he is embarrassed to be informed of his daughter's birth in the middle of a meeting. His wife's plea to him to participate in the process of his daughter's growing up leaves him unmoved because, according to him, that is not what men are supposed to do; he has provided adequately for the family, and that should suffice. As a result, he is completely out of sync with his daughter and her dreams. The hollowness of his self-image and meaninglessness of his life are revealed to him when his daughter visits him on her birthday. The story re-examines the social construct of a man as husband, father, protector and provider, and deconstructs it in the process of narration.

The story, 'The Invitation' ('Amantran') depicts the tensions in the life of a career woman, Sarita, who refuses to betray her ideals for the sake of family. It is her life's ambition to serve the cause of women, their health and education. Sarita chooses not to leave her hospital behind and accompany her engineer husband, Jayteerth, to the US. When their daughter Nishi grows up, she moves to the US with her father. Nishi invites her mother to visit her, and, though reluctantly, Sarita accepts the invitation. Once there, she spends time introspecting her relationships with her daughter and her husband. Eventually, Sarita comes to terms with their decisions and accepts their right to live life on their own terms, just as she has lived hers. She learns to accept the present, without denying the past, and keep an open mind about the future. She also comes to understand love in a new way, without possessiveness, and without surrendering her autonomy. This is yet another alternative vision of what women can want.

The novella *Another Chance* ('*Awartan*') again revolves around the institution of marriage, relationships within a family and the breakdown of communication among family members. Saniya seems to be deliberately posing a hypothetical problem: can there be a viable alternative to marriage? She then goes on to examine the institution of marriage from diverse angles: security of home, financial commitment, companionship, support and understanding. At one end is Suruchi's family—her parents, younger sister, and maternal grandmother—all suffering from tensed interpersonal relationships and unable to get any pleasure except in power play. At the other end is Suruchi's intimate relationship with Shreerang who has steadfastly refused to make any commitment to her. Afraid of possible desertion, Suruchi wants the 'safety and security' of marriage. Her attempts to analyse her family, Shreerang's personality, his relationship with his family and its own set of tensions brings out the complexity of the institution of marriage and how it subjects both men and women to the politics of power play. The alternative could be an intimate relationship like that of Suruchi and Shreerang, or a collective life devoted to close relationships with friends involved in social work. The story offers no definitive answers, yet it creates interesting perspectives on human relationship in diverse fields.

Thus Saniya's literary articulations represent issues that women's movements have raised over the last three decades in Maharashtra. Her major preoccupation is with analyses of the institutions of family and marriage, patriarchy and its machinations, and the strategies and processes operative in the ensuing power struggle. This constitutes both the strength and limitation of Saniya's work.

Saniya employs plenty of dialogue and conversation between people, or an internal dialogue of the person with herself. Her language is colloquial and candid, but its simplicity is deceptive because the words often carry an unexpected forcefulness underneath. The sharpness of tone and the underlying critique—spoken and unspoken—is powerful. The translator, Keerti Ramachandra, has been able to bring out the hidden power of Saniya's narratives and language very well in her translation.

The discussion of Saniya's narratives cannot end without taking note of her narrative techniques, which have made her stories a compelling and engaging read. Her stories generally lack a straightforward and linear narrative structure; the narrative usually moves back and forth, delving into the past from the original point of orientation in the present to unravel the map of events. Often this preoccupation with the past allows the present to slip through the fingers and keeps the future out of reach.

One area that Saniya's narratives do not examine is the sexual relationships between men and women. Sex is a major location of problems in marital relationships, and therefore its analytical and critical representation would have been a radical step in her fiction. Exploring the earthiness and physicality of sexual relationships, within and outside of marriage and family, would have perhaps rendered the introspection of her characters more effective and complex.

Another limitation of Saniya's vision is the lack of concord between the middle-class world of women and the world of 'other' women—women belonging to the working class or lower castes. Though her narratives contain a powerful criticism of patriarchy, other forces that have shaped patriarchy in India and determined women's selfhood or subjectivity, such as imperialism, class, caste and religion, remain unaddressed.

But these are issues which a writer of Saniya's sensitivity is bound to address in her later work, or as and when she feels it is appropriate to do so. Until then, this translated collection of Saniya's fiction will certainly expose English readers to an important contemporary feminist voice in Marathi literature.

1 A Matter of Choice*

It was just after eight, not at all late, but in winter the roads are pretty deserted and people go to bed early. I parked my Luna and, as I climbed the stairs, I heard the ring of a telephone shattering the silence. It came from my flat. I always thought the ring was not loud enough to be heard on the staircase, but I suppose that's because it is drowned out by the surrounding noises. I hastily unlocked the door and picked up the receiver.

"Hello, hello..." I said eagerly, because I liked the thought that someone wanted to speak to me. Perhaps because I live alone, these unexpected communications are very welcome.

"Hello, is that Vaijayanti?"

The voice sent me reeling. It was Makarand! Where had he sprung from?

"Makarand? It is Makarand, isn't it? Where are you calling from? How are you?"

"That's what I called to tell you. Found your number with great difficulty."

I pulled a chair and sat down.

"So, what's the news?"

"Vaijayanti, are you free? Can I come over?"

"Now?" I asked, somewhat surprised. He probably doesn't know that I live by myself, I thought. What does he mean by wanting to come here at this time? Actually, there's no harm if he does. Makarand is an old friend. I can trust him. He won't

*Originally published in Marathi as 'Aapaple Prashna', in the magazine *Maher*, August 1991.

misbehave. Besides, I am quite capable of dealing with anyone who dares to try anything funny. I have even learnt judo. But that's not the issue. Tai, my landlady, lives downstairs. She is a lovely lady. Caring, affectionate, helpful. I borrow lemons, sugar, even onions from her in an emergency. She remembers to send me whatever interesting dish she prepares. She will rush to me if I call out to her. Yes, she is fond of me.

She has a family, a son, daughter-in-law and grandchildren. But they keep pretty much to themselves. The son and his wife both work, the children come upstairs once in a while. That's all. Even Tai doesn't interfere in my life, though she does look out for me. We have a mutually trusting relationship. She knows if someone comes up the staircase, and I usually tell her when I have friends over, or if a girlfriend is coming to stay with me. During the day it doesn't matter, but now, at this late hour, a single man dropping in? It has never happened before.

All these thoughts ran through my head in one brief minute. "But it's almost eight o'clock! Where are you coming from?" I asked.

"I'm right here, at my parents' place."

"Which means you won't reach before eight-thirty or even nine o'clock!" I exclaimed.

"You know what, Vaijayanti, I need to talk to you. I have only today and tomorrow. You were at work all week, so I chose today. Besides, I am not coming alone. I am bringing my daughter."

I was relieved. "Daughter? How old is she?"

"Six and a half. So shall I come, then? We will take an autorickshaw. Give me your address."

I put the phone down and realised I hadn't asked him about dinner. I don't actually like cooking. Anyway, I'll ask him when he comes, I said to myself. As usual, I went and had a shower. Then I tried to tidy up the house, but didn't quite succeed. Only when the maid comes in the morning does it get a semblance of orderliness. In the evening, it is solely my domain and no matter what, there is a mess all around.

I heard an autorickshaw stop outside. Tai must have heard it, too. She must be at the window, making a note of who it was, where he was going. I opened the door and saw Makarand walking up holding his daughter's hand.

"Hello!" I said. "Where did you find such a lovely little girl?"

The child quickly hid behind her father, suddenly shy. Closing the door, I told them to sit wherever they could. "My house isn't always this untidy, just ignore it for now," I said.

The child stuck to Makarand's side. Glancing around, he remarked, "*Wah*, a very nice place!"

Then immediately he added, "I am very sorry, Vaijayanti, I had absolutely no idea. When I came here, somebody mentioned in passing that you lost your husband..."

"Yes, that was almost two and a half years ago."

"Since then, you have been...?"

"No, I was with my parents for a year, but that started becoming too oppressive. I couldn't get along with them. Then I found this place, and now I am well settled."

Makarand looked serious. Naturally. Everyone becomes serious whenever my husband's name is mentioned. He died within two years of our marriage, in an accident. No one wanted to talk about it.

To lighten the atmosphere, I said, "So this is your little girl. What did you say her name was?"

"Tell Aunty your name."

"Madhura," she said shyly.

"As sweet as the name." That's all I could say. Some people have the knack of winning over hearts with just a few words. I don't. Ravi could do that. He got along very well with kids. He would join in their games, tell them jokes, teach them tricks. Basically, he loved children. He wanted a child soon after we got married. And that's why when even after a year nothing happened, he got depressed. Neither of us was young. He was almost thirty and I a couple of years younger. Anxious visits to the doctors and treatment followed. When I finally conceived, Ravi's life was cut short. No one knew about my pregnancy. Not even my mother. We wanted to have it confirmed and then tell everyone. But Ravi's sister-in-law knew because she was my doctor. In those days of utter grief and despair I considered everything carefully and came to a decision. In this situation, what would I do with a child, I thought. Besides, I wasn't particularly fond of children. He who was, was no longer there. How would I bring up a child single-handed? A child who would never know what a father was?

I spoke to Ravi's sister-in-law and without any fuss or ado, she took me with her one morning, performed the abortion, kept me in her clinic till the evening and then dropped me home. All hush-hush, like some clandestine event. I wonder what my mother would have said had she found out. I felt nothing after the procedure. For a brief while I did feel that though Ravi had gone away from me, he had left a part of himself with me and that I was destroying it. Was I doing the right thing, I wondered. From the perspective of a traditional mother what I was doing was extremely cruel and inhuman. Had it been a film, the heroine would have given birth to the child and brought it up saying it was a symbol of her beloved husband. But I was no heroine. A modern, educated, independent woman, I had to live the rest of my life, alone. At first people would say, "At least if she had a child..." Later the same people would remark, pityingly, "Good thing she doesn't have the additional responsibility of bringing up a child and all that, poor thing!"

Madhura had brought all these thoughts to the surface. Makarand was saying, "She is a precocious child. Very intelligent. Once she gets to know you, she will chatter non-stop. All this bashfulness is only in the beginning."

"But I don't know how to chat with young people."

"Naturally," Makarand said.

What's natural about it, I wanted to ask, but kept quiet. In the course of our conversation, I gathered that he had resigned from his job. It was not the first time. He had changed several jobs. But this time his plans were slightly different. Since he felt he had no prospects in this country, he was planning to migrate to Canada. His older sister lived there and would sponsor him. It was just a matter of two or three months. Everything would be sorted out by then.

Puzzled by his words, I asked, "Now? At this age?"

"Why not? We aren't old. We are not even forty."

"But Makarand, people take such steps in their twenties. Before they acquire a family, wife, kids. It's easier then, isn't it?"

Rubbing his palms, he declared, "So what? It is not all that difficult."

Madhura was silent all this while. "Would you like to eat something?" I asked. I found out that neither of them had had dinner. "So what shall I make? I'm afraid I am not a very good cook, I can't make many things."

"But I can," Makarand interrupted. "You tell me what you want."

I was confused. He asked Madhura what she wanted to eat. "*Poori* and *alu matar*," she said matter-of-factly.

"Oh!" I gasped. "I don't think I have the ingredients."

But since I was committed to being hospitable, I decided to ask Tai. I even made a list. I showed Makarand what I had and went downstairs.

Tai opened the door at once. "I saw them come in. Very sweet child. Relatives of yours?"

Giving her a noncommittal answer, I showed her the list. "Sure, you can have it all," she said and went in to get the stuff. Madhura's presence had made everything easy. With her had come the image of a family man, a veneer of respectability. Had he come alone, it would have been quite different. I was nonplussed. Can a child, who will eventually grow up into an untrustworthy cunning adult, make such a difference to perception only because of its age and its innocence? I climbed the stairs deep in thought, and when I went into the house, I saw Makarand, apron tied around his waist, already halfway through the cooking. He had cut and chopped everything neatly, and whatever was cooking smelt delicious. Madhura was sitting on a stool by the counter, half asleep.

"I had no idea you were such a good cook. Lucky woman, your wife!" I said to him.

He had mentioned something about her work having prevented her from accompanying him.

"Oh, our distribution of labour is slightly unusual," he said, putting an end to further discussion.

Madhura had her dinner and fell asleep almost immediately. Now I have only one bedroom and a single bed. That room is out of bounds for everyone. Even Tai's grandchildren, close friends or relatives are not allowed to get on the bed. When a friend occasionally spent the night with me, both of us would sleep in the living room. Never in the bedroom.

Makarand picked up Madhura and put her on the bed. I could say nothing. If that child was responsible for giving this situation respectability, couldn't I let her use my room?

We had dinner, cleared up and came out. I had to admit that he was a gifted cook. His touch had made the food taste special.

"Can I smoke?"

I said yes and, without realising it, added, "Ravi was a chainsmoker."

"Ravi?"

"My husband."

"Strange. I don't even know your husband's name!"

"We haven't been in touch for so long! I was right here all the time, but you were travelling across the country."

"I did come on vacation, but not often."

"So how did you think of me now?"

"When one is going far away, one wants to say goodbye even to those one has lost touch with."

"I don't know about that. I haven't ever gone away. Nor thought about it, so no question of goodbyes."

"Well," he said, "I am going away alone. Things aren't exactly fine between us."

"Between you and your wife? Really? What happened to...?"

Although we had had no communication for so many years, I was surprised by what he said.

"She is a good soul, poor thing. It's me. I am at fault."

I felt like laughing. He also smiled. "It's the truth. I am not a stable person at all. I can't settle down in one place. That's why the numerous job changes, the travels... Minakshi tried hard to make it work; she gave up good jobs a couple of times, even a promotion once. For a while we tried setting up two establishments when we lived in different cities. But now she has a successful career, an excellent job, a big house, a hefty salary... but I am fated to move once again. Very far away this time! She flatly refused to accompany me. What could I do?"

"'What about Madhura?"

"That is the question. This time, I just brought her with me. The school term begins in January, so I could take her out. She doesn't know that we are separating. She thinks I am going abroad and says she wants to go with me. She is very attached to me. Perhaps because right from the beginning I was the one who took care of her. Minakshi was often too busy. I was the one who saw Madhura through all her minor ailments, attended school functions—it was always me. She is a daddy's girl, in the true sense."

This side of my friend's personality was unfamiliar to me. Naturally. We had been friends when we were in our twenties, immature, awkward boys and girls. Enjoying each other's company, chatting, debating, arguing. Drawn to each other sometimes... Those were the days. But the bonds that resulted from them grew weaker in the light of new worlds.

I kept staring at Makarand. He lit another cigarette.

"I am confused. I don't know what to do."

"Why this insistence on going so far away?"

"I tried all sorts of jobs here. Didn't work out. Perhaps there, some new opportunities will arise. Have to earn a living, isn't it?"

"But with Minakshi..."

"That is no longer an option. We tried everything. She and I come from different soils, are of a different breed. She wants stability, I need change; she prefers to put down roots, I am a nomad. With every move the bitterness grew. Now we have reached the end of our tether."

He smoked in silence, I struggled to stay awake. It was past eleven. When is this man going to leave, I wondered.

Suddenly he stood up. "Oh well, must go now. Thanks, Vaijayanti," he said.

At the bedroom door he stopped. Madhura was fast asleep. "Taking her back like this... Will I get an autorickshaw?"

"Unlikely. It's already quite late. In any case, you will have to walk up to the main road."

He went to find an autorickshaw. I struggled to keep awake. Ten minutes went by, then fifteen, half an hour. I was getting really annoyed. Why had he come so late in the first place? With a little girl, too. He has a hope if he thinks he will get an autorickshaw in the middle of the night. Even if he finds one, will the man agree to take him to where he lives?

Thirty-five torturous minutes later, he turned up. Shoulders sagging, dejected, tired.

"No luck at all. Not a single autorickshaw in sight. One fellow who was there was drunk."

"Go in the morning, then. You have no choice." Tai will know that the guest stayed the night, I thought.

And my worst fears came true. My bedroom had been taken over. Makarand lay down next to Madhura, and I, like a guest in my own house, was relegated to the living room. Sleep, which had seemed unconquerable a little while ago, vanished. Instead, angry thoughts besieged me. How dare he turn up without warning, after being out of touch for so many years? What does he mean by putting me in such an awkward position? I had been extremely careful to ensure no one took me for granted or behaved familiarly with me. I had tried hard to be correct, proper and firm so I could fend off pity—"Oh the poor thing"—or opportunism—"She is alone, let's take a chance and see..."

The day began as usual the next morning. The maid came in, saw the bedroom door slightly ajar and peeped in. Seeing a little girl curled up next to her father, she probably thought nothing of the unusual occurrence and went about her work normally. When I got ready, both of them were still fast asleep. Finally, as it was time to leave, I called out to Makarand. He was lost to the world. Impatiently, I shook his shoulder. "Makarand, will you wake up now? I have to go to office."

He sat up with a start. "Sorry! Gave you lots of trouble, didn't I? Okay, I tell you what, you go to work, I will make myself some tea, then lock up the house. Where shall I leave the key? Next door? Or shall I bring it to your office?"

I was speechless. But there was no time to think of a fitting retort. "Give the keys to Tai. I'm going."

I marched down the stairs and kick-started the Luna.

On Saturdays the office closes at one-thirty. We usually plan to get together at someone's place in the evening. Or go for a movie. On Sundays I visit my parents. That Saturday I didn't contact anyone. Nor did anyone call me. So I went straight home. As I was climbing up the stairs, Tai called out, "Ah, Vaiju, those guests of yours, is the child sick?"

Startled, I said, "Why? Who told you?"

"The father had come to borrow a thermometer this morning. When he returned it, he said the child had a fever, 102 degrees! Don't know if they went to the doctor or not... that's why I asked."

Tai was smart. She had deliberately asked me, knowing I had just come home. I found Makarand in the living room. Madhura was asleep inside.

"What happened?" I asked.

"She's had a fever since morning. That's why I didn't go out anywhere. I was putting cold compresses on her forehead. I had some aspirin, gave her half a tablet, but it's had no effect."

I was furious. "And you did nothing? Not even call the doctor? You should have asked Tai. She would have given you a number."

I was so upset because of the sick child in my house, but the father—he was unconcerned!

Makarand muttered, "I have to make a confession. I have absolutely no money. Not even for an autorickshaw. So how could I pay the doctor's fees or buy medicines?"

My god! I stared at Makarand. He looked pathetic. The same crumpled clothes, unshaven, unkempt, a picture of desolation.

"So that's why you came back without an autorickshaw last night?"

He did not reply. Just sat there staring at his feet.

"Okay, get up and do something now. I will lend you the money. Attend to her first."

"What shall I do?"

I reached for my diary. I didn't know any paediatrician. Then I remembered Ravi's sister-in-law. Should I call her? It was a Saturday afternoon.

I called. Identified myself. She came on the line and said, "How are you, Vaiju? What have you done this time?"

"A little girl in my house has a high fever. Don't know what to do. Will you help?"

"The clinics are not open at this time. Tell you what—give her this medicine to bring down the fever. Keep sponging her, and around five o'clock bring her to my clinic. I will see her because she is your guest. Or I can suggest some other doctor."

I went down once more to get the medicines. When I returned, Makarand and I undressed Madhura and gave her a sponge bath, then put the same clothes back on her. I had never done anything for someone so little—and the sight of the tiny body, the slender limbs, the small palms and fingers did something to me. I had never felt this way before.

At five we took an autorickshaw to Ravi's sister-in-law's clinic. There was a crowd of mostly women waiting their turn. Makarand walked in ahead of me, carrying Madhura. People must have assumed we were a family—husband, wife and sick child. Suddenly I was desperate to get out of this situation. I wanted none of it. How does Makarand take care of her all by himself, I wondered.

The doctor took one look at Madhura and said, "It could be measles. I will give you a reference letter to a specialist. It's better to have your own doctor in case you need one..."

We went to the other doctor from there. We were called in after half an hour. He examined Madhura and said admonishingly, "Did you not notice the rash and the red eyes? How could you not recognise it as measles?" I am certain it would not have occurred to him that I was not the child's mother or Makarand's wife.

Obviously, I paid for everything—transport, doctor's fees, medicines. Now what? Makarand spoke. "I have a small request, Vaijayanti."

"What?"

"Will you keep Madhura with you for the next eight to ten days?"

What! Was I hearing right? Very sharply I retorted, "I am at work all day, *maharaja*... And I have no full-time servants either."

But I looked at his face and softened a little.

He said, "My brother has little kids. If I take her home in this condition, that will be the end. As it is our relationship is strained. Madhura doesn't like being there at all. Besides, she is ill. You don't worry. I will take care of her. It's not the first time she has fallen ill. I can manage. Just need a place to stay, that's all."

Needs a place to stay? Free and comfortable? What about money? He came here with empty pockets and, fortunately for him, found me—living independently, in my own house, with a phone, and all conveniences. What do I owe him that I need to oblige? My eyes fell on Madhura, whimpering piteously on Makarand's lap. My mind was in turmoil. What if I'd had a child? But I hadn't let it happen. If Ravi were alive, the child would have been alive, too. About two years old now. Would I have done all this? Doctor's visits, diapers, bottles? Or would it have been Ravi? Like Makarand? Who knows!

Tai, her son and daughter-in-law were standing on the veranda, talking to some visitors. Tai saw me come in, with Makarand carrying Madhura behind me. She called out, "What happened? Is she feeling better now?"

"Looks like measles. Don't send the children upstairs," I replied.

They must have thought I meant none of them should come upstairs.

Obviously Madhura would occupy my one and only bed. Makarand warmed up the milk for her. He made tea for us. I sipped it silently.

Sitting opposite me, he said, "Vaijayanti, I am extremely sorry."

I said nothing. What could I say?

"I know what I have done is very wrong. I had no right to land up at your place like this. But sometimes circumstances make a man helpless. Abject, even."

I did not respond.

He continued, "When Minakshi and I quarrelled, I used to get very angry. It must have affected Madhura also. But it brought us very close, my daughter and me. I used to be around when I was between jobs. Even otherwise I would spend a lot of time with her. As a result she wanted to be where I was. Minakshi must have seen the advantages of that. She did not object to the child's attachment to me. What I am trying to say is that Madhura is my life. My future. I have nothing else. My parents and brothers think I am a good-for-nothing fellow, anyway."

I laughed.

"It's not funny. It's the truth. My mother does have some affection for Madhura, but of all the other grandchildren, she is the least favoured. After making up all kinds of stories, I have managed to persuade my sister in Canada to sponsor me. But I will believe her only when I get the ticket and papers from there. I feel my luck will change in a new country with new opportunities. I will be able to do some kind of work and take care of Madhura. It will be better than this situation."

I don't know why I felt sorry for him. What world was he living in? He had no concrete plans, no idea of what he wanted to do—only that he had to get away. It struck me then that no ticket or sponsorship would come. It was highly unlikely that his sister had any confidence in him, so why would she do it? "What about your clothes, then?" I asked after a while.

He probably didn't hear my question. He buried his face in his hands and his shoulders started shaking. Makarand was actually crying. I was stunned. We had known each other from our college days. He was such a carefree, fun-loving, amiable fellow, popular with everyone. He would jump at the mention of food. We teased him mercilessly about it, and he enjoyed the teasing. Makarand was also very helpful. If anything had to be done, it was always, "Tell Makarand." Whether it was something to be brought, a message to be delivered, someone picked up or seen off at the railway station or bus stand, cinema tickets to be purchased, overdue library books returned, Makarand was the man. The word 'No' did not exist for him. Of course, people took advantage, but he didn't mind it. Being useful had become a habit for him. He must have felt the need to be wanted, to be depended upon. He must have drawn comfort from the fact that everyone turned to him, that he was indispensable.

So where were all those people now? Why is this man so alone today? An uncaring wife, a sick child, empty pockets... sitting here in my living room, weeping? My mind was in turmoil.

He got up and went away. Returned after a while.

"Can I ask you something? You won't be angry?"

"Ask." I couldn't get any angrier, I thought.

"Do you have any of your Ravi's clothes?"

I couldn't believe my ears.

"Just a couple of pants and shirts will do. I will get a couple of dresses for Madhura. We left the house with just the clothes on our backs."

"But yesterday..." I managed to mumble.

"I called you after the big, final fight we had. With my brother. And then... but there's no point telling you the details."

My mind went numb. Was this ever going to end? Why should I shelter this man in my house?

In a daze I went to the bedroom, took out all the money I had and held it out to him. "Take this. Return it if you can, when you can. Otherwise... But fend for yourself."

Makarand did not take it. "Vaijayanti..." he said.

"Please, you must also understand my situation," I said, still holding the money.

"I know that. But what am I to do?"

That was true. Where would he go with such a sick child? I left the money on the table and went outside.

I am rarely alone on Saturdays. From Friday itself we make plans to do something on the weekend. Fortunately, I have many friends. But for them, how would I have spent my time? When Ravi was around, it was different. We didn't plan, but we invariably went out. People often invited us over. When he died, they came to my parents' house to offer their condolences. Too many of them, at all odd times. Till I was sick of them. Eventually I went back to work. Gradually I got back my life. And when I mentioned that I wanted to be on my own, the family started putting pressure—"This is not done." "That doesn't look good." "Those people coming here is not proper." "You going away is not right."

Finally, after much negotiation, I got this house. Through contacts. Tai rented out the place, with the telephone, for a reasonable rent to a widow. So this was my life now. So far no one had said "Get married again", but they would start soon enough. They would go out of their way to convince me how difficult it is to live alone. "Be open to making compromises", they will advise. Family, friends, colleagues, Tai will suggest suitable matches. A widower, a man divorced, or someone who has enjoyed life all these years as a bachelor but is now looking to settle down... I know it all. But I return to the immediate present: how do I spend a Saturday evening? What do I do with myself on Sunday? Whom do I visit on a holiday? As for leave, I avoid taking any as far as possible.

Makarand was lying down next to Madhura, who was still asleep. Can children with fever sleep like this without eating or drinking anything? I was so unaware of all this. For a few moments I was really worried. Then I thought, it's his daughter, let him worry.

I called a couple of my friends. One of them had gone out with family. The other had guests for dinner. Another friend was going to attend a concert that night. I went and stood by the window in the living room, watching the traffic on the street below. It had become cooler. Darkness was falling. Tai was at the gate, alone, like a watchman. As if she was leading all the neighbours in her mission. Suddenly I felt afraid of her. For no reason, really.

I went downstairs and took the Luna out of the gate. As I was walking out, Tai asked, "Vaijayanti, how is the child now? Has the fever come down?"

How would I know? I hadn't checked it. I replied, "She's sleeping."

"The child has no mother, it seems," she said.

I shook my head. What could I say?

"You carry on. If you need anything, don't hesitate. I will go and see her for a few minutes."

I took off. I felt very lonely. It was nothing new. I feel this way often. Especially when I am on the Luna. What if I meet with an accident... who is the closest relative to inform? Who knows, I may lie there for a while, like a destitute. Then they will come—my parents and others, one by one. But only after someone finds their address and informs them. We don't have the same address. What morbid thoughts! Why would I lie on the street anyway? I have been riding the vehicle for years.

I went into a shop and bought some clothes for Madhura. Not knowing her size, I just gave her age and picked out what I liked. Bought a few other things, too.

Makarand was rummaging around in the kitchen. Silently. Like a poverty-stricken housewife. I went inside without saying anything. I left the clothes on the bedside where Madhura was lying. Stood on a stool and brought down the suitcase. It had Ravi's clothes in it. I usually got all choked up just looking at it. I quickly shut the suitcase and left it on the floor. Picking up a book, I switched on the radio and sat down. This was the perfect picture of an average middle-class family. The only difference was that no relationship existed between me and Madhura-Makarand. Really? No relationship? What were relationships after all? Those that one forges intentionally? Living together in the same space, working, eating, sleeping. Who said anything about love—emotion—physical or mental coming into it? How would outsiders know whether the couple inside love each other or not? I know so many couples who don't speak to each other. I have heard of many couples staying in strained relationships because of the children. So who knows what that which looks like a home from the outside is actually like?

Tai must have already wondered whether the stranger staying upstairs and Vaijayanti were sleeping together. It only goes to show that what goes on within four walls can be different from what one imagines it to be. A little more, or a little less, but different nevertheless.

I was sitting there with the book in my hands, not reading a word. Makarand came to the kitchen door and said, "Vaijayanti, say something. Don't be so angry, please."

I was startled. Makarand asking me to speak, when in those days he couldn't stop chattering? My god! How far we have come! "What do you want me to say?" After a pause, I added, "Tell me truly, Makarand, are you really planning to go abroad?"

"I am trying. Might succeed."

"And until then..." I asked, suddenly nervous.

"Look at it this way, Vaijayanti. I will look after your house; I will do your chores. All I need is a place to stay. For me and my daughter. This is a seriously comic-tragic situation where a man goes up to a woman and spreads out a towel before her, pleading for a place to stay!" So saying, he actually unfolded the towel on his shoulder and held it out. "What shall I do? There is nowhere for us to go. Had I been alone, I would have slept on the footpath, worked as a coolie. But with the child... I want to give her a good life, I really do."

I was beginning to giggle. This was a modern-day tale, but who would understand the context? Surely Makarand was not afraid of me? Afraid that I would scream and shout and turn them out of the house? That I would refuse him everything, food, shelter, clothing, money? Or ask him for compensation? A price? A young, healthy woman like me... Makarand was not bad-looking, even smart... What if I went up and...

But no. I was too 'decent' and 'respectable' to do any such thing. I have only given shelter to a homeless father and daughter. Now my home, with a readymade family, will look like countless other homes. A little distorted, perhaps. Like a mirror image.

2 Bequest*

Mrunal was in the kitchen when she heard the doorbell ring. Wondering who it could be so early in the morning, she lowered the gas flame and, wiping her hands on her apron, went to the door. She couldn't believe her eyes.

"Milind? You?" she said, not hiding her surprise.

"Yes, me. Unexpected, isn't it? Thank goodness you recognised me," he said with a half-smile.

"Why wouldn't I recognise you? You haven't changed all that much. All of us have, a little bit... Come in, sit. I'll join you in a minute."

Mrunal went in. Milind followed her. He put the *jhola* bag he was carrying on the floor next to the wall. "Custard apples. You like them, don't you?"

Mrunal was thrilled. "You remembered? Saurabh would never think of it. He travels so much, but does he ever bring anything back for me? Of course not!"

"Where is he? Still sleeping?"

"No! He isn't here. On tour, as usual."

Milind clicked his tongue. "What a pity! I came early thinking I could meet him as well. Wanted to catch you both before you left for work."

"You got it wrong on all counts," Mrunal laughed. "Saurabh isn't in town, and I don't go out every day either. Schools closed last week. The situation is volatile. Not here,

*Originally published in Marathi as 'Varsa', in the magazine *Akshar*, Diwali Issue, 1991.

actually, but the government has directed schools and colleges to be closed for a fortnight. A law and order issue, they say..." After a pause, she continued, "There is no disruption in our lives; it's just that with no studies, the children are running wild. But tell me, how are things with you? Busy, as you should be? It's your time now..." she smiled.

"Don't take it lightly, Mrunal. The times are such. There's uncertainty everywhere. It is not much in evidence here, that's true. But where I have just come from—no one knows what will happen when."

Mrunal switched off the gas. "Will you have something to eat? Or shall I just make tea?"

Hesitantly Milind asked, "What's your plan for the rest of the day? Are you going to be home?"

"I was thinking of visiting Dada. Have you ever met my father? He lives with my brother. It's almost like going to another town. It takes about an hour and a half to get there, and the buses are so irregular. But my visit will make him happy. I am preparing all this to take for him. Why do you ask?"

"Just like that. I am quite free today, don't have anything particular to do. Thought I would ask you both to take the day off..."

"You, and free? That's surprising."

He laughed awkwardly. "Yes. Why, I will explain later. I don't want to come in the way of your plans, though. You carry on. I will leave in a bit."

She thought for a moment, then said, "I will have to go since I left a message last night that I was coming. They will worry if I don't show up. There's no telephone at their home. I will have to call my brother's factory. His place is like a farm house, actually... Look, why don't you come with me? We can catch up on the way, and Dada will enjoy talking to you. He is alone most of the time. What do you say?" Milind was quick to reply. "Yes." She packed the stuff she wanted to carry, then handed him a plate saying, "Here, eat this while I get dressed."

As they sipped their tea, Mrunal glanced at the newspaper. "Whether it's the newspaper or the television—the news is only about protests, rioting, violence... No matter what the issue, the atmosphere is tense, waiting to erupt. Lawlessness is everywhere. Don't you think so?" After a pause she asked, "Tell me, how did you get into politics?"

Milind looked into the distance. "Of course." Then slowly he added, "Your question about how I got into politics... you know it is in the family. My father was a politician and I grew up in that environment."

"But there was an ideology, principles, discipline in his politics. Today?" She stood up. "Shall we? This conversation is pointless. The three of us have spent endless nights discussing it, remember?"

"Of course!" he replied. "It's not something one can forget. Both of you teased me sometimes, and tried hard to show me how unfit I was for politics!"

"Made no difference, did it," she said as they climbed down the stairs. "You did exactly what you wanted."

"I had no choice, Mrunal."

"Really?" Her laugh was disbelieving. "And why not? Perhaps if you'd got a job, got married, had a family, politics would automatically have stayed far away. But you did none of that..."

"You know I never wanted any of those things. When I started, I had no intention of joining any party. In fact, my father and I used to have serious arguments about this. My role was purely that of a social worker. Whatever anyone else may say, it was challenging, demanding work but emotionally satisfying."

They stood at the bus stop in the pleasant morning sunlight. There was a huge crowd waiting for the buses—office-goers, young people and old, men and women, even children.

"And now?" Mrunal asked, continuing their conversation.

"I don't know. I'm not sure about anything anymore." Then he quickly added, "But I am only admitting it to you. I would never say it to my colleagues."

Mrunal smiled to herself and waited. A bus, jam-packed, arrived. A few passengers got off, many more got in. The driver patiently waited for everyone to board. The conductor, too, allowed people to get in, then exhorted them to move forward.

"What a rush," Mrunal said to Milind as they waited for their bus. "They've reduced the number of buses it seems. As if there were too many in the first place. But no one complains."

"That is the real problem," Milind interjected. "No one protests when they should."

"Indeed they do—about irrelevant things. Tell me, do you agree that these current issues are worth fighting for? Do they merit so much rage? No educated, cultured human being will say they are. It's all games that politicians play. They incite the public to violence by picking on some delicate sentiment, and then while the common man burns in the fire, the politicians reap the benefits."

Milind grabbed her arm. Startled, Mrunal looked at him, then laughed. "Oh, no! That was not directed at you, Milind. No one can question your credentials. But the herd that you have joined—they are becoming more contemptible every day. If we, the middle class, feel this way, what about the others?"

Milind stood silently, arms crossed. Just then the bus came. "Get in quickly. Look at the crowd," Mrunal said. They were literally pushed in by those behind them. She managed to grab the handrail and get both her feet on the floor of the bus. The money for the ticket was in her other hand. Conversation was impossible. As the bus moved forward, the crowd settled into the available space. "We will change buses at the terminus. At least we will get a seat there," Mrunal said, turning around to address Milind.

But even there they found a long queue. As expected, there was no shade at the bus stop and the sun was hot. "So what else do you do these days?" Mrunal asked Milind.

"There's no time for anything else."

"So how come you are free now?"

"For you both."

She felt like laughing. "Anyone will believe that!"

He didn't explain. After a while he asked, "How is school?"

"Closed now. Yes, it's good. Very good."

"What classes do you teach?"

"Class 5, 6, 7. Science—biology, physics and chemistry."

"And you enjoy it?"

"Of course. Why? Are you offering me another job?"

"What can I offer!"

"Who else can then? One of these days you will become a big shot and we will have to come to you for favours."

"Mrunal," he said, his tone changing, "you are not the kind who would."

"You mean Saurabh and me? Yes, it is highly unlikely. We already have good jobs and there are no children or anything," she said and fell silent.

As soon as an empty bus stopped in front of them, a horde appeared from nowhere and began to push in. Mrunal managed to find two seats. "Ha! Now for half an hour, we are okay. I normally fall asleep, but today I have you to chat with."

After a while, Milind said, "Mind if I ask you something? Don't answer if you find it offensive."

"What?"

"You have any regrets about not having children?"

Mrunal started laughing. "You are mad. What made you think we cannot have children? It is possible that it was a conscious decision not to have any."

Milind looked surprised. "Is that so?"

"Isn't it possible?"

"Yes, but rarely..."

"Rare it may be, but certainly possible, isn't it? We often feel that life is getting more and more difficult every day. The situation is so bleak, so hopeless. The future looks grim. Then we feel relieved that there is no one after us. What kind of legacy can we leave for them? Why bring another life into this world? Worries start at birth—first we worry about earning enough to provide for the child, then we worry about who makes the compromise with work. As the child grows up, we run around for school admissions even though we know that the education system is pathetic. And then we rave and rant because there is no alternative to it. Next, slog to make the child stand on its own feet. Instilling values like hard work and sincerity is a punishment these days. Do we therefore encourage ruthlessness and dishonesty instead to make them eligible for success? When our life itself has become a conundrum, why start another one?"

"How cynical you sound!" Milind said.

"Am I not right?"

"How can I say you are not! But then, won't things ever change?"

"Do you feel they will? Tell me honestly, not as a politician, but as a dear friend... Awkward question, isn't it?" Mrunal laughed.

"It isn't like that, Mrunal. What you are saying is partially right. You say nothing is going to change. But we don't know that. We cannot go forward believing that there is no option, no alternative. That there is only a status quo. Things must change. Someone must bring about a change. Who knows, maybe twenty years from now there will be a complete turnaround?"

"Ha, ha, Milind, there is no conviction in that statement. I told you to speak in your own voice, but that politician's tone has become a habit with you!"

"Please, Mrunal..."

"Then what? What kind of answer was that?"

"I am not as pessimistic as you."

"Good."

"I'm serious. Think of it as your and Saurabh's child. Brains, good looks, talent, sensitivity, a deeply ingrained value system, that's how it will grow up, *na*? Both of you have so much to give it. We need individuals like that today, Mrunal."

"That is nonsense. Being virtuous in today's world is of no use. It only makes you a misfit. Being principled can be extremely stressful at times."

"Don't say that."

"Why not? Saurabh often comes back from a tour thoroughly frustrated. He rarely meets people who think like him. But forget that, even in school, among my colleagues, hardly anyone has views similar to mine. If I am earnest about something and speak animatedly about it, they either laugh it off or dismiss it as impractical. They have no inclination to introduce the students to something new, to teach them something more than what is prescribed. In fact, not a single teacher thinks there is anything wrong when angry parents bring their children's answer sheet and haggle over a couple of marks. Their main concern is how to get the better of the parents. It's disgusting, their attitude."

Milind sighed softly. "I wish I had met Saurabh," he said.

"I know. He would have been very happy, too. He should be back in a couple of days. But in these uncertain times, trains can get cancelled without warning and then... Can't you stay?"

"No, that's why the regret."

"Then come again soon. Not after several years like this time!"

Neither of them spoke for a while. They appeared to have reached the outskirts of the city, but there were signs of new developments everywhere. They got off the bus and began to walk along the tarred road, lined with shops and well spaced out bungalows.

"Nice place," Milind remarked.

"It used to seem way out at first. No longer. Once the shops came up, the neighbourhood grew... There, that building you see in the distance is my brother's factory. The house is on this side."

Mrunal rattled the gate. A huge dog rushed out, barking. A boyish looking servant came after the animal to tie it up in the courtyard. They opened the gate and walked in. Dada was seated on the spacious veranda. "See that?" Mrunal laughed, "He is waiting for me!"

She introduced Milind and said, "You've probably met him at our place long ago. You might not remember, but some time back his father... You must have heard of him?"

"What do you do?" Dada asked Milind.

"Strictly speaking, nothing," Milind smiled.

"What kind of answer is that?" Mrunal scolded. "He is in the same line, Dada. Politics, among other things. Even I won't be able to say exactly what he does. But he is a good friend." So saying Mrunal went inside to meet her sister-in-law and the children. She knew Dada would keep Milind engaged in conversation. Vahini was in the kitchen and the children were glued to the TV since they had holidays. Mrunal and her sister-in-law caught up with family news, and soon came out onto the veranda. The servant had brought glasses of fresh lime juice. The desultory conversation continued until her brother came home for lunch.

They all sat at the large dining table which was neatly laid. The simple but full meal was served piping hot. Vahini served everyone once, then sat down. The servants took over after that.

"Things are going from bad to worse," Mrunal's brother said. "Our consignment has been held up for weeks. How can we fulfil our commitments if we don't get our supplies? If we cannot meet the allotted quota, we will lose business. And thanks to the cost of living going up, the workers' demands never cease. Now they have started threatening us!"

"It wasn't like that earlier. There must have been corruption then, too, but not like this. There was still respect for principles. Today from the lowest to the highest, unless a palm is greased, nothing moves," Dada said.

Mrunal was disconcerted to hear this, but she said placatingly, "Don't generalise like that. We ourselves are different, aren't we? We might complain bitterly, but we remain straightforward, honest..." She looked at Milind. He was concentrating on his food. "What do you say Milind?"

He looked up. Again he was noncommittal. "What you say is true, but..."

"How can it be untrue? I have been running this factory for so long, I know all the ins and outs."

Immediately Mrunal retorted, "Which means that we also contribute to the mess, doesn't it?"

"We have no option. To survive in business we have to adopt the tricks of the trade."

"Then why complain. Everyone is on the same path."

Mrunal's sister-in-law looked alarmed at the turn in the conversation.

"Mrunal, you haven't touched the *kheer* yet. I'm going to refill your bowl, okay!" she said, changing the subject.

"The food is delicious," Milind said, then added, "I rarely get such tasty homemade fare, for free."

"Then you must come more often. We always have someone or other over for meals, so one extra person won't make a difference," Mrunal's sister-in-law told Milind.

Milind made the right polite response, but neither accepted nor declined her invitation. He turned his attention to the children, and Dada joined in their conversation.

By the time Mrunal and Vahini finished clearing up and came out, Mrunal's brother said, "I must get going now. Lots of work... Remember us," he said to Milind, "and drop in if you are on this side of town. I will show you around the factory next time." Then with a smile he added, "It is good if people like you tread our way."

"Milind is a very good and old friend of ours." Mrunal's tone indicated her displeasure at her brother's remark.

Dada retired to his room after his son left, and Vahini took the children inside to read or play or do something other than watch TV. Only silence and the afternoon quiet were left on the veranda. "You don't come here often, do you?" asked Milind.

"How did you..." she stopped herself, then continued, "I do, sometimes. To meet Dada. Saurabh has no time. His life is always hectic. And they have lots of visitors, they entertain often... We don't always fit into their lifestyle."

"Shall we go for a walk? You said there were fields behind the house?" Milind asked.

"Sure, come..."

The two of them went into the fruit garden behind the house. There was a well, and below it there were small square patches of cultivation.

"He bought this land long ago," Mrunal told Milind. "He's smart. Land was cheap then. Now, his factory is here, they have their bungalow, the garden, enough domestic help, he lacks nothing."

"Really? I don't think so."

"You don't think so what?"

"That he lacks nothing. There is always something missing, Mrunal. Ask him when you are sure you will get a truthful answer. Not only will your brother, but your sister-in-law and even the children will give you a list of all that they don't have."

Mrunal stopped in her tracks and turned to Milind. "It seems you didn't form a very good impression of them?"

"No, no, nothing like that..." Milind hastily explained. "Don't mistake me. They were very good to me—treated a complete stranger so cordially, fed me..."

"That's nothing special. They regularly have unexpected visitors. Since one never knows who can be useful in some way, they welcome everyone equally warmly. They are very hospitable. But if you felt that way, you are not wrong. I, too, wonder sometimes..."

"About what?"

"About our relationship. It's there because of our birth. That's all. They are not indifferent or anything, mind you. They do care a lot about me and are very affectionate when I go over. But that's not everything, Milind. A relationship is when one feels a deeper connection with someone, when we know we are on the same wavelength. But such relationships are rare and not valued enough. They are not even acknowledged. Everyone is stuck on the superficial, conventional connections of birth, caste, religion, language ... So where and how do we find people whom we have an affinity with? Is one lifetime enough for that? Even if we do, can we bind them to us? Hold on to them? It is depressing just thinking about it. And exhausting."

"I was wrong to call you a pessimist, Mrunal. You are not. You want to continue searching for honesty and integrity even in this modern jungle."

"But what purpose will it serve, Milind?" she said almost plaintively. "An entire lifetime will be spent just searching."

Suddenly the peace was broken by a flock of birds that flew up, chirping noisily. Milind and Mrunal looked in their direction. They could hear faint sounds in the distance... Car horns, a muted siren, dogs barking, crows cawing, the slap-splash of clothes being washed on a stone, a voice shouting...

"I am going now," Milind announced.

"Where?"

"I told you a little while ago. I am properly trapped. There's no stepping back. All this time I was doing small odd jobs which I took upon myself. But now I am going to get enmeshed in the real thing—the big, gaudy, glittering web of politics. Full-time. I might even contest elections. I will get elected, adorn some important post. It is a point of no return—there's no getting out of it now."

Mrunal stared at him. "But that's what you were doing all this while, weren't you? We always thought of you as our politician friend."

"That was a small world where honesty and integrity still meant something. It was a world on my terms. But no longer. Now it will be a messy, tangled, deceptive world of power and intrigue."

Mrunal couldn't believe what she was hearing. "You know all this and still...?"

"And still, yes. How can I explain it? I thought only Saurabh and you would understand my predicament. That's why I came to meet you. There was little time, and I had to travel far, but in spite of that I decided to see you." Milind's voice suddenly thickened. He turned away, a lost look in his eyes. He swallowed a couple of times, and then looked at Mrunal again. "I am at that point in my life, Mrunal, from where there is no going back. Once I move forward, the way back is blocked for ever. I no longer have a choice. I don't think I ever did. I was shaped that way, right from my childhood. There were, and still are, lots of expectations from me. But then there was a conscience deep inside. For the longest time I nurtured it despite all odds. Saurabh's friendship, however brief and intermittent, helped keep it alive. But I don't think that's going to be possible now. I have been sucked into a vortex, and I will drown among those people. Having been inducted into the team—I must play the game of political expediency, of power, of exploitation—be it of circumstance, situation, or individual—for self-fulfilment. I wanted to take my leave of you and Saurabh before I lose myself completely."

Mrunal continued to stare at him, disbelieving and nonplussed.

"But Milind, if you can see all this so clearly, why don't ..."

"That's the price one has to pay, Mrunal," he said agitatedly. "I know it, I understand it. Perhaps many don't even realise it. Whenever I look at our leaders, I wonder when and how the transformation took place in them. Now, I see myself entrenched in it all. And it burns me. I can see everything that is fine and subtle within me turning into something crude and opportunistic, necessary to survive in today's unscrupulous world. I wanted to meet you before it all melted away. You will continue to live your lives—fraught with problems, despair and frustration perhaps—and yet you will keep the faith. As for me, I will be in a world far removed from yours, a world of the power-hungry, corrupt people you despise. Where some people like your brother will curse me and yet spread out the red carpet for me, feed me, for the sake of the chair I occupy, from which they hope to benefit. I will be a party to it all, Mrunal, because once you enter the playing field, you play by the rules of the game. Win or lose, play you must. And then it will not be possible for us to meet. Even if we run into each other, we will not be able to talk. Because I will have lost you forever."

Milind's face turned pale and he looked away, his lower lip clenched between his teeth. Mrunal was shaken to the roots. She understood exactly what he was saying. Even what he didn't say. He was such an old friend, different from the others who came to their home often, dined with them, spent hours talking, debating, laughing... Though they did not meet frequently, there was a close bond between the three of them. And now Milind was distancing himself. Never to meet again? Never to communicate? Even when they looked for him in the crowd, he would be lost to them—never to be found again?

He would cease to be a person for us, like those one encounters everyday but doesn't notice, like the names in drab, tasteless news reports, anonymous. What a tremendous waste of a life! A loss that could never be recouped.

Mrunal felt drained, utterly dejected.

"Shall we go?" Milind asked. "It will get late by the time..."

Dada was asleep when they returned. Mrunal said bye to the children, told the servant to inform her sister-in-law and walked out of the gate. The bus was not too crowded. The two men on the front seat were discussing the present scenario in loud voices—who was going to win the election, how the government was going to collapse, blunders committed by some leaders. Milind looked at Mrunal and smiled.

There was no sign of the bus that would take Mrunal home. She told Milind, "If you are going in the opposite direction, carry on. I will wait here for the bus, or..."

For a few moments Milind said nothing. Then he replied, "Okay, I will go then. You will tell Saurabh? What else can I say?"

She wished he could stay longer. They could go home together, he could stay the night. Saurabh would be surprised and pleased to see him when he returned. She would persuade Saurabh to take a couple of days off, and they could spend time together. They had been married for so long, but time with Saurabh was rare because of his frequent travels. This would be a wonderful opportunity to have her two favourite people with her.

She looked up at Milind. He, too, was watching her awkwardly. A young man carrying a bundle of the evening newspapers with big banner headlines rushed past them. Faint sounds of an altercation came to them. They saw aggressive men, women, even children, shoving and pushing their way past the queue. A destitute old woman was curled up in the far corner of the bus shelter. A little ragamuffin boy came slinking by them, touching them for alms. When a very pregnant young woman approached them with an overloaded basket of fruit, calling out her wares, Mrunal broke out of her reverie.

With a start she noticed her bus had arrived at the shelter. "Oh, I wasn't paying attention! My bus... if I miss this one, the next one is only after half an hour or more."

Milind looked relieved to hear her say that. "Yes, you had better go," he replied. Mrunal joined the queue. She turned around to see Milind standing nearby. As she entered the bus, he nodded and said, "Take care, both of you, bye..."

The bus was full, but after looking around, she found a seat, though not by a window. She reached across and leaned over to look for Milind. He was nowhere to be seen. The conductor gave her a ticket and moved forward, when she heard her name being called. Apologising to the lady in the window seat, she stuck her head out and looked around.

Milind, standing on tiptoe, thrust a garland of jasmine buds into her hand. "I was walking out when I saw the flowers. Beautiful, aren't they? Ready to bloom. You loved flowers... I still remember... The buds should open fully by the evening."

She took the flowers and looked at Milind with wet eyes. Words stuck in her throat. No thank you, no goodbye... He smiled as if he understood, and waved. The conductor blew his whistle. Mrunal sat back on her seat. To stifle the pent-up emotions rising in her, she buried her face in the flowers.

3 Bhumika*

Just as Vasu was leaving, Mayi said, "It's past nine o'clock, Vasu, and this woman hasn't turned up yet."

Vasu absentmindedly asked, "Who?"

"Our maid, who else? It's better if she comes before you leave."

"She will be here by nine-thirty, don't worry. The door is left open till then, so you don't have to get up. Okay, I'm going now."

Vasu turned around at the corner, waved to Mayi—who she knew was watching her from the veranda—and headed for the bus stop.

Monday morning. The start of a new day, a new week. Time was rushing past. As she reached the third floor of her office, she met Shrirang as usual.

"How are you?" she asked.

"I have to tell you something," he replied.

"So tell." She stopped.

"Not like this. Meet me during lunch hour. Here."

Strange, she thought but said nothing. In a short while she had forgotten it. Later, when she was walking down the wide, curved staircase of this magnificent five-storied building to the canteen on the ground floor, she saw Shrirang at his desk and remembered. She told her friend to carry on, and went and stood in front of him. Shrirang was engrossed in his work.

*Originally published in Marathi as 'Bhumika', in the magazine *Milun Saryajani*, 1990.

Pulling out a chair, she sat down and said, "What were you going to tell me? That you cannot get along with your wife?"

"I haven't mentioned it to anyone yet, Vasu, am feeling a bit awkward about it, but Sushama is expecting," Shrirang whispered grimly, glancing around to make sure no one was listening. Most people had switched off the lights and gone for lunch.

"It is your wife, isn't it? Then why are you saying it as if you have got a girlfriend pregnant? Congratulations."

"Please Vasu... I don't know what to do. Our Nikhil is already twelve. When Sushama wanted a second child all those years ago, nothing happened, and now this accident!" Shrirang sighed, loosening his tie. "I am touching forty... to become a father again at this age?"

Vasu still thought it was a joke. "Why are you so upset? What does Sushama have to say about it?"

"She, too, is confused. We had not expected anything like this to happen. By the time we realised it, five months had gone by. Now even if we want to do anything, it is a big risk."

"Tell me Shrirang, what do you honestly feel?"

He was silent for a while, then hesitantly he said, "Somewhere inside I do feel joy."

"That's it then. Don't people have children late in life? If anyone expresses surprise, let them say what they like. Ignore them. Enjoy it."

"You really think so?" Shrirang asked with relief and gratitude.

"Of course! You are the rising star of the agency. Who knows, the kid may bring better things with it. Boy or girl?"

There was genuine happiness in Shrirang's laugh. "Haven't thought that far ahead yet. We've both been so confused since we found out, especially Sushama. Come over to meet her. She trusts you and your advice."

"Of course I will come. Isn't that why you told me first?"

Getting up, she looked at Shrirang's smiling face and said, "Becoming a father may fill your stomach, not mine. I am going to have lunch."

"Thanks, Vasu, and don't forget to visit."

Vasu nodded and went out.

Before Vasu came home that evening, Mayi put away her books and tidied up the place. She suffered from acute arthritis and her movements were severely restricted. After she had freshened up, Vasu casually said, "Oh Mayi, I forgot to mention, Sushama is pregnant."

"Sushama who?"

"Shrirang's wife. Don't you remember?"

"Hmm." Mayi's face became thoughtful. Obviously she was doing some mental calculations. "But they have a grown-up son, don't they?" she asked.

"That's the fun of it! It was unplanned. Both of them are probably very embarrassed."

"She is quite old, isn't she? As old as you? It is difficult at this age."

"Perhaps," Vasu answered brusquely. She knew what Mayi was thinking. If only Vasu had had a husband, children, family... that's the track her mind was on.

Vasu heard Mayi sigh. "Why do you keep asking why this, why not that, all the time?" she snapped.

"When you have taken such a firm stand, what can I say? I haven't raised the topic even once recently, have I?"

Vasu turned away. She was sure her life was not meant to revolve around a husband and children, but she couldn't convince Mayi of that. Mayi thought her life was incomplete, one-dimensional, drab.

As Vasu opened the gate and walked in, she noticed Sudhatai sitting on the spacious veranda of Shrirang's bungalow. She was busy knitting.

Looking up, she smiled. "How are you, Vasu? It's been a while since you came over... Come, sit down. You've come straight from office?"

"Today is Saturday so..."

"But Shrirang isn't home yet," she said.

Vasu mopped her brow with a handkerchief. "Our departments are different, as is our work. He is in media and needs to go out often, I am in copywriting..."

Just then Sushama ambled out onto the veranda. Vasu was startled to see her gaunt and drawn face. She was seeing Sushama after a long time.

"Finished your nap?" Sudhatai asked Sushama.

"Hmm," Sushama mumbled and sat down.

"I will make tea for everyone," Sudhatai said and went inside.

"I don't want any," Sushama called out after her.

"Why not? Have a little, you will feel refreshed, it will perk you up."

Vasu dragged her chair closer to Sushama's and took both her hands in her own. "You are all right, *na*, Sushama?" she asked.

"How do I look?" Sushama countered.

"Um, you look a little tired, but that is natural."

Sushama's hand lay limp and dry in Vasu's. "You do go to the doctor regularly, don't you?" Vasu asked.

"Vasu, I don't want this, absolutely don't want it..."

Vasu was dumbstruck. Then, making an attempt at laughter, she said, "What are you saying, Sushama! You are in your seventh month, and what is this nonsense about not wanting it? Is something bothering you? Do you feel unwell?"

Sushama shook her head. "It's not that. I just feel so negative... This burden, this ungainly body, I feel like throwing it all away."

"But why?"

"What do you mean 'why', Vasu? I never expected anything like this. Nikhil is a big boy, everything was going smoothly, and now this unanticipated development—no, not unanticipated. Shrirang has deliberately done it." Sushama was in tears.

"Deliberately?"

Sushama turned her face away. Vasu patted her hand comfortingly.

"Depression is not uncommon. But it passes soon enough. Don't worry. Once the baby comes, you will forget everything. You have Shrirang's parents, Shrirang himself, so many people to care for you... Shrirang looks really happy to me."

"And why wouldn't he? He doesn't have to go through it! You tell me, Vasu, is this right? To thrust this upon me, at this age, this stage in my life?"

"Don't be silly, Sushama. Why do you say 'thrust'? It was an accident, it happened. The doctor did advise you not to do something stupid, right? It's only your second child, Sushama. And you have the resources to bring it up well. So why should you feel so negative?"

Sushama pulled her hand away from Vasu's. Dabbing her eyes she said, "I don't know why I am so depressed. Nobody understands. How will they, when Shrirang himself takes it so lightly? They are all enjoying my predicament. They think we are embarrassed because of my age, but it's more than that—I really don't want to go through this; I am worried, frightened, angry."

Sudhatai walked in with the tea. Handing Vasu a cup, she asked, "And how is everything with you?"

"All well."

"Shrirang doesn't normally talk about the office, but he was saying what a good name you have. He admires you."

Vasu smiled. Sushama was gazing into the distance.

"Have some tea," Sudhatai told her.

"I don't want it." Abruptly she got up. "I'm going in to lie down," she said.

Vasu noticed the affection with which Sudhatai was looking at Sushama's retreating back. "Although it is a little late, this pregnancy is a good thing. Nikhil was an only child, and I was not happy about it at all."

"She is keeping well, isn't she?" Vasu asked.

"Who, Sushama? Of course she is. She goes for a check-up every fortnight. The doctor said all was well. Winter will set in by the time she delivers, so thought I would start well in advance. Got nice coloured wool, too." Picking up her knitting, she smiled, "After so long I am making a small sweater!"

Vasu felt an inexplicable sense of dismay.

Despite her efforts, Vasu was not able to meet Shrirang for three days in a row. His table was unoccupied, so she thought he must be out on work. Finally when she did see him, she was leaving the office and he was just walking in.

Stopping him she said, "Wait a bit, Shrirang, are you in a hurry?"

"I am. Don't know why but it's getting late every day. Can't even go home on time."

"Come on, stand me a cup of coffee at least."

"What for?"

"What do you mean 'what for'? Just like that. At least you will spare those ten minutes..."

Since the office canteen was closed, the two of them went to a nearby café and ordered coffee.

"How is Sushama?" Vasu asked.

"Very well."

"Really well?"

"You met her, didn't you? Wasn't she fine?"

"On the contrary, I was worried. She looked scared."

Dismissing Vasu's remark, Shrirang said, "Don't be silly. That's her nature. Even when she was carrying Nikhil she was like this. She doesn't remember but I do; she used to get panicky without reason."

"Even so..."

"Vasu," Shrirang's tone was patronising, "Is she the first woman to get pregnant? The doctor also said that sometimes if you are over thirty you can get stressed."

"Then what do you do to help her?"

"To tell the truth, I am under great pressure myself, handling two very major accounts simultaneously. You know how important they are. I reach home very late and she is usually asleep by then."

Vasu shook her head. "That is so irresponsible."

Shrirang was annoyed. "What do you expect me to do, then?" he snapped. "Sit by her bedside all day? That is ridiculous, Vasu. Did she ask you to intercede on her behalf?"

"Not at all," Vasu retorted. "I just felt that way. You know what, Shrirang, I haven't gone through this process myself, but I think every pregnant woman sometimes feels resentful of the freewheeling and carefree male, along with a despair about her own condition. That's why I said *both* of you must enjoy this event."

Shrirang was angry but managed to conceal it well. Calmly he said, "Thanks for the advice."

"Shrirang..." But before Vasu could say anymore, he had gulped down his coffee and was standing up. "Want me to drop you at the bus stop or shall I carry on?"

"Please carry on," Vasu replied.

As she draped her sari, Vasu told Mayi that she was probably going straight to the hospital to see Shrirang's baby girl.

"He had a daughter?" Mayi asked surprised.

"What is this, Mayi, I told you yesterday."

"You didn't," Mayi retorted. "You are so distracted these days you don't remember what you said. What are you thinking about?"

Vasu was convinced she had told Mayi about the baby. Anyway, when Mayi asked, "So how many pounds is the baby girl?" Vasu replied, "Don't know. I didn't ask. Shrirang left the office as soon as he heard. Okay, I'm going now."

She saw Mayi's lost, confused eyes and felt a twinge of guilt. She knew Mayi was longing to hear such news about her, but she pushed the thought aside. Mayi will never understand that I have no desire to get entangled in these kinds of relationships. For Mayi, motherhood and the maternal instinct are natural and everyone has them. She must regret that it is all past me now. And she is justified in feeling that way.

Vasu had to go out in the afternoon, and when she returned it was almost four-thirty. She was told that Shrirang had called her. Before she could return his call, Shrirang's assistant came up to her and said, "Vasu, have you heard? Shrirang's wife is gone."

"Gone? Where?"

"Gone—departed this earth. She had just delivered a baby. Something untoward must have happened. We must go and see him."

A chill sliced through Vasu. For a few seconds she felt dizzy. Her mind went numb. The news that Sushama had passed away did not register.

Knowing the close friendship that existed between Vasu and Shrirang, the assistant patted Vasu's shoulder sympathetically. "Be brave. If you decide to go over, let me know. We can go together."

Vasu emptied a glass of water in one gulp. How and why had this happened? Was Sushama's fear and despair a premonition? What about the new-born baby? How is she going to live the rest of her life? And Shrirang? All said and done, he did love Sushama. Such a simple, affectionate girl. The twelve-year old Nikhil... Does he even know what death means?

Vasu was benumbed. It was decided in the office that a few of them would go over in the evening. For a moment, she thought she should inform Mayi. But then she realised that Mayi would assume she was late because she had gone to the hospital to see the baby. With this turmoil in her mind, it was a while before Vasu noticed that she had not even felt like crying, as one would be expected to.

As she opened the gate Vasu sensed the eerie calm that had fallen on the bungalow. The veranda was deserted. She rang the bell. Sudhatai came out. Vasu walked up the stairs and sat down in the nearest chair. "You here at this time?" Sudhatai asked.

"It is Saturday today, isn't it."

"Of course! I forgot. Shrirang is still on leave, so..."

"Has Nikhil started going to school?"

"Oh yes," she sighed. "Nothing stops, does it? We insisted that he go back immediately. He was getting very disturbed at home. At least in school he has company."

Just then a baby's cries were heard. "Before we know it, she is a month old already. Such a pretty child..." She called out to the woman looking after the baby. "Bring her here," she instructed. The woman brought the swaddled baby and held her out to Vasu. Taking her in her arms gently, Vasu looked at her.

"Who do you think she looks like?" Sudhatai asked.

"I can't tell."

"We think she is a carbon copy of Shrirang. Girls should resemble their fathers."

Vasu was confused. She didn't know what to do with the bundle in her arms. Seeing her discomfort, the *bai* took her back.

"She was crying a while ago, wasn't she? Must be hungry. Let me get her milk ready. I will send Shrirang out," Sudhatai said, getting up.

For some time Vasu was sitting there alone. All the conversations she had had with Sushama came back to her. They had become friends only because she was Shrirang's wife. Most people found it easy to like Sushama. She was that kind of person. Simple, warm, helpful, and genuinely happy to be a wife and homemaker. Whereas Vasu and Shrirang's friendship went back a long way. Often when Sushama and Shrirang were going out with Nikhil—be it to a movie, a restaurant, a picnic—they insisted that Vasu accompany them. On such occasions the two women would gang up against Shrirang and tease him, and get the better of him in most arguments. Sushama had so much respect for and faith in Vasu that often after a serious quarrel with Shrirang she would open her heart out and complain about Shrirang to her. And Vasu had taken it all as part of their friendship.

In spite of this closeness, the two women were totally different from each other. Sushama made no bones about her envy of Vasu being a professional with a successful career, while Vasu, though not jealous of Sushama's personal life, was certainly curious about it. Vasu had tried to reciprocate Sushama's affection with her warm friendship.

Shrirang came out with some snacks and tea that Sudhatai had prepared.

"When are you rejoining office?" Vasu asked him.

"Haven't decided."

"But leave for so long? What do you do all day?"

"Nothing. Just stay at home."

Vasu looked at his drawn face and lost expression, and felt a surge of sympathy.

"I think you should get back to work soon," she advised.

"Everyone says that..."

"Then why aren't you listening to them?"

"Shall we take a little walk, Vasu?" Shrirang asked, getting out of his chair. "Let me tell *Ai*."

There was a distinct coolness in the air, now that winter was approaching. As they walked, Shrirang said, "One asks oneself so many questions, but finds no answers."

Vasu smiled.

"Why did this happen? In this day and age how can a woman lose her life in childbirth?"

"It isn't that, Shrirang. Normally everything goes smoothly. Sometimes, though, there can be complications. That it should happen in Sushama's case was most unexpected."

"She slipped into a coma, and even the doctor didn't realise what was happening, I think. And that new-born child..."

"What have you named her?"

"Nothing yet. Don't need to address her still. When we have to, we will see." Shrirang sounded thoroughly dejected.

"How has Nikhil taken it?"

"Poor boy. Doesn't speak at all. He must be missing her the most. Fate has me in a tight clinch it seems."

"Shrirang..."

"What else? At this age, this stage in my life, to become a father, lose my wife, my career in shambles—how do I cope with it? Bring up two kids, especially that one all by myself..."

Turning to him Vasu said, "None of this was in your control. But now that it has happened, you must take charge."

"How?" he said, his tone bitter.

Vasu had no answer. Each one must find their own solutions. Are you so weak that you need help, she wanted to say to him, but held back her words. It had only been a month.

It is not easy to accept something like this; he will need time, she told herself.

With the onset of winter, Mayi's health problems increased. Vasu was busy taking care of her, in addition to all the extra chores that the cold weather brings. One day when she stopped at the chemist, she met Sudhatai, reading out from a list: baby food, vitamin drops, cotton, etc. When she saw Vasu she said, "So many things they need! We have a bai to take care of her, but the mothering I have to do."

"How is she? Must be growing up fast."

"Yes, trying to crawl now."

"You haven't named her yet?"

"That's something we missed out on. Everyone calls her baby, little one, or something. Sometimes I feel we should have a small naming ceremony, just for the family."

"There is no need for any ceremony. Just start calling her by a name," Vasu said. "What do Sushama's parents say?"

Sudhatai sighed. "What will they say? They came to visit once. They are much older than us. Besides, it is our baby, isn't it?"

Vasu waited for Sudhatai to collect all her stuff and make the payment. Then they both walked out together.

"Shrirang is okay in the office, isn't he, Vasu?"

"Oh yes. Why?"

"Nothing, but he is very quiet when he is at home, so I was wondering..."

In an effort to reassure her, Vasu said, "He has a lot of work. He was on leave, so the work piled up. It is very competitive out there; if you fall behind, you are lost."

"It's a good thing he went back to work. Otherwise he would be brooding all day."

Sudhatai took an autorickshaw and offered to drop Vasu on the way. She asked after Mayi. They had met a few times.

"Do come over, Vasu, at least to see the baby."

"I will," said Vasu with a smile. "You better have a naming ceremony for her. A nice name that will go with Nikhil."

"Suggest something."

Without thinking Vasu blurted out, "Something starting with Ni... How about Niti?"

"Lovely!" exclaimed Sudhatai. "Let's call her Niti. Now you have to come home for lunch, the christening lunch."

"Sure, I will," Vasu laughed.

In the office Vasu met Shrirang during the lunch hour. He seemed to be as busy as before.

"So what is the news?" she asked as usual.

"Going on," he replied. "Nikhil's exams are coming close; Ai insists I help him with his studies."

"That's not a bad thing."

"No advice is ever bad, is it?" he said with a laugh.

"What do you mean?"

"Now Ai says..." Shrirang paused, looked around and lowering his voice, said, "Get married again."

"Really? So soon?"

"Is it so soon?"

Vasu was embarrassed. All sorts of thoughts were going through her head. It is a business transaction, finally. One wife goes, get another one. To run the house, look after the boy, help him with homework, bring up the daughter, and also because Shrirang is still young, virile, maybe? Which means Sushama's role in this scheme of things was minor. Insignificant. But that wasn't true, was it?

"I also found the idea bizarre at first. But in day-to-day living... you know the usual issues. Why does one need a wife? Mainly for Nikhil's sake. He has become very withdrawn. Our love and affection doesn't seem to be enough. Not that he will readily accept a new mother. But if someone can treat him lovingly... As for Niti, she does need a mother."

"You are convinced of this, are you, Shrirang?"

He said nothing. Just then some colleagues joined them and the subject was shelved.

Once again Sudhatai sent for Vasu. After lunch on that Sunday, all of them went to an uncle of Shrirang's who lived close by. He had visitors from abroad whom Shrirang wanted to meet.

After a while Shrirang suggested that he and Vasu go out and stretch their legs a bit.

After walking for a while, he said, "Vasu, I want to ask you something."

She merely raised her eyebrows.

"Would you like to marry me?" he asked.

Vasu was taken aback. "What are you saying!" she exclaimed.

"Why? I'm not so bad, am I? You know me well."

"I may know you well, Shrirang, but we are not in love with each other."

He laughed. "That's not the point. One can fall in love even later."

Her voice rose sharply. "Shrirang, we have been good friends, almost since our college days. We entered the same profession, changed agencies a couple of times, but coincidentally ended up in the same office. And over the years we have built up a warm, caring, loyal and trusting relationship. Sushama became a part of that relationship so naturally. No other emotions came into it. Definitely when Sushama was around. And now that she isn't... So far we have ignored the few gossipmongers in the office who have said all kinds of things about us, and managed to nurture that pure friendship. So what is this that you are asking of me now?"

Shrirang was startled by her reaction at first. Then he said, "Don't get all riled up like this. Think over it. There is no hurry. Besides, my question is not as weird as you think it is. Does anyone say we must hold on to only one kind of relationship? If you start with friendship, then love and marriage are only a short walk away."

Vasu tried to control the anger rising within her, though she was not sure what was infuriating her. She realised that Shrirang would interpret whatever she said now as an angry reaction. Better to keep cool and give him a reply after a week or so. By then, he, too, would have calmed down.

Vasu came out drying her hair on a towel, and decided that since she had never kept anything from Mayi she would tell her about Shrirang's proposal, too.

"Shrirang has asked me to marry him, Mayi," she said.

Mayi stared at Vasu. First surprise, then excitement, followed by joy were all reflected on her face.

"When? That's what..."

"Last Sunday. That's what, what?"

"You keep going to his place."

"Mayi," she said firmly but gently, "I have not said yes."

"Why not? It's all come to your door uninvited, don't turn it away. He is such a nice boy, good family, parents, house... You are no longer young, so what if he has two children, we know the family. It will not be difficult for you to adjust." Mayi sounded very enthusiastic.

Vasu continued towelling her hair without uttering a word. "I'm talking to you, Vasu. Say yes to him. Don't worry about me. I will be fine on my own. We will get a bai to look after me. You can drop in whenever you can. Or let us look for a nice old age home. There are many such facilities for single women, I believe. All these days you did not consider marriage because of me, now that a golden opportunity has come your way..."

Vasu was stunned. Opportunity! Such an apt word. Everyone—Mayi, Shrirang, society—they all see it only as an opportunity. The pieces fit so neatly, like a jigsaw puzzle. In the one blank space, a readymade suitable object. But no one thinks about that object's individuality, feelings, beliefs, hopes, aspirations.

Throwing her towel over her shoulder, Vasu said, "I only told you what he said. I have not decided anything."

Vasu got so involved in her work that despite her efforts to come home early for Mayi's sake, she was late.

That evening, as soon as she stepped in Mayi said, "Why are you so late? Sudhatai was waiting for you."

"Sudhatai was here?"

"She said she came to see me, but was actually waiting for you."

"You know I have been promoted, Mayi, so my workload has also increased."

Mayi followed her in. "They have asked for you in marriage."

Vasu burst out laughing as she splashed water on her face. What sort of arrogance was this?

"I told them I had no objections. Everything was to my liking. They are also very fond of you. Nikhil feels comfortable with you, and I believe you suggested the name Niti? You didn't mention it to me. Anyway, such situations don't come together so easily so often."

"Shall we have dinner?"

"First tell me, Vasu..."

Vasu became impatient. "Don't put pressure on me like this, Mayi. They want a daughter-in-law, a mother for the kids. I don't fit in that mould. You know that, don't you?"

"What is there to 'fit', Vasu? A family evolves naturally. You are fond of those children, aren't you? A girl like you will take care of them so lovingly."

Vasu was stumped. "I have a career, Mayi. I have worked hard all these years to bring it to this stage. I have got used to earning, spending, behaving as I please. Should I give it all up? Motherhood is not in my genes."

"What rubbish! Any woman can become a mother. You remained unmarried for so long. Was that easy? Will you live all by yourself when I die? Be able to face the world on your own? You have a readymade family being offered to you. A home, husband, children, money—there is no dearth of anything there. Not even love. They will all shower affection on you. And this career of yours, how long will that last? One needs people in one's old age. Think of me for a moment."

Vasu's mind had gone numb. She knew exactly what was going on in Mayi's mind. She even felt a little sorry for her. But her own voice was louder. So far she had not ignored it. But this time, in spite of its persistence, she felt herself wavering.

She kept running into Shrirang in the office every now and then. Both of them behaved as if nothing had happened between them. For one thing, the pressure of work was great, so they had little time to chat.

After several weeks, when they met on the staircase, Shrirang said to her, "You haven't come home in a while. Ai was asking about you."

Vasu laughed heartily. "I am a little scared to come home, actually."

"Why?"

"You know very well why."

Shrirang darted a quick look around. "You are afraid to get involved, right?"

"We'll talk about it someday."

"I will wait for you this evening after office. Come when you are done."

Vasu was uncertain, but reluctantly she went to Shrirang's department. Some people were still hanging around as usual. Shrirang finished what he was doing and walked out with her. "People have already drawn their own conclusions," he muttered.

"Why just them? All of you are also taking a lot for granted."

"What does that mean?"

"Don't pretend to be so dumb, Shrirang," Vasu snapped. "I still feel I am not suitable to be your wife."

"But Vasu..."

"Just listen to what I have to say. I am an independent, self-centred, career-minded woman with no housewifely interests. I am not cut out for the role you are offering."

Shrirang looked at her, disappointment writ large on his face. They began to walk, purposelessly.

Vasu stopped, then said a little more kindly, "Just because I am single, you want me to give up my job and come into your life as your wife, a mother to your children?"

"Have I ever asked you to give up your job?"

"Then it's even more difficult. To walk this path of ideal wife, ideal daughter-in-law, perfect mother is just impossible for me. Think about it, Sushama was so different from me. You want someone in that role. Since you are afraid to take a chance with a strange woman, you are all trying to stuff me, a known person, into that mould. I may look perfect from a distance. But if you force me into that frame, I will not remain me. You will be disappointed, and so will I. It simply won't work, Shrirang!"

Shrirang fell behind, looking grim. A wave of sympathy swept over Vasu. For him. For all of them. But her mind was firmly made up.

Without realising it, she grabbed his arm. "Don't run away, Shrirang... the road will soon end." They had walked a fair distance. Around them were numerous structures under construction and a few scattered houses.

Shrirang stopped. Turning to face Vasu, he said, "Wait. We can think about all the other things later. Do you or do you not feel like marrying me for my sake alone?"

Vasu smiled and gave him a long look.

"What can I say to that? The question cannot be taken in isolation. It's okay for you. If you marry me, your life will not change much. That's why it sounds so tempting. But my life will be overturned. Do I continue to work? Give up my career? I will have to play whatever the role demands of me. And that circus I am not prepared to be a part of. Do you know when I decided not to marry? When I was young, I fell in love and was hurt badly. I had to struggle to rebuild my life. And I found joy in it, pride, and self-worth. I am not meant for fulfilment through being a wife, a mother, a homemaker. Why don't you understand that, Shrirang? One can't take emotional decisions at this stage of our lives. They have to be practical as well."

Shrirang was looking down, his face thoughtful.

"Tell me Shrirang, do you want me as a friend or not? If you do, then don't try to force another relationship on me. I will never be able to occupy Sushama's place. I am too unlike her."

Shrirang's expression was petulant. In that instant Vasu knew what he was expecting her to say. He thought she would admit that she was attracted to him. That she would find fulfilment in marriage to him. It would signify his triumph as a man, a lover, a husband. She was angry and sad. How hard it is to sensitise a man like Shrirang, she thought. It made her very unhappy.

When Vasu walked up to Shrirang's desk he was engrossed in writing something. She knocked on the table and asked, "Can

I take a minute of your time? I have just received some good news. Thought I would share it with you, my closest friend." It all came out so easily, she thought.

"Tell me?" Shrirang said, trying to smile.

"I am leaving this place. I have a new job. More challenging; more paying, too."

Shrirang's face fell. "In the same city?"

"Yes, but we will no longer be colleagues. We will be rivals!"

"Congratulations."

"I will have to give a month's notice, but I am taking leave during that period."

As an afterthought she added, "If you ever think of me, call, or come and meet me. You will, won't you?"

There was pain in Shrirang's smile.

"Tell Sudhatai also. I will drop by some time. Mayi hasn't been too well. She gets upset with things like this. So I am planning to take her somewhere for a holiday."

The office buzzed with visitors, phone calls, conversations, summons, as was usual for an afternoon. In the midst of that hustle and bustle, Vasu held her hand out to Shrirang with a deep sense of self-confidence. "Wish me luck, Shrirang," she said.

As if there was a sudden flash of lucid realisation, Shrirang took her hand and offered her his best wishes.

4 The Love Gene*

He picked up the newspaper but before he could read the headlines, his eyes fell on the date. It was his daughter's birthday today. He was surprised. He had not remembered her birthday before this. Nor had he noticed the date. Why would anyone notice that? Days come and go one after another, dates change routinely. From one to thirty or maybe thirty-one, or sometimes twenty-eight, maybe twenty-nine. Month after month, year after year—each day like the one gone by. Nothing new or unusual about it. So of what consequence was a date?

Birthdays were different apparently. Most people considered them special. Not him. To him birthdays were not important. Neither his own nor anyone else's. He did not recollect ever remembering anyone's birthday. Many years ago his wife had complained, he vaguely remembered. Women were known to make an issue of such things. His stock answer had been, "When I don't remember my own birth date, why should I be expected to remember anyone else's?" Was she appeased by that reply? He didn't know. But even if she wasn't, she had remained silent on the matter after that.

Then came his daughter. Invariably on her birthday he would be out travelling on work. His wife must have admonished him, "At least try to remember the child's birthday." But it made no difference. Gradually the girl also must have got used to it. Whether he remembered or not,

*Originally published in Marathi as 'Premache Januk', in the magazine *Shabda Deepotsava*, 2007.

she continued to grow up. Years went by. His wife died. The grown-up daughter went away. The dates on the calendar changed, merged into one another. There was no need to notice them, pay heed to them. Neither then, nor now. Simple.

Then why did the date scream out at him today, "It's your daughter's birthday"? He tried to ignore the voice and started reading the paper. But nothing registered. He was too distracted. The date. The birthday. His daughter's. The words went round and round in his head. He set the paper down and leaned back in his chair. Many years ago, on this day, she had been born. How many exactly? He couldn't remember. How old was she now? What did she look like? Was she tall? How did she dress? Was her hair long or short? Was she slim? Plump? He couldn't recall anything. Gradually, a series of images floated across his memory. Images of a little girl, going to school, seated opposite him at the dining table, curled up on the sofa, leaning against the kitchen door, preening in front of the mirror in her room, walking home briskly as he watched from the balcony, or throwing her jeans-clad legs across the pillion seat of a motorcycle and leaning against some unfamiliar back, and then suddenly standing before him, her face wet with tears, uttering heart-brokenly, "*Ai*!"

Those were all fragments of an old movie. He felt he had seen them before, but was not sure of the context. Nor could he recall the sequence. What was the story all about? He did not know the characters, but they seemed familiar. Nothing was clear. What was real, what imagined? A mixture.

His daughter. So what if she had gone far away. She was still a daughter. Born in this house, grown up here. He looked at the date on the newspaper again. Carefully. Yes, no doubt about it at all. It was the date of her birth. A date he had not remembered earlier.

He was not around when she was born. His wife had gone to her parents' place for the delivery. The phone call had come during an important meeting. "You have a baby girl," the secretary had informed him softly—but loud enough for everyone to hear. His first reaction was one of discomfiture.

He was not the boss then, just a bright, hardworking and ambitious young man, with the potential to go far. All eyes were on him. As if he'd achieved something remarkable. He was embarrassed. The boss and the secretary had a triumphant look on their faces. His colleagues seemed delighted. He felt a rush of anger. Why should one new life generate so much happiness and joy, he thought. The annoyance spread to everyone around him. It was an important meeting, some major issues were being discussed, and now because of this interruption, that, too, pertaining to him, there was a break in the chain of thought. Besides, what was so special about the event? When a man and a woman marry, they cohabit, they produce a child. So?

No one noticed his reactions, let alone understood them. One person thought he was impatient to see his wife and newborn daughter, while another assumed he was disappointed because it was a girl. A third muttered, "Such a bloody miser, doesn't want to give us a party and is looking for an escape route!" One man even went so far as to say, "Perhaps he doesn't like his wife, that's why he is so casual about the whole thing."

These comments reached him, but he chose to ignore them. Later, he went, as was customary, to see his wife. And the newborn baby girl. Eventually, his wife came home with the baby. And that was it. Things happened as they were supposed to, without his help. He did not need to remember anything.

In the early days, his wife would sometimes say things like, "A father should participate in the upbringing of a child" etc. Not exactly in these words, but by asking him to do some little tasks. Gradually all that stopped. Once he overheard her say to a friend, or was it a neighbour, he wasn't sure, "When he is so disinterested in the house and home, what is the point of telling him anything? He is buried in his office and his work, day and night. What to do?" He knew it was him she was talking about, but he wasn't particularly affected by it. Because it was true, and justified, too. But wasn't it so of all men? He had known it all along. A simple matter.

And now, after all these years, when another simple matter presented itself before him, he was bewildered. How is it that he had noticed the date and realised it was the day of his daughter's birthday, without any context, without any reason?

Putting the paper down, he stood up. Now that I have remembered, let me at least get in touch with her, he thought. That means call her. But what will I say to her? It's your birthday, many happy returns? Greetings? Or something like that? What will she think? If I do something I have never done before, she will wonder what the matter is. Either she will fall down in a faint, or think that her father has gone off his head. Or...

He went into the bedroom and picked up the telephone diary. Then he hesitated. The girl had become a complete stranger to him. During his long and successful career, he had come across so many people. It was his job to provide each new acquaintance with information, persuade them, instruct them, allay their doubts and fears, reassure them. As a result, they had all benefited. They had all done well. Could anything be more important, more meaningful than that? It was a chain, and through each link of this chain, so many things were accomplished, bringing with them money, enough to buy the comforts of day-to-day living—food, clothing, shelter. The best of everything.

He had been following a routine for so long, he seemed unaware that there was any other life beyond his own. So today, when he contemplated doing something out of this pattern, calling up a strange woman and saying to her, "I remembered your birthday," he wondered if it would be proper. He opened the diary. It was his wife's, so it would certainly have the girl's number. He flipped through the pages. They were full of numbers, written in a neat, round, childish hand. Who were all these people? Friends, relatives, acquaintances of his wife? So many contacts she had? His cell phone, too, had a long list of numbers. But they were all official. Besides, whenever one particular number had served its purpose, a transaction was completed, the number was deleted. In this diary not one number was struck off.

A sudden curiosity stirred within him. It must be almost two and a half years since she'd passed away. The house had been full of people that day, but his daughter had taken charge of everything. She was smart, capable. That's what someone had said to him. And added, "She's got these traits from you. She's going to have a very bright future, and great success, just like yours." That, he had doubted. He had known it even before then, for she had chosen a path completely different from his. At the age when he had been absolutely clear about what he wanted in life, his career options, objectives, goals, she was thinking of something quite bizarre, according to him. Animal welfare—that was her obsession.

He had learnt of it only because his wife had mentioned it to him. "These days, she is spending a lot of her time with some organisation. I believe they take care of stray, helpless, injured, abandoned animals. Cows, buffaloes, cats, dogs, horses, even donkeys." He had been shocked. Both by what his daughter was doing, and on discovering that institutions like this existed. Were animals ever abandoned? Wounded? He had not given it a thought. Soon shock gave way to annoyance. He considered her preoccupation foolish and mindless. He waited for his wife's reaction to his observation. He had always found her acquiescent. He expected her to be. This time, though, she was silent. Did not utter a word. Not even a "No". Her face was expressionless.

This development had taken him unawares. It unnerved him. So he said rather sharply, "What? Isn't it stupid, this obsession of hers? Why is she wasting her time on such meaningless things?"

She'd replied calmly, "I don't think so."

"What? What don't you think? Did we bring her up, educate her to serve dogs and cats? Why didn't she become a vet if she cared so much for animals? At least that would have been a profession."

"I don't agree," his wife said again.

He was furious. "What do you know of these things? Useless stuff. Did she even attend that last interview? It's a good job in a big company. I know people there. She should get it easily."

His wife remained silent, as he expected. What could she say? The girl had a job, but this was an opportunity for something better. A bigger company, higher salary—it would be good for her. Once she settled down, they would find a nice boy and get her married. It wouldn't be difficult to find a worthy groom for an educated, employed girl, his paternal confidence assured him.

Then one day, he confronted his daughter. They rarely came face to face. Their schedules were such. While he travelled on work, his wife looked after the house, the daughter and her welfare. Her coaching classes, her health, her tantrums; disciplining her, indulging her—it was all his wife's department. She managed it well. Their responsibilities had been clearly defined, simply and practically. His life was perfectly planned, efficiently executed.

The girl stood in front of him. Tall, slender, wearing tight jeans and a t-shirt with a picture of a puppy across the front. Underneath were the words, 'Save Me, Love Me'.

Blood rushed to his head. "What's all this nonsense?"

"What?" she asked, puzzled. Following his gaze, she ran her fingers over her chest and said nonchalantly, "Cute, isn't it?"

"What is all this about cats and dogs I hear?"

"I like them. All animals, not just cats and dogs. You know that black kitten we had? You would not let her come into the house, but I used to give her milk outside every day. She would come and play with me on the terrace. One day she disappeared. I cried for eight days, you remember?"

He recollected none of it. She must have been a little girl then. He had no recollection of her at that age. He was concentrating on his career then. His wife had been the only witness to all that had occurred in this house.

His head was reeling. Getting a hold on himself, he said, "So what's this organisation you are going to? And your job?

Have you given it up? Weren't you supposed to go for an interview?"

"Yes, I'll go. I haven't given up my job or anything. I go there when I have the time. It's a voluntary organisation. A lady runs it. They always need volunteers. So many people come, whenever they can. After all it's a service; they do it out of love, not for money. You don't know it, but that is real love. It is selfless, limitless, undemanding."

He was speechless. How much this chit of a girl could talk! Most of it nonsense, irrational, illogical. His knees felt weak so he sank into the sofa. The girl remained standing. Patting the space next to him, he said to her, "Sit, come and sit down." Her eyes widened in surprise. Normally, one never had a face-to-face discussion in this house. The few times her mother had sat before him, she had heard him out and nodded in agreement.

The girl remained standing. He started, "All right, now I know. It's all very well, this animal love, but what is the priority in your life? Don't you have any goals, any aspirations? We educated you, indulged you, aren't you going to do something with it? Achieve something?"

She looked at him blankly. "Isn't what I am doing worthwhile? I believe it is."

For a moment he didn't know what to say. His temper began to soar. It soon turned into a rage, to the point of wanting to deny any connection with her, have nothing to do with her. How did she become like this, so irrational, unreasonable?

"Who has put all this rubbish into your head?" he asked, his voice shrill.

"No one can 'put' these things into anyone. They are within you. Once you acknowledge them, everything becomes simple. The way forward becomes clear."

Just then her cell phone rang. She answered immediately, shrieked, exchanged a few words and then abruptly switched it off. "I have to go. It's urgent. I have been summoned," she told him.

"By whom?"

"Our madam. It is serious. A temple elephant has been ill-treated, beaten badly, dehydrated. It needs to be rescued at once. Bah! What people! Claim they are god-fearing and religious, but don't have any humanity in them. I must go..."

He couldn't believe his ears. His daughter getting so worked up about an elephant? He was almost amused by the absurdity of the situation. Then exerting his authority, he thundered, "You are not going anywhere. Not at this time, on a Sunday afternoon."

"I have a hat, my sunglasses and a bottle of water. I will take an autorickshaw. You worry about me going out in the sun. What about that poor elephant that is being tortured? It has no shade, no food, no water..."

His wife came out just then. Holding out a water bottle, she asked her, "You have change for the autorickshaw?"

Rage choked him. The words stuck in his throat. It was too much. Gradually the anger evaporated, leaving behind scars, like steam burns.

Her madness continued. She did not attend any job interviews, passed up opportunities for better prospects. He was grievously disappointed. He had never put any restrictions on her because she was a girl. He had encouraged her to do an MBA, confident that she would take after him, follow his career path. What happened to all that?

But the bigger shock had come from his wife—she was actually supporting the girl. He was not used to being contradicted by her. Once in a while he had noticed mother and daughter in close conversation, but the moment he entered the room, they fell silent. He had not given it any thought. If he ever complained about his daughter, his wife either kept quiet or obediently said, "Yes, yes." He was convinced that she respected him, was proud of his professional success, and eternally grateful for the good life he had provided her. But that day this illusion he had been harbouring about his wife was shattered. That was the bigger blow.

Had he not noticed the signs? But she had never openly confronted him; she had either very gently protested, or ignored his views and changed the topic. Was it a conspiracy the mother and daughter had hatched, he began to wonder.

How could they be so ungrateful? He had done so much for them. He had worked so hard to provide them with a spacious house, a bigger car, every mod-con to make their lives easier. Not only that, he had never refused to help her relatives, even friends, get jobs, admissions, recommendations. He had given hard cash, too. This is what he got in return. All women are like that, he was quick to generalise.

Then came her illness. At first it seemed an innocuous ailment. But then they found it was serious, life-threatening. Despite the best medical attention, she passed away. It was a blow, being so sudden, and he did grieve for her. But it was his daughter who suffered the untimely loss of her mother the most. True, she had been remarkably composed those days. Ran the house efficiently, attended to the innumerable guests, visitors, relations and well-wishers.

Then, once a decent interval had elapsed, she declared that she was moving out. She had a new job, had found a place to live in. But he believed that was not the real reason she was going away. She was not telling him the truth.

"What will happen to me? To this house?" he asked her petulantly.

"Everything will function as before. I have made all the arrangements."

"And you? How will you manage?"

"I am not a child anymore. I will get along fine. It's best this way. One must learn to stand on one's own feet. And if one stumbles, one can learn a lesson from it, pick oneself up, and carry on."

Again that foolish prattle. His head began to spin. So many changes had taken place in his life. Everything he had taken for granted—his ever-attentive wife, his well-run home, it was all gone. His daughter went away. Far away. She would call occasionally. Visit once in a while, tidy up the house, question why things had to be done in the same fashion, and leave. His routine remained pretty much the same. But his daughter had changed. Every time he saw her she looked different. If he asked her any questions, she would go off into some long-winded spiel, most of which he couldn't understand.

Once he pointedly asked her about marriage. Should he look for a boy? Or did she have anyone in mind?

"Of course not. No marriage for me," she retorted.

"Why not? All girls get married. If your mother were alive, she would have found..."

"No," she interrupted, "Ai knew of my decision. In fact she said, 'If you don't feel like it, don't get into it.'"

"Really? She said that?" He sounded disbelieving. Why, her mother had been so well-off after her marriage. Would she have had such a good life otherwise?

"Yes, Ai understood me. Mothers generally do, when their daughters grow up. It's almost instinctive. Of course, one must have the capacity to understand, *na*... Not everyone has it."

Whenever this girl speaks she confuses, no, confounds me, he thought. She is a smart, intelligent girl who takes all her own decisions, makes her own choices, but this kind of talk doesn't make sense.

Beads of sweat gathered on his brow. He slumped in his chair. His daughter brought him a glass of water. "Are you all right?" she asked solicitously. Just like her mother used to. He had always mocked her for that question. Today she wasn't beside him. His daughter, too, would go away... He missed his wife greatly that day.

Several months passed.

Then this day dawned. He looked down at the diary in his hands. There was no number against his daughter's name. How could there be? She had gone to live on her own after her mother's death. How to find her number now? He riffled through the various diaries, phone books, scraps of paper with numbers scribbled on them. Without luck. He picked up his cell phone and searched under her name. There was a number registered there. How had it come there? He had never called her, nor had she spoken to him on the cell. Now that he was mostly at home, she used the landline. Perhaps she had inserted it there, just in case... Not wasting too much time on figuring that out, he pressed the call key.

Many rings later, just as he was about to disconnect, a heavy, sleepy voice said, "Hello, how are you?"

"Did I wake you up?"

"Yes! It's my birthday, na, so I thought I'll celebrate by waking up late."

He felt deflated. It was pointless saying 'I remembered'. She would not believe him.

"So what are your plans for the day?"

"I was planning to come and see you this evening. You are at home, aren't you?"

"Yes, yes I am," he said, and then added, "I will wait for you if you are coming."

He wondered if she got the sarcasm in his tone. She disconnected. He tried to get on with his normal routine, but found it extremely difficult to concentrate on anything. An inexplicable restlessness seized him. Suddenly he became conscious of his years. It seemed as if nothing mattered anymore. He sat there flipping through the pages of his wife's diary. All it contained were phone numbers. And a few addresses. He read the names. Not one seemed familiar. He started giving them identities, relationships... This is her sister; that is the lady next door...

His gaze fell on the photographs of his wife that his daughter had placed on the telephone table. She was standing alone in a garden in one. In another, she was holding her daughter's hand ready to cut the birthday cake, the momentous occasion captured for posterity. In the third photograph, his wife was carrying their baby daughter. There was a crowd of people around her. Who were all those people? When had these pictures been taken? He realised then that he had played no part in any of these events. He knew nothing about them.

He stayed home all day. There was only one thought in his mind—his daughter was coming in the evening. He was waiting for her. Never in his life had he waited for anyone like this.

The doorbell rang several times before he heard it. He scrambled out of his chair and rushed to open it. There was a woman standing on the doorstep. When it occurred to him that it was his daughter, he heard her say, "Were you sleeping at this hour? Are you all right?"

She came in and switched on the lights. As usual, she went around the house, checking everything. "You didn't eat lunch?" she asked. "The vessels look untouched."

"It's your birthday," he said.

"I told you on the phone. I've taken leave today. My friends are having a party for me later. Thought I would come and see you before that."

"Your mother..." he stammered, "what did she do on your birthday?"

"When I was little, she used to have a party. Buy me a surprise gift and keep it next to my pillow before I woke up."

She paused. "Do you know what I gave her for her birthday? A sapling. Many of the plants in our garden are those presents. She loved gardening. We had planned that some day we would buy a big plot of land and have lots and lots of trees. I insisted that we have a shelter for animals, too. Everything and everybody there would be infected by the love gene. The place would be filled with love. We hoped that it would spread, far and wide. But none of that happened. Dreams rarely translate into reality, do they?" As she spoke, her eyes filled with tears.

As usual, he was completely nonplussed. What was she talking about? It made no sense to him.

She went in and got him a glass of water. "Here, have some. You'll feel better," she said.

He gulped it down. He struggled with the words, "What were you saying about that love gene or something?"

She stared at him for a long moment, but said nothing.

He, too, kept looking at her. A strange woman. His daughter. Grown up now. Born this day many years ago. How many? How little he knew about her.

She started to explain, "It's a science. Genetics. A person's essence is contained in the genes. It is passed on to the next generation. Love, too, is like that. If you have the love gene, you have love in your heart. If not..."

"Rubbish, I haven't read anything like that," he snapped.

"Really? Well, you couldn't possibly have read about everything, could you? Moreover what is unfamiliar today will become known tomorrow..."

He became nervous. The strength seemed to drain out of him.

"You probably don't have it," she continued. "I must have inherited it from my mother. It is not found in everyone. Only when it becomes universal will the world change. But it's a slow, gradual process. We must keep trying though, to proliferate it..."

He felt completely exhausted. With difficulty he muttered, "I remembered your birthday this morning itself."

A half-smile played on her lips. Did she believe him? Who knows. He had not known what to gift her, not even what to say to her. He just sat there with a defeated air about him. A long time passed. Neither of them spoke. Every now and then she looked at her cell phone. Pressed a few keys, then put it away. She picked up the newspaper lying on the table and glanced cursorily at it.

Suddenly the phone rang. She kept muttering, "Hm, hm, hm," into it. Then she stood up. "I am going now," she said.

"Alright. Greetings on your birthday. Many happy returns..."

She smiled. She looked so much like her mother then.

5 The Invitation*

When Sarita opened her eyes, the room was still dark. She'd had a good night's sleep and was wide awake now. She got out of bed and tried to open the curtains but they wouldn't budge. Then she realised there must be some contraption by which to part them. This wasn't her home, was it?

What she saw outside the window was magnificent. A range of mountains in the distance and lush green meadows below. A few scattered houses. And then her eyes alighted on the backyard with its trees and flowering shrubs. Everything was so charming, so serene. She was enchanted.

She stood by the window for a few minutes, then walked out. The bedrooms were on the upper floor. She went down the stairs and headed towards the sounds coming from below. At a table in the living room-cum-kitchen, with its large French windows looking out on the grassy landscape, Nishi, spectacles on nose, was at the computer, engrossed in her work. Western classical music played softly in the background.

Sarita found the whole scene strange, yet familiar. Astonishing, too.

Nishi looked up. "Finished sleeping, *Ai*? I was waiting for you to wake up." She hit a few keys, shut the computer and stood up. Pouring the just-brewed coffee into a cup, she asked, "Milk? Sugar?"

*Originally published in Marathi as 'Amantran', in the magazine *Mauj*, Diwali Issue, 1998.

"Everything," replied Sarita, sitting down at the table. "What time is it?"

"Eleven-thirty."

"Really! I slept so long?"

"Of course! Mother, it will take you three or four days to get over the jetlag. Your timings will go haywire. But so what?"

Sarita sipped her coffee. Nishi pulled out a chair and sat down next to her. "You slept well?"

"Very well." After a pause Sarita asked, "Has your *Baba* gone to work?"

Nishi smiled. "Yes, he leaves by seven-thirty. And why are you saying 'your Baba'? You always addressed him by his name, didn't you?"

"That was a long time ago. Now I don't know what to call him."

"Just call him Jay as you used to. I'm sure he'll like that."

Sarita looked at Nishi. Though she was over twenty-five, she looked like a callow young girl. In her tight jeans and short, cropped hair she is quite at home in these surroundings, thought Sarita.

"What would you like to do today?" Nishi asked.

"Whatever you say."

"Then get ready quickly. Have something to eat first, I'll show you around later."

Sarita sensed her enthusiasm. That same eagerness had made Sarita overcome her reservations and land up here. Nishi had been very persuasive—so many letters, so many phone calls—not giving up until Sarita had said yes. "Give me one good reason for not wanting to make this trip," she had insisted.

What excuses did I have, Sarita thought. I tried using work and the demands on me and my time. But her daughter wasn't convinced. Neither was I, for that matter, especially in the last few months.

"What are you going on about your work? As if there are no other doctors besides you. You must have trained several of them over the years?"

Then she tried mentioning health issues. It was true she hadn't been keeping too well. Minor nagging problems. To that Nishi had retorted, "All the more reason to come here! The clean, unpolluted air will refresh you, make you fit and fine. Eat well, relax, have a good time." Sarita had realised that herself. She needed to rest. To take a break. Nothing wrong with that.

That was all. Nothing more was said. But Jayteerth had written, endorsing Nishi's proposal. That's when she realised how long it had been. The ego problems, the misunderstandings, the emotions and sentiments, the closeness and the estrangement appeared trivial, inconsequential, after all this time. So what should I do, Sarita kept asking herself.

Finally she had gathered together her resources, her clothes and her enthusiasm, and arrived here. The place she had once chosen to turn her back on, firmly, unequivocally. Jay's world. She had entered it now.

Nishi walked into the room while Sarita was getting ready.

"You don't wear anything other than saris, do you, Ai?"

"Oh no, no! What else could I wear?"

"It is quite cool outside and the evenings get positively chilly. You won't find the sari so comfortable. How about *salwar kameez*?"

Sarita laughed. "Whose, yours? You think I will be able to squeeze into them?"

"I don't have any, anyway. I was just wondering if..."

"Forget it. Just give me a muffler and a sweater and I will be fine. Don't worry so much about me."

"*Wah bhai, wah*... If you catch a cold tomorrow, you will blame me!"

"Why would I do that?" Sarita asked a little anxiously.

"Because I forced you to come!"

"Of course you didn't. It was entirely my decision."

"All that persuasion and pressure, and now you say it was your decision!"

"That is all very well, but the choice one has to make oneself, isn't it? We are experts at making choices. Your father and I made ours twenty years ago. Five–six years ago, you made your own decisions, didn't you? And no one objected."

"That is true," muttered Nishi. "But it doesn't mean that either we are very understanding or we don't really care, does it?"

Sarita was taken aback. What is the answer to that question? Have I been looking for it all this while, or have I not given it a thought at all? Or is it because it has often been popping up in my head of late that I...

The pre-dinner conversation was animated. Jayteerth was busy chopping vegetables for the salad and Nishi stir-frying something in a pan. Only Sarita was idle. For one thing, it was a new place, and everything was unfamiliar—the kitchen, the utensils, the style of working—but what kept her from offering to help was Nishi's stern warning: "You will not do any work. You will only relax."

Nishi was telling Jayteerth what they had done all day. He was asking Nishi, Did you take her to this place, did you show her that. Through their conversation Sarita could tell that they completely identified with this place.

"So how did you find it all?" Jayteerth asked.

"Very nice. Clean, orderly and pretty. I had no idea what to expect."

Nishi interrupted, "That's it. Most people believe that there are only fifty-hundred-storied buildings, the din of traffic, and blinding lights. They don't realise that a town can be different, isn't it, Baba?"

Jayteerth laughed. "Hmm, yes."

"Those impressions are formed from what one reads in magazines or sees in movies. Or from someone's travel accounts. Hardly anyone mentions small pretty towns like yours."

"That's why I insisted that you come and see for yourself," Nishi said. "Don't keep saying no and refuse to venture out. Everything is different when you see it for yourself."

Jayteerth placed a glass of wine in front of Sarita. "No, no! I don't drink," she said, looking slightly alarmed.

"Ai, stop making a fuss," Nishi said sharply. "This region is famous for its wines. And get over your prejudice. There's no drink like wine in the world. At least take a sip and see."

"But Nishi, I haven't in my whole life..."

"That's why you should have it now. You are not going to get drunk or become an addict so soon. Try new things, learn how to enjoy at least now, Ai. There is a difference between being addicted or controlled by something, and enjoying it with awareness."

Sarita kept looking at her glass and Nishi uncertainly.

"Nishi is right, Saru. Why are you still so timid? So scared of everything?" Jayteerth asked.

Sarita gave him a startled look. What was she startled about? That he should say she was timid? Address her as 'Saru' so naturally, and continue to sip his wine and cut vegetables as if it were an everyday occurrence?

Nishi sat down opposite Sarita. "You are on a vacation with us, Ai. You will have to do as we tell you. Besides we are not your enemies waiting to pounce on you. We are your own daughter and husband."

Sarita was at a loss for words. She felt extremely awkward. What Nishi had said so spontaneously was true. Am I really as timid, as afraid of little things as Jayteerth said?

Sarita picked up the glass. She didn't like the taste after the first sip, but with the second and the third and subsequent ones, she noticed that the colour, the fruity flavour, the full-bodied liquor and the fragrance were quite enjoyable. Watching her expression, Nishi was smiling mischievously.

To divert attention, Sarita said, "We have yet to see your campus, Nishi."

"Yes, I have saved it for later. We will spend a whole day there. It's quite far from here and also very big. You will like it. We will go to my apartment after that."

"Your apartment?"

"Yes, on campus. It's tiny, but I live there."

"You didn't mention it earlier?"

"I didn't? Must have slipped my mind. It's been a year now. It's very convenient. I can work at the library and with the computers there."

"And someone special also lives there," Jayteerth added, laughing.

Sarita watched Nishi throw a slightly annoyed glance at her father as he continued to smile. She felt a twinge of envy seeing that special something they shared.

"But that's not important," Nishi hastened to add. "It's just a place of work. Wouldn't I have sent you that address if it were home?"

Am I trying to keep tabs on my daughter even now, wondered Sarita. Good thing Nishi didn't ask if she was. Even that time, she had only said, "Ai, I have made up my mind. I am going." You cannot fight or argue with a grown-up, educated daughter, can you? And yet Sarita had felt that the child who had grown up in her care, shaped by her upbringing, would be like herself. She was hardly likely to turn out like him just because she exchanged the occasional letter with him!

When it was time to clear the table, Sarita said, "At least now tell me what I can do."

"Nothing. Just relax. It will all get done in no time. What are these gadgets for!"

"Surely our gadgets need human beings to run them, isn't it?"

"Sure. It is a job. Like yours."

"What do you mean like *mine*?"

Giggling, Nishi replied, "You also 'run' human beings don't you? Like that."

Sarita frowned. "I run people?"

"What else? Haven't you been doing it for years, at home and outside? You have got people to do things for you—your domestic help, the doctors and nurses at your workplace..."

"You mean to say I haven't done anything myself?"

"Getting things done is also doing something."

"Your tone implied it was merely secondary."

"For heaven's sake, Ai! What is there to get so het up about? Just admit it now, that's all."

Confused and angry, Sarita chose to remain silent. Jayteerth continued to put away things without speaking. After a while, she turned on him. "You must feel the same way, then? All these years, I merely got people to work for me. Not just a few, but a full twenty-five, twenty-six years? I have done so much—set up a hospital, travelled to all sorts of places to set up clinics, trained staff, helped hundreds of people—all that was merely 'getting things done', not doing it myself? So what is 'doing it yourself'? Making tons of money? Is that the only yardstick?"

Jayteerth stood still. He stared at Sarita long and hard. Nishi looked up from the dishwasher that she was loading and watched her mother, listened to her. When neither of them said anything, Sarita was infuriated. So that's what both of them believed. Jayteerth hasn't changed one bit, she thought. He is as rigid about his views now as he was then, when he had made his decision to come here and outlined his plans. And here I was thinking that he invited me here because he wanted to recapture some of that which he had lost, even if it was too late to go back. I thought I was invited for my sake. Foolish of me to think so! And Nishi? My daughter, whom I carried for nine months, a recent arrival in this country, she, too, should say this?

After a long silence Jayteerth said, "What is all this? We are not here to settle accounts, are we? Nishi, are you done? I need to leave early tomorrow. I am off to bed. Goodnight," he said and walked away. Nishi went back to her half-done chores. "Will you have some coffee, Ai?"

"Now? No."

"I am making some for myself. Then I have some work to do. I didn't have any time all day."

"I will go up then," said Sarita and turned towards the stairs.

"Will you get ready early tomorrow? We will go to my campus."

Sarita whirled around. "I am not coming in the way of your work, am I?"

"No, no, not at all," Nishi said with a smile. "Luckily for me, mine is not a nine-to-five job. I can work at my convenience.

Even from home. I have more than enough time to take you around."

"I don't want anyone to be inconvenienced because of me."

"What are you saying, Ai! If that were the case, would we have insisted on inviting you here?"

Because Sarita didn't say anything, Nishi continued, "That was quite unnecessary, Ai. Why do you take everything personally and react so strongly?"

"What does that mean? What did I do?"

"Even simple remarks set you off on an outburst about principles."

"You mean there are no principles underlying all our conversation and our behaviour?"

"See, that's exactly it. Anyway, forget it. Go have a good rest. In three or four days, see how free and relaxed you will feel. And learn to forget yourself once in a while, Ai."

Sarita was totally flummoxed. How can this girl say all this so glibly to a woman like herself, who had made difficult choices, led her entire life on the basis of an ideology, had pushed aside all temptations and immersed herself in hard work and hardship, had disciplined herself to always put others before herself so it had become a habit?

Nishi had already spread out her papers and her laptop on the dining table. The music was playing and the coffee cup was full.

Sarita went upstairs. There were four bedrooms and each of them had a balcony. Because the doors were closed she had no way of knowing if Jayteerth had gone to sleep immediately or was still awake. Suddenly this house, the neighbourhood, the town revolted her. I would have been better off in my own home, she thought. A small three-roomed house it was, but one was used to it.

Malan always used to say, "Your home is so nondescript, Saru, just like yourself." Malan was not known for her tact. Though she was a younger sister, she was more of a friend. On a couple of occasions when Sarita had wanted to open her heart out to someone, the only person she could think of was

Malan. And this, in spite of having built relationships with so many throughout her life—her colleagues, people she had recruited and trained, 'guided' as they said, and the many she had met professionally. All of them treated her with a lot of respect, admired her. They gave her a sense of fulfilment.

Malan had also said, "You will never lack for people, Saru. One call and fifty of them will come running to your side." And yet when she needed a confidante, only Malan came to mind. At least then. Until recently, when she had started talking to Gautam.

When Malan heard about Sarita's travel plans, she had been quite angry. "What is that daughter of yours inviting you there for? Remember one thing, Saru, she isn't inviting you to her house. It is to her father's house. Do you realise that?"

"I know that. But after all these years, what's the point in bringing it up..."

"What do you mean? Didn't your husband ditch you and your daughter and go off on his own?"

Saru almost laughed, infuriating Malan.

"Don't take it so lightly, Saru," she warned. "Come to your senses, think it over. You have a sudden urge to travel abroad? Go to some travel agency and buy a round-the-world ticket. No harm in that. But don't go to see your husband and daughter, I'm telling you."

"Actually, Nishi is very insistent, Malan."

"Then tell her to come and meet you."

"She wants me to go there, look around a bit..."

"But there? To his home?"

"Jay's also written."

"Oh really? He's suddenly sprouted feelings for you after all these years?"

"Nothing like that. Just a simple invitation." Sarita's voice had a sharp edge to it.

Malan was furious. The same Malan who, when she had heard of Jayteerth's decision, had said, "Why don't you go with him, Saru? Why are you being so stubborn! You can study further, earn lots of money, smart doctor lady that you are." She wouldn't have understood that it was a matter of principle. And yet when Jayteerth took off, Malan was a great support. Work had been hectic and demanding. In that rush of emotion Sarita had taken on lots of responsibilities. Nishi was very little then. Every time Sarita was in a spot, Malan had come to her rescue. She had proved that after the parents, it was the two sisters who had to support each other. Malan did all this in spite of her husband's and in-laws' disapproval.

Gradually things settled down. Sarita managed to establish a routine. Success at work, name and fame followed. Nishi grew up, independent, capable. Naturally. Inevitably. People accepted her as she was. Because she was straight, firm and principled in her work. That had not changed. It would not change. And yet, when Sarita was planning her trip, Malan had said, "You want to prove your point, don't you, Saru? Go, but you will come back, won't you?"

"What kind of question is that? Why would I not come back, at this stage of my life? Is there one good reason for me not to?"

"Who knows? You might find one there."

"Nonsense! If I wanted to, I would have gone then itself. I don't regret that decision one bit. What I stayed back for, I achieved, in full measure."

"Yes, but by being alone..."

Was that Malan's punch, or her concern? Who knows. That's one thing I could never discuss with her. Not even with myself, perhaps. There was just no time. I have my whole life ahead of me, I will think about it later, I'd tell myself. But that wasn't how things played out. And now that life has sped past, do I finally see what I was missing all along?

Gautam alone had been supportive. "Of course you must go," he'd said.

"Why 'must'?" Sarita had asked him light-heartedly. "So that you can take charge of all this?"

But he became serious. "What are you saying, Madam? Don't you trust me at all?"

Sarita couldn't bring herself to say, "I was only joking."

"You involve yourself in too many things. Never take a vacation. Besides, you might reconsider..." he continued.

"That option is no longer available, I've told you that."

"Perhaps you can find out?"

"What? That I could go live abroad? Or return to my husband?"

She had been surprised. Gautam saying this?

He had quickly added, "Of course, that's not an option now. When it was there, you rejected it outright. As per your ideals. But now, a brief meeting, for yourself...?"

Though she didn't admit it to Gautam, she'd liked what he said, agreed with him. She couldn't have told Malan that... It would have set her off again. "What are you saying! You discussed this with Gautam? That youngster, your assistant? Why?"

The truth is one can never really open one's heart to anyone. She certainly didn't have anyone. She hadn't really needed to perhaps. It had been a single-track journey so far. But now?

The university campus was truly beautiful. A backdrop of mountains, lush green meadows as far as the eyes could see, buildings that looked like they had grown organically out of the verdant earth. As they drove around, Nishi pointed out the various departments and talked about the courses they offered. Nishi stopped the car and they got out to walk around.

"Quite splendid!" Sarita exclaimed.

"Of course! That's why I decided to come here. When Baba sent me the prospectus and I saw the pictures, I knew I had to be here. Couldn't let such an opportunity pass."

"So you were won over right then?"

"By Baba, you mean? No, it was by these things. How many people get opportunities like this, to study, teach, work in such surroundings? Really, Ai, why were you so adamant then?"

Sarita looked at Nishi wonderingly. "You think I, too, should have succumbed to these attractions and come here? What about all those things I had planned to do? I wasn't just another qualified doctor even in those days. You know that. I was involved with so many things. Giving it up would have been a betrayal of my ideals—to work for people who needed me, especially women, for family planning, for education... You should be saying this to me, Nishi? Surprising!"

As if she hadn't heard Sarita's words, Nishi said, "That building over there, it is an apartment block. Come, let me show you mine."

It was a small, neat, purely functional apartment. "You live here alone?"

"Meaning?"

"Yesterday your Baba was saying..."

"A friend comes over sometimes."

"American? Foreigner?"

Nishi laughed.

"No. Nandan. That's his name. I'll introduce him to you sometime."

Sarita felt a little uneasy. By Nishi's casual manner. By her own uncertainty on how to deal with the situation.

"You're marrying him?"

"Not decided yet."

Sarita sighed.

"You haven't asked about Gautam at all?"

"Oh yes, how is he?"

Sarita said nothing.

"I sent him a few postcards at first. The fellow didn't reply to even one of them. So I gave up. What does he do now?"

"The usual. He is a very intelligent, conscientious, hardworking doctor, Nishi."

"I know. Like you."

"What are you implying? Is it a flaw to be like that?"

"I didn't say that. Has he got married or anything?"

"Not yet."

"Of course!"

Sarita fell silent as if snubbed. The conversation was pointless; it would lead nowhere, she realised.

Nishi was going through the mail that was lying there. "You must have some work to do, Nishi?" Sarita asked hesitantly.

"Not today," Nishi replied. "I will work from there, home, I mean. I have a couple of lectures tomorrow and the day after. But we will think about that later."

"I don't need you to be around to look after me every minute, Nishi! I can definitely go for a walk on my own."

"That's true. Let's plan to go out together over the weekend. There's a lovely park—almost like a forest—nearby. We can stay overnight there. And Ai, it's going to get colder now, so..."

Sarita spontaneously said, "Let me try on your trousers and shirts, let's see if they fit."

Nishi screamed delightedly. "Really, Ai? Why mine? Let's get you your own. We'll do it right now, on our way home. You are a courageous woman, Ai!"

The whole experience of the drive, the speeding cars, the wide open spaces, the immediate surroundings, it was all beyond Sarita's imagination. Used to small, confined spaces, this vastness was too much for her eyes to take in. Though she travelled around on work, it was to similar, familiar places. There was no place for the flowing river in a village, or a lake in the middle of a town, the hillock in the background, in her world of pain and suffering, ignorance and superstition. Water had come to mean scarcity, misuse, pollution and disease. The same was true for fields, groves and forests. The thought that plagued her mind was how to educate the people, how to alleviate their misery, bring relief to them.

What she was seeing here was unalloyed beauty. Surely there were problems here, too. Only she wasn't going to encounter them. They did not belong to 'her' world. Gradually her eyelids started drooping. Nishi was driving. Jayteerth was in front with her. Unending roads, high speeds, and music to prevent you from dozing off at the wheel.

They called it a park, but it was really a protected jungle. There were all kinds of trees, and it was much too large to walk across, thought Sarita. Nishi had packed a picnic basket. She was offering a great deal of information, and Jayteerth was filling in the gaps. When they stopped to rest en route, he asked Sarita, "You are enjoying all this, I hope?"

"Of course. It's very different. Quite stunning, in fact."

"That's why we kept inviting you."

"So that I could see all this for myself?"

Nishi was a little distance away, taking photographs. Looking in her direction he replied, "Yes, one should, isn't it?"

"You seem to be completely at home here?"

Jayteerth laughed. "It's been so long!"

"You found everything you wanted?"

"You can say that."

"Hmm," she said. "And now she, too, is with you."

"She came of her own free will. Isn't she old enough to make her own decisions? Our Nishi is a big girl now, Saru."

For a long moment Sarita stared at Nishi. "Indeed, she is."

"She has grown into a lovely young lady. Just as I had imagined. Naturally, all the credit goes to you. You brought her up single-handedly."

"Thank you. At least you give me credit for something."

"Well, no one can deny you that. I was sure of that."

"It must have seemed easy to you?" Sarita said.

Jayteerth gave her a long look. "'Easy' means? What are you trying to say?"

"You know exactly what I mean. Yes, I brought her up. Alone. It wasn't easy."

"I didn't say that. But I helped in whatever way I could. I kept in touch with her throughout."

"And you think that's enough?"

"You are saying this now, Saru? What are you trying to get at? At that time I..."

Just then Nishi appeared beside him. "Come on, get up. There's lots more to see."

Sarita was tired after all the walking. But it wouldn't be right to say that to the two of them, so she stood up.

Sarita noticed that Nishi had reserved two rooms in the motel where they were to spend the night. After dinner, Jayteerth went to one room and Nishi took Sarita with her to the other. The long drive, the tiring walk, the wine at dinner time had all transported Sarita into a new and unfamiliar world.

"You must be tired," Nishi said.

"I am not used to these things. You probably are."

"Yes, there's so much one can see and do here. If you enjoy doing something, you can go out and do it."

"Can I ask you something?"

"Sure."

"About your father... I don't know anything, actually..."

Nishi was sitting on her bed. The lights had been switched off.

"What is it you don't know, Ai?"

"You tell me. It's been ages since we separated. I know nothing about his life after that. He wrote to you regularly. He sent for you, that's all very well. He must have done it as a father. But as a man... Nishi, I have always talked to you as a friend. You hear me, don't you?"

"Yes, Ai. I understand."

"Meeting after so many years... things must have changed?"

"Of course they have. So much time has passed. You both led your lives independently, that, too, without getting a divorce."

"That's a mere formality. Never felt the need to go through with it. If he had wanted it, he would have asked for it... At least, that's how I look at it."

"But he didn't."

"True, but even so..."

"Ai, you want to know whether Baba has a woman in his life, right?"

Sarita said nothing. She sighed deeply.

"Well then, listen. Yes, he has."

Sarita did not react.

"Ai..."

"I am listening. Carry on."

"You're sure?"

"It doesn't matter to me anymore." Sarita's voice had an edge to it.

"You angry?"

"Not at all. Go on, tell me. He has a girlfriend?"

"Yes. An American. For the last two-three years..."

"And before that?"

"I am not sure, but there must have been... I don't know for sure... but Ai, Baba is not the kind of person who... You lived alone all these years, but Baba is not one who can be alone."

Sarita was clutching the blanket in her fist. In the dark she kept repeating to herself: how does it matter to me? Reassuring herself, trying to be brave, unconcerned.

"Ai..."

"I am listening. I have no grouse, Nishi. And why should I?"

"But it is bothering you, isn't it?"

"Not at all. I am not that stupid! At that time, didn't I know... Didn't I let him go?"

"I know. Why did you do it, Ai?"

"Unh?"

"A man like him... You know how charming he is, how pleasant his manner, how likeable his personality... Any woman will be attracted to him. I saw it from close quarters after coming here. When I was with you all I had was an image of him, as a father. You kept that image alive. You never uttered a word against him or criticised him. That's why taking the decision was easy for me. Once I got here, I, too, fell in love with him, Ai. As a father, he is perfect, he will rise to any occasion, he's that kind of person. And yet... How could you let such a man go? And live a dry, arid life on your own? Why, Ai?"

Sarita was at a loss for words. She lay there stiff, her breathing ragged. After a while she whispered, "Nishi, are you awake?"

"Yes. Why?"

"This woman, your father's friend..."

She noticed Nishi had turned towards her. Though it was dark, she could see.

"She is bound to meet you, Ai. You will, won't you?"

"Of course I will. Why not? Do you know her?"

"I do. She is a divorcee. Has two grown-up boys. She's a very nice lady."

"I am sure."

"She is friendly and warm. You'll get along with each other."

"Who knows?"

"Why do you say that? Ai...Ai, are you upset?"

"Not at all."

Nishi got out of her bed and slipped under Sarita's blanket.

"Can I sleep here with you, Ai?"

Sarita was overcome. Nishi had turned into the little girl who used to snuggle up to her in the old days.

Sarita finished writing her letters. There were a couple of picture postcards of the local tourist spots, behind which she had scribbled a few lines about her journey and stay here. They were addressed to some of her colleagues who had bid her a fond farewell, happy that 'Madam' was going abroad to meet her daughter. There was a longer letter for Malan with a description of the house, the surroundings, a detailed account of Nishi's life and routine, and a passing, almost impersonal reference to Jayteerth. And of course, the assurance that Nishi was taking good care of her.

She took a while to decide whether to write to Gautam or not. Though he hadn't said anything, she knew that he would like to get a letter from her. So what if I give him some moments of happiness, she thought, as she sat in this tranquil distant place. She started the letter. And before she knew it, it was pages long—expansive, candid, almost conversational.

She knew it from the first day he came to work with her, recommended by a friend. A simple, small-town boy, highly intelligent and fearless, he had struggled to educate himself and had a head full of idealism. Oh well, there are some like this in the younger generation, too, she had thought; someone who wanted to make good use of his education, do something different, for himself, for others. It made her happy. And yet there was a slight apprehension. The initial idealism would be forgotten when opportunities for a successful career and more money came along. But Gautam had stayed. As an equal. He started coming home and soon was almost part of the family. Nishi was with her at that time. Of the many people Nishi was fond of and who regularly visited their home, Gautam was one. Sarita had hoped that the two of them would choose each other. Nishi had refused to be a doctor despite her persuasion and advice. She had decided to study Economics. But so what, one can work in any field. This way at least she would remain with her, Sarita had thought.

Was that the only reason she wanted this? So that Nishi would stay with her always? Be moulded by her, walk the path of her choice? Was that really it?

She tried to encourage the relationship. Inviting Gautam home, asking him to stay for a meal, overnight. Making sure Nishi was around when he came. Yet she felt it was all happening quite naturally, unforced by her. Even though neither of them came out and said anything openly.

How eagerly she had waited for him. Spoken about Nishi to him all the time. Praised his work, his idealism before her. She had done all she could. And then one day Nishi announced her plans to go abroad, to Jayteerth. Sarita was thoroughly confused. What was this girl saying! Discussions, disagreements, arguments had followed. A repeat of what had happened earlier between her and Jayteerth. Finally Nishi retorted, "Ai, you have brought me up to be independent and bold. Which means I should make my decisions myself, isn't it?"

That left me with no answers, but it didn't stop me from making one last effort, recalled Sarita. "I thought you were convinced about my philosophy of life, my code to live by?"

"Of course. You are truly great, Ai. Noble."

"That's all?"

"What else do you want me to say? Isn't that what you want to hear? You are used to being told that by everyone around you." How calmly she had made that remark.

"Does one get greatness by asking for it, Nishi?"

"Of course not, Ai. You have spent your whole life working for it. I have seen it right from my childhood. Entrusting me to the care of this person or that, you rushed to help someone else somewhere."

"And I was wrong to do that?"

"No, I was only describing what happened. I certainly don't mean that you were less of a mother to me. You brought me up as a friend, and you managed to help hundreds of people. That's why I call you great, not many can do what you do."

"But you still want to leave?"

"How does my going have anything to do with it? The fact that you have given me the liberty to... Surely I don't have to tell you that, Ai?"

"Have you discussed this with Gautam?"

Nishi fell silent. Until then Sarita had not needed to confront her. A good thing the opportunity came up. Maybe now Nishi would rethink her plans.

"Nishi, you and Gautam share a special friendship, don't you?" She had looked a little downcast then. I was deeply moved. Getting up, I had put my arms around her. "Have you said anything to him?"

She just shook her head. I couldn't figure out whether it was a 'yes' or a 'no'.

"Shall I speak to him?"

Nishi jumped up and retorted, "No. You stay out of this."

"At least tell me what it is?"

"Well, it doesn't look like it will work."

"Why?" My voice rose. "He is a very good boy, Nishi," I said more calmly.

"Exactly. Ai, please... do not try to pull me back. Not for something like this. It won't do anyone any good."

"But then at least tell me why."

"There's nothing to tell. I have shown you all Baba's letters. I want to go there to study. Let me go, Ai."

Naturally there was no question of preventing her. No one would have considered her decision improper. A bright girl like Nishi, going abroad? 'Wah! Very nice!' they'd say.

Gautam continued to come over as usual. In fact, he helped Nishi with everything—from running around, to getting all the documents ready, to packing her stuff. Really, what was there to discuss then?

Nishi actually departed and... And then what? Work continued as usual. That would neither stop nor change. The construction of the Trust hospital was completed, and with it came more work and additional responsibilities.

One day while she was telling Gautam about Nishi's letter describing her new home, she just happened to say, "I never thought Nishi would actually go away." Although Gautam was like a family member, he was much younger, both in years and experience, so she should not have said it to him. But she had.

He responded in some surprise, "You didn't? Why?"

"Because I brought her up." There was some unease when saying this. "Alone. After Jay went away. It was a big decision those days."

He must have known all this, but it was the first time they were talking about it.

"But you were firm in your decision?"

"At that time? Of course I was. Right from my college days. Perhaps it was because of my Gandhian father."

"And yet you did... um... marry him, didn't you?"

Had anyone asked me this fundamental question before? No.

"I married him because I thought Jay was a good boy. No one discussed things like this those days. He was an engineer, I a doctor; we liked each other. That's all. It was enough. He didn't say anything about wanting to go abroad then."

"But later?"

"Nishi was born soon after. We became a family like all others. Then Jay found a new path... one of prosperity. And that was it. He was obsessed with that one objective—to go abroad where there were plenty of opportunities, lots of money."

"And you were not in favour of it?"

"Of course I wasn't. I did not believe that success, progress, money could be life's goals. I was convinced it was wrong. But Jay was not willing to listen."

"Then?"

"Then the usual—discussions, arguments. Jay didn't have anyone he could call family besides us: his wife and daughter. In the end he was prepared to give them up, too."

With a faint smile Gautam said, "Or perhaps you were prepared to leave him."

"But I wasn't going anywhere. He was the one leaving." There was an urgent defensiveness in the remark.

"You got what you wanted, didn't you?"

"Of course. Everything went according to plan. With some difficulty maybe, but yes, it worked out."

"And yet you didn't want Nishi to go?" Gautam had laughed as he spoke.

His 'And yet' was a little puzzling, but since Nishi's name had come up, I couldn't help asking, "Why didn't you stop her?"

"Me? Who am I to stop her?"

"What do you mean? Did you ever speak to her about it?"

He had looked straight at me. Squelching the growing unease, I said, "Since she didn't answer my questions about it, I am asking you." I hesitated. "You do like her, don't you?"

Slightly startled, he replied, "What's there not to like about Nishi?"

"So why didn't you say anything to her?"

"Because it wasn't going to work out."

That caused a shudder to pass through me. Why?

"Maybe she would have stayed back. Not necessarily here, but somewhere near by. Sometimes I feel that when people you are close to leave you and go away, you can't help thinking there's something wrong with you."

Gautam was listening silently. I continued.

"But what exactly it was, I never found out. Not now, not then. Nishi and I were very close. I did not intimidate her as a mother, nor was there any distance between us. She was free to do and say what she pleased, but yet... I don't think I ever fell short as a wife to Jay. In fact we were like any other happy family. At least that's what I thought."

I could say all this, but with it came a surge of emotion. Was it because I had never articulated it so clearly before?

"Yet, people drift apart. Consciously, out of choice, or for no apparent reason."

Then Gautam spoke. "Isn't it possible that you don't see the reason?"

Startled, I asked, "What? I am the reason? Is there some flaw in me? In my behaviour? In my nature?"

That hurt deeply. My voice rose slightly, there was a tremor in it. Gautam quickly placed his hand over mine to calm me down, then clasped both my hands in his.

"No one said that!" he said placatingly. "You look at everything too critically. That is not the only truth, you know. It can be a series of little things... And one needs to have the vision to see them. That's all I meant."

His hands held mine for a long time. It was comforting. That was the only emotion. Perhaps knowing that there was this man to walk beside me was reassuring. The disappointment that Nishi had chosen a different path was slightly assuaged, perhaps. Who knows.

"I'm going to be a little busy this week," Nishi said.

"That's okay! I didn't come here to go out sightseeing every day, you know. We are doing that anyway."

"There is so much to see, to experience, especially since you've come from so far away. There's just one problem here, though... everything is spread out. Unless you have a car..."

"Is it all right for me to go for a walk?"

"But of course! Just avoid the highway side. I showed you that jogging track, remember? Lots of people walk or run there. And there are books, Ai..."

"I know there are plenty. You don't worry."

"I'll be back on Saturday for sure."

That's when it struck Sarita. "You mean you are going to stay on the campus till then?"

"Yes, for the next four to five days."

To ask if she could go there with her would have sounded foolish. Besides, that apartment was not convenient for two people.

"Why? You are asking because Baba and you are going to be here by yourselves?"

Sarita smiled, embarrassed.

"But he is away all day. He leaves before you wake up. You will meet only in the evenings. And don't bother about cooking all kinds of things. He is not used to any of that. Either he will cook something for himself, or go out or even eat a frozen TV dinner, therefore..."

"That's not a problem at all. You don't worry."

After Nishi had gone, Sarita wandered around the house. It was so beautiful, so spacious, so modern, so strange. She had grown used to the place, to the gadgets, but it was still unfamiliar. Besides, she kept asking herself, 'Me, here? Why? As what?'

She decided to explore the neighbourhood that afternoon. Though there was a nip in the air, it was bright and sunny. The huge trees had begun to shed their leaves—golden, russet, brown, yellow. Sitting on a bench, she watched them as they floated down, adding to the pile already at her feet. There were joggers young and old, men and women, children playing, mothers walking their babies in strollers and prams, kids on bicycles shouting and yelling at each other, the composite sounds of the park... she listened to them all. Some people looked at her curiously, others smiled, while a few greeted her as they went past.

What if I, too, had become a part of this life like Jay and Nishi, she wondered. It wasn't difficult to study further and practice as a doctor. So many had done it. But then she recalled all her life's work until then—the numerous clinics she had started, the seminars and camps she had conducted, the free services she had offered in all sorts of places, especially during epidemics, floods, natural disasters. These experiences had made her the person she was. Very few are fortunate to find such a clear path at such a young age. Had I not followed it, I would have been no different from the many selfish, self-centred, materialistic individuals, and my concerns would have been the same as theirs: get a bigger house, the latest model of car, collect jewellery, spend lavishly. No, that was not in my DNA. Does one really know what the real Jay is like now? If he thought the opportunity he got then was so great that he was willing to leave wife, child and country for it, surely he must be a very different kind of man? In the last few days he had come across as decent, extremely hospitable, gentlemanly. But she couldn't get any idea from the normal conversation they'd had. That Nishi was extremely fond of him was obvious, as was his affection for her, his pride in her. Nishi is actually a very sensible girl. Smart, too. She knows exactly how I feel, and she understands him as well. And yet, she chooses him and his world. Which means that, in the end, his blood flows stronger in her veins.

Sarita had barely returned home when the phone rang. Nishi had already called twice to check on her and Sarita had been amused by her concern. This time, though, it was Jayteerth.

"Forgot to mention it in the morning, but Angela will be coming over this evening. She will stay for dinner."

"Who?" Sarita asked, confused.

"Angela. Nishi must have told you about her. She wants to meet you."

"Oh yes, yes, all right. I mean, what shall I make? Our kind of food?"

"Nishi will take care of that."

"But she isn't here. She has gone to the campus."

"Oh oh, I completely forgot." After a pause, he said, "So then?"

"So nothing. I can cook. A simple meal will do, I hope?"

"Of course, that is not a problem. I had taken it for granted that Nishi would be there. You... er, don't mind, do you, Saru?"

Sarita was silent. Had she forfeited the right to mind? And even if she had not, on what grounds could she have said so?

"No, I don't mind at all."

"Oh good. Seven o'clock then?"

Sarita got down to work. She was a little rattled at first, because she thought only Jay and she would be home for dinner. But that was all right. She had got used to this house over the last week or so, like a guest in a relative's home. But now that Jay's friend was coming, to meet me, he'd said, she was a little anxious. What will she say? What will we talk about? She tried to put it out of her mind and focus on the cooking. When everything was ready, including herself, a strange apprehension gripped her once more. She kept reminding herself: I am an independent, capable, successful woman. I must behave like one. I owe no one any explanations. I will not be intimidated by anyone.

Angela arrived and Sarita found her to be exactly as Nishi had described—chatty, warm, friendly. Her accent was a little difficult to follow at first, but Sarita soon got used to it and conversation was easy and free even when Jayteerth left the room for a little while.

From what Angela said, it was obvious that Nishi had told her a great deal about Sarita's work. Angela was a librarian, Nishi had said and Sarita found her well-read and well-informed. It was amazing how easily Angela referred to her former husband and her children while talking to Sarita. Even in Jayteerth's presence. Accept the present for what it is, and the past without denying whatever had happened. That seemed to be her attitude. It helped Sarita to be more unselfconscious.

At dinner Angela praised every dish. "You've made a lot of stuff," Jayteerth said to Sarita.

"Nothing special. It's what we have every day. Besides, I rarely need to cook. One always gets someone to do it at home."

"That's the great thing about your country," Angela said. "Work gets shared. When the kids were small, I had to do everything—look after them, do the housework, shop for groceries, in addition to holding a job. At the weekend the husband would turn up to take the kids out. He had the right to do so, didn't he? It made him much more popular with them."

"One can do as much as one chooses there, but one is subjected to close scrutiny from society," Sarita said ruefully.

"And why is that?"

"Because there, divorce isn't socially acceptable as yet. Things are much better now, no doubt, but during my time..."

"And how much importance did we ever attach to what people said?" Jayteerth interjected.

"We didn't, but we paid the price all right."

"Come on, Saru! Society always gives a self-made, successful woman like you greater leeway."

"Of course you would think so! I lived in that society, you came away."

"You really had to pay such a huge price? Not financially, for sure. I always sent you money, even if in Nishi's name. I kept in touch through regular letters. We did not live apart because of a bitter quarrel or anything. We chose different paths, that's all."

Sarita did not like the turn this conversation was taking, definitely not in Angela's presence. In spite of that she added, "There's no need for you to belittle what I went through. Besides, the path I chose was dictated by my principles, my dedication to my work. That was something you could not accept."

It took a while for Sarita to realise that she had switched to Marathi in her agitation. But Jay made sure his words were in a language Angela would understand.

"Very well, madam, I concede that you made all the sacrifices, that your path was the more difficult one."

Sarita felt like she had received a slap on the face. Angela laughed and, pouring wine into Sarita's glass, said, "You should have known by now, woman, that men are essentially selfish. My husband believes I was unfair to him. He himself was an alcoholic, a clumsy, shabby man. When he went to work, he earned a lot; when he blew it up, he was broke. I slogged hard to educate the children. And yet he claims that he was unjustly treated."

"It was my fault. I got carried away," Sarita said.

Patting her hand, Angela consoled her. "Not at all. No apologies. Definitely not from someone like you. Nishi was telling me that you have taken upon yourself the education of women in your area. Must be a really thorny path, that, in your environment..."

"It is, actually." Calming down somewhat, Sarita continued, "The problem is with the men. Women are prepared to change, to learn. It is the men who are inflexible."

When they had finished the meal, Jayteerth said, "Why don't you ladies go outside? I will clear up and get the coffee."

Angela stood up at once. Taking Sarita's hand she said, "Come, let's sit down and relax."

Sarita was now quite acquiescent. She and Angela had talked about so many different things. She had to remind herself that she was the woman in Jay's life! For their conversation had been so natural, like that with a newly acquired friend. Nishi was absolutely right about her, then!

Gautam's letter did not surprise Sarita. He had written to her even before receiving her letter. Almost soon after she had left. The letter was in English. The language was easy and free-flowing, but because they usually communicated in Marathi, it felt strange. He had written about things at home, given her an update on a couple of cases and matters on hand, asked after her and then Nishi. It was almost like a news bulletin! Before signing off he had written, "And I still miss you very much." She was taken aback for a moment. How would one translate that? Perhaps it was only a formality, a manner of speaking in English. Even if he had meant it, he couldn't have said it in any other language! Neither literally nor figuratively. Sarita suddenly realised that despite all the fun, the guilt-free leisure, she, too, was beginning to miss being busy, her work, her colleagues, and Gautam. I do think about him often. I have gotten so used to having him around, she thought. He was completely dependable where work was concerned, but even for conversation and companionship. He filled the space that Nishi's departure had created. Is this what missing someone means?

When Nishi returned that evening, Nandan was with her. She introduced him to Sarita and excused herself. Sarita asked him about himself. He told her he had come there as a child with his parents. Which means he has grown up here, Sarita thought. Hadn't made too many visits to India. There was no one there, he said. Looked like he had neither knowledge nor interest in knowing more. He worked for a big IT company, with no connection to the university, obviously. Jayteerth had said something about Nishi taking an apartment to be near him, but it wasn't like that. Nishi was staying there because it was convenient for her work. When Sarita said something to that effect, Nandan replied, "Oh we do meet sometimes at her apartment. I have a spare key."

Conversation stalled. Nandan asked Sarita nothing. To him, she was only Nishi's mother—a woman, a homemaker, like his own mother. How is it that Nishi told Angela everything about me but said nothing to Nandan, wondered Sarita. When the full import of the matter struck her, she was a little disappointed.

She felt a huge relief when Nishi reappeared. Offering to make some tea, Sarita went in.

At dinner time, when the three of them were chatting as usual, Nishi casually mentioned to Jayteerth that Nandan had come by. Looking pointedly at him Sarita asked, "Have you met his parents?" Immediately Nishi and Jay exchanged glances.

"Not really," Jay answered with a shrug. "Might have seen them or bumped into them somewhere. I told you I don't normally participate in these '*desi*' get-togethers."

Nishi spoke up. "His parents are very much a part of it all. They are at the forefront of all activities, celebrations, cultural events."

"Do you also attend them?"

"Not regularly. Once in a while maybe. That atmosphere... you have no idea Ai. They believe that the only way to preserve culture is to celebrate everything much more elaborately than anything we do back home. All it means is flaunt saris and jewellery, indulge in loud chatter, serve lavish meals. That's all."

"From Nandan's words, he didn't sound very interested in those events either! But he didn't seem to know even the simple things about our country, isn't it?" The words slipped out before Sarita knew it. She immediately regretted them.

"You are right," Nishi said. "He has neither knowledge nor interest. Ignorance is bliss!"

Sarita was taken aback by her remark.

"He is a good friend of yours, isn't he?" she asked.

"Yes, he is. Should one not speak about a friend's faults?"

"Not like that, Nishi. But why call him a friend then?"

Nishi laughed. "Everything doesn't come 'made to order', Ai! You have to make allowances, give some, take some... He is a friend, yes, but I am not about to spend the rest of my life with him!"

Her words caused Sarita much unease. She fell silent. With a smile, Jayteerth said, "Your mother cannot accept that, Nishi. Don't get into some unnecessary discussion."

"What do you mean? What will I not accept?" Sarita's voice rose sharply. "I, who all those years ago decided to live on my own, I would not accept this? Neither of you seems to have really understood what kind of a woman I am."

Nishi said gently, "You say we haven't understood you. Then who do you think has, Ai?"

Sarita's eyes brimmed. Disappointment? Defeat? Sadness? She couldn't tell.

Jayteerth placed his hand on hers. It took her by surprise. That touch, after so many years, so easily, so deliberately. She was thrown off guard.

"Saru, calm down." That's all he said.

Nishi began to clear the table. "There's a good movie on TV tonight. Want to see it?" she said, as if nothing had happened.

"Sure, let's watch it," Jayteerth replied. "Tomorrow is a holiday. We can wake up late and then go out somewhere."

After they had decided to drive to the next city two hours away and see the famous museum there, Nishi declared that she would not be able to go with them. "I have to complete a project. It is urgent. I thought I would finish it but it seems like I will have to go to the university this morning."

Is she doing this deliberately, to leave Jayteerth and me alone, wondered Sarita, but did not dare to voice her suspicions. Jayteerth remained silent. "Ai, I have seen that museum four times at least. Everyone who visits is taken there. But you should go, you will like it."

Sarita got ready. Mentally, too. Throughout the drive and even after they reached, Jayteerth kept filling her with loads of information. She was not particularly well-informed about art, but when she saw the rows of paintings lined up on the walls, period-wise, she was soon lost in that world. We have nothing like this at home, she thought. As a child she must have been taken to some small historical or science museum, but had never been exposed to artists from all over the world, presented so beautifully. She revelled in the entirely new experience. At noon, they took a break for lunch in the café attached to the museum.

By the time they finished with the museum, it was evening. Jayteerth suggested a walk to the nearby park. The wide tree-lined avenues with pavements meant exclusively for pedestrians made walking a pleasure. A thick carpet of russet-brown-yellow leaves lay on the sidewalk, and in the evening sunlight they looked like burnished gold.

"Tired? Like a cup of coffee?" Jayteerth asked and went off to get some. They sat in the park, under clear blue skies and as he sipped his coffee, Jayteerth said, "There is a very popular restaurant by the lakeside. People come from all over for a meal there. Shall we go there tonight?"

"Wouldn't it be a waste on me? I am a vegetarian, also I don't eat much," Sarita replied.

"One doesn't go there just for the food, it is more for the atmosphere. Come on, I must take you there. You will enjoy the wine—you've become quite a wine drinker now!" he laughed.

What Sarita saw was something she had not ever imagined. So picturesque, it looked like the painted backdrop of a stage, or a scene from a film. Clear blue water, pretty lamps marking the bounds of the lake, the neatly manicured garden around the restaurant, night slowly stealing in upon them, a cool breeze, twinkling lights on pleasure boats, young people and old people, romancing couples and families, all in high spirits. As if there was no life beyond this... no awkward questions, no sorrows, no problems... had they forgotten them or were they deliberately denying their existence for that little while?

She stood there absorbing the sights, the sounds, the atmosphere.

"Beautiful, just beautiful. Beyond compare," she whispered.

"You like it?"

"Of course. How many are fortunate enough to enjoy this!"

He laughed. "Some have the privilege all the time."

"Yes, but maybe some people don't want it all the time. Reality doesn't disappear because of it," she replied, an edge to her voice.

"You're right. It is a matter of choice."

For a while she was silent. She kept reminding herself that this was a magical place and her reality, her life with all its attendant problems, was far away.

"This couldn't be anything new for you," she said to Jayteerth.

"Not new, but immensely enjoyable."

"You can do it again and again?"

"Why not? Can't one experience something beautiful, romantic, enjoyable, over and over again?" He paused, then continued, "Besides, this is not the only life. There is a parallel life of work, problems, everyday hassles. Each one has his share of troubles. In fact, it is much worse here. One has to be on one's toes all the time, to prove oneself. If not, one is out of the running. And to keep running is not easy."

"But that's a choice you made."

"Of course. And I have no regrets at all. What I wanted to do, and was able to achieve in my field here, I could not have done there. There was just no scope for it."

"Which means you are happy overall?"

"Yes. Aren't you?"

"I am."

After a while he said, "Shall we spend the night here? I am sure we can find a room somewhere." Then he quickly added, "Of course going back is not a problem either. Just a two, two-and-a-half-hour drive."

"Whatever you say," Sarita replied. It was no longer important whether they stayed here or went back. It was only a temporary journey. Enjoyable, pleasurable certainly. Like this short visit.

The first two places were full, probably because it was the weekend. The third place had only one room. Jayteerth was reluctant but Sarita quickly interjected, "It's okay, only one night after all. We'll probably fall asleep as soon as we lie down! Just take it."

How easy some things become after a particular age, she thought. Nishi had planned on spending a night here originally, so a small overnight bag had been packed. Sarita changed into her nightgown. The small room had two single beds separated by a table. Opposite was a TV on a stand and a lamp.

She climbed into one of the beds. And for some reason she started laughing. Jayteerth who had emerged from the bathroom looked at her in surprise.

"What happened?" he asked, puzzled.

"Don't you find this whole situation hilarious?"

"What situation? Why funny?"

"The two of us... here... after such a long time... of course it was a possibility... that a couple, after many years of marriage, at the age of fifty... but then we... almost strangers to each other if you look at it... knowing little of each other's lives... living apart, and now in this predicament... isn't it funny?"

"We are still husband and wife, remember," Jayteerth said seriously.

"How? Because we aren't officially divorced? Our marriage would be deemed dead anyway, legally."

He said nothing.

She continued, "Why didn't you ask for a divorce? You must have had women in your life. Didn't you feel like marrying again? What about Angela?"

"No. I am married only to you, Saru," Jayteerth replied.

"But you did give it up and come away, didn't you?"

"I never considered marriage. I had a wife and a child, and that was enough. Never thought of marrying again."

"But it doesn't mean there was no woman in your life?"

"No. But what about you, Saru?" he asked.

"Me?" she was shocked, as if the question was utterly offensive.

"Did no one ever come into your life?"

The question infuriated her. Why she could not explain. Agitatedly she replied, "No. Certainly not."

"Why 'certainly not', Saru? Was it unnatural for you to meet someone?"

Sarita had no answer. But she felt the full force of her anger and indignation. The path she had chosen had been for herself and herself alone. And it had clung to her, never to let go.

"You didn't meet anyone, or you deliberately kept everyone away?"

"I don't know. Maybe."

"Saru..." There was a strange and unfamiliar note in his voice as he spoke her name.

She sat up, knees drawn to chest, her arms hugging them, head bowed, as if she was far away, frightened, his voice coming from some distant place...

"Look here, look up," Jayteerth said. "Why are you so upset? I am not asking for any explanation or justification. In fact, you have the same right as I do, to do what you wish. That's all I'm trying to say. Besides, what claims do we have over each other now? Saru..."

Sarita looked up at him. She realised she was becoming afraid of herself. She was losing control over all her responses. Why? Was it her surroundings, the wine, the sharing of this room, the proximity? Why was this happening to her, the strong, capable, determined, self-made woman? Or was it a game planned by her own daughter?

"Go to sleep now," Jayteerth said to her. "We walked around a lot all day. Don't wake up in a hurry. I will call you."

She lay down. He drew the sheet over her and switched off the light.

Nishi called the next day. "How was your trip, Ai?" she asked.

"Lovely. We spent the night there."

"I know. I'd called. It is a beautiful place, worth spending the night."

"Your work is done?"

"It's going on. Dragging a bit. But don't worry. If you need anything, tell me. I will be back in a day or two."

"Nishi, I am thinking of going back by the end of the week."

"So soon?"

"It's been almost a month..."

"What month! Stay a little longer, Ai. Anyway, we'll talk about it when I come home. Okay?"

For the next two-three days Jayteerth was not home for dinner. Some visitors to be entertained, he said, so she was entirely on her own. The day would dawn, the same mountain ranges greeted her when she parted the curtains, the serene atmosphere, the walk in the park under the shedding trees, the anonymity amidst crowds, impersonal glances, casual smiles and exchanged greetings. At home, her solitary presence, no one to distract her, no cooking, no cleaning, no demands on her time or her attention... truly all alone. Sarita savoured the solitariness.

When Nishi came home, the question of Sarita's return came up.

"Stay a little longer, Ai," Nishi pleaded.

"What is little longer, Nishi? I came, I was extremely well looked after by both of you, I saw all that there was to see, but it's time to go back. I have to return sometime, haven't I?"

"You must? You don't feel like staying on?"

Sarita laughed. "Nishi, it is all so lovely here, it's true, but it's not for me. I have made a life for myself there, and you know it."

"I do."

"And even if I did consider staying back, where's the place for me here?" she said jokingly. "For a few days, it's all right. I was welcome as a guest. You have your work, your life. Your father has his own life, his people..."

"It's still 'your father', is it?"

"Only when talking to you. He is Jay when I speak to him."

"You are still as stubborn..."

"Oh really? You are saying it as if you are a recent acquaintance. Tell me, is something wrong? Your face looks drawn?"

"Nothing really. Strain of work, maybe. Once that is over, I'll be all right."

Sarita couldn't help herself, "About Nandan..."

"What about him?"

"You must have thought over things carefully..."

"Of course. I always do, Ai."

"Don't say 'always'. In one instance, you hadn't."

Nishi retorted, "Oh, about Gautam?"

"Absolutely right." Then with deep concern Sarita said, "He is truly a very good boy, Nishi. I generally don't go wrong in my assessment of people. I meet so many all the time. I think he is the perfect man for you. Since there were feelings between you two, you should have tried to persuade him to join..."

"Wow!" Nishi interrupted. "And he would have agreed, right?"

"Did you even ask him?"

"What makes you think I didn't?" Nishi retorted shrilly. "But he is your *chela*, your acolyte, isn't he? He will do what you did."

"In my case it was different. What happened between Jay and me was long ago. Times change. Circumstances change. People are different. Equations can also be different."

"Oh yeah? And you are saying this? In fact you should know better."

"What about, Nishi? I would have persuaded Gautam. If only you had told me. When I did ask, you were evasive."

Nishi looked furious. Sarita had rarely seen her like that. Maybe once or twice when she was a child. If memory serves her right, when Nishi got to know that Jayteerth was going away, far away. Though she was a little girl, she managed to keep all her emotions, anger, fear, disappointment, hurt, under control and well hidden. How she had scared me then, thought Sarita. Now, too, she was a little worried.

"Nishi, was I wrong?"

"You ask me this now, Ai? You want to hear it, don't you? Okay, so here goes. Yes, I liked Gautam. A lot. I loved him. That's why I wanted him here with me. I begged him, pleaded with him, cajoled, threatened, even wept. But he did not budge. He wanted to remain there, working for you. With you. He didn't want to come with me. And I couldn't stay with you, Ai, so..."

"Nishi!"

"You still don't get it, do you, Ai? Gautam never loved me. He is in love with you, Ai, understand?"

Sarita quickly grabbed Nishi's shoulders. Nishi shrugged her off instantly.

"You mean you don't know?"

"Don't talk rubbish, Nishi. There is nothing like that. You know it."

"Yes, I do, and as soon as I realised it, I decided I would not remain with you, no matter what. Not for him, not with you. Definitely not when you were both there."

"What Gautam feels for me is not called love, Nishi."

"Then what is it called?"

Shaking her head helplessly, Sarita said, "What can I say?"

"You don't need to say anything. He admitted it to me."

"Never!"

"And why not? What is love, Ai? Something that fits into a framework, a definition? Is love only that which conforms to some rules drawn by society? Okay, you tell me—what, according to you, is love?"

Sarita went numb. She didn't dare to ask herself the question. This conversation was getting frightening. Silence was the best option.

Nishi had calmed down by then. Sitting on the sofa, she said, "You view everything from the sidelines and draw extreme conclusions. You are aware of all the aspects, you are smart enough to see them. But you refuse to acknowledge them. Because then you have to face the failings, too. And that you cannot bear to do. You will never accept weakness of any kind. Because you are deemed great, Ai. Just great!"

Laying her head on the table Nishi burst into tears, huge, racking sobs shaking her body. Even this she had controlled so well all these years, thought Sarita. Only once had she wept like this—when, on the first birthday after Jayteerth had left, she was opening the gifts he had sent. And what had I done? Hadn't I held her close?

Sarita did the same that day. She held her and let her cry. And herself, too.

Unknowingly, Sarita reached for Gautam's letter and read it again. She pondered over it for a long time. She couldn't think clearly. Her mind filled with apprehension, but she continued remembering nevertheless.

It was about six months after Nishi had gone. I was missing her terribly. She was a big girl, of course, and one day she would definitely leave home. But this was hard to bear. How could she go to a far-off country, and that, too, to be with Jayteerth? It made no sense. I could not accept it.

The next day Gautam came over to discuss some event. As usual he stayed for dinner. Leaving the mess in the kitchen for the maid to clear the next day, I went out into the living room. Gautam followed me. "You seem very distracted today, Madam, isn't it?" he said.

I smiled. What was I thinking at that time? Worrying about Nishi? Uneasiness? Inability to make sense of things?

"You are worrying about Nishi?"

"Umm, hmmm."

"She will do well there. She won't lack for anything."

"Does one ever know what one lacks, Gautam?"

"One doesn't?"

"I'm not sure now."

"Why do you say that? We fill one lack with something else, don't we? That is the basis of our lives."

"It's so simple?"

"If we can see what we have, that's enough. Then the pain of what we don't have is reduced."

Hadn't I looked at him then, a little puzzled, a little pleased? And hadn't his expression been one of reassurance?

Presently Sarita got down to tidying up her room. It was strewn with her stuff. Better to have it all in one place instead of packing at the last minute.

When she came down to ask about her ticket, she was met with complete silence. Nishi must have gone to her room, she thought, and went back upstairs. Jayteerth's room was next to hers, and because she could hear strains of music from there she went and stood by his door. It was ajar. She stepped in and pulled the door shut behind her. The lamp in the corner was on, but Jayteerth was not in the room. Thinking he must be in the balcony, she went up and asked, "Can I come in?"

"Of course," he said, turning around. "You haven't gone to bed yet?"

"No. As I was going to my room I heard the music, so I thought I'd check what was playing."

"Just stepped out for some fresh air. See how the mountains look at night."

"Rather blurred, the view."

"Let your eyes get used to the darkness."

She did.

"It's cold. Come, let's go inside."

She looked around the room. She had come in a couple of times before, but today her eyes lingered over it. It looked different in the dim light. She noticed an old photograph of herself and Nishi on the table. Picking it up, she remarked, "How young she was then!"

"Yes, what I brought with me when I came."

Sighing, she said, "I seem to have aged rather quickly. But you haven't."

"Who says?"

"I."

"Because you were adamant about being alone?"

Smiling a little, she replied, "That has nothing to do with it, Jay. One accepts being alone or one doesn't. It's all in the mind."

"Oh well, call it stubbornness, discipline or punishment."

She was leaning against the table. When she heard his words, she looked up at him, her eyes sad. Suddenly, Jay took her hands in his and drew her close. She felt her heart thudding. Why all this? What for? Now? her mind was reminding her.

"I could never win you over, Saru," he said.

"Win over?"

"I wrote so many letters pleading with you, Saru..."

"Letters?"

"Saru," he said, his voice thick.

"Don't resist everything so strongly, Saru. You did not reply to a single letter of mine. That was your pride. What I thought was your obduracy. You have forgotten it all so easily!"

"I haven't forgotten anything, Jay. Ask yourself who has."

"You knew it well, Saru, what would have happened if we had lived together like that. Your aspirations, your goals, your reasons, your principles were important to you. I wanted to build my career in my own way. The huge opportunity I got then was a challenge. But you didn't see it like that. You only saw it as greed, for money, for the good life. You were contemptuous of me then..."

Sarita was overcome. "No, Jay..."

"You scorned my attitude. Had I been around, you would have scorned me, too. Living with you there was as impossible as bringing you here. And you could see that. That's why you could remain so firm."

"Okay. I am not complaining," Sarita said.

"But I am," he replied. "I loved you, Saru. I still do."

"Love?" she said, sorrowfully. She was still in his arms.

"You don't believe in love." He paused. "Even if we lived apart for so long, we could have spent some time together. All my letters went in vain. And the one time I came down, you spent barely an hour with me. Giving some excuse or other, you kept your distance. You allowed me to meet Nishi. That's all. I was grateful you permitted me to be in touch with her."

"What was the point of meeting, Jay?"

"There was. Do we have to live our lives in a dry, rule-bound frame, Saru? Our lives are past now, but the interim years we could have built bridges of emotion, of affection. We could have shared some moments of happiness like two friends, or like family members do. Of course, it would not have been like most families, but then you are not like most women, are you? Your achievements are so extraordinary, they have been your downfall, Saru!"

Sarita's tears broke their banks. She sobbed disconsolately. Jay tightened his arms around her. "If you had come here earlier, I would have convinced you of my arguments long ago. But you couldn't, you wouldn't do that, would you!"

"I don't understand any of this, Jay," she said trying to control herself.

"Never mind. You will, at some later date. I have implicit faith in your intelligence. That's why I could leave you so easily!"

Alarmed, she stopped his hands.

"What's the matter?"

"Jay, I... in all these years... after you left..."

"I know. You mentioned it."

"Will I be able to... will you, I, get anything from it?"

"How will we know unless we find out, Saru?" Jayteerth said. "Take it as it comes. You are not a stranger to me, after all!"

Sarita had finished buying gifts for everyone. Nishi was helping her pack her bags.

"Did you have a good time, Ai?"

"Very. Much better than I thought."

"Give my love to everyone. Even Gautam."

"I will. And the sweater you got him, too."

"That's not such a big deal. Actually, it was mine. I have used it a little. Everything here is unisex, as you must have noticed."

Sarita laughed. "Yes, indeed. I have seen much, learnt more, experienced it all first-hand. It is very different from reading about it in books."

Nishi kept looking at her. "Not bad, Ai, you put it better than me."

"So when are you coming, Nishi?" Sarita asked her with a smile.

"Let's see. What's the hurry? I've just seen you. There's nothing urgent to take me back."

"Take care, Nishi."

"Why do you say that?" She paused. "You didn't like Nandan much, did you?"

"If you want the truth, I didn't. Rather, I didn't like that he should be in your life. Anyway, what have I to do with it?"

"I have not committed to him for life, Ai. He is not that bad, really. Nor is he the kind who has some special qualities, someone you can fall in love with. Certainly not like Gautam."

Sarita blurted out, "You and Gautam need to talk."

"Ai," Nishi said sharply. "You stay out of this. It will all get unpleasant otherwise. Give me your word, you will not interfere?"

"I won't."

"Do I take that as your promise?" It came out like a threat.

Sarita smiled. "Of course, child. It is. I am not going to have any time for all that... So much, old and new, needs to be sorted out. I must get rid of this weight I have put on, but after this wonderful holiday, I feel recharged."

"See, that's why I insisted you come. You must come again. Don't worry about the tickets, money, all that."

"Okay."

"You'll come?" Sitting cross-legged on the cot Nishi said, endearingly, "Ai?"

Patting her cheek, Sarita replied, "I will."

When Nishi went down to get dinner ready, Sarita closed her suitcase and went into Jayteerth's room. He hadn't come home yet. She went out into the balcony and let her eyes feast on the mountains in the fading light. Coming in, she sat on his bed and looked around the room once more. Her gaze lingered on the old photograph. She began to open all the drawers of the chest. Not because she was looking for something. She just wanted to see them... Jayteerth's belongings. She ran her hands gently over his clothes hanging in the cupboard. Everything bore evidence only of him. No one else.

She went back and sat on his bed. She had left her imprint on it now, she thought. Mixed, dissolved into something. Or had she become one with Jayteerth all those years ago? It seemed as if he had carried it carefully up to this point. That's why he had said he had not even thought of marrying anyone else. I am already married. I have a wife and child, he had said.

At that moment she became acutely aware of her entanglement. In that totally unexpected and complete experience with him, she seemed to have found herself. That's perhaps why I came all the way here, she thought. And this need to find herself had started from the moment she made up her mind to make this trip.

"I will clear up today," Sarita said to Nishi after they had dinner. "Go finish whatever you have to do. You will have to spend all day at the airport with me tomorrow."

Nishi left the room. But Jayteerth stayed back to help her.

"Isn't it funny, by the time you get used to everything, it is time to leave? When I first came Nishi used to say, 'Leave it, Ai, you can't manage it!'"

"Once Nishi moves out, I, too, will have to find a smaller place."

"Where will she go?"

"She must have some plans. She is hardly likely to stay in this place, this job, permanently. No one does."

"Does she have any thoughts about marriage or not?"

Jayteerth laughed. "That's entirely her business... I don't get involved."

She realised that Nishi had left her past behind with her mother, but her future would probably be more closely linked to her father. I will have no part in it, she thought.

"Angela had called," she told Jayteerth.

"What did she say?"

"Nothing much. Just called to say bye, asked how my visit had been, whether I had a good time..."

After a while Sarita asked, "She won't be coming to stay here with you?"

"No such plans," Jayteerth replied.

"Why?"

"Because she is just a good friend of mine, that's all. And that's how it should remain. Should not mix up these things. It doesn't work out. Instead..."

Slowly lowering herself into a chair, Sarita asked, "Jay, will you come back sometime?"

He was making coffee. Without looking at her, he said casually, "If you invite me, I may come for a few days."

Sarita felt a tight knot forming inside her. I will write to him when I go back. Not immediately, but later sometime. If he replies, I presume he will... then I will say it's been a long time since we met... Why don't you plan to visit?... Where? My house? The space I created for myself? To visit me? For a holiday? To meet, to see? To keep in touch?

Setting two cups down in front of her, Jayteerth pulled up a chair and sat beside her.

"What are you thinking about? How and when to ask me over?"

She smiled faintly.

"There's no hurry. You don't have to return my hospitality immediately. There is no obligation on you. You do things your way. I will wait. I waited for so long, didn't I?"

He picked up her hands. Turning them up, he stroked her palms.

"Before you leave, I want to give you my definition of love," he said. "That which binds two people together is love. Everything else, like work, time, convenience, meeting, defining a relationship, giving it a name, these are all the mundane details. All of them constrain love. Restrict it. I have discussed this with our Nishi so many times. She agrees with me. Other people may not. But that's their problem. It has only to do with those we love, isn't it? So, for example, us—what we have."

Sarita laughed wholeheartedly. She remembered that before Jayteerth actually went away, she had showed how she had accepted his decision to go away so calmly, and stood by her own so resolutely. To prove how true she was to herself, she had deliberately kept him at a distance. She had shown him how normally her life would continue in his absence. When he said goodbye, Nishi had been very upset, had cried a lot. He, too, was overcome for a few minutes. While she, Sarita, had taken leave of him unemotionally, formally. Keeping at bay touch, tears and sentiment.

She was surprised that that memory should come back to her now. Holding his hands tightly, she said, "Nishi will take me to the airport tomorrow. You have to leave early, I believe?"

"Yes, I have no choice. Part of life here!"

"So is this our goodbye?"

He looked at her deeply. She could read his expression clearly now. It surprised her. Thrilled her, too. Before he could say anything, she covered his lips with her fingers and said, "When you come there to me, then. Come soon." After a moment, she added, "I will write to you."

6 Another Chance*

PART I

The autorickshaw stopped in front of the station. Abhijit and Suruchi jumped out. "You go ahead. I'll give him the money and come," said Ila, pulling out the money from her purse. Abhijit grabbed Suruchi's arm and pushed his way through the crowd. It took them a couple of minutes to find the platform where the train would arrive. For a few moments Suruchi was overwhelmed by the chaos. What train? What time? Who was going? None of it made sense to her. Suddenly she realised that it was she who was travelling and needed to get on the train.

Snatching the suitcase from her hand, Abhijit began to run. "Hurry," he said, "we have to cross the overbridge." Suruchi kept looking back to see if Ila was following them.

"She'll come. Don't worry," Abhijit reassured her. "You have a train to catch."

Ducking under luggage on the coolies' heads, avoiding elbows and knees, panting as she hurried forward, Suruchi asked, "She knows the platform number?"

"She knows. She will catch up with us. And if she doesn't..." Abhijit's words were lost in the noise.

As they were climbing down the bridge, Suruchi saw the train. Now they had to find the right bogie. She somehow

*Originally published in Marathi as *Awartan*, Mauj Publications, November 1996.

made her way into the compartment through the jostling crowd of well-wishers bidding fond goodbyes to their friends and relatives and started looking for her seat number.

As expected, someone had already occupied her seat. Abhijit was trying to push her suitcase under the berth. Frustrated, he threw it on the upper berth and muttered, "Adjust it later." Suruchi sat down on her now vacant seat and said, "You better go. The train will start moving any minute..."

Abhijit took Suruchi's hand and holding it tightly, said, "Take care. Don't worry ... think everything out carefully."

Suruchi nodded. A lump rose in her throat. No words came out of her lips. Abhijit's hand slipped away and soon he disappeared into the crowd. Just then she heard Ila's voice, "I'm here, by the window."

Suruchi leaned forward and grabbed the bar. Ila patted her hand. "Just relax, okay? Be comfortable, be free. Remember, we are here ... we are all here."

Tears welled up in Suruchi's eyes. The train had started moving and soon Ila, too, merged into the crowd, leaving only the glimpse of a waving hand behind.

As the train gathered speed, the passengers settled down. Suruchi sighed and glanced around her. There was a couple huddled in the corner of the opposite berth and next to them was a middle-aged man. On either side of her were two women, one young, one old.

Suruchi took a deep breath and stretched her legs slightly in the cramped space. In spite of the last minute rush she had made it to the train after all. She sighed. Once the TC finishes checking the ticket, I will open up the middle berth and go to sleep. Forget about everything. Tomorrow is another day, she thought. I'll deal with it when I get there. It was another world, Nini's home. Nini's—her grandmother's—house where she was brought up, where she spent her childhood, grew into adolescence. From where she had set out. And now she was returning to it. At this time, in these circumstances she needed to be clear-headed, keep an open mind. As Ila had said, she had to find her own solutions. Consider all options. Give everything a try. That's it. Give it a try.

Suruchi hardly spoke to anyone during the journey, except for the perfunctory smile when closing the window and putting up her berth. She hoped to fall asleep as soon as she lay down, and before she knew it, it would be morning and she would have reached. But that's not how it was. Sleep would not come. Instead, random thoughts rushed about helter-skelter in her mind, creating a tumult. She lay there tossing and turning, trying to lull herself in the rhythm of the train. But to no avail. Sleep continued to elude her.

The door opened. Nini's voice reached her from the hall, "You've come on time." Suruchi put her bag down. Suddenly she felt light. Free. Glancing at Nini, she exclaimed, "You look just the same!" Like the image she carried in her mind. Nini had not changed at all in six years. Still tall, lean and erect. Her hair was all white. Her eyes sharp, penetrating. The sari was expensive, with small print in pastel colours. On her feet were soft, home slippers.

Nini looked Suruchi up and down. "You haven't changed too much either."

Suruchi smiled, "Really?"

"I don't see anything different. Go and freshen up now. Your room is ready. Afterwards we will have coffee."

Suruchi would have preferred coffee first, a nice, strong, hot cup. But Nini had said "Go!" She dragged her suitcase to her room. The bed was made with a freshly laundered white bedspread and pillow cover, the mosquito net hung from above. The windows had been opened and the cupboard neatly lined with clean paper and mothballs. Suruchi looked into the mirror on the cupboard door. She almost didn't recognise herself. Hair untidily tied at the nape of her neck, a tired face, baggy cotton shirt, faded jeans and dusty canvas shoes. Nini would not have approved of any of this. Neither her appearance, nor her present situation. Suruchi looked out at Nini's small garden. Pots lined up against the compound wall, neatly pruned crotons, and the square patch of grass, all bathed in the morning sunlight.

The bathroom was adjacent to her room. Suruchi stepped in. The stone slab floor scrubbed clean, a new soap in the dish, fresh towels on the rack and a bucket filled with water greeted her. She took off her shoes and socks and dropped them into the bucket with a plop. She pulled off her clothes, threw them into the bucket, then turned on the shower. It was old and had not been used for a while so the flow was uneven. But she stood under it. The water was cold and though it prickled her skin, she stood there, hugging herself.

When she was bathed, she put on a flowing, ankle-length skirt, tightened the buckle at the waist, and slipped on a shirt. She looked at herself in the mirror as she dried her wet hair with the towel. Throwing the wet towel on the bed, she went out. Nini was reading the newspaper. Two cups of coffee were kept on the table in front of her.

For a long time Nini did not say anything to Suruchi. Then she put the newspaper aside and said, "You know they are all coming next month, don't you?"

"Who's 'all'?"

"The three of them. You haven't heard from them?"

"No," she lied. She knew they were coming: Kamala, Pradeep, Swaroop—her mother, father and sister. Coming from another country, many thousand miles away, but from their home. Like the usual once-in-two-three-years visit. Come they did, but she never knew who would come when. They made it as and when they could, when they did. But this time they were all coming together.

"Your journey was comfortable?"

"Couldn't sleep."

"You have all day to sleep now. Rest, eat properly..."

Finally Suruchi asked her, "You got my letter, didn't you, Nini?"

"Of course. How else did I know you were arriving this morning?"

Suruchi fell silent.

"You wrote that Shreerang had met with an accident. What happened?"

"Car accident."

"His own car? Was he driving?"

"Someone else's, but he was driving."

"How did it happen? Was it at night? Had he been drinking or ... drugs?"

Suruchi was stunned. She stared at Nini for a long time. Nini sounded just like the police. Alcohol? Drugs? Whose car? Licence?

She shook her head. "No. It was an accident, Nini. No reason, a mistake." Suruchi's voice grew thick. "Someone must have tried to overtake from behind. He lost control and crashed."

Silently Suruchi was screaming, Believe me. It's the truth. Shreerang never touched alcohol, forget anything else. More importantly he was a very sober, balanced kind of man, not rash. He knew exactly what he wanted. Not one to make mistakes.

"Even an accident is a mistake, Suruchi," Nini remarked. "Mistakes have a reason, a cause. Maybe a contributory factor, but always a reason."

"There was nothing."

"You won't know that for sure so soon."

"It's not like that, but..." Suruchi's voice had become shrill

"No more discussion on this subject, Suruchi," Nini said sternly. "Besides, I do not like raised voices. You know that. You have my sympathy. But that's all. You were not married to him. Therefore he was not a part of our family. So the matter is closed. Understand?"

Suruchi nodded, her mind numb.

How did Nini spend her time, Suruchi wondered. She had just retired, so was home most of the time. Her presence seemed to shadow her, her voice, her footfalls follow her. All this she did artfully, speaking in low, dry tones, walking around soundlessly, that's what she was known for. A strict disciplinarian, stern and unforgiving, that was her reputation as the principal of the school. She was extremely efficient and competent, giving no one any scope for criticism. Everyone—students, teachers, staff—was afraid of her. And yet at her farewell, they praised her lavishly. The school had acquired such a good name because of her, the students were exemplary, the results were always excellent. The school grew and flourished under her guidance and its success was attributed to her dynamic leadership. A couple of speakers even got quite emotional. Some girls invited her to their classrooms and gave her special gifts. Some actually touched her feet. And Nini? She was as usual, composed, unmoved, with a hint of a smile on her lips. That's all. She thanked everyone and took leave. Dry-eyed, unemotional. She was prepared for her retirement and took the last day at school in her stride. And from the next day, it was home all the time.

Suruchi remembered those post-retirement days. No early morning rush, no hustle-bustle to get ready for school. And she getting stifled in that atmosphere. Was it really so long ago? It seems like an age. But Nini looks the same, acts and speaks the same. How can she change? She has been like this ever since I can remember, Suruchi thought.

Suruchi did not know for how long Nini had been standing by her bedroom door. She scrambled out of bed. She didn't ask Nini to come in and sit down because she knew Nini would not want to come in.

"What are you doing?" Nini asked.

"Nothing."

"Then do something. Read. We have so many books here."

Indeed. The hall was lined with cupboards packed with books. Old, bound volumes, complete works of well-known authors, canonical texts. She had not touched any of them before. If Nini handed her something to read, she would cast it aside and run away. Eventually Nini had given up. How? By coming into Suruchi's room one day and confiscating all the magazines, comics, popular novels. Suruchi had wept and wailed because it had been done without her knowledge. "If you must read," Nini had declared, "read quality stuff. Otherwise don't read at all. It's fine if you don't. But certainly no reading this trash."

So what had Suruchi done? She had continued to read. Only she did it outside ... At her friends' place, in the library pretending to be studying, sometimes even bringing books home on the sly. But Nini found out about this, too. She did everything she could to prevent it. She looked through her cupboard, in the drawers, on the shelves, under the mattress. In a fit of temper, Suruchi had vowed never to touch a book again. If she couldn't read what she wanted, she wouldn't read at all. As for textbooks, there was no choice. She would study just enough to pass. That's all. And then Shreerang appeared. Shreerang, who read to her late into the night, who explained things to her.

Now, I can open Nini's cupboards. I can pick up any book I choose. But I won't. I don't want to. Now she tells me we have so many books. As if the past had never happened.

Suruchi remained seated, hugging her knees. Nini stood there looking at her critically.

"Are you going somewhere?"

"Where will I go?"

"Surely your old friends are here? Go visit them."

"There's nobody."

"That's not possible." Of course Nini would know. "I met Merlin recently. She was asking about you."

"I'll go some other time."

Nini raised her eyebrows and shrugged as if to say, There's nothing more I can say. Suruchi was watching her.

"My routine is more or less fixed," Nini declared. "I am out three days a week. I look after the matters of the organisation. Sometimes the women come here. For meetings. Now that you are here, you should know this. If you choose to stay in your room, there's no problem. No one should get in each other's way."

Nini walked off. Suruchi watched her retreating back. Ila would have been surprised, and she would have laughed out loud at her speech. Nini would have become a source of entertainment for her. Nini had said no one need get in anyone's way, that there should be no interference from either side. Didn't she have the slightest interest in what I've been doing all these years? Was nothing important to her? The people who were close to me, who had been around me—what were they like? Did they influence me? Or didn't they? None of this mattered? Ila had practically shaped me. Had set me on my feet then, and held me up now. Ila, ten years older, extremely intelligent, knowledgeable, gritty. Actually, Nini would have liked her. Or would she? Unlikely. What I had seen as similar traits in them were not so similar after all. Like the shades of a colour, like the meaning of a word changing with intonation, they were different.

Nini had not come to see me even once. I hadn't really expected her to. But if she had, she would have seen everything—Ila and Shreerang, their lives, my life. But no. Nini had erased everything, even my existence. In her mind, only two steps separated my stepping out of her house six years ago and my return now. Not an age.

Suruchi wandered around the house, waiting for them. Their taxi should arrive any moment now, she thought. Nini was not at home, but Suruchi felt her presence everywhere. Lakshmi was busy in the kitchen. When she looked up and saw Suruchi at the door, she asked, "Want something?" "No," Suruchi replied, and continued to watch Lakshmi at her task. She had been trained well by Nini and followed every instruction perfectly and seemed happy to be doing what she was. If Nini had not rescued her, given her shelter, she would probably have died of her husband's abuse. Her husband and his paramour had attempted to set her ablaze. Unwanted because she was barren. Now she was a part of Nini's household. She was treated very well. Given her own room, good clothes, and excellent food. Nini never looked down on her, and made it a point to introduce her to everyone as "our Lakshmi". Lakshmi would smile and join her palms in greeting. In return she did all the chores that Nini assigned her. Yes, she was grateful and loyal, content with her life. Her simple gesture said it all.

How would Ila have reacted? Should show Nini Ila's writings. The magazines with her articles were still in the suitcase. A book of essays, too. But would Nini even glance at them, let alone read them? And if she did, she would probably remark with a sneer, "These foolish, hot-headed women! What do they know about sustaining relationships?"

Suruchi went into the garden and stood by the gate. Am I really waiting for the taxi, she wondered. She rolled up the sleeves of her shirt, thrust her hands into the deep pockets of her skirt and stared at the road.

When they arrived, Suruchi was inside the house. Hearing the car stop by the gate, she hastened out. So did Lakshmi, wiping her hands. They got out of the taxi—Swaroop, Pradeep, and then Kamala. The bags were unloaded, taken in, and one by one they entered the house.

Swaroop rushed towards Suruchi and threw her arms about her. "Oh *Didi*, how wonderful that you are here!" she gushed. "I was just dying to see you! My dear Didi, how are you?" Holding Suruchi by her elbows she drew back and looked at her. Suruchi stared back. Swaroop was almost as tall as herself, plumpish, fair, with a typically 'foreign' air. Perhaps it was the clothes, the jerkin, the slacks, the fashionable jewellery, handbag, perfume, permed hair. As foreign as I am native. No, that's not true. It can't be. Just then Swaroop leaned forward and kissed Suruchi on both cheeks. "How pretty you look, Didi! Where's this gorgeous skirt from? I want one exactly like it. It's so ethnic, just perfect. Didi, why no earrings?"

Kamala followed a little later and immediately gathered Suruchi into her arms. "My baby, my little girl, how are you? You are well?" Her eyes brimmed as she hugged Suruchi even closer and began to whimper. Unbidden tears came to Suruchi's eyes as well. Resting her head on her mother's shoulder, she murmured, "I'm all right."

After a while, Kamala let her go. Suruchi looked at her mother as if for the first time. Rather short, plump but compact, in a sari, wearing the mandatory real jewellery, her hair neatly tied back, perhaps because they were here. Kamala turned to Pradeep and said, "Did you see our Suruchi? How does she look?"

Pradeep had been busy paying the taxi-driver and making sure all the luggage was unloaded and taken inside. He reached for Suruchi's hand and drew her towards him. Giving her shoulders a squeeze, he said, "She looks perfectly fine to me!" Before Suruchi could even think of responding to his embrace, he had withdrawn his arm. Kamala quickly took her hand and walked into the house. "I kept worrying about you all the time," she said. "Now that I have seen you, my mind is at rest."

Swaroop, who had been wandering about the house, asked, "Where's Nini?"

"At a meeting. Will be back soon."

Pradeep went with Lakshmi to see where their bags had been put. Kamala and Suruchi sat in the living room. Holding Suruchi's hand in a tight grip, Kamala asked again, "Tell me really, you are okay, *na*?"

"As okay as can be."

"We got your letter ... and I went numb. Was so shocked ... Worried about how you had taken it ..." Kamala became tearful once again. "Why did this happen, Suruchi? Such a fine young man ..."

Suruchi clenched her lip between her teeth. She couldn't afford to cry. Nothing was to be gained from breaking down.

There was no way of knowing if her mother's grief was real or not ... What I felt would not affect my mother's emotions, thought Suruchi.

Just then Swaroop came and stood in front of Suruchi. Pulling her by the hand, she pleaded, "Come na, Didi. See what I have got for you!"

"What's the hurry," Kamala said. "Let Nini come, we will open everything then."

Lakshmi had brought in cups of steaming coffee. Kamala picked one up. "*Wah*! This is something you cannot get anywhere in the world—the authentic *desi* coffee—except in Nini's house and made by Lakshmi."

Lakshmi was pleased. While Kamala got into a conversation with Lakshmi, Swaroop dragged Suruchi to her room. Hastily she opened her suitcase, pulled things out of it and scattered them on the bed. Clothes—skirts, t-shirts, jeans—shoes, cosmetics, perfume bottles and sundry other trinkets. Suruchi just stared at them.

"All this ... for me?"

"Why? Don't you like them?"

"No, it's not that. But where do I use all these things?"

"Oh, and why don't you use them? You will now. Got all the colours you like. Remember *Estée Lauder* ... you used to love that fragrance ... that's why I chose it. I paid for it all with my money, Didi ..."

"That's all very well, but I never use makeup."

"What do you mean 'never'? I've seen you earlier ..."

"That was long ago ... In the last two years ..."

Suruchi looked at her sister. Almost seven years younger than herself, but it doesn't seem so now. Two years ago she was a child, but she is different now. The appearance is the same ... fashionable, modern ... The same age as I was when I took that decision ... just over twenty.

Swaroop threw her arm around Suruchi. "I know, Didi, what you went through. But you've come out of it, haven't you? I knew it the minute I set eyes on you. I felt so terrible when I heard, I couldn't stop crying. I had really liked Shreerang. If you hadn't been in his life, I would have fallen in love with him myself. And then, so suddenly, so unexpectedly ..."

Her voice trailed off. Does Swaroop really mean all this, Suruchi wondered. Is she really so mature or is she just blabbering away like a typical American teenager—garrulous, shallow? Suruchi couldn't decide.

Swaroop pushed Suruchi on to the bed. "Listen Didi, before anyone, that is, Mummy or Daddy, says anything to you, I want to tell you something. Come back with us, to our home. Have a good time for a few days ... then decide what you want to do. I don't say you should stay there permanently. Return to wherever you want to be... but first come with us. What do you say?"

With a half-hearted attempt at a smile, Suruchi disentangled Swaroop's arms.

"We'll see."

"No. You must."

"Look here, you've just arrived ... there's still time for you to go back. We'll think it over, and decide..."

"Okay, but I asked you first, okay? If you decide to come, I get the credit, okay?"

"Very well," Suruchi laughed. She glanced at the mess on the bed. Because Swaroop would expect it, she picked up each item, said, "Very nice, very good" and put it down, thinking all the while that this was not important anymore. Clothes, accessories, looking good ... certainly not because Shreerang was not there. On the contrary, they weren't important because he had come into her life. And with him, came Ila, and all the others. Because of them she had learnt about the things that were valuable in life. Despite the hardships, the sorrows that came with them—or perhaps because of them. She was no longer so small-minded to be stuck in them.

They were sitting on the sofa: Nini leaning back, Kamala beside her, Swaroop on the other side, and Suruchi a little distance away. Swaroop had a plate of *sev* and *chakli* on her lap and she was stuffing herself with them. Nini threw her a couple of sidelong glances and then remarked, "Swaroop, you have been eating continuously for so long..."

"Let her eat, Nini!" Kamala's tone was indulgent. "We don't get these things there. Not that I don't make them... But she should be at home to eat it, na! She is so distracted. Anyway, she can't afford to eat so much, can you Swaroop?"

"What is she doing now?" Nini asked.

"She's just finished a course in designing. She'll look for a job when we get back. Thought we'd take a holiday first, a relaxed one. Work can wait. She is used to doing all sorts of jobs... every summer..."

Nini nodded. She had heard all this before. "And then what? After getting a job?"

"What then?" Swaroop retorted.

"She'll decide for herself, won't you, Swaroop?" Kamala replied, her voice reflecting maternal pride.

Swaroop gave her a thumbs-up. Kamala turned to Suruchi and said, "I worry about her."

"What is there to worry about when I am here, hale and hearty?" Nini asked sharply.

"That is true," Kamala said gently, "she is your daughter for all practical purposes. She is mine in name alone. I have no cause to worry when you are here and yet..."

Suruchi stood up abruptly. She did not want to prolong this discussion about herself any further. What right do these people have to talk about my life? Besides, they won't stop at this. They'll go further and further into the past and then there will be no control. As it is, I feel my life has slipped out of my hands. If it slips out through words, then what's left? Let them talk behind my back. I cannot prevent that, she thought, and went into her room.

When Swaroop came in, Suruchi was standing by the window. Swaroop plonked herself on the bed.

"Come on, Didi, let's go out."

"Out where?"

"Somewhere. Anywhere. Can't we rent a car here?"

"I don't know, I don't drive."

"Then we'll take an autorickshaw. Let's go shopping."

"You want to buy something?"

"Not particularly. If I see something I like, I will pick it up. You get lots of jewellery here, I believe? Silver, artificial, ethnic... and skirts, like the one you are wearing."

Suruchi said nothing.

"Or we can go to the beach. Marina. No, let's go to Besant Nagar."

"No, not Besant Nagar!"

"Why? I'd gone there last time. I preferred that to Marina. There are lots of houses on the beach, aren't there? Nice ones. Should buy one of them for us when we come down on a visit..."

"This house is already there. Though it is Nini's, it's yours, too, isn't it?"

"Of course not. You are Nini's pet. She's going to leave it to you, I'm sure."

Suruchi was lost in thought. Shreerang had taken her there. To his home in Besant Nagar. Not his, his parents' home. An old spacious bungalow set amidst a coconut grove. She had been worrying because they had come here, but she hadn't gone to see Nini. What if she found out? What would happen?

Shreerang's father had asked her a lot of questions. Who was she? Where from? He might have heard of Nini, she thought. As Nayantara. But he wasn't the kind of man to be impressed by a well-known, highly respected headmistress. He would have felt sorry for her rather than admired her. A simple middle-class woman, a schoolteacher who instilled values in others. And this girl, her granddaughter, whom she had brought up? Hobnobbing with the son of a shrewd and successful businessman like himself? Suruchi had wondered why she formed that opinion of him. It was not right, even if Shreerang was not exactly close to his father. A father who had insisted that the son take over part of the family business. If the man did not particularly care about his son, why would he bother about a girl who was his son's friend? Shreerang's mother, dressed in an expensive sari, laden with diamond and gold jewellery, looked like she was a simple and kind woman. "Come, let me show you the house," she had said, leading Suruchi by the hand.

The two of them must still be there, in that house of theirs amidst the coconut trees, on the edge of the ocean. What will they say if I land up on their doorstep? Will they say anything at all?

"Are you even listening to what I'm saying, Didi?" Swaroop complained.

Suruchi was embarrassed. "Okay, tell me again."

"So what shall we do?"

"Whatever you say."

"Then come on, let's go right away."

"I'm ready."

"You're coming like this? Oh, okay. Don't ask anyone. Let's go, just you and me. We will tell them we went for a loaf. No need to give any details."

Pradeep and Swaroop were engaged in modifying Nini's garden. Because Swaroop had summoned her, Suruchi was standing there silently, arms folded across her chest. Pradeep was sitting on his haunches, filling some new pots with soil while Swaroop helped him, chattering non-stop. Pradeep looked up and asked Suruchi for something. She didn't understand what he was asking for. Swaroop shook her head disapprovingly. "Oh you, Didi!" she muttered and handed him the packet of seeds.

Suruchi was puzzled. Do I not understand these people's speech or am I just distracted? No, I am not. But I can't believe that this man, sitting here, wearing a pair of shorts, with a cigarette dangling from his lips, up to his arms in soil, who I have been watching for some time now, is really my father. Why? Not because I haven't seen him often enough. He's been coming to see me, every now and then, with my mother. They would come for a holiday, take me out, indulge me, buy me whatever I wanted... that's all the part they played. Did I never say to them, Take me with you? Or when I had gone back with them, had I said, I want to stay here with you? I don't remember. Nini was my guardian, and I was used to her. It had been decided from the start that I would live with her. According to Nini, it was a practical decision. Nini knew that when Kamala decided to marry Pradeep against her wishes, Kamala was too young, too irresponsible. She hadn't even completed her education. How then would she manage a family and home? She had been swept off her feet by Pradeep. Nothing had mattered—education, financial prospects, caste... And then within the year I was born. Soon after came Pradeep's decision to give up everything here and go looking for his fortune in a foreign country. Kamala was determined to accompany him, come what may. That's when Nini put her foot down. "Go if you must, but alone. You will not put this child through any hardship. She will stay with me. I will look after her well."

Kamala acquiesced. Perhaps she, too, didn't want any encumbrances. It would be easier to keep a check on the husband without a demanding infant. Besides, how would she manage a baby in a far-off, alien land! So she handed me over to Nini and went away. Both of them faced many hardships in the early years. They lived in a tiny place, took up all sorts of odd jobs, earned very little money. Trials and tribulations in an unfamiliar country. But Pradeep was determined to stick it out and make a living there. Did Kamala ache with longing for me, the child she had left behind? For the first few years, they couldn't afford to visit us. By which time I became wholly Nini's. She gave me the best of everything. There was a *bai* to take care of me, but Nini supervised everything herself. She gave me love, personal attention. When I saw my parents for the first time, it was with my sister. She must have been about two years old then. I was introduced to them: "This is your mother, your father, your sister." I was delighted. They made much of me. And then they came, if not every year, every alternate year. They took me back with them once. Their circumstances were better by that time. They had a nice house, enough money. But I came back. I couldn't stay away from Nini. Nor she from me. Life went on. Letters, photographs, gifts. Sent through friends and acquaintances. By post. In person. Did affection diminish? No. Does affection develop only with constant proximity? Not likely. I didn't ever fight with Swaroop. She remained the little sister, cute as a doll, a playmate, and I her Didi, her dear older sister. Kamala, the mother who smothered me in her arms when we met, wept copiously when saying goodbye, and expressed deep love through her letters. Don't so many children live in hostels for years and years? Or with grandparents, even distant relatives? Either for education or because of family pressure, and some because they were given up for adoption. I am just echoing Nini's words. And through all this I hadn't given much thought to my father. What have I got from him? He, too, gave me love. He spent money on me, bought me things. Yet something seemed to be missing. What? Why?

Pradeep had finished with potting the plants. Swaroop cheerfully dusted off the mud from herself and, when Pradeep went in to wash his hands, came and stood in front of Suruchi. "Now what?" she said.

Suruchi looked at her questioningly.

"We have to go to one of Daddy's brothers' for lunch."

"I'm not coming."

"Very clever. What do you mean, you won't come? We are all going. Nini, too."

"I've had nothing to do with any of them for the last so many years. I don't want to meet them."

"But they haven't been in touch with anyone either. From the time of our parents' marriage. But now father is doing well, lives in a 'foreign country' with dollars in his pocket and imported gifts for everyone, so they invite him. Don't two warring nations make compromises? It's the same thing. I believe they have a really old house with antique furniture. Also a big carved wooden swing. I want to see it. So don't fuss, Didi, you have to come," Swaroop said, gently punching Suruchi's arm.

The matter ended just as anticipated. Everyone got ready to leave. Then Nini spoke. "Suruchi, are you coming like this? Even Swaroop has worn a sari, and look at you."

"I don't normally dress up."

"Normally, it's fine. But today we are all going out together."

"I won't come in that case."

"Don't say that, Suruchi," Kamala quickly interjected. "Come, I'll put on the sari for you. You will look so pretty. Come, my good girl."

"Please Mummy, no." Suruchi bit her lip and looked at Pradeep, hoping he would say something. His relatives, his daughter. He could easily have said, let her be. She looks nice as she is. Simple, but lovable.

All he did was shift the cigarette from one side of his mouth to the other and look at his watch. "Hurry up. It's getting late. If she doesn't want to come, don't force her."

Swaroop pleaded, "Didi you must come."

In a calm voice Nini admonished her. "Swaroop, you are not a child anymore. Why do you need your Didi around all the time? Come on, let's go. It's her wish."

A load was lifted off Suruchi. The house was quiet and peaceful. She told Lakshmi not to make anything for her. And then, for the first time since her return, she went out. Alone.

As she read Ila's letter for the second time, her emotions overcame her. She had barely folded it and put it in its envelope when Swaroop barged in. Quickly she pushed the letter under her pillow and dabbed her eyes. Swaroop lay down on the bed saying, "I'm so bored, Didi!"

"Bored of what?"

"Of this place. There's nothing to do."

Suruchi smiled. "What did you do on previous visits?"

"I was a child then. Tagged along with Mummy and Daddy, ate, drank, played... Besides, last time we came to visit you. We had such a good time. How's that Ila?"

"She's fine."

"Still single?"

"Not still, Swaroop. Always. She isn't shopping for a husband."

"But she was married once, wasn't she?"

"Yes. She's separated."

"Why?"

"Why?" Suruchi echoed. What could she tell her in a couple of words? "Incompatibility. She is a very independent-minded person. And then her work demanded a lot of travel. To meet all kinds of people. No man tolerates that in a wife."

Swaroop sniggered. "You talk as if you are never going to get married either."

"Obviously not." Suruchi's tone was sharp. "Where's the question of marriage?"

"Sorry, Didi. What happened to Shreerang apart, would you two have married some day?"

Suruchi was startled. Is this child grown-up enough now to sit and talk to me so candidly? What can I say to her? Is it easier to answer other people? Shreerang used to say we are not accountable to anybody. If you feel you are, then you are obliged to give answers. Give up that fear. Then no questions remain. And answers emerge or vanish.

"I don't know," she said in response to Swaroop's question.

"What do you mean? You were living together, weren't you? I hear it's not easy to do that here. People are very inquisitive. They love to interfere in other people's lives." Then she added, "Whenever you were mentioned, Mummy's waterworks would start."

"Tears? For what?"

"Because she was worried. How you were living alone, with someone you were not married to, that there was no direction to your life, etc., etc., etc. But let it go. What else has she done all her life but weep?"

"Meaning?"

"Forget it, Didi. I don't like talking about it. Once I get a job, I am going to live on my own. Away from all the nagging. Go home for a short vacation, that's enough. You're lucky."

"I am?"

"Of course. Okay, tell me about yourself... What have you done with your house?"

"What else? Locked it up before coming here."

"It's a rented place isn't it?"

"Yes."

"So what will you do with it now? And your job? In the library?"

"I gave it up."

"What? Will you get it back?"

"Who knows? I don't know anything, Swaroop!"

Swaroop looked thoughtful. "That means you don't have to worry about leave and all that. You can definitely come with us."

Suruchi was silent.

"Come on, Didi. You will love it there. Unless you see it you won't know what a difference there is between Houston and New Jersey. We can even go to Canada. I have a friend there, in Montreal. We can visit him. Travel around."

"A friend?"

"Just a friend, but you don't worry about all that. I will arrange it. Please come, Didi."

"I'll see."

"Say yes you will."

"Okay."

Just then Kamala entered. Pushing aside Swaroop's outstretched legs, she sat down. "What are you planning, you two?"

"She's coming back with us!"

Kamala's unenthusiastic reaction surprised Suruchi. All she said was, "Oh really?" Then patting Swaroop's back she told her, "Go, baby, and ask Lakshmi to make us a nice cold drink. Lime juice, or see if there's some tender coconut."

"You could have brought it yourself when you came in, Mummy."

"Just go. Don't argue."

Swaroop went out grumbling. Kamala shut the door. Suruchi got a hollow feeling in the pit of her stomach. Moving quickly towards the door, she said, "I'll go and see what there is to drink."

"No need. You sit here for a bit. We must talk."

"But I have nothing to say!"

"Don't do that, *beta*. Look how thin you've become. Your skin, your hair, your face... you take no care of yourself."

Suruchi was silent.

"You shouldn't take it so much to heart. Whatever happened, happened. None of it is in our hands. And once it happens, there's nothing we can do. My heart breaks for you..."

Suruchi looked at Kamala's rapidly brimming eyes. "Don't worry about me," she said quietly.

"How can I not? I've worried about you all my life. Whatever Nini might say, you are my first-born. How could I ever forget you? You are always in my thoughts."

"I am old enough now."

"So? All these days I wondered how you could be living with someone..."

"Don't utter a word about Shreerang," Suruchi said, an edge to her voice.

Kamala was taken aback. Controlling herself quickly, she replied, "That's all right. We had liked him actually, but even so..."

"Please, Mummy..."

"What do you plan to do now?"

"I don't know and I don't want anyone to ask me that question again."

Pushing open the door, Swaroop walked in with three glasses in her hands. Handing them out, she said, "I have a great idea. Let's hire a taxi and go to Mahabalipuram. I want to see the temples there."

"There's nothing there. It's all washed away."

"That's just it. I want to see the ruins. Please, let us go."

Swaroop was dragging Suruchi by the hand along the wet sand towards the water's edge. "Come, Didi, into the water..."

Kamala shouted, "Don't, Swaroop, don't go too far..."

Swaroop ignored her and pulled Suruchi further in. Suruchi stumbled slightly. The water was above their knees.

"Enough." Suruchi stopped. She had forgotten to pull her salwar up. Swaroop was trying to ride the waves on her long legs.

"Don't go any further, Swaroop."

"Why? What's going to happen? I can swim!"

"No. Wait. Look back... Mummy's waving her hands about saying, 'Don't, don't.'"

"Why look back? Look ahead. Hold my hand. Don't let go, okay Didi?"

"I won't." Resignedly Suruchi looked at Kamala trying hard to call them back, and raised a helpless hand towards her. Pradeep stood there, smoking and staring at the sky. Nini alone was far away from them all, erect, arms folded across her chest, a typical Nini pose.

That's how she had been standing on the veranda with the smooth round pillars. An old bungalow, Shrida's. A place I often played in whenever I went there with Nini. Shrida was an old family friend. Grandfather's friend. One of the few people Nini had kept in touch with. He was a doctor of the old school. His clinic was at one end of the house. The consulting room was a room off the corridor. There were a couple of benches outside for patients, and in a partitioned-off corner was the compounder. Behind him, neatly arranged on a shelf were rows of coloured bottles. If you slipped the piece of paper with Shrida's prescription on it through the tiny opening in the partition, a bottle with a vertical label and a packet of pills would appear. While Nini awaited her turn, I played with Shrida's grandchildren. A boy about my age and two younger girls. Sometimes for half an hour, sometimes longer. Then Nini would call out "Time to go" and we'd take an autorickshaw back. But I don't remember ever taking any of Shrida's medicine. I must have needed it some time. Was there any other doctor? Or did I never fall sick? Why did Nini go to him so often? After some time, I stopped accompanying her. Didn't enjoy playing with those children anymore. The boy became arrogant, the girls were too childish. But I remember seeing Nini one day, standing there, leaning against the pillar. She was looking a little disturbed, sort of confused. She hadn't called out to me, so I said, "Nini?" and she replied, "Come on."

Sometimes Shrida came to visit us. He always spoke to me, asked after me. If there was anyone Nini would turn to for advice or help, it was Shrida. To me, he was just someone we knew, who came to see us, that's all. I was too young to understand. Soon there was a perceptible tension growing between Nini and me. College gave me a good excuse to stay out longer. When the final results came, I deliberately looked for a job in another city. Shrida had come home that day. Nini must have asked him to. I didn't want to spend too much time talking to him but when he started asking about my studies, results, future plans, I had no choice but to answer his questions. I had nothing against Shrida. In fact, I was quite fond of him. He was a man of few words. Calm, pleasant, soft-spoken. But more importantly, he listened attentively whenever one spoke to him. It made a difference, because at that age one tends to think no one pays any heed to what one says. When he asked me that day, I answered him almost insolently, "I will go somewhere. Anywhere. Far away if necessary. I am quite capable of living on my own." He looked at me with a half-smile on his face. Nini wasn't around. I didn't realise at that time that she had deliberately left us alone. Had she thought that Shrida would put some sense into my head? Maybe. But Shrida said, "Go! You have my support." And then he added, "Don't tell her I said that!" Actually he hadn't said 'her', but mentioned her by name. "Nayantara" he'd said. I laughed and said, "Okay."

Nini didn't refer to our conversation or ask about it at all. I accepted the job, prepared to leave. I felt vaguely like seeing Shrida once before going, but I didn't. I didn't visit him even when I came back the first few times. Once when I thought of him, I asked Nini how he was, and she told me he had closed down his clinic. I couldn't figure out whether she'd met him or he'd come to see her. There was not much of a relationship with his family, so that was that.

From where to where my thoughts have taken me, Suruchi thought and came out of her reverie. With extra force, she dragged Swaroop back. "That's enough," she said. "Mummy has gone hoarse calling out to us. Come on."

Reluctantly, Swaroop turned back. Letting go of Suruchi's hand she ran towards Pradeep. Suruchi saw her pointing out to something and telling him something. Suruchi reached Nini's side. Nini pretended not to notice and kept her gaze fixed on the ocean in the distance.

"How is Shrida?"

Nini's face was blank.

"Must be all right."

"You don't meet nowadays?"

"Not really."

"Why?"

She just shrugged. "I have no time. Perhaps he doesn't either."

"But you just said he's closed down his practice?"

"Maybe he's doing something else, I don't know."

"He was always so helpful, wasn't he?"

"Those days are gone. Everyone's roles change. Some relationships become redundant. Maybe that's what happened. I don't know."

Suruchi was shocked. Nini's inflexibility was so obvious. Everyone says she brought me up with much love. How did I perceive that love? Not as hugging and cuddling. Not even by remembering special occasions, getting gifts, celebrating birthdays, giving rewards. Then how? People must have different ways of expressing love. But if it is never expressed, how does one believe it exists?

Suruchi followed Merlin up the stairs. She'd had no idea what Merlin did or where and how she lived. Since she had told Nini when she met her, Suruchi knew where Merlin worked. Merlin unlocked the door and said, "Come on in."

She opened the window and light streamed in. She pulled out one of the folding chairs for Suruchi and one for herself. "Sit. I'll make some tea," she said, but Suruchi stopped her and looked around. Two small rooms. Minimum furniture.

"It's okay, Merlin, forget the tea. Let's sit and chat."

Merlin smiled and sat down.

"I met Nini after a long time. When I saw her, for a moment I hesitated; then I thought, oh yes, that is Suruchi's grandmother. I went up and asked about you. Thought, if she doesn't like it, too bad. At least I will get to know where you are."

"Why do you say 'if she doesn't like it'?"

"Because it's true. Your Nini never liked me. You don't remember? Whenever I came to your house to study, she'd send me off as soon as she could. Sometimes she'd even say you were asleep, or not at home ... any odd excuse to get rid of me."

Suruchi laughed. Merlin was so candid. She's always been simple and straightforward. We sat on the same bench in class, shared our lunch boxes. Merlin brought mutton and chicken. I learnt to relish it. It tasted better for not letting Nini hear of it. Then Merlin went to the Arts College and I opted for science. But we met at least once a week. She was the only friend I had.

She felt the same. Merlin went to church every Sunday. We found it was a good place to meet, walk around or sit down quietly and talk. When Nini found out, she was furious. She didn't like my going to church one bit, but I continued to go there without her knowledge. I started evading her questions. I learnt to tell lies. After a time, her probing got to me. But then my meetings with Merlin became more infrequent. She took up a job soon after her BA. I went on to do a Library Science course. We still made an effort to get together once every couple of months or so. We couldn't meet at my place because Nini wouldn't like it, and Merlin was ashamed to take me to her home. The small house, large family, relatives flitting in and out, the untidiness ... it was not conducive to chatting, she'd say, so we would meet somewhere for coffee or a cold drink. Or we would go to the same church compound. But something had changed. She was immersed in her problems and I was involved in my activities. I didn't know when, how and why that relationship ended.

"Never mind about me. Tell me about yourself," Merlin said. "You went away because you got a job, Nini said. Why? You could have got so many jobs right here."

"That's not how it was. I got an opportunity, so I took it." After a pause, Suruchi added, "I wanted to get away."

"But you did come back now and then?"

"I did at first. On leave, during vacations. But then some things happened which came between the two of us. So much so that I left her house. I didn't see her for six years."

"What are you saying! Really?"

"Yes, it's true. But I've come back now. I had to. I had nowhere else to go. Besides, ties of birth don't break so easily."

Merlin was unconsciously chewing her nails and staring beyond Suruchi. Quickly Suruchi reached for Merlin's hand.

"You said you were married, Merlin, and had children. Where are they?" she asked.

"Viren has taken them to his mum's place. Yes, two children, a boy and a girl. They go to school. Study well."

"And Viren?"

"He's...umm, okay. He was. When I met him as Viren Braganza. We had great plans. We wanted to build a house. A future for ourselves. But accomplished nothing. Viren lost his first job. He got another one. A temporary one. Disappointed, he took to alcohol. Then he got a good job which he couldn't keep due to his drinking problem. It's a vicious circle... no job, so drink; find a job, then lose it because of drink... But he adores the children. When he is sober, he is good. Otherwise... That's why I have to work. Take dictation half the day, hammer the typewriter the other half... I can't do anything else."

Suruchi had let go of Merlin's hand and her fingers found their way to her mouth again.

"Why don't you seek the help of some organisation? There are several who can help..."

"Forget about me. What about yourself? Did you get married?"

"No."

"Very sensible. No wise person should ever get married. Brings too many headaches with it which just don't go away, and we get royally screwed. Husband, children, in-laws, house, chores, responsibilities... it is never-ending. All that happens is your ties with your own family snap."

The way Merlin kept talking, Suruchi forgot that they hadn't met for several years! Obviously she didn't have anyone to talk to either. Isn't that what had brought us together in the first place? Of course we hadn't thought of it like that then. At that time, neither of us had wanted to talk about our families. Some kind of inferiority complex, perhaps. That's why we met outside and avoided any discussion about home and family. We talked generally and casually about so many things. Inconsequential stuff. That's what our friendship was about. Today those things are still unimportant. We've met after all these years, but Merlin is going on and on about her life. What should I tell her about mine? I didn't need to because Merlin kept blabbering about herself. She must have assumed that because I wasn't married, I had no life, that mine was an incomplete existence, so there was nothing worth talking about. Was it really like that?

Suruchi took the tea Merlin insisted on serving her. Admired the photographs of the husband and children. For a moment, Suruchi felt like saying, "Come let's go for a walk, like old times." But she gave up the idea. When they had nothing more to say to each other, she took her leave.

When Kamala pushed the curtain aside and entered the room, Suruchi was lying on the bed, reading. As soon as Kamala sat down next to her, she shut the book and sat up. Kamala kept looking at her as if searching for something. As if she was looking at her daughter for the first time. After a while she spoke. "How do you spend your time?"

Suruchi shrugged. "Just like that. Don't do anything particular."

"I don't mean here. There. What do you do when you come home?"

Suruchi thought that Kamala was trying to suggest that the past was not yet dead by using the present tense.

"I have many friends there."

"That's what I meant... What's her name, that lawyer friend of yours?"

"Ila."

"Yes that one... Is she still at it, fighting for women's causes and all that?"

Suruchi was amused. What world is she living in? Even if you defined women's issues so simplistically, is it something that 'begins' and 'ends'? Does Ila even believe that these issues will be resolved at some point and that everything will be fair and just? Ila was a strong, intelligent woman with firm convictions. I still remember the first time I met her. I'd started working as a librarian in the University library, and had been given a room in the hostel there, because of Nini. Who knows, even my job could have been because of her. She had contacts everywhere. Once she accepted the fact that I was applying for jobs elsewhere, she must have spoken to someone. I don't know and never dared to ask.

Ila used to come to the library often. I noticed there was something special about her the first time I set eyes on her. It was her appearance, her demeanour, her voice, her steady gaze, that gave her an almost electrifying presence, and I was deeply impressed. Before I knew it, I started becoming like her. I dressed in oversized shirts with rolled-up sleeves, baggy jeans or long floral printed skirts, carried an oversized handbag or slung a jhola on one shoulder, and shoes. No jewellery, only a watch. I may not have been able to fix someone with my gaze like she did, or speak as animatedly as her, but yes, I did succeed in emulating her. This Ila was completely different from the Ila in the court room, or on a podium, or at a meeting. But incomparable, inimitable, all the same.

Perhaps her coming into my life was significant, momentous. We always end up becoming like those we admire or are inspired by. It's natural. Nothing wrong in it. Ila came to the library to borrow books or read or do some reference work. At first we only smiled at each other. Gradually a few words were exchanged, then came meetings for tea in the canteen. Ila was addicted to tea. As I came to know about Ila's work, I was drawn into it. From my visits to her home, her office, the meetings I attended with her, observed her at seminars, I acquired a new perspective on life. Another world came into view. On one side was a grim, disturbing world; on the other was the thrill of watching her overcome its challenges. I became Ila's friend. Many nights were spent in her house, chatting, discussing, exchanging views. And meeting new people. Not just that, so many other activities were a part of our lives—theatre, films, exhibitions, music concerts, picnics, poetry and play readings followed by discussions about them. There would be heated arguments, sometimes vicious personal attacks, earnest attempts to convince others of one's standpoint... but always, coming together in friendship and warmth.

When I went home to meet Nini after almost a year and a half, she was obviously rattled. She bombarded me with questions, who, what, where, how, why... My replies were guarded, matter-of-fact, abrupt and incomplete. Sometimes I skirted the question, or gave vague answers, and I even made up stories. Be tactful, don't tell her anything that would make her angry, that she wouldn't like, I warned myself. But I ended up saying, "I am a big girl, I am independent. I can do what I want, live as I please. I will decide what to wear, who I want to be friends with." I thought the matter would end there. That Nini would withdraw, step back, keep quiet. But no. Nini just brushed aside my tirade, ignored all that I'd said, erased it.

And yet I returned to her. Because she is my grandmother. She has brought me up. We are related, by blood. How can I deny her? Besides, I was the one who fought with her; the decision to stay away for the last six years was mine, not hers. That's why I wrote that letter. She said, "Come" and I came. This journey was at Ila's behest. She was the one who'd said, "Go to Nini," got me the ticket, and dropped me off at the station. She'd never met Nini and yet she had urged me to come here. "Think it over"; "Sort it out for yourself"; "Take control," she advised. That was Ila!

Kamala interrupted Suruchi's thoughts. "You will find such women there, too. They hold demonstrations, raise slogans, protest against all sorts of things. But tell me, Suruchi, what kind of lives do these women have? Broken marriages, abandoned husbands and children; when they cannot take control of their own lives, what will they do for others? Take your Ila herself... she is separated, isn't she?"

"It isn't like that."

"Then how is it? You tell me."

"They don't do it deliberately. Their husbands cannot handle their independence, their competence, their success. Hence the conflict."

"Don't tell me all that. They view a husband as an enemy. He has to be fought. Now you tell me, Shreerang was not your 'husband'... what difference did it make?"

"Mummy..."

"Very well. I will not say anything. You never let me speak anyway. You have no idea how I feel. I'd always hoped to see you married, have a family, a home of your own. It would have made me so happy! But no," she sobbed, wiping the tears flowing down her cheeks. "What made you live with him like that? What was lacking in your life? Sometimes I think it was good this happened. What if you had been married..."

"Mummy!" Suruchi screamed. She was trembling inside. What did she mean? It was all right that he died? It wouldn't have been if he were a husband? What a heartless, despicable thought. Didn't relationships, affection, friendship, mean anything at all? She felt pity for her mother. Her thoughts, her manner of expressing them, her tears... it was pathetic!

"So what do you expect me to do, Mummy?"

"Stay with us for a while."

"For what?"

"Because you haven't stayed with us at all."

"You're the one who left me and went away."

More tears from Kamala. "You won't understand. There was no option. I just didn't know what to do. As a wife, it was my duty to accompany your father. We had no idea where we would live, what we would do; besides, we had no money. You were a little baby. You would've suffered. I was afraid of that. Nini knew that, too. She gave me no choice. She said she would not hold it against me if I left you in her charge. You know how angry she was when I decided to get married. Had I not agreed, she would not have forgiven me for the rest of my life. She would have behaved as if I didn't exist. You don't know Nini. A woman who does exactly and only what she wants. I was in a fix. I had no one else except her. Even on your father's side there was no support. So what could I do? I handed you over to her and went away. Sometimes circumstances put one in such situations... But no one understands that."

Suruchi sat still, hugging her knees to her chest, listening to Kamala, watching her tear-streaked face.

As usual Swaroop barged in, looked first at one, then the other, wrinkled her brow and said, "At it again, Mummy? Tears and all? At least don't drown Didi in them."

"How does it concern you?" Kamala snapped. "Who are you to tell me what to do? I am talking to my daughter."

"I can see that."

"Is this the way you talk to your mother?" Kamala's voice became shrill. "Just go away."

"I won't," replied Swaroop defiantly and settled down beside Suruchi. "Who are you to tell me to go?"

"How dare you! Behaving rudely has become a habit with you. Go on, get up..."

When Swaroop showed no signs of moving, Kamala, in a fit of rage, slapped her arm. Swaroop screamed. That sent Kamala's temper soaring even higher, she began raining blows on Swaroop's body. Suruchi was shocked.

"Mummy! Don't! Stop it!" she shouted and tried to separate the two of them. Kamala stopped, took a deep breath, threw a scathing look at her younger daughter and stomped out of the room.

Suruchi was still in a daze. "What is all this?" she said.

"Nothing new," replied Swaroop, sighing.

"She beats you? Even now?"

"Oh yes, often. You are fortunate, Didi! Nini wouldn't have raised her hand on you, isn't it?"

"Never!"

"Just as well you don't live there."

Suruchi was very upset. These people were not strangers, they were her own family. Hadn't she ever noticed these things before? Maybe she hadn't, or maybe she had deliberately glossed over them. Not just this but lots of other things ... greater, smaller ...

"Why don't you listen to her?" Suruchi asked Swaroop.

"Forget it, Didi. I don't like talking about it. Just wait and see, after a while she'll be all loving and caring. Come, let's go out. You said you'd show me a church. The one you used to go to with your friend. Come on."

When Nini fell ill, the whole household revolved around her. It wasn't anything serious, just high fever, sore throat and a cold. But Kamala would not leave Nini's bedside and from there, ordered the girls around. Naturally no outings could be planned and everyone was compelled to go about their business quietly around the house.

Suruchi was alarmed when she saw Swaroop meddling around with the books in the living room cupboards. "What are you looking for? Have you asked Nini's permission?"

"No. Why should I ask her? I am not planning to take them with me. Just looking for something readable."

"Like what?"

"Something romantic."

Suruchi smiled. "How about Romeo and Juliet? In the original?"

"No, no, not that. A modern romance. The kind where the hero-heroine fall in love and straight into bed... and their exploits... That's nice and hot, good fun..."

"You won't find anything like that in Nini's library."

"You read those kinds of books?"

"No, not anymore."

"But you used to earlier? And you gave up because you met Shreerang? Did you also do all that, Didi? Tell me, Didi... how it happened. Did you fall in love at first sight?"

"It doesn't happen like that..."

"Then how?"

Suruchi was stumped. What could she tell her? If she tried to recall the events, where should she begin? The first meeting? I don't remember it at all. I remember when I met Ila for the first time, not Shreerang. I don't think we even noticed each other when we were introduced. "He manages his father's engineering goods business," they said. One was hardly likely to pay attention to a tall, sallow, easy-going young man with such a prosaic background. Or do I feel this way now? Perhaps he'd struck a chord even then. It is not always easy to explain why two people come together and settle into a relationship. We kept meeting as a group, but why the two of us became close, I cannot say. No, that's not quite true. I remember how when he started to recite poetry, I was mesmerised. I mentioned this to Ila. She laughed. "You will find out more once you get to know him better," she said. And that's what happened.

He lived in a two-room place in a seedy locality, ate his meals out, had little regard for his father, and yet did his work dutifully and sincerely. The rest of the time he spent reading, attending plays, watching movies, making friends. Shreerang loved literature and would have been perfectly happy getting an MA degree and teaching English. But his father had said no. He was stern, autocratic and domineering, Shreerang had said. As we continued to meet, I got the impression that he was quite a talkative fellow. He spoke candidly about himself, his parents, his education, doing an MBA in the USA instead of an MA, at his father's behest, and then joining the family business. Monotonous, uninspiring, demanding but profitable.

I remember one evening. Late evening merging into night. We had gone for a long walk, so long that my legs started aching, but I couldn't say that. He was talking about something animatedly and I was listening, spell-bound, half in love with him. I was engrossed, not so much in what he was saying, but in my own unravelling feelings. By the time we returned to Ila's flat on the first floor, everything was in darkness. Ila must have gone to bed. We didn't want to wake her up. I couldn't possibly go back to the hostel or to Shreerang's room at that time, so we spent all night sitting on the landing, Shreerang and I. Talking. Shreerang talked about his mother for the first time that day. His kind and hardworking mother, always immersed in household chores, either in the kitchen or in the courtyard. There was the big house to maintain, several servants to manage and a continuous stream of guests and relatives to look after.

Her husband had given her a mansion to live in, cupboards full of clothes, loads of jewellery, prestige in society, but that was all. Nothing more. She had no identity of her own. And then there was Shreerang. He used to follow her around, holding on to her sari *pallu*. As he grew older, he tried to help her in whatever way he could. She suffered from insomnia, so she told Shreerang stories. And that night, he repeated them all to me. Stories that had been told for years, some new, some familiar, some I'd read. I was finding it hard to keep my eyes open. But he was wide awake. Shreerang noticed me dozing off.

He stretched out his legs and let me sleep in his arms. That was the first time we 'slept' together. Not really, for he was awake all the while. I slept soundly. Shreerang did not touch me. Not then. And when he did, there was infinite tenderness rather than love in it. When Ila opened the door the next morning, she was shocked to see the two of us outside her flat. What could we say to her? That we spent the night on her landing, sitting there, dozing off? Would anyone believe us? Did it actually happen? Was it a dream? Another world? Would Swaroop understand any of it? Will she find it 'romantic'? Or call it foolishness? Will she believe me?

She asks, so naively, what happened, how did it happen. What do I say to her?

"Things don't happen the way we imagine them," Suruchi replied.

"What do you mean?"

"I mean, umm... you think you love someone deeply, and imagine it's an all-consuming love, one that gives you wings. But it's rarely like that. Not that it doesn't happen once in a while. But most of the time there are so many other issues around it. Simple everyday matters. You have to find love through them."

Suruchi was startled. What am I saying? Had I really felt this way, too? After spending so much time with Shreerang and hearing him talk, I had just begun to understand him. He was so unlike other men. Not one who spoke fondly about his family, had career aspirations, and dreamt of marriage, a wife, children, a home with fridge-TV, etc! On the contrary, he had contempt for these things and often ridiculed them quite harshly. Yet I fell in love with him. How do I explain that? What does 'yet' mean? Did I, too, want a husband who would provide all these things?

After meeting innumerable women who came to see Ila, and reading dozens of articles, I had started viewing women differently. At first one was an individual. A human being with an identity. Then one was assigned roles, handed down the centuries: daughter-wife-mother. Home equals family equals happiness. How misleading these premises had proved to be. I had seen them fail with my own eyes. So why was I reluctant to live as 'ME'? As an independent person? Ila did it. Her work, her conviction about her role—it had been hard at times, but she kept up the struggle. And I got carried away. I told myself that I, too, had a good job, a comfortable life, lots of friends, the freedom to do as I pleased ... Now I could set out in search of the elusive 'self'.

At that point I was looking out for a place to stay. But I found that most landlords were unwilling to let out their rooms to a young, unmarried woman. Shreerang had gone with me to see one particular place. It was a tiny, independent, outhouse kind of space, which I liked instantly. Before discussing any details, the middle-aged owner assumed that we were a couple, newly married, most likely. I was amused. As soon as the gentleman left, Shreerang asked, "How do you like the idea?"

I was puzzled. "Of marriage?"

"No, not marriage. Living together. Look, the minute you say you are single, the man will refuse to give you the house. But if we are together, he will agree. We don't have to provide any kind of proof that we are married, either to him or to anyone else. You've seen more than a dozen places so far. How many more will you try? If you have to make adjustments why not about this? My rooms are also not fit to live in. We could live here together, yet completely independent. Not binding on either party. It is purely a matter of convenience. And a ploy to get the place and throw dust into society's eyes." Then he said, smiling, "This way we can get the better of them!"

I was stunned. My mind went blank for a few moments. What he was suggesting made sense. I needed the place, but how far was I willing to go to get it? The injustice of being refused simply because I was alone stung me. But then living with Shreerang was also compromising societal norms, wasn't it? He was a man, a support, but to make a husband out of him... was it honest? What about all those other little adjustments one would have to make, day in and day out, if we lived together?

I decided to speak to Ila. "You have to decide. Do you like him enough to want to live with him? That's the only question you must answer. Don't make an issue of other things," she said in her no-nonsense way. I thought deeply over it. I had to convey my decision to the landlord quite soon. If it was a 'Yes', then the rooms had to be painted, stuff for the house to be bought, and Nini informed.

We moved in. I wrote to Nini that I had found a place, I had furnished it, and was settling down. I included the new address. But I did not mention Shreerang in the letter. Later, the fear of what would happen if Nini found out from someone else brought me home to meet her. It was the last meeting before the six-year estrangement.

Without fully understanding what Swaroop had said, Suruchi absently nodded. Just then an agitated Kamala came out of Nini's room. "One of you, call the doctor," she urged, "Nini's temperature has shot up. She is not responding to me, not saying anything ... What shall we do now?"

"Mummy, first stop all this drama. I will phone the doctor. Nini will be fine, she is a strong woman, what are you panicking for?"

Suruchi went into Nini's room, sat beside her and started applying cold compresses to her forehead. Nini was utterly silent. Even when Suruchi called out to her, she did not open her eyes or say anything. Kamala was trying to control her tears. Lakshmi stood in the doorway, looking frightened. The doctor came, advised immediate transfer to the hospital. She will need a drip, he said, but nothing to worry about.

When Pradeep, who had gone out of town for ten days, returned, Nini was still in hospital. Her fever had come down but she was extremely weak and because she was dehydrated, they had put her on a drip. As Nini needed someone by her bedside all the time, everybody got busy with either hospital duty or taking care of household chores. Suruchi could not remember the house ever being run without Nini. But because of Lakshmi everything was taken care of—meals, phone calls, visitors, guests. For the first time Suruchi realised how well Lakshmi had been trained. A simple illiterate woman like her would have been done for by her husband's ill-treatment, had

Nini not extended her a hand of support and transformed her life.

Now in Nini's absence, she managed the household efficiently. She kept meticulous accounts, buying what was necessary, planning and preparing meals for everyone. Had I ever given Nini due credit for this tremendous achievement of hers, for helping Lakshmi to realise her potential?

Suruchi was sitting with Nini when Pradeep came to visit her in the hospital. Nini hardly spoke to him. Nini didn't like talking to visitors, Suruchi noticed. She hated the thought of being ill. In fact, she told them not to inform anyone. If someone wanted to visit her, she would tell them to come to the house later. Even to the family she hardly spoke. Only with me she is a little more communicative, thought Suruchi. I was surprised when the nurse asked, "Who is Suruchi?" Evidently Nini had asked for me. Me? When all the others, including Kamala, were present? I noticed that she became very uneasy when Swaroop or Kamala were around, and suggested that they go home. But she didn't mind if I sat with her. She said little to me, and yet I couldn't help think that she did love me after all. She had been upset with me then, but so what? She had brought me up, cared for me, hadn't she? She couldn't have erased those years from her memory later, could she? I can't do that. It isn't possible. It was the most important, life-changing period of my life.

Kamala was due to spend the night in the hospital, so when Pradeep got up to leave, Suruchi accompanied him. There was really no cause for concern, and in a day or two, Nini would be home.

Suruchi was preoccupied when they got into an autorickshaw and she did not hear what Pradeep said. When they stopped, she asked, "Where are we going?"

"In here. You haven't met them in a while, they all asked after you, so I thought..."

Suruchi recognised the place as her uncle's house. Pradeep's brother. She hadn't seen them for years. Why were they so eager to meet her? Was she a specimen from some zoo to be exhibited like this? They were her father's relatives. Blood relations. So? Suruchi felt the anger rise within her. She was not used to being told what to do.

The conversation was general. No one directed any questions at her. In between, someone asked her what she had studied, what she was doing, that's all. She didn't bother to find out who was who, how they were related to each other, to her, but she did notice that Pradeep was enjoying himself in their company. They also seemed to be pleased with him. Could it be because he now had money? Living abroad, a dollar income, status and style. But what did he get out of them? He was the one who had broken all ties and gone away. Never to return, according to what Kamala often said, no matter how difficult life there was. He was prepared to put up with the hardships. They must be doing very well now, at least that's the impression she'd got from Kamala and Swaroop. Then why this yearning to reconnect with 'my family'?

Someone interrupted her thoughts with, "So you don't have a family, a home of your own yet?" Obviously the person had taken her age into account when asking this question.

Before she could answer, Pradeep said, "All that is not for her."

One elderly lady asked, "Why do you say that? She is such a lovely girl..."

Suruchi was taken aback, both by Pradeep's reply and the lady's comment. The hollowness of the two remarks struck her. The conversation would drift into inanities, she felt. No, it would degenerate into insincere platitudes. Not saying what was on one's mind, using words one did not mean, not speaking the truth. Trying to please someone with flattery. Why do people enter into conversations at all if they cannot say what they mean? If they did, there wouldn't be so much time wasted in decoding each other's statements.

As they got up to leave, almost everyone said to Suruchi, "Come again." She couldn't bring herself to say, "I will," so she just smiled.

"You could, you know," Pradeep said.

"What, visit them?"

"Yes, why not? Good to, once in a while."

"I don't think so."

"Don't forget they are our family, yours and mine."

"So what?"

"One needs to maintain these links... You will understand eventually..."

Suruchi understood nothing, but was angry. Nini had told her, disapprovingly, that Pradeep had enticed Kamala. He was a smart man. She was a simple girl, young and naïve, the kind who got carried away by the littlest attention. How long then before she fell in love? She was happy to give up college and get married. How quickly it had all happened—marriage, child, going abroad... It was hard to accept the sequence of events the way Nini described them. Suruchi was rather annoyed. "They are my parents, aren't they?" She'd wanted to say. Those were the days when Suruchi had felt intense hostility towards Nini, so she reacted violently to anything Nini said. But she kept her anger well hidden. She would find out the truth some day.

As soon as they entered the gate, Swaroop ran up to them. "Where were you all this while?"

Suruchi's face flushed. Pradeep replied, "Everyone has seen you. They hadn't met Suruchi so..."

"There was no need for them to... Had I known earlier, I would never have come with you," Suruchi snapped.

Suruchi had not spoken to Pradeep so rudely before. She may not have been affectionate or confiding, but this outburst surprised even her. I still haven't been able to figure out who this man is, she thought. Who exactly is a father and what is his role as one? What kind of bond is there between a father and child? I don't know. To me this was a stranger who I met once in a while. At first I looked upon him as someone who used to get me gifts. Not any longer. Gifts are what Swaroop brought. He hardly ever asked me anything about myself. He had not wanted to find out what I had studied, what job I was doing, where I lived, how much I earned... He and Shreerang had met only once. He took Shreerang out for a beer. He was surprised to see Shreerang did not drink even beer. I asked Shreerang when they returned, "What did you talk about?" His reply:

"We have nothing in common." There was little Shreerang could say to him. Having lived in the USA himself, he was not impressed by any stories that Pradeep had tried to tell him. It was the same Pradeep who had been so talkative with his relatives! Expressing an opinion on everything, pulling stories of adventure and romance out of his American bag. There are so many people in the world, all have the same physical attributes and yet it is impossible to say who will get along with whom. Maybe it's this unpredictability that is the charm of relationships. Pradeep chose to ignore Suruchi's outburst. Swaroop had distracted him by throwing her arms around him and cajoling him to get her something. Suruchi turned away involuntarily. She found all this quite distasteful. She marched into her room and flung herself on the bed. As usual she pushed her fists under her pillow, a habit which Shreerang had noticed. So he left small objects, notes, under the pillow. On her birthday, he had put a card there with the poem:

My true love hath my heart and I have his,
By just exchange one for the other given;
I hold his dear, and mine he cannot miss
There never was a better bargain driven....
My true love hath my heart and I have his.[1]

Suruchi had been amused. Shreerang admitting his love? As a gift? So romantically? He didn't have to, but that's the way he was. Bringing colour into life. Shreerang travelled quite often but all his trips were unplanned, whether it was to meet his father or on business. She never knew if he would be at home when she returned. Sometimes when she woke up early in the morning, she would find him snuggled in bed next to her. The door couldn't be locked or bolted from the inside because of this. At first she was afraid. Then she got used to it. If she reached under the pillow, she often found billets, messages from him, even things that she had misplaced and had been looking for frantically, sometimes a pen, handkerchief, cassette or book. She used to say in jest, "Will you never get me anything larger than the pillow?" His standard reply used to be, "When you have the whole of me beside you..." That was true. But what when he was not? That was the price. Freedom was paramount; obligation, rules, bonds, none of them applied. No demanding them, no expecting them either.

When I worked myself up about this one day, I found a scrap of paper under the pillow. It said, "NO". Crushing it into a ball, I wept into my pillow. Stayed indoors all day. Took leave without permission, ate nothing, did nothing. And Shreerang, who was due back after a couple of days, turned up the same evening. Seeing my dishevelled appearance, my tear-streaked face, and red, swollen eyes, he drew me into his arms and murmured, "I knew you'd do this to yourself. That's why I came back. In fact I never went." Which meant he knew, he cared. But that 'NO' was definitive. It offered no option. Was this its horrible ugly face then? Of death?

Death, be not proud, though some have called thee
Mighty and dreadful, for thou are not so[2]

I can still hear Shreerang's voice read the poems, every one of them. Line after line after line. He was probably fulfilling his desire to teach poetry. It was an enchanted world... One that I had not even peeped into because of my resentment against Nini. I didn't read even now. I would make him read while I listened. And the words became meaningful. If I listened to this, I had to listen to the 'NO', too. Naturally.

Suruchi set out to post the letter she'd written to Ila when she noticed Nini sitting in the living room. The women from her organisation had just left and Suruchi had overheard Nini telling them not to elect her as an office-bearer the following year. Suruchi was surprised. Why had she said that? It was not just the others. Nini, too, had tremendous confidence in her own abilities, and her vast experience of running schools, enforcing discipline. She was working in a similar capacity in this organisation, wasn't she?

I had never shown any interest in her organisation, her work, and the women she dealt with. I had some idea because of what I had heard and read, but Nini did not talk about it herself. The women were either destitute or abandoned by their husbands, or had been cheated by someone. Providing food and shelter for them, giving them training in some skill, getting employment for them—in short, rehabilitating them. It's a lot of work Nini is doing. Perhaps Ila knows more about it than I do since she is in a similar field. But the two of them are so dissimilar. Why? Nini's work is considered social service, whereas Ila is branded a feminist. Because Nini helped them, but did not free them? Does it imply that Ila doesn't offer the women assistance, and Nini doesn't give them freedom? Who made these distinctions? But help means support. Independence is inherent in liberation, so does one abandon support? Is that where the difference lies? Does this difference manifest itself in everybody's life? Shreerang always wanted independence. I wanted it, too. That's why I left Nini. But did I find independence? I got involved with Shreerang. And despite reiterating it to myself over and over again, being convinced of the need for independence, I couldn't give up that longing to make Shreerang mine forever. He could do it. He was much more demonstrative in showing his love, through his words and deeds. And yet he was firm. He knew what he wanted right from the start. And he didn't lose his focus even after the bitter quarrels we used to have later. I was the one who vacillated. Because I was making the demands. Which meant I was not independent, nor liberated. He was. Free meant alone. On one's own. He was fully aware that the other side of freedom was loneliness. That's what he wanted. But I was afraid of being alone. Does that mean he who is afraid of being alone can never be truly free? That fear comes in the way of liberation. Once you get rid of the fear, you are free! But that's not how it turned out. And I was enslaved for life.

Suruchi was walking along the gravel-strewn path, lost in thought, when she stumbled and fell. Because she tried to break the fall with her hands, both her palms were badly grazed and bleeding. The skirt had ripped and exposed her skin, causing one knee to be severely bruised. She somehow got to her feet and limped back home. Swaroop saw her and dashed to the gate. She lifted the skirt and found blood trickling down

Suruchi's leg. She quickly got water, Dettol, cotton wool, and started cleaning the wound. "Didi," she said softly, "someone has come to see you."

For a split second Suruchi thought, Shreerang? And then checked herself. Was she mad? How could she even think the impossible?

"Who is it?"

"He's seated inside, chatting away with Nini. Nini herself asked him in."

Just then Abhijit appeared at the door. Suruchi smiled. "Before I could get a description of you, you came out," she said. "You've been introduced to Swaroop, I suppose. See what a good nurse she is!"

Despite Suruchi's protests, Swaroop plastered band-aids all over the wounds. "Didi, if you have difficulty eating with your hands, I will feed you, but no taking these off," she warned, and went inside, taking all the first-aid paraphernalia with her.

Suruchi asked Abhijit what had brought him to Chennai. He had come with his script, he said. Someone must have tempted him with an offer to produce the play here, she thought. None of the plays he had written so far had had more than five or six shows.

"How are you, Suruchi?" he asked. "Ila insisted that I visit you. She said you hadn't replied to two or three of her letters."

"I just posted one," Suruchi replied, adding, "I'm all right."

"I didn't know your entire family was due to come."

"You didn't? I must have mentioned it. You must not have paid attention. You never do, anyway!"

Suruchi felt good teasing him. She'd met Abhijit before she met Shreerang, because he was Ila's friend and assistant. He often wrote things out for her. He was an intellectual, reticent, lost in his own world. Suruchi knew that Ila was very impressed by his commitment and focus on his work. Besides, he was very useful to have around, to do odd jobs like book tickets, receive or see people off at the railway station, carry messages. In addition to managing his job, he also single-handedly took care of his elderly mother.

Swaroop came in, carrying coffee for everyone. Abhijit was to return the next day, so the three of them planned to go out that evening. As he took leave, Abhijit said he would wait for them at the Parry's Corner bus stop at the designated time. That would be most convenient, he said. It probably hasn't occurred to him that we might take an autorickshaw and not the bus, thought Suruchi, but she said nothing.

Kamala and Pradeep, who had gone out, came in a short while later. Kamala went into Suruchi's room where the two girls were. "Finished whatever shopping was left to be done," she said. "This way there won't be any last-minute rush and we won't forget anything. Who knows when our next visit will be," she sighed.

She always said that, as if she didn't quite trust the future. But they had been coming every two–three years, even earlier, of late. Perhaps the uncertainty of the early years was responsible for her apprehension. She had had no assurances then, and now uncertainty had become a habit.

After a few minutes Kamala turned to the two of them and said rather seriously, "I have to tell you something," and waited for their reaction.

"Then say it quickly," Swaroop urged.

"Okay, listen. There is a very nice boy. He's done his PhD, has a good job, no family responsibility, has a married older brother, a sister..."

"Is it a marriage proposal? For whom?" Suruchi interrupted.

Kamala hesitated. "Umm, it is... actually the only information we have. If you are agreeable, Suruchi..."

"For me?" Suruchi's voice was thick with contempt. Kamala was flustered.

Quickly collecting herself she said, "I just asked. Only if you are willing. Think about it. He seems perfectly suitable for you. There might be a couple of years age difference, but that we can..."

Suruchi glared at Kamala, her face flushed. "Okay, okay, we will consider him for Swaroop," she added hastily. "He seems perfect for her in every way. The boy is good-looking, based in London. Presently in India for some seminar. He's coming here tomorrow. So if a meeting has to be fixed ..."

Suruchi shuddered involuntarily. She turned to see Swaroop's reaction, but it was most unexpected. Instead of flaring up, Swaroop calmly asked, "Any photo available?"

Suruchi couldn't control herself, "Swaroop, you agree to this?"

"Why not? I want to get married anyway, and Mummy's description sounds excellent. But Didi, if you like him, I won't come in your way, okay?"

"Shut up, Swaroop!"

Swaroop shrugged. "Mummy, photo?" she said nonchalantly.

"No, no child, we haven't got a photo. We heard about it when we had gone out just now. I have the phone number. I deliberately didn't mention either of you. Thought I would ask you both first and then decide. I will call them tomorrow and then plan to meet somewhere convenient for everyone."

Suddenly Suruchi felt the strength leave her body. A lassitude overcame her. All the enthusiasm for the evening's outing evaporated. There was no way of contacting Abhijit. Besides, Swaroop was quite excited about going out with him.

They reached the bus stop much before time. Suruchi said, "I didn't think you would agree to this business so easily."

"What business?"

"This ... proposal, girl-viewing, planning ..."

"Why not?"

"I don't mean marriage. Whether you do or don't get married, it's a personal decision. But these practices? You are an American girl, Swaroop. You like all these things? Getting married to an unknown man on the basis of his appearance, his educational qualifications ..."

Swaroop laughed. "To tell you the truth, Didi, what one wants and what one gets in life are two different things. Aren't they? You tell me."

Suruchi was stunned. To hear Swaroop speaking so seriously was unexpected, to say the least.

Swaroop continued, "Yes, I grew up there. I am American, but in name only. One doesn't forget one's roots. At least Mummy and Daddy didn't let me, the way they brought me up! All said and done, one is an outsider there. No matter how much you try to assimilate, you can't. But then one feels like a misfit here, too. So what does one do? And Didi, I want marriage. A home of my own, a husband, children, I want it all. Where I will feel safe, cherished, comfortable ..." Swaroop's voice was charged.

Suruchi became cautious.

"Who do I want to marry? I have many friends there. But none of them talk about a lifelong commitment. And I am scared of anything short-term. You don't feel you can trust it. One should at least start with the feeling that it is forever. Then one can work towards making it last. I will definitely make the effort."

"But Swaroop, why do you feel the need for it? Has something happened?"

Swaroop opened and shut her purse with a snap. "You really don't know, Didi?"

"What?" said Suruchi her heart lurching. "About what?"

"Mummy and Daddy?"

"No, what about them?" Suruchi asked hoarsely.

"Mummy is always so high-strung. Constantly complaining. Blaming her fate. When I was a child, I used to be terrified that either she would leave me and go away, or Daddy would. But I have grown up now. I am going to leave them."

"They fight a lot?"

"All the time. Mummy is suspicious and Daddy ... he is the same."

"Meaning?"

Swaroop looked into the distance. "Any woman will do for him."

"What are you saying?"

"If you don't believe it, drop it. I don't like talking about it either."

Suruchi felt weird. I wish Abhijit comes quickly, she thought. But there was no sign of him.

"You never mentioned any of this to me?"

"I was a child until now, Didi. I felt suddenly grown-up when I met you."

"How long has this been going on?"

"Ever since I can remember."

"What else?"

"Didi, what else can there be? Mummy made this huge sacrifice for him. She remained by his side. She even left you behind, didn't she? And today what has she got for it? In the home, and outside it?"

"And you want marriage in spite of this?"

"Because of it. I understand that there is no guarantee it will work even if you find your own husband, even if you fall in love. Suppose it comes your way and then something happens like ... what happened to you ... There's no guarantee of that either. What do you say?"

Against her will, Suruchi's eyes filled with tears. Swaroop hugged her sister tight, as if she was the older one. "I am not as young as I look, Didi, or as immature. I will weigh everything and then make my decision. That is the only way."

Suruchi envied her confidence. But then wasn't I also like that at her age? Or was I? Maybe she is a little more firm. She knows what she wants. I didn't. Everything was vague then, but there was curiosity. How does one acquire such self-assurance? And discover what one wants so early in life? Like Shreerang knew, too. Is there any similarity between his and Swaroop's situation? He had seen how his father had treated his mother. He spoke about it in a sort of cold, dispassionate way. Such experiences had not come my way. I always wished I had known my parents better, had been a greater part of their life. Only then would I have understood relationships—theirs, and, indirectly, those between husbands and wives. When Shreerang spoke about his parents, I could see them, but not clearly. There was nothing of my parents in that image. Mummy and Daddy were far away, almost like strangers, slightly formal, but always viewed as a couple who came and fussed over me, although not often.

And now Swaroop tells me something else. Their relationship was not what I had imagined it to be. It was possible to see it objectively now. Two young persons, deeply in love. Especially Kamala, in her innocence, her immaturity, struggling to give the man she loved everything. I can see that now as an outsider. She ended up being Pradeep's wife alone, fulfilling that role far better than the role of a mother. She had a hard time. And must have spent the better part of her life weeping. What had she got out of their marriage? Out of being this 'wife'?

Is this what Shreerang had been trying to tell me? He hadn't said much about my parents. Only what was necessary. Never discussed them. But whenever they were mentioned, he would make cynical remarks about his parents' marriage.

He must have thought deeply about these things. Had I failed to understand him? I kept asking myself, Why is he so adamant? Why doesn't he agree with what I am saying? My reasoning was long gone; what was left was simple obduracy. It all boiled down to one pathetic issue. He didn't want it while I insisted on having it. What really lay behind it, I was not sure. Will it become clear to me at least now?

Abhijit arrived and the sisters quickly ended their conversation.

Kamala's packing was accompanied by copious tears. She always got emotional when leaving Nini. She and Pradeep were to return earlier, Swaroop was to follow later. She would try to persuade Suruchi to go with her. This time Kamala's anxiety for Suruchi added to her grief. Besides, she didn't know when she would come again.

Nini was calm and collected as always. Suruchi had never seen her shed a tear. She was back to normal now and had resumed her routine. Suruchi felt sorry for Kamala and kept hovering around her. Every now and then Kamala, overcome with emotion, would hug Suruchi tight and say something to her. "Take care of yourself"; "Don't worry about anything"; "Start a new life," etc. Suruchi had decided not to reply, only nod. It would make no difference.

Swaroop and Suruchi dropped their parents at the airport and returned home in a taxi. Nini had stayed back. She did not go to receive or see off anyone. The atmosphere in the house ought to have been the same as far as Suruchi was concerned. Pradeep and Kamala were not really a part of her everyday life. Even if they had been, she would have, at this age, been living away from them. Did Swaroop miss them? She was often impatient with Kamala, but it was obvious that she was close to Pradeep and he, too, doted on her. Before leaving, he had hugged her and whispered something in her ear. But he only patted my shoulder, and said, "Okay, bye," Suruchi thought. Kamala had held her tight in a soppy wet embrace. She kept turning back and waving after they went inside the terminal, until Swaroop muttered impatiently, "Go now, that's enough!" How easily the words slipped out. Would I have also spoken to her like that if I had lived with her all my life? They say familiarity breeds ill will. The less time you spend with someone, the sweeter the encounter is. And yet one longs to have the person one loves constantly by one's side. Once they are there, then what? Wasn't Shreerang living with me? All his belongings were beside mine. We slept on the same bed. And yet I felt that this man was never wholly mine. Was it because he came and went as he pleased, never gave an account of his whereabouts? No. Most people would do that. Kamala was by her husband's side all the time; did she feel secure about him? Swaroop had given me concrete examples of his philandering. What assurance had Kamala got? Was it because Shreerang was not really my 'husband'? That is even more pathetic, laughable, in fact. Because who thought he wasn't my husband? We had maintained our distance with the landlord, had not bothered to make friends with our neighbours. We owed no one any explanations. Ila, Abhijit, our friends knew. They respected each one's privacy, gave them their space. So it was only my insistence then?

When I came to see Nini the first time and described the house in detail, answered all her questions and told her about Shreerang, she stared at me with her cold clear eyes. I held her gaze defiantly.

"Do you know what you are doing?"

"Yes."

"You know what people will think of you?"

"What people?"

For a moment she was lost for words. But she came back with, "And yourself?"

"What about myself?"

"Today you are just sharing the house, tomorrow..." Nini's eyes pierced me.

I knew what she was trying to say. What could I say to her? How would she react? She would never approve of anyone having a relationship with a man you were married to only in your mind. I was furious with Nini, and all that she represented. Society. People. Norms. Why make such a big issue of something so insignificant, something which was a purely personal matter. One that occupied a tiny fraction of one's day. Yet, on it was built the edifice of relationships, reputation, morality, honour. Nothing beyond that.

I remained silent. Defiant almost. The decision had been made. That itself must have given me the courage. And love, too. Shreerang and I had just started living together and I was savouring the experience. Besides, I had a full day's work at the library, Ila's friendship, the excitement of learning new things from her, and all the usual activities. Shreerang wasn't always there when I returned home. Sometimes a note awaited me. I'd spend my time planning what to do in his absence. When he was home, his presence filled the house. Shreerang was not a very tidy person. Nor was he demanding in any way. If I was late returning, he would have cooked dinner for us. Having spent so much time with his mother, he had learnt to do many things around the house... cook, clean, wash clothes, mend tears and sew buttons, even do *rangoli*. And he could tell stories and recite poetry. From what he said, I guessed that he was very attached to his mother. It made me extremely jealous. Does he have an Oedipus complex, I wondered. Would he ever be able to break away from her? For quite some time this thought troubled me. When he snuggled up to me, I wondered, 'Is he looking for his mother in me?' Such thoughts were so unnecessary. They caused me to pick unnecessary quarrels with him. Fortunately that stage passed; possibly because I met his mother. It gave me a kind of peace. Some answers can be found. We know them, yet regularly forget them. Ever so often I would remind myself of the bond between Shreerang and his mother, the tenderness in it and, through it, her repressed, pitiable womanhood.

What was my connection with that womanhood? A hapless woman's identity, lost under the dominance of her husband in an institution called marriage. Was it possible that Shreerang did not want any woman to suffer the same fate as his mother? Was this his way of protecting me from it? What would my life have been like? Difficult even to imagine. I hadn't been able to figure out clearly how Shreerang and I were different from any ordinary husband and wife. Our being together did not come in the way of our independent existence. Yet when we were together, we were good friends. But in company, when interacting with others, there was a feeling of unease inside. What was this man to me? Did I have any right over him? Possess him? Although I rationalised to myself the fragility, the hollowness of such questions, I still wanted answers. I needed some assurance, something to hold on to—the same thing that Shreerang mocked at. Only natural relationships were real. Like that of mother and child. Not those created by society, like marriage and husband-wife. So what is a relationship you can hold on to? Could you ever lay your hands on it? Did only the uncertainty of the relationship keep growing in my mind?

After Pradeep and Kamala left, Suruchi decided that she needed to sit down and think with a clear head about the future and the present. About what had happened thus far and how and why. Nini's routine had resumed, albeit at a slightly slower pace. Lakshmi was managing the household and Swaroop was whiling away her time as usual. Because she had insisted and Kamala had given in, a VCR appeared in Nini's home. Swaroop spent much of her time watching movies on it, munching snacks that she got Lakshmi to prepare or reading all sorts of books, magazines, comics that she borrowed from the library. And Nini said not a word to her. In fact she didn't even bother to ask what Swaroop did all day. She did speak to Suruchi occasionally, though. And sometimes even introduced her to people who visited her. Suruchi sat with them but did not show undue interest in their conversation. Their world was alien to her, she knew. She could never become a part of Nini's world, and with her in it, never! No taking that route again. Nini had erased the intervening six years quite coldly. How could she?

As the days sped by, she had felt a growing exhaustion every now and then. Her appetite was poor, she was losing weight. And then one morning, she was nauseous, feeling so sick she couldn't get out of bed. Shreerang was not there, she recalled. I lay there for a while and then when I felt slightly better, I went to the doctor round the corner. He advised me to get a blood test done. "I am almost sure you have jaundice," he'd said. I went straight to Ila's house and decided to stay there for three–four days till Shreerang came back. But Ila's three-room flat on the first floor was more like an office. People walked in and out all day long, the phone kept ringing, and strangers used the bathroom, the kitchen. It became too much for me. I just couldn't take it. I had become very weak. Then Shreerang came back and took me home. I had to be in bed all the time. There was nothing much to eat, and whatever there was, was bland, tasteless. I couldn't even read. I gave Shreerang Nini's number. Wondered what she will feel when she hears. What will she do? Will she come and stay here for a few days? She had even taken leave and nursed me through my childhood illnesses. If she says, "I will take her back with me," I will go. Even if I feel the journey will take its toll.

"I told her, but she said nothing," Shreerang said to me.

"Nothing? Not even 'How is she, what is wrong?'"

"That I had already told her."

"And she didn't say a word? She didn't say she'll come, she'll see me? How is it possible?"

Her indifference hurt me so badly that I cried my heart out. I accused Shreerang of not explaining my condition properly to her. "You two have never met, you wouldn't know how to speak to her," I'd said angrily. I wished my illness would become so serious that I would die. Then Nini would know. Then she would realise that there was someone called Suruchi in her life.

Shreerang thought all this drama was unnecessary. "So what if she didn't say anything? That's her problem. It is okay, accept it. Whether she says anything or not, getting better is your problem. You have to do it yourself. No one can do it for you."

Those days were spent in anger, self-pity and loneliness. Every time the thought that Nini had rejected me came to mind, I was consumed with grief. If she could, then what was Shreerang to me? He refused to be tied down. Because he wanted the freedom to move away from me any time he wanted to. Why this emotional tug-of-war? One struggling to hold on, the other desperate to let go, and in the end neither has anything to hold on to. As it happened between Nini and me. Is nothing left between Shreerang and me? Is that the truth? Or is it very much there but one fails to see it? Is it something one must feel and accept, not define?

I love thee with a love I seemed to lose
With my lost saints. I love thee with the breath,
Smiles, tears, of all my life; and, if God choose,
I shall but love thee better after death.[3]

Despite Swaroop's constant grumbling, Nini had insisted that both girls accompany her. "What do I have to do with that Shrida?" Swaroop had exclaimed angrily.

"But of course you have," Suruchi explained. "He has been of great help to Nini."

"So what, Didi? I don't even remember what he looks like, whether he is dark or fair, fat or thin. Nini is so unreasonable at times. How do you put up with it?"

"What else do I do?"

"Rebel."

"I did, didn't I?"

"It's not enough to do it once and forget about it. Every time you need to, you must protest. I thought you were like that. But this time you seem to be giving in too much, too easily. Without reason."

"Not really, you are mistaken."

"It's not true?"

"Perhaps... Who knows... Besides, one changes, Swaroop. One doesn't remain the same."

"I know that."

The servant led Nini and the two girls into Shrida's room. He was sitting up in bed, but looked quite weak and frail. None of his family members—his sons, grandchildren—seemed to be around. Busy with their own lives perhaps. Nini said, "This is Suruchi and this is Swaroop. You do remember them?"

Shrida looked at them and shook his head. Swaroop immediately nudged Suruchi as if to say, "See, I told you; we came here for nothing". Suruchi recalled the Shrida of her childhood... His warm smiling face, his affable manner and his ability to listen to you.

Nini made polite enquiries after his health, and Shrida, who had earlier not been talking, began telling them all about himself. His ailments, his routine, how most days he was confined to his room, how the servant looked after him well, took him for a walk in the evenings, but he was not able to walk much, it tired him, reading was a strain on the eyes, he slept very little and did not know how to pass the time.

"I don't know what to do." This sentence disturbed Suruchi.

The formalities over, Nini and the girls stood up to leave.

On the way back, Swaroop remarked, "I still don't understand why we were dragged here."

Suruchi turned to Nini, "For how long has he been ill?"

"Several months now," Nini replied dryly. "I just wasn't able to go see him."

"What about his children? His sons and their families all lived in that bungalow. But no one was around?"

"Each one has his own preoccupations. We also went over for just a few minutes. He is now a part of their routine life. They get used to it."

"Even you didn't visit him until now?"

"Where do I have the time?"

"And what did we come here and achieve?" interjected Swaroop. "Got bored in that sick old man's room. Didn't you feel suffocated in there, Didi? And that peculiar smell... did you notice it?"

"Swaroop, don't talk like that," admonished Suruchi. "But Nini, why didn't you at least visit him, tell me?"

"Swaroop, you are my granddaughter. I can take you anywhere I want, understand? I do not wish to hear another word on this. Can't you do this little thing for me?"

"Let it be, Nini, Swaroop is young..."

"You both have a lot to learn. There are many sides to everything. Even human beings. We don't always know all the sides. Remember that. You must always leave a little room whenever you form an opinion about someone, express a view on something. How that space will get filled up, you can't tell."

Swaroop and Suruchi were stunned into silence. Nini rarely spoke so much these days.

"When are you planning to leave, Didi?" Swaroop asked. "I want to go with you."

Suruchi was relieved. She had more or less decided, but Swaroop compelled her to fix the date. They went and booked tickets on the Mail. Then they completed some formalities for Swaroop at the Consulate. When they got home, Nini told them that Kamala's friend who had brought the marriage proposal had called. Behind some flimsy reasons, the very attractive alliance had rejected the proposal.

Swaroop stood still for a few moments, and then rushed inside. Nini shook her head. Suruchi followed Swaroop into the room. She was standing by the window, chewing her lower lip. Suruchi laughed out loud. "What are you getting so upset for? What's the big deal?"

There was no response from Swaroop. Suddenly, she turned and fell into Suruchi's arms, sobbing. Suruchi felt sorry for her. Stroking her back, she said, "Look, Swaroop, all girls here face this kind of rejection, it is normal. When one is put on the market, then a Yes or a No is inevitable."

Suruchi realised she had been a little harsh, but it was all her pent-up anger against the system that had spewed out. She continued more gently, "Don't think there's something lacking in you. He must have found something else he was looking for. How can we decide what someone's priorities should be? Tell yourself that this was not meant to be and move on. Perhaps something better is in store. Don't let some stranger's rejection undermine your own sense of self-worth."

As Suruchi spoke to Swaroop, her words took on a special meaning for herself. She couldn't say anything more.

Part II

Suruchi and Swaroop got into the autorickshaw and told the driver where to go. It was a cool, grey morning, bright but not sunny. Trying to hold down her hair that the breeze was tousling, Swaroop exclaimed, "Didi, it seems to have rained here!"

Suruchi noticed the damp earth and muttered, "Hm." She didn't feel like saying anything more. They reached the house, paid the autorickshaw driver and carried their bags in. Suruchi fumbled for the keys in her purse, found them, opened the door and walked in. Dank, stale air and a musty smell greeted them. By the time Swaroop got all their luggage inside, Suruchi had opened the windows and pulled the curtains apart. She glanced at the unmade divan bed on one side, the four cane chairs lying haphazardly on the other, papers, books, magazines scattered all over the living room, and then went into the kitchen. Unwashed utensils lay in the sink and on the counter were used cups, plates, glasses. Suruchi threw the window open. She went into the inner room where Swaroop had kept their suitcases and stopped in the doorway. She suddenly felt suffocated, her breath stuck in her chest. She put her hand on her stomach to quell the rising feeling, but it wouldn't stay down. The bile rose into her mouth and she ran into the bathroom, clutched the upturned bucket and sank to the ground.

"What's the matter, Didi? Are you all right?" Swaroop was by Suruchi's side.

Suruchi shook her head in reply.

"You feel better now? Want water? Come outside."

Suruchi wanted to be left alone, but Swaroop didn't understand that. After a while Suruchi came out and lay on the divan, her arm covering her eyes. "I want to sleep for a while," she said.

"No tea-coffee?"

"You'll have to get milk."

"I know where to get it. I'll go."

"Don't forget to take the key."

Suruchi turned towards the wall and closed her eyes. I should have told Ila to get someone to clean the house. Clean it or empty it? But would tidying up or removing things have got rid of Shreerang? His presence was everywhere, not only in his books, his clothes. One leaves one's imprint on everything one comes in contact with. The walls, the furniture—why, even I have absorbed his smell. Can one get so completely immersed in another human being? When was I swallowed up by that wave? I was probably taken unawares.

I had never harboured the dream of marriage, home, husband, children. Knowing it would never happen, I rolled it up and put it away. Then why the sudden urge to experience it all? I mentioned it to Shreerang. I expected him to show surprise, or maybe joke about it. Who knows, I thought, he might even consider it. And why not? But Shreerang had very calmly said, "You are totally free. We can part ways this instant. You can marry any man you choose and have a child."

His ice-cold words sent a shudder through me.

"You can leave me so easily?"

"You know the answer to that."

"I don't believe it. Shreerang, have you no involvement with me at all? Is there nothing between us? You will be able to leave me, at this moment, without a qualm?"

"Once one decides, how does it matter whether it was a difficult decision or an easy one? Yes, I will be able to leave."

"No. I don't think it's possible." My voice rose needlessly.

Shreerang smiled. "Why should it matter to you whether I can do something or not when I am confident of it myself?"

"So our relationship is meaningless? How important can it be if it can be broken in a minute?"

"Do you feel it's less important?"

"It's not about me."

"Can a relationship be one-sided?"

"Why are you speaking in riddles? Answer straight."

"You know very well that you can never get me to say what you want to hear. Don't be stubborn, don't insist on it."

"Me? Stubborn? You are adamant. Adamant for what! Because you don't want to make a commitment. If I can be deleted so easily from your life, then... then..."

"Go on, say it."

But I couldn't speak. I broke down, and Shreerang, who had lately expressed contempt for such tearful scenes, just walked out of the house. He did it all the time. Came and went as he pleased. Where he went, when he would return, I never knew. Did he have another lover? If there had been someone else, I would have known after he was no more... someone would have mentioned it. No, it wasn't that. There was no other woman. Of that I was sure. Was there someone before me? What difference would that have made? Would it have changed anything? He had begun to go away a great deal on work. He could have done anything with anybody then.

Commitment would not figure in those relationships, would it? Being a husband would not have prevented him from having an affair and then coming back to me. But Shreerang, though not a husband, always came back. He had ignored the arguments, the tantrums, the accusations, the tears; he had forgotten them so easily and come back. Was this not commitment?

The fault probably lay with me. I was not able to understand what commitment really meant. I kept listening to my inner voice. Now that I was looking back at the years with him, I began to understand that there was a bond between us, a bond which was no less than any commitment.

He had set up this home. He lived here. The house is full of his things. One's surroundings, the people one shares space with, all of them are impacted by one's personality. Haven't I set down roots in Nini's house? This is no different. But what's the use of all this wisdom now, after he has gone? Why now?

Thus let me live, unseen, unknown;
Thus unlamented let me die;
Steal from the world, and not a stone
Tell where I lie.[4]

Suruchi opened her eyes when she heard Swaroop calling out to her. Her neck and back were stiff from lying awkwardly, her mouth felt bitter and her heart heavy. Holding out a cup to her, Swaroop said, "Here, have this, Didi, it will make you feel better."

Suruchi sat up.

"What a mess your house is in," Swaroop said. "We'll need four days to get things in order again." When Suruchi did not respond, she continued, "Did they bring him here?"

Suruchi nodded.

"His family members came?"

"Hm."

Swaroop sensed that Suruchi did not want to talk, so she fell silent. But Suruchi knew that she wanted to ask her many questions. Perhaps she feels that I should talk about it, get it off my chest. But I don't feel like it. I cannot open up to anyone because they are not my family. They never were. Shreerang's parents and a couple of others had come by train. I was scared how his mother would react. What would she do? But she turned out to be very strong, composed. She sat by Shreerang's side, one hand resting on his head, the other clamped tightly across her mouth as if to prevent any sound from escaping. That's all. She looked utterly forlorn. I couldn't bear it, and almost went to pieces. I stood in the inner room, away from people. Shreerang's father came in, and my heart missed a beat. How much like Shreerang he looked! Tall, dark and dignified. Shreerang would have looked just like that when he reached that age. He walked up and put his arm around me, just like he had done the first time, drew me close and asked, "What is your wish, my child?" Even the voice was the same. A tremor went through my body. Here was this man, a carbon copy of Shreerang, someone Shreerang had held in contempt all his life. I couldn't speak. He patted me and said, "We will do exactly what you want. Would you like to do everything here and not take him back?" I mumbled, "Yes." With some fear and hesitation I added, "Shreerang did not like any rituals or ceremonies." It seemed to me that he gave a half-smile and replied, "I know my son. We will do only as much as his mother wants. Nothing more." He gave me tremendous support during that time. He stayed beside me. When they were taking Shreerang to the crematorium and I said, "I want to go, too," he quickly made some place for me. He did not bother about what people would say. I went inside and stayed till the very end. It felt like Shreerang was with me, giving me courage. I witnessed the raging fire inside the furnace and as we consigned him to the flames, I said, "Go, I am setting you free."

Why did I say that? Or was it Shreerang telling me, "I am letting go of you"? Who was holding on to whom? Who was setting whom free? Or was it not like that at all?

One short sleep past, we wake eternally,
And Death shall be no more;
Death, thou shalt die.[5]

As Shreerang's parents were leaving, his mother had said to me, "I'll be happy if you came home sometimes."

I had nodded, but I knew it would not happen. I would not go to Shreerang's house again, alone. Ila was with me. Abhijit came over. Someone was there all the time. But day dawns, night follows. People go back to their routine. Each new day brings new happenings. Soon I sent everyone away. They felt I was handling the situation well, I was in control. I had accepted it once I realised one has no choice. One cannot undo what is past. One's grief is one's own. It will always be a part of one's life and no one can share it. It's entirely personal, and should remain that way. While convincing myself of all this and keeping it bottled up inside, I must have reached rock bottom.

Swaroop suddenly seemed enthused about something. "I'm going to tidy up," she declared. She wouldn't let Suruchi do anything. Though there was a maid to do the sweeping, swabbing and washing utensils, she did not know she was supposed to come that day. Her absence didn't bother Swaroop at all. She put on a pair of shorts, picked up the broom and started sweeping, not only the inside but also the yard. The few flowering plants looked quite healthy. Someone must have been watering them. The back of the landlord's house faced Suruchi's kitchen window, beyond which was a tap and the stone for washing clothes. Seeing some activity in Suruchi's house, a couple of faces appeared at the windows. It must have amused them to see a young woman in shorts holding a broom, thought Suruchi. But that was all. The bounds of a formal relationship. She could have reached out to them if she had needed anything, but she hadn't let that occasion arise. They had been there that day. Also people from a couple of houses in the neighbourhood. They had come only because they thought it was a public event, thought Suruchi, and that had upset her deeply. It was natural for everyone to be curious—who were these two? What exactly had happened? They needed to be eye-witnesses to it, to ask questions, seek details.

Suruchi knew she ought to offer to help Swaroop, but she didn't feel up to it. Swaroop didn't seem to mind either.

Ila came that afternoon. Suruchi knew it was her as soon as she heard the scooter outside the gate. She entered, exclaiming, "You've changed everything!"

"Swaroop has," Suruchi explained.

"Oh my, how big this girl has grown!"

"It's been two-three years..."

"So what? She looks so responsible and all that! Hmm, so have you made any arrangements for meals?"

"Swaroop is taking care of everything."

"Okay, and before I forget, as per your letter, I checked up. There is a vacancy for a librarian in the institute. You should go meet them. Only, they will have all technical books. Not like the University library. It's not even very big."

"That's all right. I'd prefer a new place."

"Then better hurry and go see them. And your sister, what's she going to do?"

All this while Swaroop was listening quietly.

Suruchi replied, "Why don't you take charge of her, Ila?"

"Will you come?"

Swaroop wasn't sure. She seemed a little unhappy, too. But then Ila was not to know that.

"Yes, do come, at least till you go back. What will you do by yourself here? I won't eat you up!" she smiled. "Once your Didi starts work, you will be alone. With me, you will not have a moment to spare, not a boring minute. People, phone calls, piles of material to read ... Your Didi, too, was bewildered at first. She knew nothing about anything. She thought hers was the whole world. But then she entered mine, and her eyes opened. Isn't it, Suruchi? After that she never left my side. Look at her now ... So, you will come, won't you? Okay, I'm off, lots of things to attend to..." said Ila, pulling her goggles down from her head. As she walked out, she asked Suruchi, "Are you okay?"

"Yes."

"You did feel like coming back, didn't you? You didn't jump into the sea!"

"Don't be funny!"

"That's how you were behaving. What would Shreerang have said?"

Suruchi was silent.

"You must not get rattled every time his name is mentioned, Suruchi. He did mean something to you, didn't he? You cannot avoid mentioning him as if he was nothing to you. You know what I mean, right? Imagine what he would have said. I don't have to tell you, you can think for yourself. I knew both of you equally well, but you were closer to him. So then ...?"

Ila kick-started the scooter as she spoke and, with a wave and a 'Bye', rode away. As usual, Suruchi went in with her head bowed to avoid seeing anyone as she walked from the gate to her door. That remark, "What would Shreerang have said?" was going round and round in her head.

Last year his father had drawn up some elaborate business plans for him. Travels to Europe, USA, trade fairs, exhibitions, a four to six-week course, meetings ... there was no way Shreerang could have avoided them. The thought that he would be away for so long caused a sinking feeling in my stomach. For a moment I wished he'd said, "Why don't you come along, too?" If he had, I would have managed it ... applied for leave, arranged the money, made some plans. But because he didn't ask, I was gripped by a sense of insecurity. He didn't ask me and I didn't have the courage to mention it. As it is, I felt he was getting increasingly impatient with my tantrums, my tearfulness, my persistence. The more I panicked, the faster he was slipping away, I felt. When that happened, an intense fear of losing him would take hold of me. I needed him. There was no alternative to his goodness, and his failings I wanted to deal with myself. Finally, though my insides were churning, I casually said, "So you are going to leave me and go away for so long?"

With a laugh, he retorted, "Leave you? Are you my lawfully wedded wife to be abandoned?"

Normally I would have made an issue of this as well. But that day I became so emotional that the words stuck in my throat. The worst thing was that it happened in Ila's presence. A couple of others were there, too. So what if they were old acquaintances? I did get choked up at that moment. The moment passed. Someone made a joke and everyone laughed. I did not hear it. Shreerang, too, had joined in the merriment. I must have had a silly, uncomprehending grin on my face. And the big lump of emotions remained stuck in my throat. I swallowed hard but it wouldn't go down. I was so afraid I would erupt and that's exactly what happened. He was packing, I was helping him and without warning, unexpected and unintended, I broke. I was sure that he would stomp out of the house angrily. But he didn't. Taking me by the shoulders he shook me and said, "Come to your senses, Suruchi. Don't hold me back at every step. I have explained all this to you several times over. I cannot, will not be able to cross the bridge you want me to. But if you keep insisting, I might have to ... we might have to part ways. You had better accept it. You will be deeply hurt. I don't want that." What did I do then? Pushed it aside and went back to packing his stuff. We went out, did some chores, had dinner, made love. Shreerang was not one to sulk or to prolong a quarrel. The day he was leaving he spent talking to me, making me laugh. I went to see him off at the station. He was to visit his parents for a couple of days and then take the flight from there. As the train started moving, his hand slowly slipped out of my grasp. And as I stood on the crowded platform watching the train, a strange calm descended on me. I was baffled. Calm? When he was going far, far away?

I tried hard but could not remember a word of what he had said all evening. No. That's not true. What was it he did not say all evening? Will no one be able to hear more than what one is saying? Of course they will. One should never forget that. In that case there is so much more to what he had been saying.

Perhaps I had not understood the significance of his unspoken words that day. Does that mean I would never comprehend them at all? I had not been able to hold on to Shreerang, nor could I stop him. When his time came, he had to go. Not before, not after. Before, after, meaningless words really. Now is the only truth. That's what Shreerang had been trying to shove down my throat. Despite my pigheadedness, my creating tension, my outbursts, the quarrels, the bitterness, the fights—he had remained calm. As if he had known what was coming. The travel, the stresses, the difficulties: he had overcome them all. That's why he couldn't stop, he wouldn't stop. Only I would be left behind. He probably couldn't say all this, he didn't have the right words. But even if he had, would I have accepted them? Reconciled with them? He knew I wouldn't, that's why he said only what he had to say, firmly and unequivocally, leaving the rest unsaid. So it would make sense to me later. Now. The necessity of his presence, the ties of his love, and after he went, all these unanswered questions that left me restless, uneasy, to make sense of, all by myself.

When Suruchi entered the clean, bright house, she, too, noticed the change Swaroop had wrought. After a long time, she actually smiled.

Suruchi started her new job on the first. The building was modern and compact, the library small but neat and well organised. The institute conducted regular courses for people from the industry and finance sectors and catered to local students as well as outstation ones. The faculty, too, comprised permanent and visiting staff. The library was always buzzing with activity. Suruchi felt that these people were more old-fashioned and conservative than those in a university. She gradually got to know the staff members, even those who were short-term employees. She liked the novelty of the experience. The only snag was that the institute was far away. The bus service was poor and she had to change buses to get there. Or take an auto to and fro. Even otherwise, she often had to take it part of the way and it cost her quite a sum. But what was the alternative? Ila had been after her for a long time to learn how to drive, but Suruchi had ignored her. She had not even tried riding a bicycle, convinced she would never be able to. It was some irrational fear she had. Here, practically everyone had their own vehicle, either a moped or a scooter. She wished she, too, had learned. But she had made no effort to learn, so it remained a wish. Shreerang used to get around a lot, usually on vehicles borrowed from friends. When she had once asked him why he didn't get one of his own, it would be so much more convenient, he had brushed her question aside with, "I get one when I need it, don't I?" He was right. Someone or other always lent him their vehicle. If not, taxis and autos were always available.

Gradually I realised that he did not want to tie himself down with anything ... neither house, nor wife and children, not even furniture or vehicle. I have seen how lovingly people take care of their cars and scooters. They won't even let anyone touch them! But Shreerang would never have done any of that. Why was this man so detached? What had taken him to this extreme? But for his mother ... he had come far away from her, too, now. Even with me it was the same. My head would spin trying to figure him out.

But it was not just a matter of detachment or self-denial for him, I think now. We had gone to see a movie together once. A love story. Passionate love and then the lovers separated by death. It was a foreign language film, unsentimental and matter-of-fact. As if this was an inevitable fact of life. Shreerang dismissed most things with a flippant remark or made a joke about serious matters, but this film stayed with him, and he made a reference to it a couple of days later.

"I thought you didn't believe in these things? How do you say it is inevitable then?" I'd asked.

"But death is inevitable, so certain isn't it?" he replied, almost seriously.

Now I recall the intensity with which he had spoken about death. I had remarked, "But that was the most convenient way to end the film. They could have parted ways and that, too, would have been a separation."

"There is a basic difference between being separated by distance and being separated by death."

"How?" I had asked cautiously, almost nervously.

He had smiled. "If one knows that one is going to die, then what's the point of forming attachments? Whereas it is possible to get attached and remain so even while living apart."

I did not like his tone and ended the discussion. I feel bad now for doing that. What else would Shreerang have said? Was there a deeper meaning in his words? I am sure he had not dwelt much on his own death. But was it possible that he might have? Was there some basis for his reluctance to form attachments? It is pointless speculating. After his passing, the very basis of existence has been shaken. Everything has assumed a new significance. Is it possible to view past events from a different perspective?

Suruchi did not think Swaroop was particularly happy working at Ila's office. She did go there, but did not observe any schedule. She had taken complete charge of the household chores and seemed to enjoy doing the cleaning, cooking, shopping, ironing, etc. Suruchi was surprised to see this side of her personality, which had not been in evidence in Nini's home. When she commented on it, Swaroop replied, "I feel like doing it in your house."

"What's so special about this place? It's just these rooms that we call a house."

"To tell you the truth, Didi, when we came last time, I really wanted to stay here, but Mummy and Daddy said we should stay in a hotel. It would have been inconvenient, of course, but still..."

"Why didn't you say so?"

"How could I? Shreerang was here!"

"He wouldn't have said no."

"Yes, but I didn't want to come between you two. I really liked the place, small, simple, not intimidating. The bad thing about America is that you get used to conveniences. Everything is easy, readily available. You think, oh my god, I don't have this, how can I live? We have so many things. You and Shreerang managed happily with so few ... especially Shreerang."

"Meaning?"

"I never heard him complain or grumble about anything, which was surprising because he had lived abroad for so long. Really, Didi, he was so happy with you ..."

"With me?" Suruchi's voice stuck in her throat.

"Of course! We all liked him so much. Mummy was thrilled, except that you were living together ... Only Nini was the cold, hardhearted one. Never even met ..."

"Swaroop!"

"What else? What kind of stubbornness is that? So she has all those principles, but what of it? Had she met him just once, she would have changed her mind."

"She wasn't against Shreerang *per se* ..."

"That's what it is. And why do you always take the other person's side, Didi? Anyway, the time is past, Nini should understand. And they say you are her favourite!"

"Perhaps that's why ..."

"That's why what?"

"She felt I let her down. If you had behaved like that, she would have accepted it. How could I, brought up by her, go against her? Just like her own daughter had done?"

"Even so, she is wrong."

"No Swaroop, it's not like that."

"Amazing! In spite of all this, you will not let anyone find fault with her!"

"You remember, don't you, what she said? You must always allow yourself some space before you form an opinion or make a judgment."

Swaroop let the matter drop. She's still young, inexperienced; she'll learn, thought Suruchi.

In her first letter after returning to USA, Kamala had expressed some reservations about the two sisters staying together. She wanted to know when Swaroop was planning to return, what Suruchi was doing, and then mentioned another proposal. Same criteria, highly educated, 'good' family, settled abroad, looking for a bride in India. Swaroop took the letter and tore it in two. "Mummy and her proposals. Don't even bother to reply," she said.

"How can I do that? She believes it's for your own good," Suruchi said with a smile. Both of them had a good laugh over the proposal. Suruchi thought now everyone would blame her for corrupting her younger sister. Secretly, she was happy. Swaroop was finally doing something productive. She would not discuss her plans for the future but she wasn't complaining about the present either. Every now and then Ila, Abhijit, and the two of them met up, chatted, went out, and life went on smoothly. Suruchi decided that if the question of her going to the USA came up, she would firmly say, 'No'. She wasn't going anywhere.

Then one day Suruchi received a letter from Shreerang's bank. They had always maintained separate accounts though they shared the household expenses. Shreerang spent more sometimes, but it was never discussed. Suruchi knew her limitations. She had to manage on her salary. She did not have to send any money to Nini nor did she expect to receive any from her. She had not once asked Shreerang about his financial health. It was bound to be very good. She had seen for herself how well-off his father was, and Shreerang, too, had mentioned it. Besides, he worked very hard, so if he did spend lavishly sometimes, she did not make an issue of it.

When she went to see the bank manager, she learnt that Shreerang had made her the nominee for his savings bank account and three fixed deposits, totalling about three lakhs. Her first reaction was puzzlement. Why had he done this? Quickly she composed herself, signed where she was told to, and came out. She was so overcome that she started walking without thinking where she was going. She needed to sit down somewhere and think about this. But think what? Whether it was the money he had earned or whether it was given to him by his father, he had left it to her. Why? Because he wanted her to be comfortable? Or was it security for some future untold eventuality?

He knew that I was a working woman, that I had a reasonably well-off family that would support me. There was no need for such a security cover. So then? Was it a gift? Or did it mean what was his was mine? Didn't all his belongings move in with him when he came to live with me? Not that he had much in those dingy rooms. Most of it was old, ramshackle, worth discarding. What was precious were his books. They are with me now. Mine. Along with his clothes and items of everyday use. In that sense, it is true what they say, that no one takes anything with them when they go. In the end, all that belonged to him, including his money, is what is left with me. Mine. Even if he resisted giving me what I wanted all his life, all his stuff is now in my possession. That, and the box hidden at the bottom of the cupboard.

A shiver went down Suruchi's spine as the memories crowded her mind. Trying to push them away, she quickly crossed the road, got into an autorickshaw and headed for the library. Though she had taken an hour off, there was not much work pending on her table. She tried to involve herself in it. She had recently got to know her colleague Prabhakar a little better. He came to her desk for a chat, since he, too, had some spare time, and casually mentioned that his daughter was back home.

Suruchi remembered that the girl had been recently married, so she said, "But she just got married, didn't she?"

"Six months ago. Since then she has come back twice. Now she says she doesn't want to go back to her in-laws again."

Suruchi went on her guard. She was not sure if she should say anything more. But he looked like he needed to talk.

"I am tired of explaining to her. It's still early, you will take time to adjust ... All you modern girls, are you all extra impatient or what?"

Surprised that he should include her in 'you modern girls', she asked, "Why do you think so? What does your daughter say?"

"Nothing. Just makes excuses to come home. We have spoilt her a little. She is not used to doing any work."

"Don't brush it off like that. Ask her. There must be a reason."

"No, no, there isn't. We found a suitable match, gave her a decent wedding. They are good people. I know my daughter.

Spoilt. That's the problem. I am going to take her back there tomorrow."

Suruchi was about to say, "Don't do that. Ask her again, talk to her, make proper enquiries", but she swallowed the words. She felt Prabhakar was not taking the matter seriously. Nor was he likely to take advice from her. Anyway, she didn't speak out. "How does it concern me?" The remark that infuriated Ila came to mind. "Don't ever make such an irresponsible statement," she used to say. "It concerns all of us. Listening to that voice, extending a hand, at least finding out what the matter is. Just one small gesture from us can change someone's life. Just as our indifference can destroy it."

Prabhakar stood up. "I will be on leave on Monday. It will take all day to take her there and come back."

"You have asked her seriously, haven't you?"

He laughed. "I have," he said. "But she can't tell me exactly what the problem is. There seem to be no issues. I'm not such a heartless father, you know," he said with a laugh.

Suruchi couldn't even smile. She felt her gut wrench as she stared unseeingly at the open page in front of her. How come someone just appears and raises a subject one is avoiding? As if deliberately trying to make one focus on it again? A cruel game played by whom? One's own mind?

It was the first time Shreerang had said, "Come, let's go home." To his home. I had not stepped into Nini's house since the day I had left it. There was no question of going there this time. We would go and meet his parents and come back. He did not say where we would be staying, but that was a small matter. Something could easily be arranged. That was the first and only journey I made with Shreerang. We took the night Mail. I couldn't sleep at all but he slept soundly. The next morning we didn't go straight to his parents' house. Instead he took me to his aunt's place. She was his mother's sister and had two college-going daughters. Shreerang didn't quite explain who I was but all three of them welcomed me warmly. They had hot coffee and breakfast ready for me and arranged for hot water for my bath. Shreerang must be a favourite, I thought. And why not? He was eminently likeable.

The way he conducted himself, the geniality he displayed, the consideration he showed, who could resist his charm? But with his father ... why? I was curious. A short while later I realised that these women had assumed that I was Shreerang's wife, that we had married quietly without informing anyone. Typical of Shreerang, he was just that kind of person. Bright, competent, but headstrong and self-willed. One couldn't hold it against him, doing as he pleased, refusing to obey his parents. Besides it was obvious that I was the object of his love, and who but a wife could qualify for that honour? This was the general tenor of their behaviour, I thought.

Then we went to his house. A big sprawling bungalow by the sea, set amidst a coconut grove. My heart was thudding with fear and anticipation as we alighted from the autorickshaw, but Shreerang was his usual carefree self. There were a number of people milling around and by the time I figured out who was who, his father appeared. I was taken aback by the striking similarity between father and son. He had the same pleasant expression and his voice, too, was warm and affectionate. I hadn't expected that. When I was introduced to him, Shreerang said nothing more than my name. Immediately his father put his arm around my shoulders and drew me close. Shreerang stood there, expressionless. His father asked me about myself. I mentioned Nini's name. He seemed to recognise it. Before he could say anything more, Shreerang almost dragged me away, and the arm around my shoulders slipped off. Shreerang's mother was inside. I noticed a fair, petite, pretty woman wearing a heavy silk sari and lots of jewellery, as if she was about to go somewhere. The first thought that came to mind was, 'If only Shreerang had looked like her, he'd have been handsome'. She smiled at me and as if on cue, Shreerang left me to her and disappeared. She showed me around the house. They had guests, so the kitchen was bustling with activity. All that Shreerang had told me about his home came flooding back—especially of his mother caught up in the endless stream of guests, supervising servants, entertaining, surrounded by prosperity, pomp, position. She asked me, "You will stay for lunch, won't you?" I didn't know. She continued, "He is so unpredictable. I don't think he will stay. Even normally he's hardly ever at home, and now that his father is here ... We should consider ourselves fortunate that he didn't exit through the back door when he found him at home."

As she was showing me the house, Shreerang's mother suddenly stopped and started looking around. "What's the matter," I asked anxiously. "Are you looking for something?" She was still for a moment and then took off one of the several gold chains she was wearing and placed it in my palm. "Tell Shreerang I gave it to you," she whispered, "but don't mention it to anyone else."

I was taken aback. Before I could react, she placed a finger on her lips as if to say, "Don't say anything", grabbed my closed fist and almost dragged me outside, down the staircase and into the courtyard. In the meantime I had relieved my fist of the rather heavy old gold chain which now rested at the bottom of my purse. Just then Shreerang appeared and said, "Let's go." His mother stared at him. She may have said something, too, but I didn't get it. Shreerang gave her a gentle hug. She looked really tiny in his arms. She reached up and stroked his face, overcome with emotion perhaps. As we walked out, I asked, "Shouldn't we take leave of your father?" and he replied brusquely, "No need."

We had lunch in a restaurant and went back to his aunt's place. Hers was a small house but still she had prepared the inner room for us. Saying, "You can rest here. We were supposed to go out anyway," all three of them departed. I had been embarrassed by their hospitality but Shreerang seemed quite at ease. I looked around the room—a steel cupboard in one corner, a pile of rolled up mattresses beside it, some decorative calendars on the walls, a groaning fan above, and on the floor Shreerang, lying on the mat, his head resting on a pillow, quite at home. I opened my purse and took out the gold chain; Shreerang took one look at it, sprang upright, grabbed it from me and held it tight in his hand. I was telling him how his mother had given it to me and what she had said, but I found his strange expression undecipherable.

"It was my sister's," he said gruffly.

"Sister?" I exclaimed. He had never mentioned a sister. He was an only child. So where did this sister come from?

"Where is she?" I asked, my voice becoming sharp. This was not something one hides. So why hadn't he told me?

"Dead." His face was turning pale.

"You haven't spoken about it. Why?" I snapped. "How old was she?"

"Older than me. By two years."

"When did she pass away? How?" I persisted.

"I was in college then."

That means she was quite old. Although I was very angry that he had kept this fact from me, I felt there was something more to it. Again I asked him, "How did she die?"

Shreerang exploded. In fact he became almost demoniacal in his rage. I had never seen him like this before. Nor ever again. He told me his sister's story in that state of anger. His young, beautiful, loving sister, just like his mother, protected, suppressed, bullied because she was a girl. But that he realised only later. So when he told me about his childhood and how he used to trail his mother, his sister must have been around, too, submissive, silent, obedient, no words escaping her lips except to talk to Shreerang and tell him stories. They weren't only memories of his mother; they included the sister as well. As he grew up, he began to notice his father's unfair, discriminatory treatment of his mother and sister. He was his father's pet and was given complete freedom to do as he pleased. His father was proud of him and was determined to make Shreerang as successful as himself. He would spare no expense to achieve that.

Then Shreerang's father got his sister married. He spent a lot of money on a lavish wedding. By that account she should have been very happy. But she wasn't. When she came home a couple of times in the first year, she looked unhappy but dared not complain about anything. Her mother tried to ask her, but the father had never consulted anyone on anything. He forced her to go back every time. Fulfilled her in-laws' demands for jewellery, cash, clothes, articles. When she came home the last time, there was a scene. The father refused to listen, the mother was helplessly silent and no one paid heed to the poor girl. When I was listening to this saga, the truth of all that I had heard since coming to Ila's struck me. The same common strand ran through each story. Until now they were other people's stories. I could never have imagined that one of them could have been the story of Shreerang's sister, whom I had never seen. And then she died. Within a year of her marriage. She had suddenly taken ill at her in-laws' place. No one got to see her body even. Imagining what they might have done to her almost drove Shreerang insane. But such incidents had to be kept under wraps, especially in his father's circle, and it was not difficult to erase her presence from their home, their lives. There was a blanket ban on every sign, every memory of her, even her name. The father had issued a stern warning—what happened to her was an unfortunate episode, one best forgotten. How had the mother coped?

She had taken off the chain she had worn for so long and, giving it to me, said, "Tell Shreerang I gave it to you." And here I was fuming because he hadn't told me he had a sister. A wave of shame swept over me, washing over the shock and the bewilderment at Shreerang's fury. I put the chain back into my purse. It would lie in a box at the bottom of the cupboard. It was Shreerang's heirloom. Now mine? What was I to do with it? It would stay there at the bottom of the cupboard, like something that lies at the bottom of the ocean. You cannot bring it out without getting your hand wet, but you can't leave it there because it keeps haunting you.

Suruchi returned late that evening, and lay down, claiming a headache. Swaroop had done everything, and grumbled, too. But Suruchi just ignored her.

Suruchi was surprised to receive Nini's letter. Nini had written that Shrida was visiting his daughter there, and Suruchi should go see him. Swaroop read the letter and stormed, "There's no need for you to go see him, Didi."

"Why not?"

"What for, but?"

"Because Nini says so."

"You want to go all that way just for that? The old man won't even recognise you."

"How insensitive you are, Swaroop! We saw him that day. Didn't you feel sorry for him?"

"Not at all. It was a big house, there were servants around, I thought everything was perfect. Old age means illnesses. Everybody has some problem or the other."

"It's not so simple."

"Really? Then how is it?"

Suruchi wanted to mention loneliness, but stopped. Someone in the flush of youth, with the panorama of an exciting life spread out before her would not understand what loneliness meant, she realised. She said nothing about going or not going to see Shrida. But she kept the thought in her mind.

It took her a while to find the address. It was an unfamiliar area—a new extension with new bungalows, narrow untarred roads, unfinished structures. Shreerang generally accompanied her, usually on a borrowed scooter, either for her work or his. His endless meetings, a visit here, a drop-in there, at any time of the day. He never said to her, "Don't come". As long as he had a vehicle, he would insist that she go with him. So, as long as he was there, he was hers, wasn't he? So what was she complaining about? He was so good at locating places, no matter what the colony, what the layout. Once they got there it was all main roads and crosses. She had been amazed at his ability.

When she received Nini's letter with Shrida's address, the first thought that came to mind was, Shreerang would have told her exactly how to get there. Had I asked him to take me there, he would never have refused. I was so dependent on him, meaning I was certain that if he were with me, I would never get lost. He was the confident, stable one. Sure of where he wanted to go, what he wanted, how to get it. That kind of confidence, that stability was important for me. It was there, by my side, and yet I was not sure of it. What would have given me that reassurance? What would have been the evidence of it? All the while I fretted about it. Why? What made me so disbelieving?

Once I had gone for a late-night movie with a few friends. Shreerang was not with us, but was supposed to pick me up after the show. I was so sure he would come that I didn't ask them to wait with me. One by one they left. It was getting really late. The place was soon deserted. Only a few loiterers hung around. My courage began to ebb. What if he didn't turn up? No, that would never happen. I was sure of that. Shreerang would never not keep his word, he would not forget, would not allow himself to be delayed or distracted, and yet ... On the one hand I feared for my safety, on the other, a terrible anger started building up inside me. If anything untoward happened, it would be entirely his fault. This was utter stupidity, standing alone on a lonely street outside a cinema hall that had closed for the day. Anything could have happened. And then he arrived. I assumed he would make some excuse, so without giving him a chance to explain, I lashed out at him. "I'm not late," he said, surprised. "I'm on time."

Then what about all that time I'd waited, alone? Terrified? "It wasn't long, just ten minutes," he said. He was right. It was only ten minutes, but it had seemed much longer. It was true my anger had stretched those ten minutes to an eternity. But the fear, the tension, the uncertainty, were they not true? So how does one decide what is true and untrue?

When Suruchi rang the door bell she assumed that Shrida's daughter would open the door. But it was opened by a fair, plump, middle-aged woman. The moment she entered the house, she saw signs of the family's affluence—garish décor, ornate furniture, gaudy upholstery, mirrors, chandeliers and innumerable knick-knacks.

The woman asked Suruchi who she was, where she had come from, what she did, and then said, "We know a doctor, I mean a *vaidya* here. We brought him here to see if the vaidya's treatment would give him some relief."

"A vaidya? But Shrida is a doctor himself?"

"What good is that now?" the woman said, standing up. "Come in. You can see him in his room. He rarely comes out."

Suruchi went inside. The woman pulled up a chair for her. She said something to Shrida and left.

"I'm Suruchi."

"I recognised you. Nayantara's granddaughter."

Suruchi was surprised. Though his body was shrunken, his face was as she remembered it and his gaze, clear and gentle.

"I came because I got a letter from Nini."

"Hmm, I met her before coming here."

"She didn't mention that. Only said that you were here."

"I've given up that house."

"Meaning?"

Shrida just looked at her. Suruchi was taken aback.

"But," she exclaimed, "You've come here for treatment ..."

"It's of no use."

"But she ... that lady, your daughter said ..."

"All of them say the same thing. Give me false assurances. To put me off. At this age, all this is expected. But they don't understand. They only want the satisfaction of having done their duty."

This garrulous Shrida was not the silent, reticent person she remembered. And then she recalled her last meeting with him and she softened.

"You will get better and go back home."

"No. I won't go back. Ever. I didn't want to leave. How could I give it up when I'd spent all my life there. I told Nayantara, 'Give me a little space, however small ...'"

Suddenly he went silent. Suruchi was speechless. His eyes filled up. His lined face, the look in his eyes, blurred by the tears. Suruchi was aghast. She was furious with Nini. How could she have refused him? He said he'd met her before coming here. He must have gone to her house. To ask for a place to stay. And Nini? She remained firm and unrelenting. Said 'No' to him. She had never made any allowances for anyone. Not for me. Not for herself. I could say to her, "You should have said yes to him. Nothing wrong in that. So what if people in your circle or his family had talked? In the sunset of your lives, what would it matter? You could have dealt with it. Didn't I handle all those questions? It was not easy but I faced them, didn't I?" How could Nini have refused him? Such determination, so much self-control! She must have realised that once Shrida went away he would not return, and she would never see him again. Had she been a little generous, they could have spent their last days in everyday interactions, sharing something a little more than words ... emotions perhaps ... Even for her, it would have been a good thing. But no. What she had not done for anyone in her life she would not for a moment agree to do for herself. What use was such resolve, such obduracy?

Before Suruchi could say anything, Shrida closed his eyes and lay back. Even when she took leave, saying "I will go now," he remained silent. She came into the gaudy living room but no one was there. She wondered how to call out to the woman who had let her in. She would have asked for a glass of water, but there was no sign of anyone in the house. Fed up, Suruchi walked out of the house. She kept thinking, if my father or someone close to me had been in this state, what would I have done? I certainly would not have behaved like this. Would never have neglected them, made them feel so alone. And yet in the end each one of us is alone in our own way—Pradeep-Kamala, Nini, Shreerang's father, mother, and I myself. Have I made any effort to reach out to them, regardless of what has happened? That's the important word. Regardless.

When Swaroop heard that Suruchi had made the effort to go looking for Shrida's address, she was flabbergasted.

"Did you have to go, Didi?"

"Have to? Of course."

"Don't be evasive. You and Nini ... I just don't understand what the two of you are about."

Suruchi smiled.

Swaroop continued, "Why are you people so devious? Why don't you come out openly about what you feel, what you do? Say what you will, this keeping everything bottled up inside is not good."

"Sometimes a little reticence is necessary, Swaroop."

"Very well, if you say so, Didi. I will never get your wisdom."

Many days later Suruchi ran into Shrida's daughter quite unexpectedly, in a store. She didn't recognise Suruchi. At least she pretended not to. But Suruchi couldn't help herself. She walked up to her and asked her how Shrida was. There was a man with her, perhaps her husband. She didn't bother to introduce him to Suruchi. He was telling her to hurry up. But Suruchi would not budge until the lady answered her question.

"He is in an old age home. Actually you can say it's a nursing home. They take good care of him."

"But his treatment? You said that ..."

"What could we do? He was just not cooperating. He himself asked to go to this place. He has people his own age ... there's nothing to worry about. We also visit him sometimes."

Without giving Suruchi an opportunity to say any more, the woman and her husband walked away. Their expression suggested feelings of guilt, Suruchi thought. But then it could have been the satisfaction of a duty done. They had done whatever they could. It was each to his own fate. So easy to say that, wasn't it? When Kamala abandoned me at Nini's, she must have explained it away in the same way. When I left Nini's house, she must have felt the same way, and when Shreerang left this world, that must have been his thought, too: she and her destiny.

When Suruchi returned home from the library that evening there was no sign of Swaroop. Since she rarely went out so late, Suruchi got a little worried. She waited for a while, then to distract herself, she began to potter about in the kitchen. It struck her that she had hardly entered this area, now appropriated entirely by Swaroop. She was neither fond of cooking nor particular about what she ate. But Shreerang was not like that. He was so enthusiastic about everything. He loved to try out new dishes when he was in the mood and then he didn't care if he made a mess, or bother about leftovers. One shouldn't worry about trifles, he'd say. Life was really simple with him actually. In all my interactions with Ila's group or my colleagues in the library, I found their personal anxieties, their dilemmas, arose from just such trivialities. I had always stayed aloof from their narrations about everyday problems, compromises, demands, expectations, just to avoid any probing questions they might ask me.

Anyway, how many people really cared? Did they know or believe that a girl like me was living with a man? I had been quite reserved, it is true, so I could get by somehow. A couple of times when someone slipped up and referred to "your husband," I had tacitly acknowledged it and carried on. Most of the time, people around me chattered on without including me in their conversation, and I was quite happy to keep it like that. Once one woman dared to say to me, "This is what people say about you. Is it true?" I had replied calmly, "It's my life." But I was angry. I fumed inwardly against them, society, the whole world. Tried to explain to them how much simpler, less complicated my life was compared to theirs. But was it them I was trying to convince or was it myself? Really, was it that different?

That is precisely what Shreerang had been trying to say all along. We mould ourselves into a standard societal framework. It's prepared for us from birth. We never question it. Gradually our emotions are drawn into it. Marriage, a husband and a wife, a man and a woman, domination, possessiveness, love, envy, expectation, compromise, adjustment ... When he put it so simply and clearly, made it sound so natural, she was convinced. And yet questions plagued her, caused her endless distress. Rational thought, reasoning gave way to intense emotional outbursts.

"The gap between your rational thought process and your emotions is widening, Suruchi," Shreerang had often said, half seriously, half in jest. "Don't treat them as two sides of a coin!" What had she done?

She thought she had been very practical. She'd lived her life, if not in happiness, in Shreerang's love. When he went away so unexpectedly, this practicality showed itself starkly.

He had left her not one or two but three lakh rupees. Why? It would buy her a flat. A home without her having asked for it. Four walls. Security. A permanent place. He'd said, "Go! I set you free." Is that what he'd really meant?

Suruchi heard a knock. Swaroop had a key, so who could this be? She opened the door and found Swaroop standing there. She looked tired, dishevelled and distraught. Before Suruchi could finish saying, "What happened?" Swaroop burst into tears, huge sobs shaking her body. Suruchi was shocked. She waited for the tears to subside. After a while Swaroop wiped her eyes, blew her nose and asked, "You were worried?"

"Of course. Where were you?"

"I was at Ila's."

"*Dhat*! That's all? But I didn't know that. You're not normally so late. But why the tears?"

"There was a case at Ila's today, Didi. A young woman, maybe my age, with children, too. She was so badly beaten, Didi, by her husband, mother-in-law and sister-in-law. We took her to the hospital. Filed a police complaint. It took all day. That's why I'm late."

"And so?"

"So what? Oh, she was so brutally beaten, her blouse wouldn't come off." Again the tears started. "Are people so cruel, Didi? To beat such a little girl ... she was so pretty, I just can't get over it."

Suruchi held Swaroop close.

"This is the first time for you ..."

"You've seen it before?"

"Many times. Domestic violence is Ila's field. She gets many such cases."

"You don't get upset?"

"Of course I do. At first I'd also get worked up like you."

"Then you got used to it?"

Suruchi had no answer. Does one really get used to it? Yes, the initial anger, helplessness, frustration becomes less. One looks around and seethes inside at what is going on. But it is a fact that with repeated exposure to something, the intensity of the response is reduced. During those days, though I had a job, I had started helping out at Ila's, sorting, classifying, filing case papers, but it was just another job. I began to wonder as I read the papers, does this kind of injustice prevail everywhere? They came from diverse backgrounds—economic, social, caste and religious—yet there was a shocking similarity in all their experiences. Especially after hearing about Shreerang's sister, I realised with horror that it could happen to anyone. Even to people close to us. I had not dared to broach the subject with Shreerang again. I did wonder though, whether Ila knew about it. But I felt it was best not to bring it up again.

How did we deal with it? We read poetry together, Shreerang and I, or went to a movie. Or went on a picnic with a few friends. Chatting, laughing, eating. Ila, too, joined us sometimes. Obviously that was not the only world, of oppression and violence. We divide our existence into compartments, and yet deep down, there is an awareness of the other reality. Is this what 'getting used to something' means?

Suruchi stroked Swaroop's face. "Come, don't brood on it," she said. "We are doing what we can, isn't it? Even if one or two of them do get help, it's good. Think of it like that."

She told Swaroop to have a wash and change while she served the food she had cooked. She would wait for her. Swaroop remained standing there. Suddenly she asked Suruchi, "Do you get mad at Mummy and Daddy?"

"No. What for?"

"Because they dumped you like this?"

"They didn't dump me! They left me with Nini."

"So what? If they didn't want you, why did they give birth to you?"

Suruchi felt like laughing. Swaroop's indignation was on her behalf!

"They could have taken you with them later on."

"Oh yes? Would Nini have let me go? Who else did she have, other than me? At least they had you."

"So people need children like they need a toy of their own?"

Suruchi looked at Swaroop. When had this girl grown up so much? Two years ago, when she came down, she was a child, just out of school, spoilt. Her life revolved around clothes, dressing up, strutting about, going out, food. Shreerang enjoyed pulling her leg whenever they were together. And she loved it. Soon after she arrived this time she'd said, "Shreerang was so nice! If you hadn't been in his life, I would have fallen for him." Even then I did not see that she had matured into a young woman. I always thought we were two different individuals because we'd been brought up in different environments. She in a free, affluent, alien country, I under Nini's thumb. But in the end, are we really so different? Are sibling bonds deep and strong? I could defy Nini and move in with Shreerang, and Swaroop, who had come from abroad, was quite willing to have an arranged marriage to a man she did not know. She, too, had been moved to tears by the violence she had seen. Was there any point in saying, "You'll get used to it"? The core is the same, deep and stable, connected, even across oceans.

"Didn't you ever feel you wanted a child, Didi?" Swaroop asked.

For the first time Suruchi voiced her feelings. "Sometimes, but not much."

"You were going to marry Shreerang, weren't you?"

"Perhaps."

"Then what happened?"

"We decided not to."

"To have a child?"

Suruchi nodded.

"But why?"

"It's not so simple. Will tell you about it sometime. Anyway, it is irrelevant now."

Swaroop looked searchingly at Suruchi's face. Suruchi turned away. She couldn't deal with that gaze. There was neither need nor point discussing such a personal matter with anyone, least of all her kid sister, she thought.

Suruchi sat in a corner, idly flipping through a magazine. When Ila got a few minutes between visitors, phone calls and work, she looked at Suruchi. "Are you just going to sit there or are you going to tell me how things are with you?"

"Everything is going well."

"You haven't been coming here of late?"

"I will."

"What kind of answer is that? You have lost interest in everything, that's the truth, isn't it?"

"Maybe."

"Come on, now. Are you enjoying your work?"

"No complaints."

"Good. Then start coming in. You can see how my work is increasing day by day, in spite of my not taking any more cases. Very often I have to do the briefing myself, though the case is handled by someone else. Can you spare some time to help me out?"

Suruchi remained silent. Ila exclaimed, "I thought you were better now!"

"I am better."

"So then why don't you make a fresh beginning? Life doesn't wait for you. Look at your sister. Didn't think that girl had much substance to her. At first she was nervous about getting into this field. But look at her now, she is fully into it."

"Really?"

"Doesn't she talk about it?"

"She does, but I spend so little time with her."

"She is intelligent, sincere, committed. American traits. I haven't noticed anything negative yet."

They were interrupted by a visitor. The phone rang. Suruchi tried to concentrate on the magazine she held in her hand but couldn't. She found it uninteresting. She had gone beyond this phase. When Ila had introduced her to this world, she, too, had responded like Swaroop, with trepidation, enthusiasm and then total commitment. Attempting to yoke her two worlds together. But she couldn't halt here. She was grateful to Ila. She admired her work, her perseverance, her selflessness and her struggle. She supported Swaroop, but personally, she had outgrown this work. She could not continue here nor could she do anything else. Why this dilemma?

When Suruchi looked up, Ila was standing in front of her, smiling. In that instant, Suruchi realised how much Ila had aged. Her hair was greyer, her face even more sallow than her own, her appearance changed. Suruchi had not noticed when Ila gave up the skirts and jeans (that Suruchi had taken to wearing after meeting Ila) for cotton saris worn with long-sleeved blouses or ill-fitting salwar kurtas. If anyone commented on it, she said it was age catching up or the demands of her profession. She looked not only older but wiser, too, with the vast experience behind her. Ila rarely spoke about her personal life. She only said her marriage had broken up. Suruchi had not dared to probe any further. She had been a great support to Suruchi, be it getting her the house, helping her manage her money or giving her moral support when Shreerang moved in with her. Suruchi had never kept anything from Ila. So why did she feel this barrier now? Who had erected it?

Suruchi was sitting down, leaning against the wall, her feet tucked under her.

Ila sat down on a stool in front of her. "So you will join me? Sure?"

"In what?"

"In my work, of course. There is a lot to do. The trouble is no one stays long enough to see it through. Either they lose interest or change their views. But you are not like that. Are you listening to me?"

"Yes."

"There's a meeting on Saturday, the usual. Come in. Participate. You'll feel better." She paused. "So then, I take it you are in with us, Suruchi. Okay?"

Without waiting for Suruchi's reply, Ila started telling her about the various cases that had come to her. The same problems, differing slightly in the details. The battle, too, was the same. For how long would one fight the same war over and over again? Was there any guarantee of victory? And how does one deal with failure? There was no point saying any of this to Ila, Suruchi thought. Her reply would be, "You've spent so much time with me, but it's water off a duck's back".

Lucky Ila. She knows exactly where she is headed.

Swaroop had told Suruchi repeatedly to attend the meeting on Saturday, but Suruchi did something else that day. As she was leaving the library at lunchtime, it being a half day, she saw Prabhakar. He offered to give her a lift, so instead of going home she decided to wander around on M. G. Road. To make conversation in the car, she casually asked Prabhakar about his daughter. With a happy laugh he said, "Oh, she's fine. Had a letter from her recently. She's going to be a mother. Didn't I tell you all would be well? Girls today seem to find it difficult to get along with anyone. What do you think?"

For a moment Suruchi was nonplussed. She didn't really want to speak, but couldn't let his question go unanswered either. "Girls have changed a lot now," she said. "They don't believe that they should take everything lying down."

"*Wah*!" he sneered, "you also seem to be one of those 'women's liberation' types? Make enough noise to attract attention. All for what? What is it that you are denied, tell me? What?" he asked belligerently. Suruchi was used to such reactions. She expected people to get nasty at the slightest opportunity, but she would not listen to them silently, she would tell herself. She would answer every accusation, demolish every allegation, but do it calmly, rationally. It was the only way to silence them. I will not let them make light of everything, she'd resolved, because in their silence is our victory, she believed.

And yet Suruchi said nothing. Why, she didn't know. A deep despair overcame her. She knew her silence was an injustice against her, her principles, the people she believed in. And yet she couldn't awaken her spirit. When they reached her destination, she asked Prabhakar to stop. As she was getting out of the car, he said, "Come home sometime. You generally don't like to mix with anyone, do you?"

"No, no, nothing like that. I will come."

"Good, I'll take you myself one day. Let's plan it."

Suruchi nodded, waved to him and walked along aimlessly. She'd walk into a shop, look around, wander out, enter another ... like my life at present ... drifting, not knowing where one is headed, what one is doing, what one wants ... She had told Shreerang once that his free-spiritedness bothered her. "You have no routine, no discipline, no bonds, no ties, no restrictions of time or place, I never know where you are or what you are doing, when you will be back, if you will ..." she'd complained.

"It's nothing new, is it? Why does it trouble you?"

She couldn't explain it. At first it didn't bother her so much. But as the days went by, it did. Why? Did I not know about it? Of course I did. The only possibility was that I was in love. But am I not anymore? No, it's not that. In fact, I still want him, more than ever. But I also want security. The security of our relationship. And stability. I've had enough of uncertainty. I do not want a situation where I have no right to question anything. But this was precisely the opposite of what Shreerang's life was. Things kept getting more complicated. There was no solution in sight. It caused me tremendous stress, not him. It made no difference to his lifestyle. Perhaps my faith in him was misplaced. Maybe there's another woman in his life, and that's why he cannot be committed to one person. He probably has no problem flitting from one relationship to another. Maybe he even enjoys it. Suspicion reared its head. Bitter quarrels ensued. I was miserable. I could see myself destroying what I held in my hands. The more I wanted to keep it whole, the more I was ripping it to shreds! What's going to remain from all this? Often I stormed off to Ila's, alone, after a bout of anger, tears, recriminations. A couple of times it was late at night. Ila was smart. She let me vent, let me cry. But gave no advice. It was only later that she said, "Think over it carefully, and before everything gets broken, becomes distorted and ugly, take an informed, independent decision. Step aside. Don't get at each other like this. No good comes of it. Lashing out at the other person to secure your own independence will only leave both of you bleeding." Had she been through this herself? Perhaps. But there was no way of knowing.

Shreerang was not home when I returned that day. As usual. But after a couple of days it seemed as if something was missing, more than before. Why? Involuntarily I checked to see if he had taken more clothes and other things this time. Where could he have gone? Wasn't he coming back? But he wouldn't do anything without telling me. Was he somewhere here? With someone else? Or in some other place? In spite of all my efforts not to get upset, I was very distressed. All sorts of thoughts plagued me. I fretted, I fumed, I cried, I lamented. I relived every day, regretting some, agonising over others, but there were moments when I felt strong, in control. Well, a choice had to be made. If it hurts, cut it off. No point in letting it fester. What do you want from life? It's time to answer that question. Work, money, satisfaction, or security, a home, a future?

Shreerang returned that night, unexpectedly. I was still in a muddled state. From his point of view, nothing had happened. Everything was the same. Convenient. It suddenly struck me—I, too, was a convenience in his life. Nothing more. Again there were words. A little acrimony. Resentment and lots of introspection. I was not really angry. Almost in control. The next morning was pleasant. We talked. Had coffee together. I got ready, and went in to say bye to him. He was lolling on the bed. I told him I want to talk to him that night, about something important. "Hmm," he replied, which meant that he would be at home that evening. I looked at him. I saw a tall figure sprawled across the bed, a sheet drawn up to the knees, his familiar bare upper body, tousled hair, the evening stubble ... watching me through half-closed eyes, a half-smile on his lips. That was the last sight of him. At home, relaxed, smiling as usual.

By the afternoon, my world had turned upside down. My world had stood still. Views, discussions, decisions became meaningless. I rushed to the hospital but I had not expected to see him so grievously injured. I was sure it was a minor accident. Ever since I heard about it, one thought kept going round and round in my head—"Shreerang, I need you, I want you, don't go ..." After seeing him I knew those words would not reach him as words. And yet, I held onto his hand muttering, "Don't go, Shreerang, please, don't go ..." Of course he would listen to me, he would understand. It didn't take very long. The head injury was fatal. In a short while, he was just a body. The police enquiries seeking information, Ila and Abhijit comforting, giving courage, informing Shreerang's parents...

Too late he would the pain assuage,
And to thick shadows does retire;
About with him he bears the rage,
And in his tainted blood the fire.[6]

I didn't know what to do. Would I have really eliminated Shreerang from my life? And then? What then? Or is he so enmeshed in every fibre of my being that it was impossible to extricate him? When his existence was being annihilated by the fire, at that very instant, I distinctly heard him say, "I have set you free." The words rang in my ears. That was Shreerang. Freedom. Release. What did the words mean? Why was I bewildered by them? Was it refusing to be tied down? To exercise a choice, that was also freedom. One had not even remotely considered this possibility. Perhaps breaking up, opting out, saying goodbye.... Death certainly didn't figure in this equation. It was in a class by itself. What does one do with the kind of freedom death gives? What must Shreerang be thinking? Is he nearby somewhere, hovering around? Is it his soul or his memory? Or is he within myself? These thoughts tormented me day after day, night and day. They drove me crazy. I gave up my job and just stayed at home. Couldn't do anything, couldn't think straight. Ila tried coaxing, cajoling, scolding. Finally, I wrote to Nini.

A deeply concerned letter from Kamala arrived. She was angry because the girls had not clearly explained their plans. They were being persuaded to go to the USA. Some references were made to suitable proposals. She was trying even there. Pradeep had hastily scribbled a few lines at the end of the letter. Although they appeared to be general comments, Suruchi knew they were meant for Swaroop. In fact, he had never written a letter to Suruchi.

"You go there every day, you do some work also. Do you like it?" Suruchi asked Swaroop one day.

"I've begun to like it."

"Shouldn't you look for something where you can use your education?"

"I will. I'm thinking of working somewhere as a designer."

"And what do we write to Mummy?"

"Didi, I might as well tell you ..."

"I'm listening."

"I've decided not to go back."

"What? Have you thought over it carefully?" Suruchi looked disbelievingly at her. "Don't go by this job you have. You will find it monotonous after a while. Then if there are issues with your visa or something ..."

"That won't happen, Didi. Abhijit has asked me to marry him."

"Abhijit?"

"Why are you looking at me like that, Didi? Yes, our Abhijit. He's a nice boy, isn't he? You know him so well!"

Suruchi was perplexed. When and how did this happen? How come I was oblivious to it? It was not about Abhijit; he was intelligent, simple, sincere. He actually liked Swaroop? Enough to propose to her?

Swaroop smiled and said, "I knew you'd react this way. Why? You don't approve?"

Suruchi collected herself. "No, no ... it's not that. He is a fine boy. But Swaroop, do you really know him? Have you been to his home? Met his mother?"

"I know what you are getting at. He comes from a modest background. So what? That can change very quickly. I will also work. Together we will change our circumstances."

"But... what will Mummy-Daddy say? Mummy is looking at boys from New York and London for you!"

"Let her. I wanted to tell you first, and then inform her."

"They're going to be very upset. First me, and now you. They will blame me."

"Not they, Didi, *she*. Mummy will be furious. Blame you also, perhaps. But not Daddy."

"How do you say that?"

"I just know. When you first wrote about Shreerang, Mummy created such a scene, I can't tell you. Though I was much younger, I didn't think it was a big deal. Didi had found herself a boyfriend, that's all. It's so common there. But Mummy! She raved and ranted, she cried and scolded. Daddy didn't say a word. 'She is old enough to take her own decisions', was all he said. So she ranted some more, 'Naturally you will think nothing of it, you are the same kind', etc. I don't even want to be reminded of it. Just to tell you that Daddy was on your side."

Suruchi's lips twisted in a wry smile. Had he ever felt close enough to her to 'take her side' she wondered. Swaroop would not believe her, she knew. She'd remind her how he had shopped specially for her before coming here, how he'd taken her around sightseeing when she had visited them, let her buy whatever she wanted, just to show her he cared. How can I make Swaroop understand that in all this, I didn't get the one thing I really wanted? Oh well, I'll just have to let it go, she thought.

"So it's not about Daddy?"

"I think so, and as for Mummy, to tell you the truth, Didi, I don't care."

Just like me, the 'I don't care' attitude, the decisiveness, Suruchi thought as she smiled. She reflected a little on Abhijit, and on Swaroop. Will they be happy together? Who can answer that? Can one be certain about anything in life?

"So you've planned everything?" she asked Swaroop.

"What is there to plan, Didi? It will be a registered marriage. No one will be invited. So ..." she said with a shrug.

"It means you will definitely not go back?"

"Yes. But tell me, Didi, did you want to go? I was the one who kept saying, 'Come back with me, Didi ...'"

"That's not it at all."

"Didi..."

"What?"

"What are your plans?"

"My plans? Why, everything is going smoothly, that's enough for me. You stop worrying about me. Think about yourself. Have you applied for a job? Where will you stay? In the same place? Together with ..."

Suruchi could tell immediately that Swaroop had thought it out seriously. She seemed to be aware that life, lifestyle, home, love could not be romanticised; they had to be viewed practically. Solutions had to be found for the problems that would definitely arise, with one's head firmly on one's shoulders. Swaroop was able to do it, Ila does it, Shreerang had done it. Then why can't I? How and where did I go wrong? Or did I? In the end, I am left with nothing.

Although the University library was closed, I was stuck there because it was raining. For a minute I wished the rain would go on and on, never stop. But then it started getting dark and I couldn't get out. I had no umbrella, and I didn't know anyone who could give me a lift. Getting an auto was out of the question. The bus stop was quite far away. Of course there were people loitering about in the corridor, the veranda, on the steps. I wished intensely for Shreerang's company. Then I laughed at myself, was even slightly vexed. This was an evening like any other, so what if there was a sudden downpour. Where did Shreerang come into it? And then ... I couldn't believe what I saw—Shreerang, wet and shivering, had turned up at the University building with an umbrella. He had tramped through puddles and slushy roads to get here. Before I could say, "What are you doing here?", he'd said, "I knew what was going on in your head, so thought I'd surprise you." Oblivious to our surroundings, I took his hand and together we walked and walked, sharing one little umbrella. I couldn't control my giggles. The darkness deepened. Streetlights came on. Finally we found an auto to take us home, paying double the normal fare. It was too dark to even fit the key in the lock. When the door opened, we were greeted by a huge puddle of water. An open window had let the rain in. There was no electricity, and we had no candles in the house. I struck a match, but it went out in a whiff. So I lit the gas, and discovered, to my dismay, there were no vegetables, no fruit, no bread even. Now what? Surprisingly, it didn't bother either of us. Nor did practical considerations like what to do for food, light, how to mop up the water, occur to us. I got out of my wet clothes and was groping for my towel when I slipped and fell. I was shaken, but before I could support myself against the wall and stand up, Shreerang grabbed me in a tight embrace. "What do we do now?" I wailed. "Do nothing. Make love, go to sleep," he said, and carried me to the bed. And that's all we did. Till the next morning I didn't think of anything. That was bliss.

How had we lived those moments? By keeping the mind at bay, wasn't it? Those days I had been so inefficient, so impractical. I didn't plan for anything—time, money or objects. And when it was too late, the regrets ... if only! Maintaining the house, buying the groceries, paying bills on time, none of it happened. Milk routinely boiled over, food went bad, the iron was not switched off, the radio left on through the day ... But Shreerang put up with it, sorted things out. Was he actually there? Was he part of it, or did he feel totally detached from household matters? A temporary resident, a mere guest? But how could that be? He took care of everything, chores and expenses, uncomplainingly, quietly. And yet there was a kind of detachment. He came and he went. Perhaps it was meant to be this way. I was destined to share only a part of his unfinished life. Like the fleeting touch of a bird in flight. Leaving no external mark of name or symbol. What was imprinted was inside, where no one could see it, understand it. It was not my lot to live as Shreerang's widow, or as the mother of his child. I have internalised Shreerang's part in my life. And there is no way I can erase it.

Reactions to Swaroop's marriage were worse than expected. Thought Kamala would write a weepy, whiny letter, but she never did. Pradeep wrote on her behalf. Instead of expressing his own feelings about the matter, he described in detail how badly Kamala had taken the news. As soon as she read Swaroop's letter, she had become hysterical. Raved, ranted, fainted. Then fell completely silent. Went into a severe depression. During that time Pradeep had looked after the house, taken care of her, and accompanied her to the psychiatrist. The sittings continue.

Swaroop started laughing as she read Pradeep's letter. Waving the sheet about, she exclaimed, "What a drama Mummy creates! Hadn't she done the same thing? Without a thought for Nini she eloped to marry a man from another caste, didn't she? Or has she forgotten?"

Maybe that's why she reacted like this, thought Suruchi, but couldn't say it. She knew Swaroop was very attached to Pradeep. She wouldn't have liked it if Suruchi had spoken up. It is possible that Kamala realised she'd made a mistake. What had she got from her decision? She ran around him all her life and yet she was not sure of him, couldn't trust him. She was separated from one daughter who had moved far away from her. Now the other one, too, was slipping from her grasp. What could be a greater tragedy for a simple, ordinary woman? All your life you struggle for marriage, home, family, and what are you left with? Nothing.

"Let her make her scenes," Swaroop continued. "What's the worst that can happen? She will come around eventually. What do you think, Didi?"

"You've made up your mind, haven't you?"

"But of course! You think I'll change it for Mummy's sake? Never! But Daddy hasn't said anything... You think he is also unhappy?"

"You were sure he wouldn't be."

"Yes, but he should have said something."

Though she did not show it, Suruchi noticed Swaroop was a little unnerved. She wanted some backing. Pradeep's, no doubt. Why? She was his favourite, naturally. She'd grown up with him. He must have indulged her every whim. He was part of her growing up, her education, her life. A father's beloved daughter. And me? They needlessly kept me away. It wasn't my fault. Mummy gave birth to me without thinking, and gave me away equally thoughtlessly. Maybe Daddy hadn't approved of it. Surely he must have felt some affection for his newborn daughter? Mummy had made the decision and run after him, leaving me here. I am paying the price. The gap between father and daughter can never be bridged. Years have gone by, childhood is over, youth is on its way out ... The time for communication has passed. Swaroop enjoyed everything—the company of parents, their love, their indulgence. All that was denied to me. Only because she was born later. Could there be any other reason? Am I jealous of her? Since when? Now, or always? Me, jealous, of a younger sister who dotes on me?

Suruchi felt very uneasy. She walked away from Swaroop, who continued to babble. Suruchi heard none of it.

Both Swaroop and Suruchi thought Nini would not respond at all. They were wrong. She sent a two-line letter, curt and impersonal. "What could anyone expect from a girl like her," she'd written. Swaroop was furious. "I shouldn't have told her at all! Who is she to me anyway! I never meant anything to her. You were the favoured one."

"Sure, it's obvious, isn't it?"

"You may say anything, Didi, she may be angry with you, but her anger is not genuine. I know it, we all know it."

"We all?"

"Yes, all of us, Mummy, Daddy, me. You think we haven't noticed how much she cares for you? You are forgiven everything, but about me she says, what can one expect ... Oh, let her go fly ..."

Things did not pan out as Suruchi anticipated. The wedding was performed according to Vedic rites since Abhijit's mother wanted it that way. Only a handful of people were invited, though. Pradeep wrote another letter, not Kamala. Swaroop ignored all that. Nini did not attend. Which meant that from the bride's side, there was only Suruchi and their friends. But Swaroop looked happy. She'd even done a bit of shopping before the wedding. Clothes and some essentials for the house. She hadn't found a suitable job yet, though she'd been trying very hard. Suruchi had paid for everything. She was quite happy to do it at first. But then she realised she was being taken for granted. Parents in another country, an upset mother, no other relatives—who else would take on the burden but the loving older sister?

Ila's mother was quite old and she lived with Ila's brother. When news came that she had passed away, Ila closed her office and went home for four days. Suruchi had no idea how close they were or how often they interacted because Ila chose not to speak about her past. She'd mentioned casually once long ago that they were not in touch. But Suruchi went to see her as soon as she heard the news. She would have accompanied Ila, too, if Ila had asked her. She obviously didn't even think of it. She seemed to be treating everything as a formality. Suruchi was surprised at the way Ila kept giving instructions to her colleagues ... remember this date, those papers are to be put in this drawer, what is to be done when ... It seemed as if she was loathe to go away for even those four days. When Suruchi offered to go to the station with her, Ila snapped, "Why? There's no need." And continued with her work. That's all she thought about, cared about. For the first time Suruchi wondered if her obsession with her work was making her boring and tiresome? She seemed to have a one-track mind, the path she was treading, narrow, long but straight. No forks, no turns, no bends. No distractions, no diversions. Was it a road or a tunnel, dark and deep? A light was visible, no doubt, but would it lead to a new world or remain a dot that moved further and further away as one approached it?

Ila gave the spare key to her assistant. The others would be coming in to work anyway. Suruchi just stood there. There was nothing for her to do. Her mind went back to those early days when there was so much she had done, first out of curiosity, then to help and finally because she enjoyed it. She used to feel so grateful to Ila for helping her find her feet, for setting her on a path she could follow, opening up a whole new world for her. We were together then. Now I am here, but she is not. Why? Because she knows only one road? Had I been on that same road, we would have trod it together, without a doubt. But was it not possible for us to be friends as two women, two human beings, outside that path? That's what I had hoped for. That's what I needed, maybe. But none of that seemed to matter to Ila. She could do without it.

There were still a couple of hours before Ila's train. She was still bustling around, so Suruchi asked her, "Is your bag packed?"

"Not yet. It's not a big deal. Will just throw in a few clothes and it's done. What else do I need?"

"Shall I do it for you?"

"Oh Suruchi, why do you worry so much for nothing? I will do it. I told you, it's not a big deal."

Ila was going through the papers in her hand. Suruchi asked, "Was she ill?"

At first Ila paid no attention, then replied, "Um ... who? What did you say?"

"Your mother ..."

"Mother? What about her?"

Suruchi shook her head. "Nothing," she muttered.

"I'll try and come back in a couple of days. Will get a bus ticket any time. Must get here by Saturday. Oh yes, good thing I remembered!" she exclaimed, turned around and started looking for something among the stack of books.

When I first met Ila, her work was comparatively less demanding. She was very motivated, of course, and very busy. But gradually the office space started eating into her home. One day Ila sent me home to fetch some papers. I had a spare key and I was rushing back when I met Shreerang. On a borrowed scooter or motorcycle, I'm not sure. He offered to take me there. Those were early days. I was pretty certain I was falling in love with him. When we were together at some programme, or bumped into each other somewhere, or on those rare occasions when he came to the library or the hostel to convey a message... Just thinking about him would make my heart race, but there was no way I could gauge his feelings. I knew how he viewed the world but not what he felt about me. How to find out? Do people like him know what love is? Is it unimportant for them, or are they beyond such sentiments?

I was rummaging through the piles on Ila's desk. Shreerang was standing in front of the shelf, glancing through a magazine. I found what I was looking for. I picked it up and said, "Let's go."

He put the magazine down, and gave me a funny look. Must be amused by my dishevelled appearance, I thought. Before I could say anything, he took the notes and papers out of my hands, then the handbag dangling from my shoulder. My breath caught in my chest. He cupped my face in his hands. "Shreerang!" I exclaimed, but no sound emerged. I was trapped in his embrace, in this very pleasurable sensation. Later, when gathering all my stuff together and locking Ila's house, I wondered what Ila would say. She'd want to know what took me so long. Actually it was only about fifteen minutes, and yet that brief span had revealed to me what Love was. His, mine. I saw him, myself anew. When he dropped me off, I stared at him for a long moment. When he smiled so reassuringly, I was convinced he was a serious person. Not as carefree and frivolous as he appeared, and certainly not irresponsible. He did not belie my trust. He had his own rules for living and he had laid them out clearly and openly. With him, you got what you saw. No secrecy, no dishonesty, no deception about anything. One saw so many people who showed different colours at different times, so many instances where they cheated, made false promises, loved under false pretences. But Shreerang was not like that. And that's what made him so lovable. So desirable. Someone to call one's own. Yes, he was staying with me, at home, coming there soon after he finished work, sharing everything, from poetry to soap! His response was always, "But I am all there, in front of you, aren't I?" But the seed inside me had sprouted and kept growing. Possession. Ownership. Forever. Mine. I could not get rid of it. The big dilemma ... the more I loved him the more I wanted to possess him. The more demanding I became. And finally?

Suruchi was startled out of her reverie when Ila declared it was time for her to leave. They went down together and Suruchi helped her get an autorickshaw. Ila waved a peremptory goodbye.

Swaroop and Abhijit had come over the previous night. Swaroop had been for a couple of interviews, but she didn't seem keen on any of the offers. Suruchi asked Abhijit about his play, the production, and performances if any, and whether he had written anything new. His answer to all her questions had been in the negative. Said he was slightly caught up in something he had offered to help Ila with, as usual. Besides, he had his regular job.

Suruchi scolded him. "Don't make excuses for not writing anything."

"Not excuses, I do have an idea. Thought I would compile the four–five plays I have written so far and publish them myself."

"Isn't it a great idea, Didi?" Swaroop asked enthusiastically. "Of course it will mean investing some money. You'll lend it to us?"

Suruchi's response was spontaneous. "Of course, I'll give it to you. How much would you need?"

"You certainly will not," retorted Abhijit. "Swaroop is just joking."

"But I am serious. You can give it back when the book sells."

"What if it doesn't?"

"We'll see then. You can return it slowly. I am prepared to wait. Tell me when, how, and how much. But do consider it. I, too, feel your book should be published."

Swaroop's joy made her throw her arms about Suruchi and kiss her cheek, exclaiming, "Didi, you said yes so readily?"

Suruchi sensed Abhijit's embarrassment. To put him at ease, she said, "Abhijit, is ours a recent friendship? Besides now you are a relative. So don't act smart."

True to type, Abhijit said no more. He just smiled. Suruchi went in to get them something to eat. Swaroop followed her. "Didi, I have something else to tell you."

"What?"

"I'm pregnant."

Suruchi spun around. "What! So soon?"

"Not soon, Didi, it's been six months since we got married. You thought we did nothing these six months?" She giggled.

Placing a hand on her shoulder, Suruchi said, "Will you be able to manage everything?"

"What kind of a question is that? You think I'm still a child, do you?"

"But naturally. You are my younger sister."

Swaroop laid her head on Suruchi's shoulder. "You will help me, won't you Didi?"

"Do you need to ask?"

"I was just dying to tell you, Didi. I feel so nauseous in the mornings, so sick, I feel like weeping."

"You want to come and stay here for a while?"

"But you are out all day ..."

"So what? I am there mornings and evenings, aren't I? And Abhijit's mother, how is she?"

"Ya, she's there."

"What does that mean? Speak clearly."

"What can I say, Didi... Actually nothing's really happened, but she just doesn't like me. She criticises everything I do. What would you know, you've lived there, she says. She makes these barbs about Mummy-Daddy as well. Claims we are not like normal families. That I am like this because they didn't bring me up properly. That her children are all so well behaved and so good because of her efforts. It's annoying to hear this kind of conversation all the time, Didi."

"Then why do you sit at home all day?"

"I don't. I do go to Ila every now and then. She doesn't like that, though Abhijit doesn't mind. Besides, how can I take up a job now?"

"So it was a bit hasty then, this pregnancy?"

"I want a child, Didi, want one very badly. To have something all one's own... so nice, don't you think?"

Suruchi was flustered. Swaroop seemed truly happy. She was blooming.

"Look," Suruchi said. "Any time you need anything, come here straight away. And don't pay any attention to these little skirmishes at home. Keep yourself busy as far as possible. And don't forget, if there's anything ..."

"Oh ho, Didi, you don't have to tell me that. If it were not for you I would not have even considered staying back here, forget about marrying Abhijit."

"That's nonsense. You did fall in love. Or didn't you?"

Swaroop looked grim. "It wasn't like that."

"Then like what?"

"Would I have found someone like Abhijit from among those proposals that came for me?"

Suruchi was baffled.

"Those guys had everything in Mummy's list of specifications. But you tell me, you know Abhijit ... Would anyone of them have given me that sobriety, that dependability?"

She is right, thought Suruchi. I know Abhijit. People like him have integrity. Loyalty to values, institutions, ideology. He would never give any woman cause to complain about him as a husband. What he would give was a life of stability and commitment. He is a man of principles. Steady and calm. Such sincerity was rare, and Swaroop had recognised that quality in him. She had been looking for that all along. Just as I was looking for love. At least to start with. Swaroop was way ahead of me. Progressive. Coming from a land of material abundance, her perception was sharp, her mind firm, her ideas well thought out. She knew exactly what she wanted and she had chosen accordingly, with a clear mind. Good choice. She says my being here helped. Perhaps. She had nothing to gain from agreeing blindly to spend her life with some PhD from London or New York. She had experienced that life. Besides, she was not lazy. Some day she would go back to fulltime work.

Right now she was able to help Ila out. Against this backdrop had appeared Abhijit. Maybe he did profess love when he proposed to her. A love that was like a pillar, solid. And she saw it for what it was. Not only was it her own astuteness, her destiny, too, played a part in her decision.

"Okay, Didi, we'd better get going," Swaroop said. "Don't bother to prepare anything. I just came to meet you and give you the news."

Suruchi patted her back, and accompanied her outside. Abhijit was reading a magazine. "Swaroop told me," Suruchi said looking at him.

He looked shy. But there was happiness in his expression.

"Swaroop must run to me even if a nail drops!" Suruchi said with a smile.

"Of course," he replied.

"Take care of her. She is still quite childish sometimes."

"Didi, that's not fair!"

Suruchi continued to address Abhijit. "I hope you are reading some books? It's not easy becoming a father. You have to share the whole experience of parenthood. Understand?"

Swaroop was flitting about and twittering like a sparrow. "Sure, Didi, I'll do as you say. Promise. Why should I worry when you are there?"

When Swaroop noticed Suruchi staring at her, she said, "What are you looking at?"

"At you. Your huge big stomach. You've really become nice and round."

"And who's responsible for that?"

"Go on, get fat, I'm not saying anything. Who's hungry all the time? Not me."

"Didi, do you think Mummy would have fussed over me?"

"Of course. She keeps asking, advising, through her letters."

"That's not the same. It's easy to say do this, do that from a distance. She just doesn't have it in her. Always shrugs off responsibility. She did that with you. And when I was barely old enough, she was in a hurry to get me married off."

Suruchi was amused. "You criticise Mummy too much. None of these things ever occur to me. In fact I thought Daddy was the slightly detached one."

"No way. He is very affectionate. A fun person actually. We used to have a great time together. But if Mummy was around ..."

Suruchi said nothing. It was a strange world and she had no place in it. She had insisted Swaroop stay here with her and Abhijit only come to visit. She had collected all the books she could find on pregnancy, childbirth, motherhood, baby care. Not that Swaroop had shown much interest in them! To her it was all fun and games. So Suruchi had to insist that she read some of the articles and do certain things like watch what she ate, how much to exercise etc. She had no time to supervise though, what with her job, the everyday chores and Swaroop's constant presence in the house. She realised that she was the one getting more jittery, more apprehensive as the date of the delivery neared. Even when she was at work the thought uppermost in her mind was, Swaroop is alone at home. Hope nothing happens ... Of course she can call from the neighbour's if necessary. Actually they are not bad, those people. I was the one who was very formal with them when Shreerang was there. But Swaroop is much more outgoing. She sits on the steps in the evenings and chats with them. They will certainly help if need be. Besides, the first baby takes a long time coming, they say. So I will get time. Nothing's going to happen in the house, she assured herself.

And yet the anxiety refused to leave her. And then one day Swaroop said, "I'm feeling funny. Shall we go to the doctor?" It was early in the morning. Both of them hurried to the hospital. The doctor laughed and said, "Now that you are here, you might as well stay, though I don't expect anything to happen before tonight." Abhijit arrived with his mother. So Suruchi didn't need to take leave, but she didn't feel like going to work. Swaroop, too, was clutching her hand. Suruchi stayed all day. Early the next morning, Swaroop's son was born. But before that Suruchi felt she was going through the labour pains along with Swaroop. When she held the baby in her arms for the first time, it hit her—I have missed this entire experience in my life! It was denied to me. It's all over now. It's too late. My paths were meant to be different. And they would remain so. Even though one had accepted the reality of the situation, at moments like this the truth looms before oneself, that one had bypassed this experience.

After this, Suruchi found there was never enough time for anything. She asked for leave as often as she could. But it wasn't easy. There wasn't anyone who could handle her job. So she had to go. It meant rush, rush, rush ... She tried to get someone to do the cooking, cleaning, other things. Abhijit's mother was prepared to organise everything at her place, but Suruchi was unwilling to let Swaroop go there. We will manage, she kept saying. More importantly, she couldn't deny the joy it gave her. If she could, she would have stayed home all day watching Bharat grow, instructing Swaroop, referring to the books on how and what to do.

When Abhijit left, Swaroop came inside to find Suruchi playing with Bharat, talking to him.

"Didi, when do you think I can go home?"

"Why? What's your hurry?"

"What do you mean, 'What's your hurry', Didi? Abhijit says come soon. In fact, tomorrow."

"Then leave him here!"

"Be serious, Didi," Swaroop admonished.

"Okay, but not tomorrow. Sunday."

By then I can get all the things that she may need, thought Suruchi. And give her some more instructions. Didn't I know this all along, that someday Swaroop would have to go to her own house? To her family ... husband, child, herself ... bound together... How can anyone else break into that circle? Permanently?

Suruchi escorted Swaroop and Bharat home. Abhijit's mother had asked her to stay and have lunch with them. She seemed very happy. When Abhijit accompanied her to the autorickshaw stand, Suruchi told him, "If you need anything, let me know at once. Also, I expect you to do your share of looking after the baby."

"Swaroop will make sure I do," he laughed.

"What progress on your book?"

"It's gone to press. All thanks to you."

"That's okay. No need for flattery. I do what I do because I want to, because it makes me happy. Understand?"

When Suruchi was tidying up the house she remembered she had to write to Nini. There was a postcard from her, but no mention of visiting. How can she be so hard, so unfeeling? Doesn't she feel like seeing Bharat, meeting all of us? If we land up there, she will do what is proper and expected of her. Stay as long as you like, she will say, instruct Lakshmi to take good care of us, make sure we are comfortable, but the minute we step out of the house, it will be as if we have stepped out of her life. How can she be so independent, so self-sufficient for so long? On the one hand she got respect, affection, success in society, but personally she kept herself isolated in her ivory tower. How did she manage to handle things entirely on her own after grandfather passed away? Where does one get that grit from? Is it inherent or acquired? Or does one have to cultivate it? How? Suruchi lay on her bed staring at the ceiling.

Suruchi realised her fist was tightly clenched under the pillow. Opening out her fingers, she turned on her side and tried to recall Bharat's face, his tiny body, his cry, his smell, but it would not come to her. All that kept coming back was the memory of her walking home from somewhere, perhaps Ila's place, after the usual evening session of conversation, discussion, food, drink ...

It was a winter evening and the breeze had begun to bite. Tensing my shoulders against the cold, I walked faster. Shreerang might have put his arms around me, made me warm. But I was angry. I wouldn't let him touch me. I felt I didn't know this man at all. He had not revealed himself to me. I had met his parents just once and that, too, very briefly. Had it not been for the chain incident I would not have known he had a sister. Which means the past was a mystery; with his kind of lifestyle, the present was uncertain, and the future?

I kept my distance from my colleagues but they most likely had some inkling about my life. This girl lives alone? No? Then who lives with her? Her husband? When did she get married? Or did she not marry at all? Without marriage? What about her parents? Where do they live? What kind of a girl is she? Her character? I took my anger at this gossip out on Shreerang by keeping him away. Not a word was spoken even after we reached home. Banging doors, clattering vessels, loud enough for him to hear, grabbing my pillow and blanket and sleeping in the other room. In that tiny house, my sniffling and sobbing must have reached his ears. I was wide awake. I don't know if he came to me himself or I let him. I wasn't really sleepy. "Why do you behave like this, Suruchi?" he asked me. I noticed the despair and helplessness in his voice. I told him what I felt, what I wanted to know about the past-present-future.

"Will that make you happier, Suruchi?" he asked. "Think over it before you reply."

I did. He had spoken so seriously that I had to reflect upon it. No, it had nothing to do with my happiness.

"So? Do you only want some information that you can store?"

No. That's of no use.

"Do you think that will bind me more closely to you?"

No. It doesn't work like that, I was sure.

"Then are you afraid? For your own security, is that it?"

I wasn't sure. Maybe it was. How else could I explain this unease, this uncertainty, this unsettled feeling? Are we so selfish that we only think of ourselves? It is true. We're self-centred and as a result, miserable, making ourselves unhappy and others, too.

I probably said little or nothing. Shreerang understood. It wasn't in him to trouble anyone. Ignoring my tantrum, he started talking normally about something. Got me to respond, too. Sometime later I switched on the light and looked at my watch. It was a quarter to three in the morning! He, too, was awake. Insomnia, like his mother. Or because of her? He often came home very late, sometimes from a long journey, walking all the way for want of transport. I'd seen him sitting up and reading through the night. His chatter kept me awake for a while, but soon I started yawning, my lids began to droop. I nestled in the crook of his elbow and shut my eyes. It felt so right. Everyone needs an arm, a body to cuddle against. Ultimately it all boils down to that. Someone to call one's own.

With this thought, I fell asleep. When I awoke, later than usual, Shreerang had gone. This was the man who believed he was not obliged to say where he was going, when he was going. He guarded his right, his freedom to come and go as he pleased. I fell back on my pillow, disappointed, when I found his note. It only had my name on it, nothing else. And that, too, as a mirror image. What does one do with this man, laugh or cry at his craziness? He would expect me to laugh, but invariably I cried. Such a contradiction in perception. In understanding. For what? So futile. So unfortunate.

Suruchi felt as if Kamala was standing in front of her and reading out the letter in a voice thick with emotion. "It is our misfortune, Swaroop's and mine, that I wasn't there with you. But Swaroop wrote that you took care of everything. It was a very big responsibility. Actually, all this should have happened to you first. I would have been so happy if you'd had a baby boy. But it was not to be. Who can quarrel with one's fate? It is not right that you two believe Nini is angry with you all. That's the way she is. We must adjust to it. She took care of you, didn't she? Fondly, too. So how can you assume she doesn't care? She is getting on now, and even if she looks fit, you can't prevent the ageing process. Take care of her, go and visit her. She will not admit it, but I know she has some health issues. Ask her, show some concern. I think you and Swaroop should take Bharat to see her. Who knows when we will get to see him! Things are a little tight here just now. But next year we will try to make it. My heart breaks thinking of you all, but you know how it is. We are not always in control."

It was a Sunday. For want of anything better to do, Suruchi started tidying up the house. Not that she enjoyed doing it, but how would she keep herself occupied the whole day? She'd asked Swaroop to come over, but they were busy, getting some guests, she'd said. So Suruchi had stayed at home. Going there too frequently was awkward. Besides there was nothing much she could say to them. Their house was quite small and it often felt cramped. She could have gone to Ila's but her mind vetoed that idea. Instead she rearranged her cupboard, climbed a stool and removed the cobwebs, changed the sheets.

When the doorbell rang, she hadn't even had a bath. She was wearing an old shirt of Shreerang's. It was baggy, and dirty. Anyway she opened the door and was startled to see Shreerang's mother there. So much time had passed since then, but she looked the same. "Please come in," Suruchi said. "Everything's a mess, was trying to clean up ..."

Suruchi went in and had a quick wash. When she came out she saw Shreerang's mother sitting on the cane chair in the front room, looking around her. Is she looking for something, wondered Suruchi. The one and only time she had come here, her son's white sheet-wrapped body was lying on the floor. She had sat at his head, looking crushed. Could not have noticed anything else. Why has she come here now? What relationship do we have with each other now, what connection?

"We had come here to attend a family wedding. Couldn't avoid it. I told him 'Give me the car, I'll go and see her'," Shreerang's mother explained.

Suruchi noticed her heavy sari, the jewellery and thought, they have become a part of her body now. Her daughter died of unknown causes, her son in an accident, and yet she has to keep up this show of wealth. It's a wedding, a social occasion; she must have got used to it ... The body has to deal with the demands of society. But what about the mind? Is there one? Or is there nothing left of it anymore?

Shreerang's mother enquired after her parents, her sister, asked her what she was doing, where she was working. Not that she needed to know, but as a formality she asked. Suruchi did not know what to say. "Will you have some coffee?" she said.

"No, just water will do."

When Suruchi went into the kitchen Shreerang's mother wandered around the house. She even went into the inner room where clothes, torn up papers, sweepings, lay in haphazard heaps. Taking the glass from Suruchi's hand, she gulped down the water and then said, "I want to ask you something." After a pause, she continued, "Do you have anything of Shreerang's that you can give me?"

"Something to give you?" Suruchi thought it was stupid. What can I give her! Shreerang was her son. I had him, but now he was lost. How much of him did I really have, if at all I 'had' him? He was so attached to her even after he was grown up. Doesn't she know that? She must. A mother knows it instinctively. In fact, it was because of her that Shreerang didn't give himself fully to me, I often thought. And now she says, "Give me something of his"!

When Suruchi didn't reply, the lady continued, "If it's difficult for you, it's okay. The truth is in that house of ours, there is nothing of his. The day he left the house, it was forever. He would come to meet me, but never stay at home. It was either at my sister's place or with friends or in a hotel. That's why he left nothing at home. He gave away everything—books, shoes, games, racquet, bat, even the little study desk he used as a child." She choked as she spoke. "It is as if I never had a son."

Suruchi kept biting her lips. What ultimately is left of a person? Nothing. Her daughter, too, had gone out of her mother's life without leaving anything behind. How devastating it must be to have this happen to you. And yet this woman is standing here in an expensive sari and laden with jewellery. That is her worth ... as much as the jewels given by her husband. And the face she was born with. Apart from that, nothing. But she must live. No escape from that. Live in that house as that man's wife, working, looking after guests.

"What would you like?" Suruchi asked.

"Oh, anything, even a shirt will do," she replied.

Suruchi opened the just-tidied up cupboard. In place of the shirts that used to hang there, it was her stuff. His clothes had been folded and put away in the bottom-most shelf. All his other belongings had been pushed to the back. Suruchi reached down and drew out a shirt. She felt a strong urge to bury her face in it, but she steeled herself against it and held it out. Shreerang's mother took it and clutched it to her bosom. After a few moments she said, "Give me a plastic or paper bag, something not transparent."

Suruchi found one. There was nothing more to say. They went to the sitting room. Shreerang's mother spoke, "One more thing I want to ask you. Don't take it amiss. We may or may not meet again ..."

"What?"

"Did you, umm, ever consider having a child?"

"No."

"That's the only thing I used to feel bad about. There's nothing left of him now. Why? I used to say to him, 'Get married, have a family, then I can come spend some time in your house.' It would have been a haven for me. Where else, if not in a son's house, will a mother have her rightful place? But he never agreed. When he was in college, when he went to America, even after he returned, I used to ask him, 'Don't you have any girlfriends? Tell me, I will choose one.' But he invariably laughed it off. I used to be so worried about him. Just as I worried when his father forced him to join the business. But he paid no heed. Then one day he said, 'I'll bring her home.' And he brought you to meet us. He didn't say much, but he was like that at home. Always angry. It was his father's house, wasn't it! But when you both came, he didn't need to say anything. I knew at once that he cared about you. I would often wonder, what will happen to this girl. With someone who said 'No' to everything, how would she deal with it?"

Tears were coursing down her cheeks as she spoke. Every now and then she dabbed her eyes and nose with the end of her *zari* sari pallu. "Don't be angry, my dear. Forgive my son. I apologise on his behalf."

"What are you saying!" Suruchi exclaimed as she shrank back, afraid Shreerang's mother would advance towards her.

"Get on with your life. Don't give up. Get married, have a family, be happy."

"No."

Shreerang's mother continued as if she hadn't heard. "Time waits for no one. We shouldn't either. Nothing's to be gained by that. Please don't mind all that I've said. Ignore it. Forget about it if it has offended you. I will not come again."

She turned, picked up her old-fashioned handbag from the floor, put on her slippers and reached the front door. Suruchi couldn't move. She felt numb. She was aware that Shreerang's mother had reached the gate, got into the car, the driver took the left turn and drove away, but she remained frozen. Slowly she sank into a chair and squeezed her linked hands between her knees. "He cares about you, you are part of his life", she'd said. Where is that life now? It must be somewhere. Deep within me. Inside this body, this mind. I should have thrown away those pills when that urge came over me. Maybe then a real life would have taken root. A girl. Just like Shreerang, but entirely mine, my own. He would not have denied her once she was conceived. And even if he had, I wouldn't have let her go. She would have carried a little of Shreerang's mother in her, too. Her colour, her features. When the lady had stood up to leave, I should have moved forward instead of shrinking back. I could have put my arms around her, held her close. Like Shreerang had done once. Her fingers would have caressed my face, too, as they had his. How long it was since anyone touched me like that, with affection. For my sake. Mine alone. But I moved away. "Forgive my son. I apologise on his behalf" — the words echoed in Suruchi's head. She began to sob.

Although Suruchi had read about it in books, she could not believe how quickly children grow up. She lost track of when Bharat flipped over, began to crawl, sit on his own, when his first tooth appeared, he stood up, started to walk, string words together ... It all happened so fast, she was left speechless.

Swaroop had not lost much weight since her pregnancy, in spite of doing all the housework and running after Bharat.

One day, she came to visit. After a while, she said, "Didi, I want to talk to you about something."

"Then speak. Surely you didn't come for nothing."

"That's not fair! Don't I come just to see you?"

"Not as often as I'd like. You always have a hundred excuses."

"Didi, you have no idea how many things I have to manage. Only when this child starts going to school will I get some free time."

"So what did you want to talk about?"

"Did I mention to you that this landlord of ours wants us to leave? He harasses us for nothing. So we have seen a flat."

"Where?"

"Vijayanagar."

Suruchi's shoulders drooped. "So far away?"

"What to do? You know how high prices are now. Renting is not an option. You were lucky you got this place when you did. It's impossible now."

"So then?"

"It's a nice flat. But we will have a tough time finding the money. Don't know what to do."

"What does Abhijit say?"

"He says we will manage somehow. Get a loan from LIC maybe, or try some other sources. But we have to come up with the amount. This place is getting impossible."

"How much more do you need?"

"We're short of about a lakh."

"I'll give it to you."

"You? I didn't mean to ask you, Didi. If you know anyone who will lend it to us ...?"

"I said I'll give it, didn't I?"

"You have that much?"

"Yes."

Swaroop stared at her for a long moment.

"But then what about yourself?"

"What about myself?" Suruchi smiled.

"What are you planning to do?"

"What does one do?"

"Are you going to continue here in this outhouse? The two of you didn't plan to buy your own place?"

"I haven't thought of it yet. But why are you worrying about that, silly? You need the money now, you can have it. That's all there is to it."

"But returning ..."

"Did I say anything about that?"

"No, no. We will return it with interest. We must. Only, I cannot say exactly when."

"Very well. Tell me when you want it and how. Cash, cheque, in whose name, etc ..."

"Didi, Abhijit will speak to you about it. But I am so embarrassed."

"Stop being silly. Forget about it. Tell me, how is the child? What is he up to now?"

Suddenly Swaroop opened up and the two sisters had a long chat over a meal. By evening, Abhijit arrived. They all went out as usual. The centre of attention was, of course, Bharat. He chattered continuously and refused to sit still. They were completely enchanted by him.

Suruchi decided at the last minute to go to the function where Ila was the chief guest. There were a few speeches followed by a short variety entertainment programme. Ila stayed back for a little while after that. Suruchi did not leave her side. She was amazed by the number of people who came up to talk to Ila—about her work, extend invitations, exchange information, make requests.

Ila said to Suruchi, "Let's go to your place, it's been a long time," as Suruchi climbed on to the pillion seat.

"Wah! Good you remembered!"

"I made myself remember, unlike you."

Both Suruchi and Ila enjoyed the long chat session. Ila told her what she had been doing, whom she had met, little incidents, routine happenings, future plans. Then she told Suruchi that she was accepting an invitation to attend a conference abroad. She would speak about her work and try to get some funding from there.

"It's nice and quiet here. No one to disturb you. I must come more often to relax."

"Come any time. My house is always open for you, you know that."

"Don't you get lonely sometimes?"

"I've got used to it. But you live alone, too, don't you, Ila?"

"That's different. Besides, I'm hardly ever alone. Either I am zipping around somewhere or people are hovering about me."

"You enjoy that?"

"Like you, I, too, have got used to it."

"Isn't there a difference between wanting something and reconciling to it?"

"You've started sounding like Shreerang now. He used to throw such challenges all the time. He could silence anyone with his arguments. You may not believe it, Suruchi, but we used to quarrel a lot when we first met. He used to tease me, pull my leg. But I wasn't going to let anyone make jokes about my work. It would hurt me deeply and I would retaliate. Wait and see, I'd say, you will meet a girl who is much worse than me, then you will come down to earth."

"And then?"

"Then what?"

"Finish ..."

"Well, he met you."

"But it isn't as if I was undemanding."

"I know, Suruchi. That's natural. All of us have to go through it. When people see me they think this woman is a fireball. She doesn't bother about anything. Has a one-track mind. When I look back at myself, I see myself as an ordinary woman. I grew up like middle-class girls do. Got an education, dreamt of love and marriage, tried to get and hold on to security and stability in life. For that I made an all out effort. Because our society is structured this way, all these things follow naturally. There's no alternative. Nobody is born saying 'No, no,' to everything. Refusal or denial is a reaction to the established system after it has pulverised you. Most people ignore it or conveniently forget it, believing it to be the unpleasant voice of protest. They don't stop to think why it has become so."

"You have any regrets, Ila?"

"Of treading this path? Not at all. Sometimes I feel a little sad that I have missed out on certain things. But only for a brief moment or two. Immediately I think of who I am, what my mission is, and that is truly important for me. I feel I am going forward with a powerful new ideology because of which many women are benefited, there is hope for them. It's true I am not always successful, but then no one is assured of it every time. Losing a few cases, feeling helpless at being unable to provide assistance sometimes is all part of the deal. What I have been able to achieve is more important, isn't it? That thought gives me the strength to go on. Now the way forward is very clear for me. No doubts, no confusion."

Suruchi stared at Ila. How could she say so confidently, "No confusion"? No matter what path one treads, it is impossible not to be plagued by uncertainty. Perhaps I am inexperienced, raw, even. But there were signs of uncertainty and confusion even in Shreerang, who was so clear-headed and decisive most of the time. Especially in bonds with his mother and sister, the stubbornness of decisions, the intensity of his relationships, of love or hate ... I had begun to see them. And Ila says she understands it all. Who is she deceiving? Herself, or our friendship?

Suruchi sighed. "You are really fortunate, then."

"You are on the same track, Suruchi."

"Far behind."

"Each one has her own place. Think about how you were. You have changed a lot, too. You are independent, you live alone ... Shreerang gave you a lot, didn't he?"

"If someone can 'give' you something, anything, of course he did."

"There are always options. But we can never say which is the best. Because until you choose that option and live it, you can't tell what comes with it. And once you have chosen it, then it is no longer an option—it becomes reality."

So saying Ila stood up. She fetched a glass of water. Suruchi stared at Ila, at her hard, resolute face. Ila, who could say with absolute confidence that she had complete clarity about where she was heading, about all the events that had shaped her. She was fully focused, absorbed in that one single mission.

"You have this ability to think rationally," Suruchi said.

"No," Ila replied. "You think so, Suruchi, but it didn't come naturally to me. I told you, I am always surrounded by people. They think, 'this lady is way above us'. It's true in a way, but not entirely."

"Were you never puzzled by the options before you, the choices?"

For a moment Ila's face flushed. Her eyes sparkled. Suruchi continued to hold her gaze.

"Once, a long time ago ..."

"What happened then, Ila? You must have considered an alternative. Perhaps that, too, would have taken you on the same path. With all the accolades and success you are getting now, but through a different route. It's never happened to you?"

Ila was silent.

"Tell me."

"It has happened, Suruchi. But I have left it far behind. What I wanted at that time was clearly delineated in the future. There was no place in it for personal relationships, emotions, tender feelings. I worked hard to convince myself of it. That's why I could get where I am today. It's all right. I have made a choice. This is my life now. There's nothing else one can do. But Suruchi, it's very lonely at the top."

"It doesn't have to be, Ila."

Ila became indignant. "It *has* to be that way. Except for this one rare day, I have neither the time, the energy, nor the inclination to come here and chat with you. Nothing is to be gained by that. My way is forward, my goal to get ahead."

"But even so ... we gained a lot from these moments. We have so much we can share."

"I decided to refuse that a long time ago, as I mentioned earlier. I have deliberately suppressed my softer side. Rejected the relationship. Denied the very possibility of it happening. One seed sprouts, you are attracted by its bright green leaves, then you are drawn to other plants and flowers. But you know these saplings are not for you. What do you do? Pull it out—roots, shoots, green leaves and all. It's easier at that stage. That's what I chose to do."

Ila stood up.

"I must go, Suruchi. Can't afford to waste time chatting. There's so much to do."

Suruchi accompanied her to the gate. Ila started her scooter and roared off. As Suruchi turned back, the lady from the neighbouring house said, "So how are you?" She asked about Swaroop. Said she had seen her and the baby. Knowing full well that she would appear snobbish, Suruchi did not say much. Silently she went inside.

It was a Sunday and Suruchi had reached Swaroop's house early in the morning. All day she had helped pack, transport, unpack and arrange everything in the new house. It had been decided that Abhijit's mother would take care of the food since that was all she could manage. Swaroop, of course, was tied to Bharat's routine. Not that Suruchi had minded. In fact, after seeing the newly painted flat, the surroundings, the neighbours, her disappointment that they were moving so far away from her decreased slightly. But there was no doubt that it would require some effort to come visiting. One would get used to it, of course, like one gets used to everything. The natural tendency is to resist any change at first. After all, there is security in the familiar, so one wants to hold on to it.

When I had first moved out of the hostel, I, too, experienced that apprehension of entering an unfamiliar world. In the hostel, everything was at hand, there was the company of other girls, even if they weren't really friends; there was nothing to worry about. But then I moved and was on my own. Added to it was the pressure of Shreerang wanting to share the house with me. How would it work out? What would people think? Would they suspect something? Shreerang was a carefree sort. He didn't really bother about anything. He had the house all cleaned up and ready for me when I reached there. Four cane chairs, a cupboard, gas cylinder, stove, utensils, storage containers—everything was in place. I was taken aback by it but felt strangely comforted by the presence of these everyday things. The fears that had troubled me when I had seen the house as mere walls, rooms, bathroom, disappeared, and the feeling of 'home' began to grow. Besides, the thought of sharing it with Shreerang only made it stronger. If asked to mention one occasion when I was supremely happy, I would have no problem naming it. Shreerang had been reciting some poetry at the top of his voice, I had been laughing wholeheartedly, all the stuff we had bought was lying around, everything was a mess ... but there was a sense of sheer joy. He had brought some food which I began to serve onto a plate by the kitchen counter when Shreerang entered, still quoting some verses, pushed the plate away, encircled me from behind and began to move his lips gently, over my hair, my neck, my ears. And I laughed. Delighted, happy. Though my lips kept saying, "Stop", my heart said, "Don't". I wanted that moment to last forever. No questions asked, no answers sought. This was it. This was the Truth. The difference between us was that for Shreerang, this was enough. He had implicit faith in the moment and did not ask, "What next". Whereas I, despite knowing it was the truth and cherishing it, could not put my faith in it. I kept faltering. I kept emasculating it by dragging thoughts of the future into it, the 'What if?' with it. Had I known that death was going to cut short my association with Shreerang like this, what purpose would have been served by worrying about the future? But if I had known that this was the reality, the truth, would I have savoured it fully? What Ila said made sense. No point wondering which would have been the better option. Because one cannot tell what its full implications are until it happens. And then it ceases to be an option, it becomes a reality. So then?

Swaroop was tired but happy. Once she had put Bharat to bed, she started rearranging the furniture and other knick-knacks, muttering to herself.

"I want some potted plants in the balcony," she said to Suruchi. "Will you get them for me, Didi?"

"Take it easy, Swaroop," Suruchi told her, "you can't set up everything in one day."

"But you like it now, don't you, Didi?"

"What do you mean now? I always did."

"You know what? I've found a nursery school close by, for Bharat."

"There's still time for that!"

"It will be upon us before we know it. Oh, and the market, too, is nearby." She looked at Suruchi, "You will stay tonight, won't you, Didi?"

"No, I must go back. Of course I'll come again."

It was quite late in the night so Abhijit offered to accompany her to her house. Suruchi did not want that. She would take an autorickshaw, she said, but they wouldn't hear of it. Perhaps they were feeling obliged to her for all her help, financial and physical, and were reluctant to let her go alone, Suruchi thought.

Abhijit accompanied Suruchi into the house to collect the sheets and pillow covers Suruchi had put aside for Swaroop. She switched on the lights and suddenly the house felt quiet, desolate almost.

"The house looks just like me now, the proverbial older sister," she laughed.

"Why do you say that?" asked Abhijit.

"Isn't it an apt simile?"

"Not at all. There is no need for you to make such statements in a moment of despair. The special qualities you have are exclusively yours."

"Really?" she smiled with tight lips.

Abhijit stood in front of her, arms crossed, the bag slung from his shoulder.

"You are not aware of it?"

"How would I know? I am old now. In body and mind. I don't remember what I say, in what context."

"Would you have said 'Yes' to me, Suruchi?"

"Yes? To what?"

"To spending your life with me, to marry me?"

"Abhijit, what are you saying?"

"What I did not have the courage to say at that time. I struggled so hard with myself but just couldn't speak up. I was almost certain of your refusal. And I did not want to lose your friendship by saying something out of line."

"Abhijit ..."

"Today, after so long I can dare to speak. Because now it won't make a difference. Suruchi, don't think I am being unfair to Swaroop. I love her. Besides, she knows that I did not have the courage to ask you then."

Suruchi gripped the back of the chair, her heart sinking.

"You're not angry ... are you, Suruchi?"

"Angry? For what?"

"I was your friend then, I will be your friend now. What happened or didn't happen in the past is of no consequence any longer. Don't hold it against me, Suruchi, please?"

"No."

"Look at me and say that. Please?"

Without looking up Suruchi just shook her head.

"Shall I leave, then? You will be okay?"

Suruchi merely nodded. She heard him close the door, then open the gate.

Although it wasn't cold, she wrapped herself in her blanket. What was this boy talking about? He hadn't dared to speak then, so why did he bring it up now? I've known Abhijit for a long time. Longer than I'd known Shreerang. He was always around Ila, doing whatever needed to be done. Slightly reserved, calm, helpful, quite different from Shreerang. At least that's what I thought. I had looked upon him as a good friend. And that's what he will always be. Nothing had ever happened to suggest anything else those days. It just wasn't possible. So then?

When Shreerang passed away so unexpectedly, leaving me alone, devastated, my world falling apart ... Abhijit had been as helpful as Ila. Sympathetic, caring, compassionate. Was it just his response to a dear friend's grief? Even at that time, I never felt there was anything more than genuine concern. Were his actions, like lending me a hand, helping me stand up, supporting me, signs I had not read? What would I have done if he had proposed to me? He said he was sure I'd refuse him. And he's right. I would have said "No". Definitely a 'No' after Shreerang. But just for argument's sake, what if I'd said yes? He would have ensured marriage, family, children, a home. Stability. Security. What about love? No guarantee of that. I never thought that he was in love with me. He didn't say "I love you" either. He couldn't. What does one really need in life? Security. Stability. Love really has no place. One can get all that, even happiness, comfort, without love. And yet we crave it. Why? Shreerang loved me deeply, immeasurably. In body and mind. But he gave me nothing else. Home, security, family, stability. That love left me perpetually frustrated and anguished. Why did it never seem enough? Why this desperate hankering after what was out of reach? Ultimately, everything went wrong, and life passed me by. That's the truth.

No later light has lightened up my heaven,
No second morn has ever shone for me;
All my life's bliss from thy dear life was given,
All my life's bliss is in the grave with thee.[7]

Although it was early in the morning, Suruchi was perspiring profusely as she reached Nini's house in an autorickshaw. Lakshmi opened the door and was surprised to see her standing there.

"Nini is sleeping," she said.

"So late? She normally wakes up at five o'clock?"

"Umm... She hasn't been feeling very well this past week," Lakshmi said hesitantly.

"What's the matter?"

"Nothing serious. The doctor has already given medicine. She's a little weak."

Suruchi sat down and asked Lakshmi to get her some coffee. Had Nini been awake, she would have insisted on my bathing first, thought Suruchi. But she isn't, so there. Suruchi drank the coffee, glanced through the newspaper, then went into her room and lay down.

When she went into Nini's room later for coffee and breakfast, she noticed that Nini was suddenly showing her age. Come to think of it, Suruchi didn't remember how she'd looked as a young woman, because she'd always been a grandmother figure. Besides, her erect and severe bearing and her piercing eyes made her seem more formidable. What she now saw was slack, dry skin, wrinkles around the eyes, and the scalp showing through thinning white hair.

"How is Swaroop?"

"Fine. Happy."

"You are doing all right?"

"Oh yes."

"So you have some special business here?"

"No, just a break. A four-day vacation."

"Very well, then. I must go in now. Even though I don't go out much nowadays, there's a lot to do. I must attend to some important paperwork."

"Okay."

Suruchi stared after her slowly retreating back. Swaroop was right. Suruchi had tried to persuade her to come along, but Swaroop had said that she wasn't interested in making the trip. If she had agreed, Abhijit wouldn't have objected. It would have been good to spend a few days at Nini's, all of them together. But Swaroop was adamant. "Besides, Nini doesn't care about me," she had repeated her refrain. Well, I came because I have nowhere else to go, thought Suruchi. I will spend my time eating, sleeping, reading ... all those books in Nini's cupboards. And then go back, rested. I need this break.

Nini told her later that her friend Merlin had come to see her. "She asked when you were coming here next," Nini added.

"What else did she say?"

"Nothing much. I told her I would convey her message, if you came."

Suruchi wasn't particularly keen on meeting Merlin, but since she had come home, she thought she should visit her. When she went over one evening, she found the front door open. Merlin was standing with her back to the door and shouting at the top of her voice. Her son and daughter were standing opposite her, defiantly, chewing their nails, waiting for her to stop ranting. They noticed Suruchi and, seeing their averted gaze, Merlin turned around. Taken aback, she quickly collected herself, and smiled.

"Suruchi! Come on in! You've come after so long!"

"I haven't been here for a while."

"It's good that you've come. I went to see Nini some time ago."

"She told me."

"Go away now, you two, run off," she said to her children.

Oh ho! I should have got something for the children, thought Suruchi. But I had forgotten all about them. Last time nobody else was there. Actually, Merlin is the only one I think of. A friend from school and college. Her family and children seem to have been obliterated from my memory. The last time I came to this city with Shreerang, he took me to visit a friend of his who had a wife and two children. They had a beautiful house in Adyar. Shreerang had stopped on the way and picked up a box of chocolates—expensive ones, in typical Shreerang style. Soon after we were introduced, all of them started chatting as if they had known each other for a long time. Joking, teasing. The children were playing around. A boy and a girl. They roped Shreerang into their games. Shreerang was completely absorbed in them. I felt isolated, left to the couple to entertain. So he did like children. I felt a lump in my chest.

But he would still say no—obstinacy, what else. Although I behaved normally enough, inside I was vexed.

We decided to return the same night. We had no reservation. Just managed to get sitting space. The compartment was crowded, passengers and luggage everywhere. No place even to move a hand or leg. Outside the window, pitch darkness. A cold breeze blew in through the window, making me sleepy. Some passengers had dozed off, their heads resting on their chests; others were cuddling their children, a few were staring out of the window. There were those who carried on a conversation, or surveyed co-passengers, watched the passing scenery. The crowd was getting to me. Oppressive, intrusive. Unconnected. Who are these strangers? I want nothing to do with them. Why are they here? Who am I? Except that we were headed in the same direction, packed into one compartment, we had nothing in common. I rested my head on Shreerang's shoulder. "Sleep. I am here, you won't fall," he said, putting his arm around me, in spite of all the people around. He was the only one who was mine. Mine alone, in that unfamiliar, scary group of fellow travellers, in the dim, flickering yellow light of the train.

So much had happened that day ... my meeting with Shreerang's parents, his mother giving me the chain, friends, relatives, going away without so much as whispering a word to Nini about our visit ... Everything dissolved into a blur in my head. Had I dreamt it all? Was it *déjà vu*? What was real, what was true, what untrue ... I couldn't tell. I broke out in a cold sweat. I wanted to scream but no sound came out. I opened my eyes to find that the train had stopped in the middle of nowhere. The breeze had dropped and it was stifling in the packed compartment. My throat was parched. I was suddenly gripped by panic. I was all alone. Where was Shreerang? Where had he gone? Why? How? "Suruchi, Suruchi, what happened?" I let out my breath when I heard his voice. I shut my eyes tight and gripped his fingers in mine. I knew the two people sitting on the upper berth opposite were watching us curiously. But I didn't care. What was important was that Shreerang was there, next to me, his reassuring touch restoring my confidence that I had someone of my own in that crowd. In that moment, everything—a home, children, the evening spent elsewhere—became irrelevant. Was that path forgotten? Not at all. It was very much in my consciousness. Even now I could recollect it vividly. So then? Wasn't that important?

Merlin's voice interrupted her reverie. "And how are you, Suruchi? You look a bit different, like you've changed slightly."

"In what sense?"

"Can't say exactly. Have you done your hair differently?"

"Of course not! And how about you? What are you doing?"

"Me? What could I be doing? Everything is as always. Not good. These brats, getting more and more disobedient, not studying properly..."

"Oh no, really?"

"As for Viren... what can I say? The drinking has only increased. Says he has a job, but gives me no money. Where he goes all day, who knows. If I ask, he gets aggressive. The other day he almost got physical." Merlin began to cry silently and wiped her nose on her sleeve.

"How come you went to Nini's?"

"I thought I'd check whether you were coming. I wanted your advice. You said some people ..."

"There are organisations which can help Viren with his alcoholism. But he must visit them. If not him, at least you could go. They provide help to families, too."

"How can I? It's so embarrassing. I've stopped visiting family and relatives now. Though everyone knows, they still ask, 'Where does he work? What does he do? Have the children passed?' I feel so trapped!"

Suruchi was not surprised. She was familiar with such cases. The women, young and old, who came to Ila were all in similar situations. Afraid, suppressed and oppressed. Bearing the burden of their predicament, and yet not quite prepared to put it down. Because they are ashamed to admit openly what has happened to them. They feel guilty, blame themselves. They would be held responsible. They couldn't acknowledge their humiliation even to themselves, let alone others. But Suruchi had also seen how, once they started talking, facing the truth, they became self-assured, confident, frank. She felt like she had assumed the role of a counsellor, helping sort out Merlin's case.

"Look, Merlin, is anything going to be solved by your sitting at home like this? You need to sort it out yourself. Bring Viren with you. I will get the address of the local organisation and go with you to their meetings. Once you go there, you will see that everyone has some problem or other. You won't feel so dejected. On the contrary, when you exchange stories, you will get strength. Will you come?"

"I'll speak to him."

"Ask him when he is sober. Otherwise you come on your own. Do it while I am here."

"You're going back right away?"

"No, I'm planning to stay for a few days."

"You will help me, sure?"

"Of course."

"You are so much better off than me, isn't it? Nini was telling me you have a good job, earn well. You live alone, I believe? Must have that kind of courage. What's the use of having a husband, children, marriage? Why does one need them? They never give you true happiness, I tell you. In fact, it's only mental tension and stress. You were smart; you stayed out of it all."

Suruchi tried to smile. Merlin insisted she eat something and have tea. The children came back and, under the mother's stern, watchful eyes, sat quietly in a corner of the room with their books. Every now and then, they stole glances at Suruchi. With blank, expressionless looks, they sat there chewing their nails. Merlin, too, was doing the same, unconsciously. In spite of the groaning fan overhead, it was hot and sticky inside, and a stale, gloomy air pervaded the room. Suruchi wanted to get up and leave. The thought of returning to this place depressed her. But she had promised to help Merlin.

Nini did not ask, and Suruchi did not tell her that she was going to visit Merlin, every morning and evening. Since Nini did not venture out of the house much, she had a constant stream of visitors to meet her, to seek her advice. But Suruchi noticed there was an air of detachment about her now. She spent most of her time in her room, reading. She had always worn bifocal glasses, but now she seemed to have some problem with her vision. Suruchi couldn't ask her about it though.

Suruchi felt an urge to contact someone who was connected with Shreerang. But who? His parents, aunt, friends? How would they react on seeing her? With surprise, perhaps, and then a pretence of pleasure. They will be cordial, exchange pleasantries. That's it. What's to be gained from such interactions? Why does one keep in touch, keep up relationships? Is it only to show one's face and conduct desultory conversation? How does it matter whether one does it or not? If I go away tomorrow, it will not make the slightest difference to this city, these people, their lives. If I meet them and spend time with them, will it matter? Just another hue added to the day's events. Good or bad, dark or bright will depend on how they view me: Suruchi. This body, this physical presence. Nothing beyond that. These thoughts made her dizzy!

Suruchi went out in this agitated state. Nini was in her room; Lakshmi was engrossed in chopping vegetables. The road opposite the house was all dug up, littered with fallen leaves, garbage, paper. Except for the autorickshaw stand at the corner and a few people at the bus stop, four women and a couple of children, everything was quiet. The small grocery store was deserted, the owner sitting idly in front of the shop display. A sad-looking mongrel lay panting on the step. It was hot and humid. Streams of sweat trickled down Suruchi's back.

She paid the autorickshaw driver and stood for a moment surveying the scene before her. It was the same old rambling house surrounded by coconut trees. An unexpected gust of sea breeze swept over her. She rang the doorbell. The man who opened the door told her Shreerang's mother was not at home. For a moment she was nonplussed. She had just assumed she would be in. "But Sir is here," the man said. "Please come this way. He is in his office."

Had Shreerang's mother pointed out the office to her? She couldn't remember. She'd probably ignored this part of the house since she had nothing to do with it. Suruchi looked around. A large room, air-conditioned, wall-to-wall carpeting, a table with a stack of files, papers, chairs around it ... "How did I get here? Why have I come?" Suruchi asked herself.

Shreerang's father was standing behind the table. Surprised? Annoyed to see me?

"I ..."

"Sit, sit... sit down. When did you come?"

"I ... to meet ..."

"How are you? All right? Where are you working now? Very good. I have restricted my market in that region. I have some people there, but not like before. Shreerang looked after it very well. He was very bright, very intelligent. I have lost much of my enthusiasm. For whom should I grow the business now?"

Suruchi forgot the heat and the humidity outside and relaxed in this cool room. She felt reassured seated in that chair. Felt like putting down the burden she had been carrying within herself all this while.

Shreerang's father rang the bell and the same man entered. He told the man to bring some coffee. Immediately he reappeared with a tray and two cups. Suruchi couldn't believe what she was doing in Shreerang's father's office, sipping coffee with him, the man whom Shreerang did not like. Shreerang had been very, very angry with his father. He had contempt for his father's unfairness, his insensitivity, his inflexibility. He'd hardly spoken about his father, merely referred to him in passing. It was mostly about his mother that he talked and later, after she found out, about his sister. They were in the same mould, the two women—loving, sensitive, oppressed, subjugated. Between them, they shaped Shreerang, his personality. And yet he worked hard to make money for a father whom he did not respect. He had done his father's bidding in terms of his education and his employment, resenting it all the while. Is that all there is to human relationships? Those light and dark threads of fabric. Do they unravel sometimes, do they get tangled, do they break? How do we make sense of them?

Suruchi stood up. "I'll go now," she said. Shreerang's father got out of the swivel chair and came around the table. Wonder what went through his mind on seeing me land up like this? Did he think I had come to ask for something, to take or demand something? I shouldn't have come. Is my embarrassment, my foolishness showing on my face? My coming here was a mistake. I had no business bringing my pain, my despair, my loneliness to them.

Shreerang's father came up to her just as he had done before. He put his arm around her shoulders. It was as if Shreerang stood in front of her—the same height, the same look, the same voice. "Shreerang, don't go!" The words escaped Suruchi's lips as a sob! She clung to him involuntarily. He patted her. "Take care, my child," he said gently. "It's hard, I know. It's very difficult for me, too. Nobody believes me, but I hope you will understand. That boy bore me a grudge, only resented me ever since he grew up. He never gave me an opportunity to explain, to talk. In spite of that, I had hoped that one day the two of us would be able to speak to each other, that we would understand each other. Erase those unpleasant intervening years. But it was not meant to be. He just left us and went away. Not one chance ... Of what use is all this now?"

Suruchi remained standing close to him. She freed her hands and wiped her eyes, then looked around. His father's words "all this now?" came back to her. On either side of the door were two glass-fronted cupboards, full of books. One had thick hardbound volumes; the other held an assortment of big and small colourful publications. Piles of magazines. Shreerang's father led her to the cupboards. She noticed the titles—all books of poetry, plays, literature. She turned to look at him. It was Shreerang's face, well past fifty, tired, dejected, hopelessness writ large on it. He smiled a wan smile.

"You probably didn't know that I had preserved all of his stuff here in my room."

She shook her head. No. She wasn't even aware that this treasure trove had existed. Come to think of it, she knew only about his love of literature and books. His mother had said, "There is nothing left of him." Then what about all these things that belonged to him, that he loved ... How and why has his father kept them so carefully? What is the connection between us and those material things which we cherish, which we hold dear, which we are attached to, which we put away so carefully? So what relationship do all these objects that belonged to Shreerang have with his father?

"Shreerang wanted to become something else, but because of my insistence he followed the course I had charted for him."

Finally she found her voice. Making bold, she asked, "Why have you preserved all these things?"

For a long moment he looked at her, not saying anything. Then he said, "Keep coming over like this, my dear."

Suruchi was taken aback. All the anger Shreerang had harboured for his father seemed to have filled her up and was waiting to burst forth. Why do people wait so long? She felt like shouting. But then for the first time she became aware of something else. How had his father and mother, the two extremes in his life, accepted her so easily? I had tortured myself to gain the acceptance of others, made excuses to myself, and in the process tormented Shreerang, too. Was I deliberately not seeing something that was not easily visible? Did I not make enough of an effort to understand?

All the anger and bitterness seemed to drain out of Suruchi. What more is there to say, she thought.

Shreerang's father said, "A person gets used to everything, my girl, working, making money, even living. There is no desire to find an option. What was my son's fault? It was his prerogative to hate his father, wasn't it?"

He opened the door and summoned the same man. "Tell the driver to drop her," he said. Suruchi could not bring herself to refuse the offer.

Swaroop had no time to sit down and have a proper chat, so caught up was she in her affairs. She barely managed to ask, "How was your trip? Nini okay? What else did you do?"

"Oh nothing much, rested, ate what Lakshmi prepared, and read Nini's books," replied Suruchi.

"Good thing I didn't come, right?"

"Swaroop, come on, let's go out somewhere."

"Why, Didi, it's fine right here, at home."

"You've become lazy."

"Oh really? Who does the running around all day? Besides, Bharat will wake up any minute. He has to be fed after that ... let's just stay here."

"I'll get going, then," said Suruchi.

"Why in such a hurry? You've come after so long and we haven't even talked properly."

"I gave you all the news, didn't I?"

"Was that all?" After a pause, Swaroop continued, "What's the matter, Didi?"

"Nothing, nothing's the matter."

"Then stay. Abhijit will drop you later tonight."

"No."

"You're angry with him?"

"Not at all! Why should I be angry?"

"He thought you were. You hardly come over these days. Don't talk much. Has Abhijit offended you?"

"No."

"He tells me everything. He had mentioned this a long time ago. I was not surprised. I told him anyone would be interested in my Didi, she is that kind of person ... But Didi, his intentions were not bad. He did say that he had expressed his feelings to you. It was not improper. One shouldn't keep anything locked away inside. He cares about you, is concerned about you, just as I am. You are a part of our family, Didi."

Suruchi was at a loss for words. Swaroop got up suddenly. "Let me finish off some chores while Bharat is still asleep," she said. Abhijit's mother was sitting in the small balcony adjoining the hall, watching what was going on in the compound, in the other buildings.

Once Bharat woke up, Suruchi found it difficult to leave. He was throwing a tantrum and would not listen to anyone, would not even go to Suruchi.

"Tell *Mavshi* we have forgotten her. Unless she keeps coming, we will not get used to her."

"That applies to you, too," retorted Suruchi.

"Yes, but for whom is commuting easier, Didi?"

"That's true."

The days rolled by. Suruchi found an invitation to the function where Ila was going to speak lying at her house. She picked it up and smiled to herself. So now I am just another name on the mailing list, she thought wryly. No participation. No prior intimation. Not being involved in it from the beginning as before. Ila had the gift of oration. Her speeches had always been very forceful. She was articulate, committed, passionate, even aggressive. She would pick up the mike, take the audience into confidence and speak to them in a conversational manner. But she was firm, precise, and clear in her exposition. Her fiery manner was new to me and I used to be mesmerised by her.

On the way back to the hostel, the group gradually dispersed till finally only Shreerang was left. That was the time when I wanted him to myself. For the road to never end, the hostel to go further away. I longed to find out what he was thinking. But the discussion was obviously about the recent event. "At this rate she will get to the top. And at that level, there is place only for one," Shreerang declared almost casually.

"Who are you talking about?"

"Ila, who else?"

"Rubbish! She will always have dozens with her. She will never be alone."

Then Shreerang laughed. As if he had seen into the future. I was furious. I snapped, "How do you know?"

He had no answer, but he did say, "Because I say so. When one chooses to tread a different path, one has to walk it alone. One should be aware of that. As I am."

I wanted to be a part of that. I was just about starting to understand his views, and yet I wondered why he wouldn't let me be a partner in his journey. A silent companion. His words about being alone stayed with me. Was he possibly aware of his own destiny? His future? Such foolish thoughts. He was of a rational, scientific temperament and here I was thinking of premonitions and forebodings. And yet! When we reached the hostel, I felt a little uneasy. We had only argued without sorting anything out. We could have changed the topic, laughed it off, one of us could have given in. But we did none of those things. When I was about to go in, all I could think of was when and where I would see him again. I was dejected, despairing. We had reached a significant moment for the first time that day. I could have got to know a little more about him. But did I ever? Did I understand him that night when I lay on his lap on Ila's doorstep? But that was later. That particular night, I said "Bye" and turned away. He caught hold of my hand and made me face him. It was the first time he had touched me. He said nothing, just kept looking at me. I did the same. For that instant, all my disappointment, despair, uncertainty evaporated and pure joy took its place. He let go of my hand; once more I said, "Bye", and floated towards my room. When we look deep into the crowded events of the past, all such moments begin to play out before our eyes, one by one. But that is *now*. Didn't I see it *then*? Does one need special insight? Or is it that only when you put distance between you and the moments, when you have gone ahead and then turned back, do you see them? What's the point of thinking about it all now? Everything has become meaningless, hasn't it?

It is not that I love you less
Than when before your feet I lay:
But to prevent the sad increase
Of hopeless love, I keep away.[8]

It had been a while since Suruchi had had a chat with Prabhakar. He would come to the library, smile, say a cursory, "Hello, how are you?" and go away. She had kept her distance from most people and had no desire to increase her acquaintance with him. As she was leaving, he approached her. "I'll drop you home," he offered.

"But I live on the opposite side," she protested.

"Then let's do one thing, let's go to my house. Have a cup of tea and then I'll take you home."

"Some other time."

"When, Suruchi? Come on, it's not good to be so aloof. My daughter is here for her confinement. She had a baby girl."

"Really! I had no idea."

"It's been a few days. We haven't actually met lately, so I did not get an opportunity to tell you about it."

It was a Saturday, a half day. She couldn't say no to Prabhakar. She went to his house. A typical middle-class home, nicely furnished with curtains, a showcase, some magazines on the centre table. The daughter came out and sat down for a while, chatted desultorily. She looked the quiet, reserved kind. Then the baby woke up, so she went inside. The maid brought tea. Suruchi noticed a family photograph on the TV—Prabhakar, his wife, son and daughter. Prabhakar noticed Suruchi gazing at the photo. "It's been seven years since my wife passed away."

"I didn't know."

"You didn't? Cancer. It was in the terminal stages when we found out. We could do nothing. My son is in USA, studied there, has recently got a job, and then this girl, my daughter..."

"Hmm."

"It's been so long since she came here, yet she doesn't talk about going back, nor has anyone come from there to fetch her. I just don't understand what's going on."

"Why?"

"Only if she speaks will I know, is it not? She only says, 'I won't go back'. And now there's a child to complicate matters."

Suruchi suddenly wanted to get away from there. She could have said, "Let me speak to the girl", given her the advice she had picked up at Ila's, even suggested sending her to consult Ila, but Suruchi said nothing. Quickly draining her cup of tea, she stood up. "I had better get going. It's very late."

"Let me drop you."

"Why? I'll take an autorickshaw."

"No, no, I can't let you do that."

Prabhakar walked out with her. In the car, he spoke a little more about himself. His life, his wife, the children, the present situation, fate, the hard times he had had to deal with.

Before she got out, he said to her, as if he had come to a decision, "Suruchi, can I ask you a question?"

"What?"

"Will you marry me?"

Suruchi drew in her breath sharply. "That's not possible."

"Wait, wait. Don't misunderstand me. I have known you for so long. I really like you. I don't know much about your personal life. But that makes no difference. I will keep you very happy. I am a simple, straightforward man. I do not impose my will on anyone. Definitely not on you. Don't say no so hastily like this. Think about it. Please. I will give you time to think it over."

Suruchi held open the car door and said, "Don't wait. My answer will not change."

"But Suruchi..."

"You know nothing about me."

"That makes no difference, I told you. I want your friendship. I am a very lonely man. Till I met you, I had no desire to make friends with anyone."

"Even so..."

"Please, don't refuse me like this. Think it over. Take your time. I will not bring this up again if you like. We will treat this incident as forgotten, as if it never happened. But keep an open mind. Please."

It was well after daybreak when Suruchi woke up. She could not remember anything. Her body ached, as if battered. Her head was heavy. She was feverish, there was a bitter taste in the mouth. She continued to lie in bed. She was rarely unwell, and that, too, when alone. Once when she had jaundice, she asked Nini to come but Nini had refused, so it was left to Shreerang to take care of her, with her irritability, her impatience, her tantrums. Why was I so angry and mean? Because he was there, I suppose. Now who should I be angry with? No option but to lie in bed, alone. Till I feel better.

When the maid came in, she asked her to do some of the basic chores. The rest of the days she was by herself. She didn't feel like reading. Or listening to music. Nor could she sleep. Even if I die, no one will know, she thought. But do they need to know? What will happen? Swaroop will gather my few meagre belongings. The house is anyway rented. Whatever money there is will go to her automatically, as my legitimate heir. Or will it go to Nini? She doesn't need it. She is happy, has her own house and all her savings. She must have willed her money to her institution, for the use of abandoned or abused wives, single women, widows, women who want to live despite their afflictions. Her funds would help rehabilitate them. Who am I to her? Do I fit into that category? Am I also needy like them? Of shelter, support, family, a man. Like Prabhakar. A widower with grown-up children, yet lonely. Troubled. He says he wants my friendship. Friendship! Wife—a body, a home, a status symbol. That's all I am reduced to now. A perfect match for Prabhakar. Suruchi, single, past her prime, whose mind and body will make do with anything, anyone, an ordinary, commonplace woman.

That evening, Swaroop arrived along with Abhijit and Bharat. She took in the situation and started shouting, "Why couldn't you send a message to me, Didi? You could have called Abhijit's office. Are we nothing to you? Lying like this, alone, burning with fever..."

And she burst into tears, muttering something between sobs. Abhijit took her outside, trying to calm her down. Bharat clung to his mother. Entering the room, Abhijit asked, "Want to come home with us?"

"No."

"Why are you doing this? There's always place for you in our house."

"I know that. But I'll be fine. I'm much better now."

"Shall I bring you a mirror?"

Suruchi tried to smile, but didn't succeed. After making a great effort at convincing Swaroop that she was all right, Swaroop got ready to leave. "Look, if you aren't better by tomorrow, I will bundle you up and take you home," Abhijit threatened.

As if to prove her point Suruchi accompanied them to the gate. When she turned around, in the dark, she thought she saw someone standing near the door. For a couple of moments, she stood staring. Who was it? Shreerang? "Shrreeerang!" It took her a minute or two to realise that she had called out his name. What foolishness is this! It would not be true to say "Go, I set you free." Because he was free even then. Because he wanted it that way. But now I have bound you to me, forever. Irrevocably. There is no escape. For either you or me.

Suruchi remained standing in front of the door, in the dark. She could hear voices, sounds of vessels clattering and the TV from next door. She did not sense that presence again. Slowly she made her way inside.

Ila was sitting amidst a scattering of books, papers, magazines, spectacles on nose, eyes focused but searching. For a few moments Suruchi stared at her, only her, apart from all the mess surrounding her. Ila looked up.

"Why are you standing? Sit down, please."

"When are you leaving for abroad, Ila?"

"Next week."

"For how long?"

"Now that I am going, thought I'd stay for a couple of months. I have all these conferences, seminars, etc. to attend, but I've finally convinced myself that I ought to take at least a month's vacation."

"Have all the arrangements been made?"

"Of course. No problem there. I've received a heap of invitations to stay, to visit..."

"Everyone wants to have you."

Ila laughed out loud. "Suruchi, what kind of mood are you in?"

Suruchi wished this would be the moment when Ila would say, "Why don't you come along, too? Your parents are there. Take that opportunity and come." And I would have said yes. Because Ila asked me. A change, holiday, foreign travel. She would have told Kamala and Pradeep that she'd gone because Ila told her to. And to the others, the excuse would be, "I'm going to meet my parents. They've been persuading me to visit them for so long."

But nothing like that happened. Ila was engrossed in preparing her speech.

"So, Suruchi, what's all the news?"

"Nothing much."

"How's Swaroop? Madam's disappeared lately. But she's assured me that she will come back to work once Bharat starts going to school. Abhijit drops in occasionally. I haven't seen such a loyal character, ever."

"True."

"His book has come out really well. Dedicated to you! I was amused."

"Why?"

"He is such a serious person, isn't he? Interesting how sometimes one catches a glimpse of some unexpected traits in an individual."

"When you return, Ila, I may not be here."

"What? Where are you planning to go?"

"Back to Nini. I haven't informed her yet. She won't say 'don't come'. Even when Mummy left me with her, she just accepted me without question, didn't she? Now, too, she will take me back."

"That's not the point. What will you do there?"

"Something to earn a living, I guess."

"And then?"

"Then nothing."

Ila took off her glasses and put them in the case. Marked the magazines and books and shut them. Gathered all the papers together and placed a paper weight on them. Getting up, she said, "Let's go out."

She parked the scooter, and both of them entered the cool precincts of the tree-lined park. A few people were sitting around. Some children were running about. Some were exercising; others had formed a circle and were immersed in conversation. But the park was spacious; it had lots of old, gnarled trees with canopies of green foliage.

As they walked, Ila asked, "You do know about Shreerang's sister, don't you?"

"I found out, accidentally."

"When Shreerang and I first met, I had just chosen to get into this field. I used to deliberately pick up cases like hers. I had just separated then and had managed to find a place. Shreerang used to drop by sometimes for a chat. The support of my friends and my own will power kept me going. This boy used to be bitter, angry, disgruntled. He was argumentative, sarcastic, contemptuous of everyone and everything. It used to puzzle me. At first I thought all men were like that, and he was one of them. But I soon discovered the reason for his bitterness. His bitterness and despair came from not being able to do anything for his sister. When you know that something is not right, but you can't do anything about it you feel helpless. A failure. Finally one day, when just the two of us were in the room, he opened up. He told me everything. About how his father had always been unfair to his mother, his sister and, to some extent, himself. As he got more and more involved in his father's business, his resentment grew. He felt like a trapped animal, he said."

Every word of Ila's story unfolded before Suruchi's eyes.

"We talked for a long time that day. I thought I'd understood him and his personality fairly well after that. His tendency not to get involved, be detached, to live fully but for the moment, in the present, had become a way with him. And then you came into his life."

In a flashback Suruchi visualised herself entering Shreerang's life.

"Was there anyone before me?" she asked.

"Maybe. There were girls in his life. He was an attractive man. And he was free. Then he met you and when I watched the two of you together, I knew this was something different. You grew close, began to mean something to each other and ..." Ila hesitated. Suruchi was looking at her expectantly.

"Shreerang came to me and said that he wanted to distance himself from you. I told him, 'You have come so close that you want to go far away now, don't you? Then don't test the poor girl.' In any case, I wasn't going to drop you like that. But you needed to be independent, self-assured, capable of standing on your own. The decision was yours. And you took it. You both remained together. And you evolved through that relationship. None of us are solid, unbreakable like a rock all the time. Sparks fly, hurts happen, jolts shake you up. But there is no choice; one has to go through it. And you did."

Suruchi listened to every word, spellbound. When had Shreerang wanted to break away? Was it before they decided to live together? She could have asked Ila for a clarification, but what purpose would it have served? What was important was that Shreerang stayed with me. We quarrelled bitterly sometimes. Argued, said nasty, hurtful things to each other. But he didn't go away. When he went, it was like this. When death took him away from life. And yet he stayed with me, by my side, all the time. The meaning of his words is becoming clear, now that he is far away. Through his desire to live fully, his engagement with life, through a million little memories of him.

"Suruchi, there is no option but to go through this," Ila said. "That's what I've been saying all along. But you will come out of it. Successfully. What if neither I nor Shreerang had come into your life? You would still have been you, right? What if you hadn't quarrelled with Nini and come away? There is no point in speculating 'What If' this or that ... Just let it be."

They stopped and sat on a bench under a tree.

"I received a letter from Shreerang's father, Ila ..."

"Oh! What does he say?"

"Nothing really. Seems caring in the letter. Heartfelt."

"Don't forget this was the man Shreerang hated all his life."

"That's the point. Nini says before judging anyone, one must leave some room for allowances. There could be something we don't know."

"But suppose what we do know is all negative?"

"You are just spoiling for a fight!"

"Wah, Suruchi, you sound like Shreerang now. He didn't fight with you, did he?"

"Rarely. Thinking back, it was I who always started a fight."

"You stayed together despite that, didn't you?"

"Ila ..."

"Come on, speak up, don't hesitate."

"I had almost decided that I had had enough. It was really difficult ... Instead of being miserable, it was better to speak out frankly and get it over with. Separate from Shreerang ..."

"Don't cry, Suruchi! You believe all this happened because that's what you were thinking? Forget it! He wouldn't have let go of you so easily."

"How do you know? He used to say, 'If it makes you so unhappy, let's break it off.'"

"One says a lot of things. When the actual moment comes, it's different. I remember when you were in the hospital, you cried out in anguish, 'Shreerang, don't go!'"

"Aloud?"

"Yes. You didn't know what was happening. Suruchi, you were never apart from him. Get those thoughts out of your head."

"But he didn't stop for me!"

"He didn't? Tell me?"

Suruchi took a deep breath. The cool refreshing air. Dark clouds crowding the sky. And the unmistakable fragrance of rain on the hot earth. Ila hasn't gone so far away from me after all, Suruchi thought. Such moments are rare. But then so are most significant events of our lives. That's why they are special. Ila has understood that I have captured Shreerang forever. When I finally set him free, he came back to me to stay permanently, just as I wanted him to. That's where he will remain. And our lives will go on, routinely, like the lives of all the people we know.

Suruchi stood at the front door of her house. It was pitch dark outside. The wind was sweeping leaves, paper, garbage, hither and thither, and bringing with it the scent of wet earth. She inhaled deeply, taking in the fragrance ... Her mind went back to one night when she had woken up and found Shreerang missing from beside her. Strange. She was used to not finding him in bed early in the morning. But this was in the middle of the night. She got out of bed and went out without switching on the light. He was standing by the window, gripping the bars and looking out into the night. She had put her arms around him and rested her head on his back. He must have been startled but he said nothing. She was only half awake. She wanted to say, "Come", but had stopped herself. Before she felt them, she became aware of his wet eyes. Why was he crying? Why like this, alone, by the window? She turned him around to face her, asked, but he refused to say anything. Muttered, "Nothing, nothing" and then accompanied her to the bedroom. He snuggled up to her like a child and she felt dismayed. He is looking for his mother in me. I am not her. But who am I, friend, lover? Definitely not mother. Because of those resentful thoughts, did my hand that was lifted to caress him fall back limply, denying him the comfort he needed? She had never found out why he had cried that night. Why?

Nini says make allowances for everyone. She will not show her happiness on seeing me, but I will go nevertheless. That huge house, the garden, the books—they are all mine after all. Getting a job there will not be difficult. Even without my asking, Nini will put in a word for me. The humidity, the heat all year round ... one can get used to it. After all I have spent my childhood there. The bus service is good, getting around will not be a problem. And then there are autos. And there is the sea. Even if most of the beaches are spoilt, the water is fine. Besides, the sea is visible from the Besant Nagar house. Even if Shreerang's father's office is cloistered, I can follow his mother up to the terrace. There is no need to reply to Shreerang's father's letter. When we meet, even if I have reserved judgment, I will be cautious. I don't know why Shreerang was so hostile to him, but perhaps eventually I will understand and overcome it. He wanted to speak to his son? Wanted to bridge the gap, perhaps? Well, I am ready to talk, on Shreerang's behalf. From one unfinished life, another new one emerges, yet unfulfilled, but as a chosen option. And another journey begins.

It began to rain, and the scent of the earth pervaded the atmosphere.

And, even yet, I dare not let it languish
Dare not indulge in Memory's rapturous pain
Once drinking deep of that divinest anguish
How could I seek the empty world again?[9]

Suruchi stepped outside. For a couple of minutes she stood there, letting the raindrops fall on her body, the fragrance envelop her. For a fleeting moment she felt Shreerang's presence beside her.

Notes

1. 'My True Love Hath My Heart'. *Arcadia*. 1580, Sir Philip Sydney (1554–1586). Quoted in the original Marathi text.
2. 'Death, Be Not Proud' (Holy Sonnet 10), 1633, John Donne (1572–1631). Quoted in the original Marathi text.
3. 'How Do I Love Thee?' (Sonnet 43), 1850, Elizabeth Barrett Browning (1806–1861). Quoted in the original Marathi text.
4. 'Ode on Solitude', 1735, Alexander Pope (1688–1744). Quoted in the original Marathi text.
5. 'Death, Be Not Proud' (Holy Sonnet 10), 1633, John Donne (1572–1631). Quoted in the original Marathi text.
6. 'The Self Banished'. *Poems*. 1645, Edmund Waller (1606–1687). Quoted in the original Marathi text.
7. 'Remembrance', 1846, Emily Brontë (1818–1848). Quoted in the original Marathi text.
8. 'The Self Banished'. *Poems*. 1645, Edmund Waller (1606–1687). Quoted in the original Marathi text.
9. 'Remembrance', 1846, Emily Brontë (1818–1848). Quoted in the original Marathi text.

Some Questions, Some Answers

Keerti Ramachandra in conversation with *Saniya*

KR: First, let's get to know Saniya the person. Tell us something about yourself, where you are from, your education, your working life.

S: I was born in Sangli, in Maharashtra and educated in many Marathi-medium schools all over the state. My father was an engineer with the state government so he was transferred every two–three years. Every time we went to a new town, I learnt to adapt to the new surroundings and observe a different way of life. I enjoyed these frequent changes. These experiences played an important part in shaping me.

I got a postgraduate degree in Commerce from Bombay University and worked in the corporate sector for some time as an accountant, but gave it up because it did not really hold my interest.

I have travelled considerably with my husband. We lived in Japan for several years. Those were some of the best years, and I cherish the experiences I had there.

Now I work as a voluntary counsellor and trainer with an NGO in Bangalore, where I live.

KR: Do you come from a literary background? Do you think a literary pedigree helps?

S: There was no literary background or atmosphere around me. My father liked to write but couldn't pursue his interest. I learnt, very early on, to observe people, their behaviour, their way of life, the surroundings. I would often make up stories on the basis of this and share them with my friends. I wrote my first poem when I was ten years old. I continued to write poetry and stories and had them published in school and later college magazines.

I don't know about literary pedigree. Talent is individual, I think?

KR: How did Saniya become a writer?

S: Writing just happened to me, as I loved to imagine and dream. I don't think I ever consciously decided to be a writer, nor did I have any ambition to be a writer.

KR: Where do you normally write? At what time? What is your preferred medium—paper-pencil/pen or computer?

S: I used to write on paper with pen or pencil, usually seated on my bed with a pillow on my lap. But since the Marathi font became available, I started writing directly on the computer, and for that I have to sit at my desk.

There is no fixed time or routine. I have written continuously for days and nights when I was totally involved in the work. But at times, days and weeks pass without my writing anything. It doesn't bother me though. I have written so much and for so long, some published, much not published. So when I don't write, I don't get stressed.

KR: How do you view the writing process—as pleasurable or painful?

S: The writing process is a part of my life, a part of me. It is very pleasurable. Even while writing about difficult experiences—suffering or death—the process of transforming them into a story or novel helps me. It gives some kind of relief and is a sort of escape. The process of creating characters and giving them a life of their own is the most the satisfying aspect of writing.

KR: Coming to your own work, how would you describe your writing?

S: My writing depicts the internal struggle of the character. The how and why of human relationships. The question my characters always ask is "What if..." It is their constant search to find out why things are the way they are, can they bring about a change, and if so, how. It delves into deeper questions of existence, love and relationships, life and death. It is important for the characters to arrive at some understanding at the end.

KR: Do personal experiences suggest themes or plots? How much detachment from the experience is necessary before it can be translated into a work of fiction?

S: They often do. The personal experience plants the thought in the mind. One needs to create a fiction out of real life. For me that is literature. So you can be attached to your experience yet your mind is transforming it into something different for your characters. That is the creative journey.

KR: Do real-life people turn into characters in your work, or are most of them created by you? How much control do you have over their lives and destinies as the work progresses?

S: The people get created in my fiction. Some aspects of their personality may be similar to real people. I first see my characters in my imagination. Later, I may realise how they have taken some elements from real people. Once they are born thus, they take over their own forms and destinies. It is fun to see them 'alive' in the words. So I let them be.

KR: Does that mean you enjoy playing 'god'? Would you describe yourself as a 'control freak', then? Do you take full charge of your characters' lives and fates? Did Suruchi, in *Awartan,* behave exactly as you wanted her to? And what about Nini?

S: No. They behaved exactly as they wanted to. I start with an idea of how I want the character to be, but once I start writing, the characters take on their own personalities. So I can't really play god!

KR: You write about strong women and their dilemmas. But Shreerang in *Awartan* is also a very credible character—a free spirit, compared to Suruchi. Do you feel it requires a different state of mind to portray powerful men?

S: Not really. To me there is no obvious 'gender' bias... they are all people and I see them as individuals with their own mental makeup and dilemmas and challenges and their coping mechanisms.

KR: Do you sometimes feel you are too severe on your characters? Nini, for example, or even Kamala, a sentimental, weak woman, and Swaroop—the ultimate self-centred 'user'?

S: No. I really like my characters. I am never judgmental of them. They endear themselves to me, give me a new perspective on life.

KR: Does the state of your mind/heart affect the way you write? What if it changes in the course of writing?

S: It does. When I start writing I detach myself completely from the real world. However, if there is something deeply disturbing in my surroundings or in my life, then I may not feel like writing at all. Sometimes, the state of mind helps me to reflect deeply. At other times, it may take me away temporarily from writing. So the mind can vacillate in the course of writing.

KR: Does a work in progress tend to haunt you? Or do you get away from it once you leave your desk?

S: The work in progress always stays in the mind. It does haunt me, especially when I am at some crucial points in the story.

KR: Do you re-read what you have written before you take a break, and then continue? Are you tempted then to revise and rewrite?

S: Some re-reading may be essential to get into the stream. I find that I rewrite more now that I work on the computer because it is easy. When I used to write on paper, I rarely made major changes. I preferred to discard the whole piece and start afresh.

KR: Which book/story/novel that you have written is your favourite/best work so far?

S: Difficult to mention just one. Some of the favourites—*Awartan* (novel), *Omiyage* (story), *Pravas* (a travelogue).

KR: What is the one very important theme that you would really like to write about?

S: I don't choose themes when I write. It is the human predicament that fascinates and inspires me.

KR: Which authors do you admire? Any favourite works?

S: Too many to name! In Marathi, I'd say the one person who influenced me, whose name comes immediately to mind is the short story writer G. A. Kulkarni. I admire all his writing. I often wished I could write like him.

KR: Are writers born, or can they be 'made'?

S: Difficult to settle on this issue. They may be born but inherent talent is not enough. There is a lot of work which goes into writing. To sustain oneself as a writer one needs to keep sharpening one's faculties all the time. Imagination, curiosity, an open mind—these need to be cultivated.

KR: Do creative writing and literary appreciation courses help one to become a writer/reader?

S: Perhaps they help to make sensitive readers, but whether they help someone to write, I don't know for sure. There are no such courses in my language, Marathi.

KR: How important is craft for a writer? In your own writing?

S: I have not paid much attention to the craft of writing. I always believed in intensity and spontaneity in writing. Of course, some basic craft, the technicalities of language, structure, form come naturally to most people. So that does not require any special effort. There may be other writers for whom craft is important and a laborious process.

KR: What, for you, is the main function of literature? To persuade, inform, instruct or entertain? If you were to rank them, in what order would you put them?

S: Actually, none of these. For me, literature is primarily expression and later, once it reaches the readers, it creates the bridge of dialogue and understanding and enrichment. If I must rank the above functions it would be—inform, entertain, persuade, instruct.

KR: If you were asked to list five qualities one must have to be a writer, what would they be?

S: Curiosity, observation, empathy and compassion, plus imagination to make a story, then expression and language.

KR: What quality or qualities give a 'soul' to one's writing?

S: The same as above. One cannot write from the outside. There has to be total involvement, empathy and affection. That, I think, gives the soul.

KR: What are the three things you look for in a piece of writing, whether it is a novel, short story, essay, article?

S: Engagement—it needs to hold the interest, make you turn the page; the story—what is said and how; enrichment to my understanding; the writer's viewpoint which may or may not be explicit in the piece but which is sensed while reading.

KR: Do you believe there is something called 'writer's block'? Have you had to deal with it? How?

S: It happens, I suppose. One just gets stalled. As if the mind is blocked. When it does, I just let it pass. The best thing to do, I find, is not to worry about it. Sooner or later, the mind starts working, ideas keep coming, solutions suggest themselves, characters take shape. One can then sense the story and the direction it will take.

KR: How do you react to the habit of identifying/classifying writers according to their religion/community/region/gender/political affiliations?

S: This kind of classification is not fair to writers. It is like looking at them through a tinted glass. It does not give a clear, real picture of the writing. As someone said, you can classify books, not writers.

KR: Your work has been translated into several languages. Do you think translations serve any major purpose?

S: Translations help your work reach across language barriers. Others get to know what is happening in that particular region. It is a good way to bridge the gaps.

KR: What do you expect of a translator?

S: A translator needs to tune in to the feel of a story or novel. Apart from being good in both the languages, s/he is expected to understand what is not being said in the piece. So the job of a translator is quite challenging and demanding.

KR: You are quite proficient in English yourself. Have you ever wanted to translate your own work?

S: You know, translating my own work is like getting another chance to rework the original. So it can become a trans-creation. I did try my hand at translation, but then I thought why translate? If I want to communicate in English, then I will write in English.

KR: Does an editor have any role in Marathi writing and publishing?

S: There is no tradition of editing in Marathi. The writer's work gets published as it is handed in most of the time. Yet there have been some good publishers who were also good editors. They helped the writers to get the best out of their work. Shri Pu Bhagvat was one. I was fortunate enough to be published by him.

KR: Do you think writers today should concern themselves with socio-economic, political issues in their writing?

S: As a citizen living in a society, one is always concerned with socio-economic and political issues. But it is not necessary that one has to write about it all the time. It may come naturally at times in fiction, but the real struggle of a human mind may transcend the reality around, and the writing may be dealing just with the inner struggle, as my writing does. I think societal trends and currents do get reflected in a novel. But a novel is not a case study, nor is it a comment on or representation of society.

KR: Would you like to introduce us to the trends in Marathi fiction today? Is it any different from when you started writing? What are the three most important changes you see from the way fiction was written in the 1980s, 2000s and today?

S: Marathi fiction has a rich heritage. The short story form has always been popular, but was more so in the 50s and 60s. There have been changes since. The most significant one is that fiction writing is not limited to the middle-class, urban scenario. There are many writers from different backgrounds who are writing at present. Dalit literature has contributed considerably to the body of work in Marathi. Writers are using dialects and regional variations very comfortably and are being accepted and appreciated by readers. Social reforms in the region are reflected in the literature. Though there are the usual complaints about the reading habit going down, the number of books getting published is ever on the rise.

KR: How much has the audio-visual media and social networking affected the relationship between reader and writer?

S: I believe that the modern technology and social media help both readers and writers. There is greater scope for interaction, they get to know about each other, writers get more publicity and have more avenues for their work to get read and heard. Things change, but then nothing remains static anyway. Except the urge to tell and hear a story, which is eternal.